NAOMI JACOB

HONOUR'S A MISTRESS

Complete and Unabridged

CHARNWOOD
Leicester

First published in Great Britain in 1947

First Charnwood Edition
published March 1986

British Library CIP Data

Jacob, Naomi
  Honour's a mistress.—Large print ed.—
  Charnwood library series
  I. Title
  823'.912[F]   PS6019.A29

  ISBN 0-7089-8321-9

Published by
F. A. Thorpe (Publishing) Ltd.
Anstey, Leicestershire
Set by Rowland Phototypesetting Ltd.
Bury St. Edmunds, Suffolk
Printed and bound in Great Britain by
T. J. Press (Padstow) Ltd., Padstow, Cornwall

A MESSAGE
TO THE CHARNWOOD READER
FROM THE PUBLISHER

Since the introduction of Ulverscroft Large Print Books, countless readers around the world have confirmed that the larger and clearer print has brought back the pleasure of reading to an ever-widening audience, thus enabling readers to once again enjoy the companionship of books which had previously been denied to them due to their inability to read normal small print.

It is obvious that to cater for this ever-widening audience of readers a new series was necessary. The Charnwood Series embraces the widest possible variety of literature from the traditional classics to the most recently published bestsellers, and includes many authors considered too contemporary both in subject and style to be suitable for the many elderly readers for whom the original Ulverscroft Large Print Books were designed.

The newly developed typeface of the Charnwood Series has been subjected to extensive and exhaustive tests amongst the international family of large print readers, and unanimously acclaimed and preferred as a smoother and easier read. Another benefit of this new typeface is that it allows the publication in one volume of longer novels which previously could only be published in two large print volumes: a constant source of frustration for readers when one volume is not available for one reason or another.

The Charnwood Series is designed to increase the titles available to those readers in this ever-widening audience who are unable to read and enjoy the range of popular titles at present only available in normal small print.

HONOUR'S A MISTRESS

A story about a family of wealthy city grocers, the Masters, and of their eldest son, Flight and his marriage to Alicia. Flight goes to France on the outbreak of war and is reported missing, presumed dead, after Dunkirk. But he is only wounded, and works with the French Resistance Movement until escaping back to England in a small boat. Learning that his brother Chris has married Alicia, thinking him dead, sends him back to France to work with the Maquis. Only his sister knows of his existence, and he determines to remain dead to the rest of his family. Eventually he marries again, the mother of a French friend and together they work and wait for the liberation of France.

Books by Naomi Jacob
in the Charnwood Library Series:

THE GOLLANTZ SAGA:

FOUNDER OF THE HOUSE
THAT WILD LIE
YOUNG EMMANUEL
FOUR GENERATIONS
PRIVATE GOLLANTZ
GOLLANTZ: LONDON, PARIS, MILAN
GOLLANTZ & PARTNERS

HONOUR'S A MISTRESS

Honour's a mistress all mankind pursue;
Yet most mistake the false one for the true;
Lured by the trappings, dazzled by the paint,
We worship oft the idol for the saint

Paul Whitehead (1710–1774)

In affection to YVONNE ARNAUD,
generous alike to her friends and her audiences,
with sincere admiration.

Mickie

Part One

Part One

1

EDWARD FLIGHT MASTERS walked slowly down the beautifully kept drive from his home to the village green. He moved a little self-consciously for he knew that people watched and noticed him. Not that he either objected to being watched or noticed, but he admitted to himself that he liked to give his watchers "value for money". That was one of his own private jokes, one which he had never voiced even to his wife, to whom he was devoted. Frances would never have understood a great many of his private jokes; had he voiced this particular one Edward could imagine how blankly she would have stared at him, and after a second's silence, said, "Edward, my dear, what rubbish! Anyone who didn't know you would think that you were conceited."

In imagination he carried on the conversation, "But I am, Francy!"

"You! The least conceited man I know!"

He was conceited, to himself he admitted it; he frequently told other people, their reaction was much what Frances' would have been.

Passing the trim little lodge, he nodded and smiled to Mary Noakes, who smiled in return and wished him good evening. Edward felt that on

3

returning to the kitchen she would say to Noakes, "Just seen the Major pass!"

To which Noakes would reply, "Did yer ... aye?"

Everyone called him "The Major", although he never failed to protest:

"I'm not a major, you know. Oh, I left the Army with that rank, but I was a strictly 'temporary gentleman', believe me. I'm a hard-working and moderately honest grocer."

All quite true, but people always laughed as if he had made a joke which might be old but which had worn remarkably well.

He was a grocer, a successful one too. His father had left him the wholesale business in Clark Square, EC4. He had never changed its trade name—Masters and Son—and had congratulated himself when his elder son, Christopher, had proved willing and even anxious to enter the business. A good business, and Chris was active, interested, and had a fertile brain. It was since the advent of Chris that they had added all kinds of foreign commodities to their price list. Chris spent his holidays on the Continent and rarely returned without some new addition to the firm's lines.

Edward was proud of his business, proud of his son, proud of his own ability to know exactly the right and correct attitude to take with customers. To old Henry Portman, of Portman and Wilsons, he was deferential but never subservient; to Fred Porter, who had a high-class grocery establishment in Sydenham, he was friendly, and ready to be amused at Porter's rather indifferent jokes. When Henry Portman said, "Nice place you've made of it, Masters. Half the grocers in England imagine that their places should be covered with dust and stink of mice!" Edward smiled tolerantly and replied, "Very early in my business career I saw the stores at Portman and Wilsons, sir. What is good enough for them is good enough for me." Little Fred Porter rubbed his hands and said, "Like a palice, Mr. Masters. I always say to the wife it's like goin' to Buckin'am Palice, going to Masters and Son!" Edward shook his head and protested. "Oh, come! Still, we try to keep the place decent."

They were fine rooms, exquisitely neat, beautifully clean; samples were laid out attractively, in complete ranges; prices were properly recorded, the amount of goods noted carefully and correctly. Edward believed that it satisfied a customer to hear him say, "Ah, this particular line? Um . . . we're low, I make no bones about it. Expecting a fresh consignment from Portugal next week. I say 'expecting', because our good friends the 'Pork and Beans', as we called them in the war, are not always very prompt in their deliveries. If four and a half gross will carry you over . . . ?" Better to be frank about matters, no use pretending you had goods when you hadn't. Only brought you a dissatisfied customer. Not that he attended to any but the most important customers himself in these days. He sat in his office, which shone with good and well-kept

5

mahogany, his Georgian decanters in the admirable cupboard with the old drop handles, and offered glasses of fine sherry and first-class port to customers. Recently many of them said, "D'you mind if I have a whisky-and-soda, Mr. Masters? Suits me better. Thanks." Edward gave it to them, but he felt that they were lacking in dignity to ask for it when they could have had a good wine. Times changed!

There were cigars, too, kept in a special cabinet which Henry Portman had given him for a Christmas present. They ranged from the superlative to the ordinary, and Edward reserved the choicest for the customers who would appreciate them. There was Bagshot from High Wycombe, not a particularly profitable client, but Bagshot knew a good cigar when he smoked one, which, Edward fancied, wasn't often. Poor old Bagshot, his orders were scarcely worth having in these days. He once said to Christopher when the old fellow left, leaving the scent of an exquisite cigar behind him, "No profit for us on his bill! The profit has all"—and he laughed—"gone up in smoke!"

Well, he could afford to do such things. He had married a rich woman; Frances Melton, the only daughter of old Percival Melton, of the Melton Galleries in Bond Street. Not that the knowledge that she would be rich had influenced him; he had married her because he loved her; he had never regretted it either. He got on well with Percival Melton, who dealt in pictures and made a success

6

of his dealing, though Edward felt that he bought and sold them with no imagination, but with a sound knowledge of what the public wanted.

Melton had said more than once, "The public don't know anything much about pictures or painting; they only know that there's a vogue for this or that. At the moment they want Guardi and Canaletto. The next month they want the greatest slices of sentiment Italy can give them. I'm here to find and offer them what they want. I don't lose. Put the ones that are out of favour into the stores, their turn will come round again."

He had died in 1914, leaving everything to Frances, with Edward as executor. The Galleries had let at a huge rental, and now Flight, the second boy, had decided to become an art dealer.

Edward's thoughts turned to his children, as he walked slowly round the village green, now and again raising his forefinger to his cap-peak when someone saluted him. He'd been lucky in his children. There never had been a nicer, better girl than Eleanor, who was twenty-eight, and engaged to the local doctor, George Charlton. She might have done better, Edward reflected, though Charlton was a good fellow and clever; but she seemed wonderfully happy, completely contented, which was the main thing. Christopher, six years younger, had never given any trouble at all. As a baby he had eaten and slept, slept and eaten, grown and thriven. Flight hadn't been so easy. Queer lad, clever—there was no doubt about that—

attractive. People assured him that Flight had fascination. He'd not exactly given trouble, but he had "mooned", and was given to moods of depression; read queer, heavy books and became absorbed in them. Difficult to understand. Had a mania for learning languages other than his own; had insisted upon going to France and Germany instead of to Cambridge, as Christopher had done. He brought foreign friends home: Jules Matot from Paris, Mario Minotto, that astonishing couple M. and Madame Lara. Still, he was doing well in his Gallery, had redecorated it, and planned his exhibitions with taste and care . . . and made handsome profits.

Now Flight had fallen in love; wildly, completely in love with the Rector's daughter. Nothing wrong in that. The Hon. Stanley Lockwood was a personality; his wife Sophia was the elder daughter of the Earl of Rusmere; plenty of money, good family. The girl was attractive too—Alicia. But, Edward frowned, somehow he couldn't see Flight fitting into that family. Rigid, that was what they were; correct, and always doing the right thing at the right time in the right way. Still, Flight seemed happy enough, except when he came back from dining at the Rectory with one of his black fits on him, went straight to his own room and only reappeared the following morning.

Ann was not unlike him, only her moods ran to tempers, rudeness, and being cheeky. His frown faded. Edward smiled again. She'd grow out of that. What was it old Nanny called her? "That one's going to be a proper madam, she is, mark my words." He still called Ann "Madam" when she was in a good mood and they were talking amicably. He was devoted to Ann, not even her tempers really worried him.

He turned homewards again. He had taken his customary stroll, he had registered the fact that he was back at Little Manor to the inhabitants of Baddock St. Mallory; he would walk slowly home, bath and change. He would enjoy his excellent dinner, his eyes would be satisfied by the sight of Frances, Eleanor and Ann wearing attractive dresses, pleased with the correct black and white of Christopher's and Flight's clothes. He sighed, life was very pleasant.

He had been right to buy Little Manor. He had seen it first in 1910, just after Eleanor was born. He had mentioned its existence to his father-in-law, who said, "If you're going to have a family, you and Frances, you should live in the country. The town's no place for children. You can afford it. Take Frances down to look at it."

When Frances saw it she had been delighted, her only objection being that it "seems a little large for two people and a very small baby". He remembered now how he had squeezed her arm and said, 'Well, it's a small baby at the moment, but it will grow, and there might be other small babies to take her place, eh?"

9

He had only stipulated that he should design his own bathroom; after twenty-eight years he still thought that it was the best and most efficient he had ever seen. In 1920 the house came into the market and he bought it. He was back in harness, doing well; Percival Melton had left him a large sum of money, the house was well worth what he had paid for it.

There were plenty of pleasant people living in the district; his children had been brought up in a good atmosphere, his family were practically "county". They dined and were dined in turn by Sir Wilberforce and Lady Cummins, with the Hon. Wilfred Horton and his wife; his son was engaged to Alicia Lockwood—their position in and around Baddock St. Mallory was assured. Edward's lips under the small grizzled moustache curved. He thought, "Edward, my boy, you're a snob!" then mentally refuted the idea. "Not actually, I admit that I like pleasant people, cultured people, but I like them for their qualities, not their social position."

He entered the drive, this time nodding to Noakes and asking how his marrows were doing? Noakes replied gloomily that if the Almighty didn't send a bit more rain he'd have about as much chance of winning anything at the show as pigs had of flying. He added bitterly, "Not even placed, that 'ul be me, sir! T'fust time fer over nine year. It's 'ard!"

Edward answered, "Noakes, you've made that

same statement to me for over nine years and you know it! I'll bet a pound you've some giant marrow hidden away somewhere, ready to bring out and astonish the multitude!"

Noakes grinned, but muttered, "Nay not this year I've not, sir."

"Well, we shall see. Don't grudge me and Mr. Flight and Mr. Chris fine weather for our week-end holiday. We work hard enough in town all through the week, you know."

"Nay, if it 'ud start ter power down Monder mid-day, fer a good twenty-fower hours," Noakes said, "I might contrive ter make a show wi' summat as won't be mistook for a pickling onion. But I doubt it, doubt it very much. Good night, sir!"

Edward moved on. He enjoyed Friday evenings, with the thought of a peaceful Saturday and Sunday to follow. London was stuffy in summer, so stuffy that he found himself more and more frequently making some excuse for slipping down to Baddock St. Mallory during the week.

"I'm getting old, Chris! This London air is no good to me; makes my wretched leg ache. We fellows who go 'dot and carry one' feel the heat more than you spry young fellows."

Chris always looked sympathetic and said, "That's right, Dad, get down to Baddock, do you good!"

Edward knew that it was an excuse. His leg really didn't bother him much, a wound in 1917

11

had left one leg less than half an inch shorter than the other; the flat in town was comfortable enough. Hill and his wife looked after him and the two boys admirably, but sometimes he realised that in his heart he grudged the fact that Chris and Flight were young, apparently tireless, and that he was fifty-two, and at the end of the day too fagged to go anywhere except to an occasional theatre, or down to his club. It was a relief to get down to Frances, to sit quietly, talking or reading, now and then driving over to the Rectory, to Cummins or to Horton House.

He knew that he had very little interest in Christopher's new discoveries, in some remarkable firm in Lucca who produced super-excellent oil, or some out-of-the-way place in Spain where the olives were bigger and better than any others. Flight's Gallery was a sufficiently pleasant place to walk into on a hot afternoon, to sit and stare—scarcely realising what he saw—at some Madonna or a Dutch painting of people skating on a pond.

He told Frances one evening, "I'm tired. Feel sometimes that I've lived too long, seen too much. I'm a back number, Francy."

"Dear Edward," she expostulated. "You only think that now, because you've had a long day. You are most certainly not a back number! I never heard of such a thing. Really, my handsome husband, a back number!"

Her indignation pleased him; he liked to know

that she thought him handsome, though he knew very well that he was only a moderately good-looking man. She always soothed him. He used to say, "You iron out all the creases!"

He stopped, and stood staring at the house; not that he was thinking about it, his mind still turned back to Frances. Queer how love went through stages, changed its shape; not that it grew less, it took on a new aspect.

He remembered when he met her first, in her father's Gallery, where he had gone with a friend; he remembered the fellow's name quite clearly—Maurice Phillips. A Jew who dabbled in pictures, knowledgeable chap. He had introduced Edward to Frances. When they left Edward said, "I should like to marry that girl!"

Phillips laughed. "I have thought the same thing myself several times, but I fancy that I shall let thinking suffice."

He had called at Melton's Galleries again. The old man asked him to "come down to my little place at Chislehurst". Edward had gone, and felt that he made a reasonably good impression. He asked Melton to bring his wife and daughter to dine and see a show; he spent a good deal of money on flowers and a box at the theatre. He sat next to Frances; his heart beat so heavily that he thought his breath must be coming in gasps, as if he had been running. He sent her books, took her flowers, finally asked her father if he would be willing to allow her to marry him? Melton gazed at him with

13

his slightly protuberant grey eyes and said heavily, "If she wants to. If you can keep her as she's accustomed to be kept, I don't see why not."

Edward took her on the river one Sunday. He brought the most expensive luncheon basket that Portland and Wilson's could produce; there was sufficient food for ten people. He laid a huge box of chocolates on the seat beside her. As they sat on the bank eating *pâté* and smoked salmon, chicken and crisp lettuce, and some elaborate cold sweet of which he did not know the name, he stared at her, feeling breathless at the thought of asking her to share his life with him.

"I've been thinking about you a great deal," he said at last.

Frances smiled at him. "Have you? What have you been thinking?"

"That I wonder if you'd marry me? You see, I do love you terribly!"

She said very quietly, "I love you, Edward, too."

"Do you? Do you really mean that?" It seemed incredible that he should have heard aright. "You really love me?"

"Of course."

"And you'll marry me?"

"If I don't marry you, I shall never marry anyone," she answered. She spoke with the quiet confidence of twenty.

"Neither should I!"

Their engagement had been a time of perpetual

wonder to him. He worked with a kind of passion, felt that every penny that he earned made him in some way more worthy of her. It was only by a violent effort that he could concentrate on his work, make himself interested in pickles, various makes of flour, colourings, red peppers and so on. There were times when the effort was almost too much for him, when it became physical as well as mental.

His wedding day seemed endless. He had glimpses of Frances in white, Frances coming down the stairs wearing pale grey and a hat with a long curled feather, Frances closing her eyes and going to sleep in the train to Dover, Frances standing in a room filled with gilt furniture in Paris, laughing and looking round, saying, "Oh —really! It's very gorgeous, isn't it?" Of Frances in a long nightgown, thin and silky, her hair falling on her shoulders. Of himself saying, "Darling, it's all a miracle!"

During their honeymoon, the first change had begun. He loved her as much as ever—more—but into that love had crept a sense of protection. He must take care of her. She was rare, precious, weaker than he was. He loved her moments of indecision. "That hat, Edward, it's very lovely! Yes, I'll have that one." Then a second later, "Or, Edward, do you think that perhaps this is more charming? Yes, I believe that it is. This is the one, I'm sure!" She was the same in a restaurant. She wanted this dish, then decided that after all another was nicer. He smiled; felt loving, tolerant and superior.

Two years later she had told him that she was going to have a baby. She had cried a little, had laid her head on his shoulder. He had known that he was proud, self-satisfied, that his sense of protection surged up in him. He petted and praised her. It was later that fear gripped him; he grew nervous and irritable, took to rushing back from the office because he had felt that she might be ill. With his fears growing, hers seemed to disappear, to die away completely. She treated him as if he were a dear but foolish child.

"Dear silly one!" she said, "of course I'm quite all right."

When the child was born, he sat, his fingers held between his knees, to prevent them from shaking. The doctor had come into the room and rubbed his hands.

"Is it over?" Edward gasped.

"No, not over! Scarcely begun. But she'll have an easy time."

Edward glared at him furiously. An easy time! Hours, years later, the fool came in again and said, "Well, proud father! Would you like to give me a drink? Nice little girl. Everything quite easy—as I predicted. Thank you!"

Edward watched him; he hated the man.

"Easy time!" he said. "D'you think I'm deaf? You silly, damned callous brute!"

Four years of tranquillity, interest in the growth

of the baby, coming home to listen to long stories regarding her brilliance. They had agreed soon after Eleanor was born that they would never recount at great length and with a wealth of detail the progress and cleverness of their child.

"People are such bores about their children!" Frances said.

Edward agreed. "Intolerable! I suppose all babies are more or less alike, eh?"

Frances replied energetically, "Of course they are! Little animals, dear little animals, but still . . ."

It appeared, in fact it was obvious to them both, that whatever other children might be, Eleanor was most certainly quite extraordinary.

Then the war, and Frances made no attempt to hide the fact that she was certain that Edward would be killed; it was inevitable. No happiness such as theirs could be expected to last, she said bitterly. She cried when first she saw Edward in uniform, she cried when he went to Salisbury Plain for training, she was completely abandoned in her grief when he went overseas.

He heard with something like dismay that she was going to have another child. Frances wrote, *Eleanor is a darling, but only children are never the happiest children, and she will love to have a sister or brother. I am so happy.*

He was wounded in 1917. As he waited for the stretcher bearers he thought, "This is possibly the end. I'm glad she has a couple of nice children,

17

pigeon pair, boy and girl. Dear Frances, what a darling!" It wasn't the end. He went home to limp a little, to go to one hospital after another, where Frances visited him and cried a little when she noticed the mechanical devices they had used to make both his legs the same length again.

He was discharged in January 1918, and felt that he had been defrauded in not being allowed to "see the end of the show". He even missed the Army, his friends, the routine, the danger. Not that he enjoyed danger better than any other man. Major E. Flight Masters would go back to be E. F. Masters, Esq., of Clark Court, EC4.

Lovely to be with Frances again, but he missed being with men. He missed the silly jokes, the dirty jokes, the hearty drinks, the visits to towns and the slightly disreputable accounts of how time had been spent. Little Manor, which he had loved so much, stifled him a little. Once or twice he snapped when she said, "Darling, there is an ash-tray there! Not on the carpet!"

He said, "Blast! does it matter where the bloody ash goes?"

Later he was contrite, held her close and told her that he was sorry. Slowly he fought it down, the longing for crowds of men, the ache of men's company, men's talk, men's oaths. The City caught him again and he was almost startled to find that he went home excitedly to tell Frances that he had signed a contract for a firm to deliver specially made Strasbourg pies at Christmas, and with another to make regular deliveries of genuine Scottish haggis.

Ann was born in 1920. Life ran smoothly, Edward was prosperous. In 1928 the boys were at expensive schools. Eleanor was to go to a finishing school in Paris. Until the term began she was to study French at home with a governess.

Frances decided upon the governess. Edward pulled down the corners of his mouth and said, "Oh dear, a 'school marm' in the house?"

Frances laughed. "Don't be old-fashioned, Edward! In these days there are no 'school marms'; they are all champion hockey players and classical scholars and all the rest of it. Mother wants me to take Ann down to Bournemouth. Dear mother! You don't mind, do you?"

He smiled. "Of course I mind, mind horribly. I shall have to invent all kinds of excuses to come down to Bournemouth to see you. How long do you want to go for?"

"Mother suggested three weeks, but . . ."

He groaned. "Three weeks! Very well, but remember, one day longer—I say one day longer —and I shall be unfaithful to you with this new governess, even if her teeth stick out and her toes turn in and her complexion is like mud. I warn you!"

"Edward, really! You say most dreadful things!" But he knew that she was delighted. "I don't suppose that you'll see Miss Richardson. She'll be with Eleanor all the time."

"I couldn't be better pleased," he assured her.

"Anyway, you'll be in town all the week . . ."

"Thank heaven for small mercies!" he said piously.

Frances departed with Nanny and the infant Ann. Edward saw them off from Victoria and declared that he should come down at the week-end. Frances pursed her lips doubtfully.

"What's wrong?"

"Well, naturally I shall be anxious about the children. You didn't see Miss Richardson when she came last night. I like her. She's bright, and I am sure she's capable, but the first week-end I am away I should like to know how everything is going. If Eleanor seems happy, if the two boys are being good? I think, perhaps, that you ought to go down this first week-end, Edward."

"Butchered to make my wife's holiday, eh, Nanny?"

"Nay, sir," Nanny said. "Ah dean't see wheer butchering starts. You'd like ter see the little lads and Miss Eleanor, sur*lie*?"

So Edward went down to Baddock St. Mallory. Flight and Chris came to meet him at the station, for in those days he came down from town by train.

"I say, Dad! Eleanor's new governess is a stunner!" Chris announced.

Flight scowled. "She likes me better'n she likes you anyway."

Chris said, "Oh, shut up! You are a jealous little beast. She does not like you best!"

20

Edward asked if Eleanor liked her?

"Eleanor's mad about her. She's got a pash for her."

Edward nodded. "I must see this paragon," he told them.

That evening he met Monica Richardson at dinner. Eleanor spoke very little, she admitted that it was "marvellous taking French with Miss Richardson". Miss Richardson, on her part, praised Eleanor's pronunciation and ability to learn.

She was tall, with very dark red hair. Her eyes were set wide apart, her skin was very white and clear, her mouth curved and generous. Edward liked her voice, liked her hands. In a few moments she would go—she and Eleanor would go, he added hastily—and the evening would be very long and rather lonely. He wished that he were down at Bournemouth with Frances.

He said, "Can't we have some music? I have spent vast sums of money on your music, Eleanor. Can you play something?"

"I don't play really well, Daddy, but Miss Richardson"—she blushed deeply—"plays most beautifully."

"I should be in Miss Richardson's debt if she would play to us, Eleanor," Edward said with the mock gravity which his children always found irresistible.

Eleanor said, "Will you, Miss Richardson? Oh, please, will you?"

"Of course."

In the large quiet drawing-room, with its pleasant chintz covers in which Frances took such pride, Edward lay back in a huge chair and listened. Did she really play very well? He didn't know. He didn't really know much about music. He liked it, but he did not pretend to understand it or to appreciate it technically. He knew that the light was soft, the room quiet. Out in the garden he could hear the last cry of the birds as they prepared for the night and sleep. He knew that a queer sense of excitement was growing in him, growing as he watched this woman playing. He thought that she was weaving melodies which were enveloping him, binding him slowly and surely. Who was she? Where did she come from? What was her life? Had men loved her? Did she love some man? He moved, suddenly restless.

She looked up, taking her hands from the keys. "You're tired?"

"No, no, not tired at all. But"—he spoke quickly—"I have some work to get through, work which I brought down from town. Will you excuse me?" He smiled, his expression embracing them both. "Good night."

He hadn't worked, he hadn't slept, he had lain awake trying to keep his mind away from thoughts which were dangerous.

The next morning he felt tired, mentally feverish. The boys stood with him on the lawn, chattering like jays; he only heard half of what they said.

22

Then, through the wide front door, he saw her coming towards them.

Christopher said, "Oh, here she is! She's a peach, isn't she?"

Edward snapped, "Christopher, how dare you speak like that of a lady! Kindly hold your tongue."

She said, "Good morning, Mr. Masters, could I have a word with you?"

"Why, yes!" Then, realising that she wanted to talk to him alone, he turned to the boys, "Cut along, both of you!"

She told him that she was disturbed about Eleanor, she complained of a headache, there were suspicious spots on her chest and behind her ears. Should she send for the doctor? It might be measles.

Old Charlton came. He nodded. "Measles, m'dear. Keep warm. Light food. I'll pop in tomorrow. Don't try to read too much. Keep the boys away, Miss Richardson."

A mild attack, but Edward refused to go to the City for a few days, and wrote to Frances that it would be unwise for him to travel for he might carry infection to Ann, even to Frances herself. Charlton said that you could have measles half a dozen times. He stayed at Little Manor, and in three days he had ceased struggling; he had known that he was wildly, crazily in love with Monica Richardson.

They dined together in the dignified dining-room over which he had taken so much trouble. The whole world could have heard every word they spoke.

"Beautiful chairs . . ."

"Yes, I looked for those chairs for a long time. Knew exactly what I wanted. I found them eventually in a shop off the Marylebone Road."

"And that picture, the one above the mantelpiece?"

"Well, they say it's a Lawrence. I'm not certain. It is my great-grandmother, she was a Miss Flight of Hereford. My father told me that she was a 'Toast' in her day. Attractive creature, isn't she?"

Nothing more personal than that. Wednesday came, Charlton was pleased with Eleanor, the attack had been very mild, no cause for anxiety. Charlton had screwed up his small bright eyes and added, "So now , my devoted father, you can go back to work without any sense of worry as to the health of your offspring."

Edward remembered that he felt suddenly sick and frightened. Had Charlton noticed anything? Heard some note in his voice when he spoke of the admirable manner in which Miss Richardson had looked after Eleanor?

He mastered his fear, and said with overdone heartiness, "That's good . . . really good news!"

Then gloom had descended upon him, gloom which changed to a sense of desperate urgency. It

24

was over. Over . . . before it had begun.She didn't realise that he loved her, dreamed of her waking and sleeping, didn't know that she was consuming him. And tomorrow he must go back to London, and in a few days join Frances in Bournemouth.

That night, when dinner was ended, Monica said, "I must go and see that Eleanor is all right. Poor child, she has been so good, hasn't she?"

Edward licked his lips. "Must go . . . ?" he said. "There is no 'must' about it. Come and play to me. I'm leaving tomorrow."

She smiled. He noticed how the smile not only touched her lips, but lit up her eyes. "I will, when I've seen Eleanor. I'll tell her to listen. She loves music. Five minutes . . . and I shall be back."

He waited. She came back and walked to the piano, saying, "What is it to be?"

Edward said, "I don't care, whatever you like. Go on playing, I want to talk to you." She glanced at him quickly, then began to play. He stood near her, talking quickly. "You know what's happened? You must know! I've fallen in love with you. I can think of nothing else—only you. You must have known what had happened to me . . ."

Without looking at him, without ceasing to play, she said, "I didn't know. I am very, very sorry."

"What am I going to do?" His tone held indignation.

Her voice was even. "You are going to London in the morning, you are going to join Mrs. Masters

25

at the week-end and . . . you are going to forget all about me."

"No! No! No!" he whispered violently. "That's impossible. Come with me to London . . . Monica."

She took her hands from the keys, and stood up facing him. He thought, "She's all I've ever wanted, ever shall want. I'm turned forty and I never realised that love was like this. It's not peaceful and charming, it's fierce and hungry."

"Listen!" Monica said. "This won't last. I *know*. 'Sudden storms are short,' you know. You must forget all about this. It's something that died as soon as it was born. If it struggles to live, be brave and kill it."

"You don't even like me?"

"You sound like Christopher when he's sulky." She laughed softly.

"You can make jokes about this?"

"Christopher, when he is sulky, isn't a joke! Mr. Masters, I scarcely know you. You've been very kind, I've enjoyed the last few days. I'm engaged to a man who is coming home from China to marry me. I love him very dearly. There!"

Again that sense of physical sickness swept over him, there was a queer acid taste in his mouth, his throat and eyes smarted.

"Coming from China!" he repeated. "Some third mate on a merchant ship! Who has slept with a different woman in every port. . . ."

He pressed his hand against his mouth, and met

26

her eyes, suddenly afraid of what he had said. She watched him coolly, dispassionately.

"No, in the Diplomatic," she said. "Shall we change the subject?"

"I'm sorry that I said that. I don't quite know what I am saying."

For a moment he fancied that he saw amusement in her eyes, thought that her lips softened. "What a good thing that you're not in the Diplomatic!" she said. "It might lead to grave international complications. Good night, Mr. Masters, and believe me, it will pass."

She was going. He might not see her again. Frances had only engaged her for the holidays, until Eleanor could go to Paris. He said, "No, don't go!" in a hoarse whisper, then caught her to him and kissed her, again and again, satisfying his hunger, conscious that he was holding her body close to his, that he could feel the soft coolness of her skin, the faint scent of her hair. She made no attempt to struggle, to break away from his arms. She remained passive while he rained kisses on her face and neck. At last, exhausted, he let her go. Still she didn't move, but continued to watch him with a kind of detached curiosity.

"Are you going to say again that you are sorry?" she asked.

"No, I'm not," he retorted. "I did what I wanted to do. I shall never forget it, never."

This time the smile was unmistakable, her eyes danced.

She laughed softly. "Ah! I respect that attitude," she said, and leaning forward kissed him lightly on the cheek. "Good night!"

He left early the next morning. He joined Frances at Bournemouth for the week-end. She said that he didn't look well. Tired, worried? He felt that he had come through a terrible illness which had left him weak and uncertain. He longed to go back to Baddock St. Mallory. He knew that to return would be madness, disaster. When Frances asked if he would be down for the following week-end, he temporised.

"It's difficult to say. I have an idea that old Carter may be coming down; he's promised himself a week-end with us for months. I don't want to offend the old boy." He would let her know in good time.

All through the week he fought, he wavered, he argued that not to go down was to show Monica Richardson that he was afraid to meet her, that to go down would be too much for his self-control. There was his duty to Frances—and his reply was "Damn it! I've a right to have some life of my own. I shan't hurt Francy!" Running into danger, or running away from love? He scarcely slept, he wrote countless letters to Monica and burned them without attempting to post them. On the Friday evening he went down to Bournemouth.

As they sat at breakfast the next morning he heard Frances give a little clicking noise of

28

irritation, and looked up enquiringly.

"Really, Edward, listen! Miss Richardson wants to leave immediately. She's engaged to some man who arrives in England next week, and they are to be married at once by special licence. How very trying! We shall have to go home early next week."

The words in *The Times* danced. He laid down the paper because his hands shook suddenly.

"Yes, she told me he was coming home." He took a sip of coffee. "He's something in the Diplomatic, I believe."

Frances said, "The Diplomatic! Really? I liked her, didn't you?"

He laughed. "She is a pleasant girl, I thought. I only saw her at dinner-times. Yes, quite pleasant—attractive, even. Better send a wedding present. Yes?"

Frances went home on Tuesday; he returned to London. When he went down to Baddock St. Mallory, Monica had gone; Eleanor was inclined to weep at the mention of her name, but recovered with the excitement of going to Paris.

He stood staring at the flat-faced dignified old house, the smooth lawns, the neatly clipped hedges; he heard the voices of Christopher and Flight, the smack of tennis balls. A dog barked. Edward shifted his weight from his shorter leg, and sighed.

Ten years ago. He didn't even remember the name of the man Monica had married. But she had been wrong. He hadn't forgotten, he never would forget. Yet what was there to remember?

The stable clock struck seven. He glanced at his own watch, the clock was three minutes fast, he must tell Noakes to put it right. Ann was coming towards him, calling, "Daddy, you'll be late for dinner!"

He smiled and waved his hand. The sight of Ann always gave him a sense of pleasure. She was so slim, moved so easily, was so certain that life was going to give her everything.

Edward said, "I shan't be late. You've never known me late for anything, and what about you? You'll spend half an hour prinking!"

"What a word—prinking!" she mocked. Then slipped her arm through his and together they walked towards the house.

2

ELEANOR stood looking out through the open window of her bedroom. She loved to stand there quietly in the early evening and watch the changing lights, loved to notice how everything altered, softened, became more tranquil. Not only colours, but shapes and sounds. Her love for Little Manor almost amounted to a passion. George Charlton had once said to her that he believed she was only marrying him in order to stay near the house.

She answered him with that gravity which had nothing in common with either lack of humour or understanding. "That's not really true, George. I'm marrying you because I love you, but I love you more because you have the good taste to like Baddock St. Mallory."

"Then you don't want me to slave to get to Harley Street?"

"I don't want you to *slave* to get anywhere."

"And you'll be content in a flat-fronted house, built right on the street, with a good fanlight, and a worn brass-plate that was put up by my grandfather?"

She smiled. "There is a wonderful garden at the back of the house and I don't mind the street. I like to live in the middle of things."

"The middle of things! The High Street of Baddock St. Mallory!"

"It's the middle of—my things," she said placidly.

Eleanor was placid, not because nothing affected her, but because she had, from her childhood, made a world which was complete in itself, a world which was filled with the people and things she loved; in that world she lived and worked and found contentment. Where, as children, Christopher had sulked if he was denied anything, where Flight had allowed depression to overwhelm him, and where Ann had indulged in tempers and rages, Eleanor, when refused something for which she asked, could be relied upon to accept the refusal and to set about quietly to find something else which would give her equal pleasure. Nanny often said, "Nay, if Eleanor asks fer t'sun and mayn't have it, she'll find a star that she'll like joost as well, bless 'er!"

Years ago, fired by the ability of Monica Richardson, she had asked her father if she might go to college and take a degree when she left Paris. Edward had stared and said, "Well, if it will make you happier. But why?"

"I think that I should like to be a teacher, Daddy."

She remembered how he had wrinkled his nose, and said, "Oh, darling!"

She had gone to college, and for three terms had done very well, almost brilliantly, then she broke

32

down. Her mother had been sent for, she had gone home, old Doctor Charlton had looked grave, and she had been taken to London to see Sir William Something or Other. They had talked of anæmia, and rest and freedom from strain, mental or physical.

Young Charlton asked her once when they were alone, "Do you mind terribly, Eleanor, giving up this career?"

"I did at first," she admitted, "but the minding is growing less, and there are plenty of things to do."

"As interesting as the things you wanted to do?"

"How can I tell? I never did the things I once wanted to do. Perhaps that is where I am lucky, it would have been worse if I had taken a degree, a good one, begun teaching, and loved every minute of it, and then broken down, wouldn't it?"

Now she stood at the window and thought what a pleasant life it was. The house—she smiled, because instinctively she put it first, though she knew really that it was additionally lovable because it held the people who were her nearest and dearest. The house really meant her father, her mother, Chris, Flight and Ann. This room— she turned from the window and glanced round it—had been the old night nursery. There were still Flight's initials on one of the window-panes. He did that when he took one of his mother's diamond rings and scratched F. M. There was the funny little cupboard in the wall where Nanny used to keep what she called, "Nurs'ry medi-cines"—Collis Brown's Chlorodyne, syrup of figs, iodine for cuts, nitre for colds, camphorated oil for congested chests, and so on. The cupboard still smelt rather like Mr. Green's, the chemists in the High Street.

There was a mark on the broad banister rail where Chris had caught it with his boot heel when he was sliding down, a thing strictly forbidden. He had crashed into the hall and cut his head badly on the corner of an old chest. Their father had heard of the accident when he came down at the week-end. He had interviewed Chris, who lay in bed with an interesting bandage bound about his brows.

"If I did right," Daddy said, "I should give you a good beating for disobeying orders. As it is, you've got your punishment in another way." Daddy had always said that. "If I did right, I should beat you but . . ." Then the reason for not administering chastisement was added. "You have to suffer this" or "The fact that you have distressed your mother will be, I hope, sufficient punishment."

The marble bust of Napoleon still showed a chip off one ear where Ann had flung a stone at it because she disliked Napoleon's character. There was scarcely a place in the house which did not have some memory for Eleanor, memories which she treasured and loved and rarely talked about.

She loved the gardens, the ancient twisted

mulberry tree, the lazy little river which ran at the lower end of the tiny wood, the sundial which Flight had found in some old yard near Lincoln's Inn and had bought from the housebreakers for thirty shillings.

"On condition as yer remove it at yer own cost an' no further obligations nor questions. No guarantee as it is reely old, mind!' Flight knew now that it was old, very old, and worth more than thirty shillings, worth a great deal more.

She loved the old espaliered fruit trees clinging to the warm brick walls in the kitchen garden, and the summer-house where Ann had scrawled in pencil, "I hate Miss Goring." No one had washed away the pencil marks, though Ann had eventually come to love Miss Goring dearly and had wept when she left.

When people who lived in London said to Eleanor, "But what do you find to do in the country?" she could have laughed at them for their foolishness.

Gravely she would tell them, "I keep fantails; there is a huge cage of canaries in the greenhouse behind the drawing-room. Ten canaries need a lot of time I assure you! I won't allow anyone else to look after the eggs. I make pickles, not jam—Cook does that—bottle fruit, find old recipes for making 'simples' and herbal ointments from an old book which belonged to my mother's grandmother. I have a girls' club. Oh, it's a bore sometimes, but there are other times when it's quite amusing. I run the village library, and—what else? I forget, but I know there are other things. What do I do!"

Yet she had never become "busy" or "managing", the women in the village liked to talk to her because she always gave them advice which was tolerant and wise. "Like talkin' ter one of ourselves, talking to Miss Eleanor! No patronising nor nuthink of that, just friendly and in-ter-ested. Never ''Ow h'is your daughter, the one as went inter service wi' Lady What's-it?' as if my daughter 'ad three 'eads an' all on 'em mucky! Luke at the Major now, 'ow friendly, an' yet allus the gentleman!"

Then just a year ago George Charlton's father retired and went to live in Harrogate because his rheumatism had got the upper hand. He left George in complete control and George had come to Edward Masters to say that he loved Eleanor and did Edward approve?

Edward had approved, not because he didn't think that his elder daughter could have done better, but because he liked George Charlton and knew him to be a decent, hard-working fellow.

George had asked her to marry him one evening when they had walked over to see that the hens were safely locked up for the night. She was startled, and without turning, said, "*What* did you say, George?"

"I asked if you would marry me?"

She smiled. "Really, George? You want me to say that I will?"

"I shouldn't have asked you if I didn't want that more than anything else in the world. Will you?"

"Darling, of course I will!"

He held out his arms. "Come and kiss me, and let me kiss you." Her mother had cried a little and hoped that George would be good to her. Chris said, "Of course he'll be good to her, Mother. What do you think he's going to do, beat her?" Ann had watched them, her eyes wide, obviously expecting to see some sudden and visible change in them both. And Flight had gone to the piano and played the Wedding March, and then suddenly relapsed into silence and into one of his strange fits of depression.

She said to him that evening when George had left, "Flight, what's wrong, dear?"

"I don't quite know. The feeling that this is the beginning of a change. It won't ever be quite the same. You'll go and live with George, Chris will marry, Dad and Mother will get older . . ." He shivered.

"Why can't things stay as they are now?"

"Darling, you know that's unreasonable. New generations cannot always cling to the older ones; it wouldn't be right or fair. We've all got to make our own lives, get experience, grow."

"I hate it; changes are hateful."

"You might want to marry one day?"

He stared at her; she thought there was fear in his eyes.

"Me? Never, never."

Yet here he was, scarcely a year later, bound hand and foot to Alicia Lockwood.

The door burst open, Eleanor's thoughts were shattered, she could almost feel them being splintered and broken into little pieces. Ann rushed in. Eleanor said mildly, "Darling, you ought to knock at bedroom doors!"

Ann said, "Well, you're dressed, it's all right."

"All the same . . ."

"Oh, Eleanor! listen—an awful, frightening thing has happened!"

"What?" She was not disturbed. "Awful, frightening things" happened to Ann at short and regular intervals.

"I've fallen hopelessly in love! Now don't say that I've been in love before, of course I have! But I never shall again. Never. I'm eighteen and I know love, *now*, when I meet it."

Eleanor looked at her sister. She was so eager; not pretty, but possessed of great attraction, with a short, faintly tip-tilted nose, eyes which were almost incredibly bright, and a skin which was quite perfect, both in colouring and texture. She remembered the long list of "only loves"—Ronald Colman, the Duke of Windsor, Anthony Eden, Owen Nares, Arthur Prince, Kreisler, were names which came to her at random.

She did not smile, she only said, "Tell me, Ann darling, who is he?"

Ann giggled suddenly at some recollection. "Do

you remember when I was so in love with that prize fighter? . . . I've even forgotten his name! This is quite different."

Eleanor said, "I wish you'd tell me about it, Ann."

Ann wriggled, laughed self-consciously, then said, "Well, I met him first at the Rectory. They are snobs there, you know! They were making such a *restrained fuss* of him. You know, completely well-bred and correct, but you felt that if he had wanted to play marbles on the drawing-room carpet they'd have said, 'Of course, it's our favourite game!' However, he didn't, he was just deathly bored, and talked to me. Then he was at the Cummins'; he was sweet, and asked if he might come over here and play tennis. He's stationed at Colchester. Eleanor, he's got a Mercédès Benz that just eats up the miles! Well, he drove over this afternoon, and I was standing where the wall is quite low, beside the road. He saw me and stopped, and we talked. He couldn't come to play tennis, he'd got some duty or other. Yes, he's a soldier. Darling, he is sweet! Not a bit good-looking, almost ugly. With a big jaw like Mussolini's—only not so objectionable. When he smiles! . . . oh, he's adorable. He says . . ."

Eleanor sighed. "Ann, could you possibly tell me what his name is?"

"His name?" Ann blinked her eyes rapidly. "Didn't I tell you?"

"No, my dear. He's sweet, he has a big jaw, and

his smile is adorable. It might be interesting to know his name."

Ann nodded. "Yes, that's just where it all gets so difficult. His name is Sholto Archibald William. His surname is—or I suppose it is—Claverley."

"*Lord* Claverley?"

Her sister nodded. "Lord Claverley."

"But he's the son of the Duke, Ann."

"I know, but as he says, neither he nor I can help that. It's just a pity, that's all!"

"But, Ann . . ." Eleanor rose and moved restlessly about the room, while Ann watched her. There was no distress in her expression, she looked interested, almost amused. Twice Eleanor stopped and opened her lips as if to speak, then closed them and moved away to straighten some fold in the curtain or rearrange some flowers in the big brightly coloured vase which she had bought in Capri and brought home with such care.

Ann said, "Eleanor, do say something."

Her sister made a small gesture of helplessness. "Darling, it's so difficult. I don't mean about you, you've fallen in love so often, but this man. Have you any reason to think, to imagine, that he—well, likes you?"

"If he doesn't," Ann retorted without rancour, "he's the world's best liar. He's coming to see me tomorrow—yes, here. Why not? It's a lovely house, lovely parents, lovely sister and brothers. Again, why not?"

"Oh, darling, because it's all quite stupid and

romantic and impossible. Ann, do be sensible. Please, dear, please!"

Her sister came towards her and laid her hands on Eleanor's shoulders. Suddenly she seemed to have gained in years, her eyes danced no longer, they were steadfast and grave. Eleanor longed to catch her close and hold her, to whisper, "You're lovely, but you're the daughter of Edward Masters, a wholesale grocer, and you can't marry the son of a duke."

"Listen," Ann said quietly, "Sholto and I love each other. He isn't clever, but he's sincere and decent. It's just—happened. I'm not a silly child any longer. It's real. Believe that, Eleanor!"

That night during dinner, when Frances smiled equally on them all and praised the table decorations which were Eleanor's work, when she asked Christopher intelligent questions about his work in the City and refrained from asking Flight any questions regarding Alicia Lockwood—who had, she felt, been more than usually difficult for the last week, which accounted for Flight's long silences and lack of appetite—Ann flung in her bombshell.

"Mother, do you mind if a friend of mine comes to luncheon tomorrow?"

"No, darling, of course not. Who is it, Griselda Cummins?"

"It's a man," Ann said calmly. "I met him at the Rectory. His name is Claverley."

Edward glanced up from the piece of roast duck

41

which he was dismembering.

He smiled. "Some relation of the Duke's, no doubt?"

Still calmly, his younger daughter answered, "Son, Daddy."

Edward repeated, "*Son?*"

"Only son, Daddy!"

Edward exploded, "What's he coming to lunch here for?"

With an air of patience Ann explained. "I think that he would like to meet you and Mother, Daddy."

"But I've arranged to play golf with Chris!"

"Then he must come again some other time when you're not playing golf."

Even Flight had been shaken out of his gloom. They were all watching Ann—Ann who could not have been more self-possessed. She smiled at them all, then said, "Then that is all right, Mother? I'll telephone to him tonight."

Her father laid down his knife and fork, he wiped his lips carefully with his large, well-laundered napkin, then he laid that, too, on the table.

"Ann, if this is some kind of a joke, then it is one which neither I, nor your mother, appreciate. What is this? Lord Claverley coming to luncheon here? Why, what for? I want this matter straightened out."

"Daddy, dear, Sholto Claverley is a very pleasant, unassuming young man. I've met him several times. I was talking to him just before I met you tonight. He'd like to meet you—like to meet us all, and I've asked Mother if he may come to luncheon. That's all there is to 'straighten out'. Don't make any fuss of him. That kind of silliness bores him desperately. Just one of our ordinary, nice luncheons, and you and Mummy just your own charming selves. That's all."

Edward stared at her, he said, "Well, well—really!"

Frances followed Eleanor into her bedroom. The evening had been difficult. Not because anything had been said, but because Ann seemed to treat this unexpected visit from an important young nobleman as the most ordinary thing in the world. Edward had made one or two tentative remarks, followed by still fewer questions; to them all Ann had replied coolly but with complete poise and politeness. Frances said, as she closed the door behind her, "Eleanor, what *is* this? I'm completely bewildered!"

"I don't know, Mother. Ann talked to me this afternoon. She has met Lord Claverley several times, and apparently they like each other very much indeed."

"You don't mean . . ." Frances sighed deeply, "that Ann imagines that she's in love with him."

"I'm afraid so."

"But this man—what does he think, imagine? If he fancies that your father is going to tolerate

43

anything in the least underhand, he is making a very great mistake. Your father is most disturbed. Lord Claverley coming to luncheon! Did you hear Ann speaking to him on the telephone? 'Is that you, Sholto? My mother will be delighted to see you at luncheon tomorrow. Yes, at one. Good night.' That was my daughter, talking to a man who will be a Duke one day!"

Sholto Claverley came. He was a tall young man, with fair hair, a rather high complexion, blue eyes and a pleasant voice.

He stammered a little, as he thanked Frances for allowing him to come to luncheon at such short notice. He praised the oak panelling in the hall, commented upon the beauty of the garden, he pulled the ears of Mopsy, the setter, gently but firmly, in a way of which Mopsy approved.

"A splendid bitch, sir," he assured Edward. "If you don't t-think me impertinent, I f-fancy there is a touch of canker in that ear. I've some powder that is incredibly good. M-might I perhaps send some over?" Then he smiled suddenly and Edward Masters decided that he liked him. "Or, better still, from my point of view, bring some over."

At luncheon he noticed the picture of "Miss Henrietta Flight". "A Lawrence, if I'm not wrong," he said.

Edward pulled a grimace, implying doubt. "They *say* that it's a Lawrence."

"I think they—whoever 'they' may be—are

44

right. That tone, the brushwork. We have two at home, the treatment is exactly the same."

"Maybe, maybe, I know nothing about pictures. My son, Flight, is the knowledgeable fellow on art. Eh, Flight?"

Claverley said eagerly, "Oh, b-but I know. I've spent quite a number of pleasant hours in your Gallery. It's a charming place. The collection of da Vinci drawings, that was a wonderful effort."

Flight's thin, sensitive face brightened suddenly. He leaned forward, looking younger and less absorbed. Eleanor watched the corners of his mouth curve upwards. That was how Flight should always look!

"Oh, you saw them? It took a tremendous amount of persuading to get people to lend them. Then there was insurance, and transporting safely, and special detectives on duty day and night. Oh, there were moments when I felt like throwing up the whole thing." He laughed.

Claverley said, "But you didn't, eh?"

"No, I didn't. There was something rather exciting in walking through the Gallery and thinking, 'I've brought you here together, you're under one roof again! I wonder if Leonardo is pleased?' and I used to feel . . ."

He stopped suddenly, his face flushed, he had seen Christopher's eyes on him, half-puzzled, half-scornful.

Flight said, "I expect that it all sounds fantastic."

45

Christopher said, "Well, I admit I can't imagine feeling like that."

Edward frowned. He wished that Chris would keep such observations to himself, realise that what Flight could and did feel was one thing, what Chris could and did feel, another. Wished, too, that Flight didn't colour up so easily, and then retire into silence. He ought to stand up to his brother. He was clever, really more clever than Chris. He just lacked something. What was it? He shrugged his shoulders and turned to Claverley.

"What do you feel about this German business?"

The younger man did not reply for a moment, but made bread pellets with a kind of deep concentration; then, pushing them into a neat little pile, he said, "I think that we're playing a dangerous game and playing it very badly, sir."

"Ah! Playing it badly, eh?"

Christopher asked, with a certain truculence in his tone, "What else could we have done?"

"Several things, surely?" Claverley said mildly.

"War? We're not ready!"

Claverley smiled. "But if you are going to argue on that assumption surely you begin a c-completely new set of reasons. You've altered your ground, p-premise?"

"Not much use rushing into a war to defend a country when you know that your power is so limited as to be little better than useless . . ."

"Oh! I wasn't altogether thinking of what was

useful, perhaps I was thinking selfishly."

Christopher said shortly, "I'm afraid I don't follow you."

Ann retorted, "Of course you don't, Chris. How could you?"

Frances rose. "You all know that I dislike politics being discussed at the table. Edward, we'll have coffee outside. Yes?"

Ann and Eleanor followed their mother. Together they walked down the steps of the terrace which led to the lawn, where coffee was waiting, the silver catching the rays of the sun which slanted through the leaves of the big elms, the china glinting as the light touched the gold and deep rich blues of the Crown Derby.

Frances sank into a chair and sighed. "What a tiresome luncheon! First Flight and his pictures, then Chris longing to talk politics. I wish that people could hold a reasonable conversation without making everything uncomfortable."

Eleanor said, "Oh, I don't really think that it mattered, Mother." But Frances Masters was disturbed, and when she was disturbed she became faintly irritable, in a childish fashion, seeking for something or someone upon whom she might fasten her grievances.

"Of course it mattered, Eleanor! Conversation at a luncheon party ought to be general, at a small party like this. Ann never opened her mouth . . ."

"I did, Mother. I spoke to Chris."

"Yes, in a way which was not calculated to mend

47

matters! Ann, I don't understand this visit of Lord Claverley's at all. What on earth does it all mean? You're very young—eighteen. He must be considerably older."

"He's . . ." She paused, and said thoughtfully, "How old is Sholto? Oh, he's twenty-four."

"You call him Sholto."

"He calls me Ann."

Frances made a gesture. "Well, really! And what does it all mean?"

Eleanor caught the note of anxiety in her mother's voice, and thought, "Darling Mother, she's terribly worried and puzzled, and rather afraid. Only Ann won't understand, she'll just believe that she is being very difficult."

Ann smiled calmly. "I expect it 'means' that Sholto wants to marry me."

"Has he asked you to marry him?"

"Several times. That's what, I imagine, he is discussing with Daddy now. He's discussed it with the Duke . . ."

"You haven't met—the Duke?"

"Not yet. Sholto wanted to talk to Daddy first. The Duke is quite willing. He told Sholto that he didn't give a damn who he married so long as she was sound in wind and limb, had straight legs, and wasn't going to try to dodge having a family!"

Frances gasped. "Well, I must say . . . Eleanor, give me some coffee!"

In the dining-room Sholto looked from one man to another. Edward was intent on his port, Christopher looked slightly sulky, Flight stared out of the window.

He cleared his throat nervously and addressed himself to his host.

"Well, sir, I suppose that you have formed some idea as to why I wanted—at this p-particular moment—to cadge an invitation to luncheon? It's more or less 'official'. I hope in the future there will be many invitations which won't be 'official', but now . . . Can I talk to you about Ann and myself?"

Chris pushed back his chair. "I'll get along, you don't want me here. Come on, Flight."

Sholto smiled at them both. "I don't m-mind in the least, you can hear all that I have to say . . ."

Edward Masters interrupted. "No, no! Better to be alone, eh?"

"As you wish."

As the door closed, Edward said, "We'll have coffee here, yes?" and ringing, gave the order to the maid who entered the room. He turned sideways in his chair, twisted his moustache nervously, and then said, "Now, is this business serious? If it isn't, then it's a damned insult. If it is—it's a very grave matter. You understand me?"

"Perfectly. It is completely serious, sir."

"I'm a wholesale grocer, and not ashamed of it. Clark Square, EC4. My wife owns the Melton Galleries—oh! you know about that. We're not rich people, we're comfortably off; stable, safe people. We've no distinguished relations, no ancestors worth bothering about. My elder daughter is going to marry the local doctor, and a very good fellow he is. My younger son is engaged to—or"—suddenly, testily—"I suppose that he's engaged to, Alicia Lockwood. Her father's the rector here . . ."

Sholto nodded. "I know the Lockwoods very well."

"Umph! Well, there's the position. Your father is the Duke of Alcaster. You're the only son. How is your father going to take this?"

Claverley laughed. "Frankly he is delighted. My father is a plain-spoken kind of chap. I won't repeat word for word what he said, but he intended his words to c-convey that he had not the slightest objection. I was born when he was forty-five, I'm twenty-four now. He's not young and he wants to see me m-married. I've never been what you might call a wild fellow, I've imagined myself in love a couple of times, but there was really nothing to it. I do love Ann: I believe that between us we can make something pretty good out of l-life. I've a good deal of money. I should like our lawyers to meet as soon as is convenient to you, and discuss settlements and so on. Now—have I your consent to go ahead?"

Edward drained his coffee-cup, sighed and said, "I don't know how you feel, Lord Claverley, but I could do with a brandy."

"So could I!" He wiped his forehead. "I'd no

50

idea what a ticklish business it was asking a girl's father to allow her to m-marry you! I'll swear that I'll never do it again as long as I live!"

Returning to the table with a decanter Edward poured out two generous brandies and offered one to his guest. His self-assurance was returning to him, and with each sip of the good mellow liquid he felt his certainty and confidence growing stronger. He nodded to Claverley above the rim of his glass.

"I suppose that I am no more or no less a snob than other men," he said, and his voice was the voice of Edward Flight Masters, of Clark Square and Little Manor. "I have never truckled to anyone in my life. I believe in the aristocracy of brains. I believe in the reward that sweetens labour. I believe in the justice of being able to enjoy the fruits of achievement. Place and power do not impress me, and yet . . ." he sipped his brandy with relish and appreciation, "the idea that my daughter may one day be a Duchess is a staggering one. I admit it, freely and frankly."

Sholto leaned forward and spoke confidentially. "Sir, when I remember that one day I shall be Duke to your daughter's Duchess, I too am s-staggered! I mean it. She's a grand person, she's going to be a great woman. You can trust me to appreciate her."

They joined the group under the elm tree, Ann, sprawling in her chair, called, "Hello, Sholto! was it frightening?"

"I was p-petrified, my sweet. But it's all right!"

51

"Were you pompous, Daddy?"

"Only justifiably so, I think," Edward admitted.

"Admirably so!" Sholto added.

Frances looked from one to the other. "Edward, dear, I know that I am only Ann's mother, but I really think that I might be told what has happened?"

"My dear," Edward said, "you know perfectly well what has happened. Claverley wants to marry Ann, Ann is apparently ready to accept him. I have no objections to make; he assures me that his father has none. That is all, except for you to embrace them both and shed a few tears in a discreet manner!"

That night Frances watched her husband undress in his usual orderly fashion; she noted with a certain satisfaction how neatly he did everything; his movements were swift and precise, and when he came and stood at the end of the bed and smiled at her, she thought how attractive he still was, how well groomed, how slim and erect.

He said, "Happy, Francy?"

"Bewildered, Edward. Ann—a Duchess!"

"What matters most is that Ann should be a happy woman. I like the young man, he's honest, simple and direct. Got a sense of humour."

"Eleanor's happy with her George, Ann with Lord Claverley. One day Chris will find some nice woman. I wish that Flight were more content. Edward"—suddenly, as if she had forced herself to speak—"I don't like Alicia Lockwood!"

"I know. Only, Francy, you're not going to marry her, Flight is."

"I wonder . . . my poor Flight! He never talks about it to me, but I often wonder if things are right between them. Tonight he looked wretched."

Edward kicked off his slippers and prepared to climb into bed.

"Probably by tomorrow night he'll be in the wildest spirits."

3

FLIGHT had known Alicia Lockwood for years, ever since they were children; they met at Christmas parties, when he was home for the holidays, and later when he returned from France, Germany or Spain. He had always liked to watch her. As a child she had been taller for her age than either Eleanor or Ann or Griselda Cummins. Her legs, encased in smooth black silk stockings, were long, slim, and, Flight thought, very attractive. Her pale gold hair seemed to him to catch and hold the light, he felt that it had a particular quality of being more "alive" than the hair of other girls. Her pale, matt skin, her large dark grey eyes with long lashes, so many shades darker than her hair, all went to make her indisputably lovely.

In the summer of 1937 he had returned from France, bringing with him Jules Matot. Flight had met young Matot in Paris at the house of Louis Lara, the well-known art and picture expert. Jules was to enter his business, and although he was, Louis Lara declared, a good pupil, possessing taste and discrimination, Jules confided to Flight that he longed to become an actor.

"For reasons which I shall not discuss now, this is impossible—sufficient to say that my mother was against it. But"—and Jules smiled, showing his incredibly white teeth, "one day, mark my words, I shall be an actor. You, my dear friend, shall see me act and be filled with admiration."

Flight asked Matot to come to spend a holiday with him. Frances was only too willing to have the young man and to attempt to repay all the kindness and hospitality which the Laras had showered upon Flight. Edward, too, was interested at the idea of meeting a specimen of French youth at close quarters. Christopher scowled and said, "For heaven's sake, can't Flight find some English chap to bring home? He'll probably be frightful, wearing most awful clothes and hopeless at games."

Ann flashed out, "Listen to our insular Britisher!"

Matot arrived. He was tall and thin, his face lean and very much tanned; he brought with him tennis racquets in elaborate cases, and his suitcases were superb. Frances liked his manner, Edward liked his air of respectful deference, Eleanor found him sympathetic, and Ann, with her air of wide-eyed innocence which always boded evil to someone, asked if he really played games.

Matot said, "Games—please?"

"Tennis; I see you've brought racquets, Mr. Matot."

"Oh yes, of course."

"Golf?"

He pulled down the corners of his mouth, and

Flight, watching with amusement, thought, "He's got an actor's face, this Jules!"

"Golf?" He spread his hands wide, palms upwards. "I have so little time. I play, oh yes, but that is just what I do—*play*, you understand? When I was last in this country—two years ago—I was at Hoylake. My handicap was ten. Imagine! I was mortified."

Christopher was obviously growing restive. Flight remembered that his brother's handicap was eight, after several years of genuinely hard work and continual playing at every possible opportunity.

Chris said, "Anything else, Matot? Cricket, football, billiards, bumble puppy, old maid, rummy?"

Matot looked blankly at him. "Cricket . . . no. Football—I was in the team which was sent to Italy last winter, then I broke my ankle and that was the finish. Billiards, of course; and the rest I am afraid that I do not know. What are they?"

Ann smiled sweetly. "They're games of which my brother is inordinately fond. Perhaps he will teach you."

Even Chris, who could be generous enough when it came to giving admiration to someone who played any game better than he did, admitted that Matot was in the professional class as regards tennis, that his golf was definitely good, and that in a game of billiards he was "dangerous".

"But you still don't like him?" Eleanor asked.

Chris said, "Oh, he's all right. I don't *like* foreigners, you see."

It was after a small dance on the lawn at Sir Wilberforce Cummins' that Matot and Flight sat talking in the early hours of the summer morning on the terrace at Little Manor. Jules, like Flight, hated to go to bed. He grimaced and always said, "But such waste—those lovely hours spent in sleep! Perhaps there might be circumstances which would make leaving the night, and lights, and stars, for bed worth while. Until those things arrive, let us sit here and talk."

Flight, his hand clasped round his slim ankle, laughed. "Don't air those sentiments before my family, Jules!"

"No, no, naturally. Though the little sister, Ann, would only laugh if I did. How very sweet she looked tonight and how well she dances!"

"Yet she isn't really pretty," Flight objected.

Jules snapped his fingers. "Oh, pretty! What is—pretty? Dolls are pretty, so are kittens. Your elder sister has beauty of a kind which comes from the mind and the character; your mother has beauty, too, of heart and affection; but there was only one really beautiful woman there tonight. Oh, she was exquisite—incredible!"

"And she was . . ."

"Miss Lockwood. Ah, there is beauty of a rare kind! Figure, face, everything. That is the kind of woman for whom a man might die. Indeed," reflectively, "she herself might kill him. Not actually, you understand me; but there is something about her which is aloof, withdrawn, cold—yes, cold. But what beauty!"

Flight said slowly, "Alicia Lockwood. I've known her since we were children."

Jules laughed softly. "My dear blind friend! And you have never *seen* this lovely creature? How strange you Englishmen are, to be sure."

Then Jules returned to France, and from that country sent presents to the Masters family; no one was forgotten, and even Christopher had to admit that Matot must have not only spent a great deal of money, but a great deal of time and thought, on the choice of his gifts.

Flight missed him, thought of the long talks which they had had together, and most frequently of the night when they had sat on the terrace speaking of Alicia Lockwood. He had acquired a rowing-boat and spent long hours on the smooth flowing river which ran through the broad lands of the county, where willows dipped and trailed their leaves in the water, where suddenly a kingfisher would swoop from bank to bank like a sudden flash of precious stones. For hours Flight would row lazily and come at last to some quiet place where he could lie and read, or perhaps only stare upwards through the branches of the willows to the pale blue of the sky, watching the white clouds which seemed to swim in the sea of sky, massive, dignified and beautiful.

Then his thoughts would go back to Alicia

Lockwood, to her pale hair, her slender neck, and those wide-apart grey eyes with their dark lashes. He knew that he had always felt her attraction, even when he was a rather lanky boy wearing his first dinner-jacket, and longing for "tails" such as his elder brother wore. Half closing his eyes, scene after scene came back to him. He saw himself standing before Alicia, asking if she would dance with him. Heard her say coolly when the dance was over, "You ought to dance better than that, Flight!" Remembered how, the following Christmas, he had again asked her to dance, and she had raised her eyes, in which he fancied a kind of lazy amusement danced, and asked, "Have you improved?" Flushing but determined, he had answered, "Come and find out!"

He had danced with her at the Cummins', so had Jules Matot. She danced, as she moved, with a sort of smooth ease, and firmly refused to dance some of the ultra-modern dances, which she stigmatised as "hideous".

Two nights ago she had dined at Little Manor with her father and mother, and had devoted herself almost entirely to Christopher. Later, Flight had walked in the garden with her for a few moments, and she had said how beautiful everything looked. He had been sulky and scarcely spoke. She asked, with that same lazy amusement, if he were annoyed.

"Not actually annoyed," he said. "I think that it's a pity to devote yourself completely to one

59

person at a dinner-party, don't you?"

"Meaning that I did so with Christopher?"

"Of course. Do you find him so interesting?"

"Interesting? Not particularly. But easy; he presents no problems."

"You don't like problems?"

"Only when I am capable of solving them. Only when I feel that it is sufficiently interesting to attempt to solve them."

He stopped abruptly, watching her intently; he knew that his heart was beating, beating so heavily that it seemed to suffocate him. She looked as he had thought the fields looked when he was rowing home before dinner. Drenched with soft light mist, grey and quiet.

He said, "Let me take you out in my boat, will you?"

"Is it a nice boat?"

He laughed. "Charming! Very comfortable. When will you come? Tomorrow?"

"Yes—unless Mama wants me to go out with her paying calls."

They went back to the house.

Lady Sophia said, "Alicia, dear, I do hope that you've not caught cold. It grows chilly in the evenings."

Her husband, a handsome cleric possessed of great dignity and a distinct presence, said in his rich mellow voice, "No, no. It's not chilly this evening, Sophia."

Alicia walked forward until she stood in the ring

of bright light where the party were gathered.

"Mama, may I go boating with Flight tomorrow?"

"*Boating?*" her mother repeated. "Why, yes, I think so."

"I thought that you might want me to go calling with you."

"No, dear, I don't think so. Yes, go with Flight. Don't tire her, Flight, will you?"

"Rather not, Lady Sophia. I'll be ready at half past two, Alicia. At the end of the garden at the Rectory."

When they had gone, Edward had said: "Somehow, although I respect him, I never feel completely at ease with the Rector. He may be the Rector, but he never forgets that he was the Hon. Stanley Lockwood first. The girl's a beauty, isn't she?"

"Ye-e-s," Frances assented, "I suppose so. I always feel that she lives completely within herself. I wonder if anyone really knows Alicia?"

Flight had lain awake half the night, his thoughts turning again and again to Alicia. Jules was right, hers was a beauty so rare, so exquisite, that many people missed it completely. Tomorrow he would talk to her, show her the places that he loved along the river bank. She had talked of "problems"—did she mean that he was one of them? The thought was not unpleasing.

He waited for her at the end of the Rectory garden, waited without impatience, only longing to catch the first possible glimpse of her as she came across the well-shaven lawn. What a satisfactory house it was, this Rectory! Little Manor had its own beauty, but this magnificent piece of Georgian architecture far surpassed it. Mellowed, cared for, admirably maintained—for Lockwood had considerable means apart from his very ample stipend —it glowed in the afternoon sun. She came through one of the french windows, turning to speak to someone in the room, turning her head so that again he could see the lovely setting of her neck and shoulders. She stooped to caress a little Cairn terrier, and Flight heard her voice, clear and distinct, "No, my sweet, I can't take you today."

He sat, his hands between his knees, watching her move over the clipped, smooth grass. How easily she moved, swiftly and yet unhurried. He sprang to his feet and stood waiting. Alicia came to him, holding out her hand. As he took it, he knew that he wanted to say, "Alicia, it's true. I love you, you're all I want in the world. You—and your beauty." Aloud he said, "It's awfully nice of you to come. Do you know our river?"

"The Twardle? My father says that it should have been called the Dawdle, it moves along so slowly. No, I don't know it well, so this is a voyage of exploration for me."

"And for me," Flight said.

"But you know it so well!"

"I've a feeling that I am seeing it for the first time today."

62

That afternoon was the first of many; again and again that summer Flight persuaded her to come with him, not only for a few hours, but for whole days, when Eleanor packed elaborate luncheon-baskets and filled flasks with cold drinks. She had never known Flight so happy, so free from those fits of depression, those long silences, and apparent inability to find interest in anything except his work.

Now he looked younger, laughed, and teased Ann, was always ready to join in discussions, and talk of his plans for the Gallery, which he had just taken over. His visits to the Continent were over for the time being at least; his French was perfect, his German serviceable, and his Spanish admirable.

One evening Edward Masters stopped him as he came across the hall.

"Flight, come into the study, I want a word with you."

"Yes, Father, of course."

Edward seated himself at his desk, and Flight realised that in some way the conversation was to be "official". His father always occupied that chair when he was preparing to talk seriously.

"Sit down, my boy. That's right. Cigarette? Now, Flight, I don't want to be intrusive, but is there anything between you and Alicia?"

Flight's hands opened and closed with a movement which was almost convulsive.

"At present, Father, nothing."

"You'd like to marry her?"

"It's the only thing I really do want."

"Does she know?"

"Honestly, I'm not sure. Sometimes I think that she does, then again I can't tell. I think that she likes me—likes me quite a lot."

Edward nodded. "You're very young—nineteen—just starting on your career. Oh, I know that you've all got the money your grandfather left you, but how far is eight hundred pounds a year going towards keeping a girl like Alicia? Remember who her people are—her uncle is the Earl of Rusmere. Her father's people . . ."

Eagerly Flight said, "I know, I know, but I don't believe that Alicia would care."

"No, but the Rector and Lady Sophia might," Edward said drily. "How old is Alicia?"

"Two years older than I am—twenty-one."

Edward nodded. "All right; I trust you to do the proper thing. Ask her father. And good luck to you, my boy!"

"Thank you, Father."

The next day, as they had drifted along the idle little river, Flight rested on his oars and sat watching Alicia. She was trailing her hand in the water, her face was serene, content. He wondered what she was thinking. They seemed cut off from the rest of the world, they might go drifting along like this for ever, he felt. On and on, oblivious of everyone else, indifferent to the passing of time, to obligations and plans, to projects and designs.

"Alicia," he said, and his voice in his own ears sounded harsh.

She looked up. "Yes, Flight?"

"Do you like me?"

He saw her slow smile soften her lips. "Should I be here if I didn't?"

"How much do you like me?"

Alicia leaned back against the cushion. Flight could see the lovely line of her throat, right to the little hollow at the base of her neck. He thought wildly, as he had done once when he was ill and running a high temperature and all kind of strange things had come crowding into his mind. "If only we could land here, under that willow, and I could take her clothes off slowly, gently, and see the full and complete loveliness of her ... If only ..." Then their eyes met, and he knew that he was panic-stricken for fear she had read what he was thinking in his eyes.

He said, "Yes, how much? Enough to make you willing to marry me?"

"Do you love me sufficiently to want to marry me?"

"Good God, Alicia, don't talk rubbish! You must know, you must have known for a long time that you are the only thing that really matters, that makes life wonderful."

"Dear Flight!" Her tone was very tender and for a second he wondered if he were going to cry. "Dear, dear Flight," she repeated. "Have you spoken to my father?"

65

"Not yet, I had to speak to you first. Alicia, will you marry me?"

"If my father consents, Flight, yes."

"And if he doesn't?"

"Dearest, don't let us even imagine that he may not consent."

"You evidently imagined it first."

He began to row again, pulled the boat to the bank, scrambled out and tied it safely to an overhanging branch. Then, holding out his hand to her, he said, "Come along. I can't talk to you with you half a mile away in that damned boat. Come, Alicia."

Obediently she took his hand, and stood side by side with him in the deep summer grass, where meadowsweet and shepherd's purse, dog-daisies and buttercups grew. The scent of the meadowsweet seemed to rise up in a great wave of sweetness and envelop them. Flight flung down his jacket, and without speaking she sat down, while he threw himself down beside her. Catching her hand he held it to his lips, whispering, "Alicia . . . Alicia, my beloved, my dearest."

She bent her head and touched his hair with her lips.

"Dearest, dearest Flight! I love you."

He reached up and pulled her down beside him, so that he could reach her mouth. His whole world seemed to be rocking, to be spattered with bright lights, the sound of music, and over all the scent of meadowsweet.

He felt her lips against his—soft, wonderful, even passionate. His arms were round her, and he held her closely, his fingers touched her neck, reached the little hollow at the base of her throat, then the soft roundness of her breast; he whispered, his lips still against hers, "My wonderful sweetness," and heard her breath come like a long sigh, breathing, rather than speaking the word—"No!"

"Darling, you're beautiful!"

"Flight! Don't, Flight!"

Then, before he realised it, she had twisted away from him, and stood looking down at him as he lay there, her fingers dragging together the folds of her light dress, her eyes wide and cold.

"Flight—what happened to us? Flight!"— more urgently—"that must never happen again! I'm frightened. I didn't know that I could be swept away like this. Like being caught in a great wave, a wave which swept over me, submerged me, drowned me. Flight—never again!"

He sprang up and stood beside her, his arm round her shoulder; he was tender, gentle, reproaching himself.

"Alicia, darling, forgive me! It was too much for me. Your beauty, the relief of knowing that you do love me. It's all right, my sweet. There"—he kissed her softly—"there, my darling! Don't hold it against me, don't!"

"No, no, against myself, only myself. To lie in

the grass like some village slut, to let even you . . ." She shuddered.

His nerves were overstrained—he had not known how badly—and her words struck some sense of the ridiculous in him. He threw back his head and laughed. Laughed until his sides ached and tears stood in his eyes. He recovered himself to find her eyes watching him, grave and cold.

"Alicia, I'm sorry!"

"I wish that I could share your amusement."

"But, darling, surely we can both forgive each other? The great moment of our lives . . ."

"That is what I feel, a great moment—and we debased it."

"Oh, Alicia, don't take it so seriously! We did nothing wrong."

He saw her hands go instinctively to her breast, as if even now she felt that she must protect herself against him. He caught her hands, spoke softly, scarcely above a whisper.

"Listen, my sweet, it's over. The unrecorded minute. Forgotten. Just tell me that you love me, and I'll be content, completely content."

The strain left her eyes, her mouth softened, she leaned towards him and their lips met again.

"I do love you," she said, "love you dearly. But—forgotten?—no, Flight, you don't want me to forget, do you?"

Without making any reply he helped her into the boat and rowed home in silence. He was disturbed; somewhere in the depths of his heart a little cloud

68

of dismay was rising. Dismay—at what? He didn't know. He loved her, she was everything he longed for most in the world. They would be married soon, soon. Alicia said, "Flight, smile at me!"

That night he went to see her father. An invitation to dine at the Rectory had come by telephone, Lady Sophia offering well-bred and restrained apologies for the short notice, adding, "But you will understand how anxious both Alicia's father and I are to have a talk with you."

He dressed with great care; his hands shook as he tied his tie, and Eleanor, coming in, stood watching him.

"You're making a mess of that tie," she said. "Let me do it."

"Thanks. I'm nervous."

"You're going to marry Alicia, you've told her that you love her?"

"Umph. It's her father—he always has put the wind up me."

"Rubbish, Flight, why should he?"

"I don't know—he just does."

As he was leaving the house, Ann called, "Good luck, Flight!" and he turned and gave her a grin which made him look like a schoolboy.

Edward said to Frances, "The boy is nervous. He ought to have had a stiff whisky-and-soda before he left."

She replied, "Edward, of course not! Lady Sophia would have smelt it and decided that he was a confirmed drunkard. That long thin nose of hers misses very little."

He nodded. "Perhaps you're right."

Flight was admitted and shown into the Rector's library. There he stood waiting, staring uneasily at the tall bookshelves filled with well-bound books, wondering vaguely if the Rector ever read any of them, or if it was true that he really only became interested in thrillers. Who had told him that? Eleanor? He couldn't remember.

The door opened and the Rector entered. Again Flight remembered that he had once heard his father say that Lockwood never "came into a room" but that he always "entered" it.

He came forward, holding out his hand, saying, "Ah, Flight, my boy!"

Flight said, "How are you, sir?"

Lockwood nodded graciously, as if to infer that he enjoyed excellent health, "Sit down, my boy, sit down. Now I believe in going straight to the point and not beating about the bush. What is this that Alicia tells me—that you have asked her to marry you, and that you are deeply in love with each other? That is so?"

"Yes, that is so."

"You're both very young . . ."

Flight smiled, he looked even younger than his years when he smiled.

"Time will cure that, surely?"

"Quite so. Alicia has seen very little of—er—the world, she has not had great opportunities for

70

meeting eligible young men. Those opportunities are to be given to her during the coming months when she will pay a round of visits to Rusmere, to my dear mother's house at Callington, and so forth. I may tell you in confidence that already my old friend, Sir Thomas Brewster, has hinted that he would welcome Alicia as the wife of his son—his eldest son—Malcolm."

The smile had faded. Flight's face looked pinched and haggard. He licked his lips as if they were suddenly dry. He stared at the handsome clergyman, who sat with his legs crossed, displaying a remarkably neat ankle encased in fine silk. He had made his pronouncement with such urbane finality, he had made certain plans, decrees, and they would be carried out.

Flight said, "But Alicia loves me, sir!"

"That I do not dispute, Flight, but I am determined that Alicia shall be given opportunities of seeing other young men; she must not even contemplate marriage until she is in a position to make comparisons. Remember, too—though this is a matter to which I should very gladly not refer, but it is necessary—Alicia is an important person. My dear mother has left Alicia, so she tells me, a very considerable fortune, to say nothing of property and family jewels. Her grandfather, the Earl of Rusmere, also left her sufficiently well-endowed. My family, and that of my dear wife, are two of the oldest in England—two of the most highly respected. No, no, my boy. Well disposed as we are towards you, I cannot permit any actual engagement until Alicia comes to the end of her round of visits and her stay in town, which she will spend with her mother at the Earl's house in Portland Place. That, I am afraid, must be my last word."

"But when Alicia comes back, what then?"

The Rector rose, he laid his large white hand with its huge signet ring on Flight's shoulder. "Then we will talk of this matter again."

"Can I see her—often—before she goes away? Can I write to her while she is away? Can I . . ." He was almost inarticulate in his distress.

The large hand pressed a little more heavily on his shoulder. "I have always wished to temper justice with mercy," Lockwood said, "and this case shall be no exception. Only I ask you, on your honour, to promise not to try to influence my daughter. Certainly you may see her. In fact"—he removed his hand and smiled kindly, if pontifically—"come along and see her now."

Flight followed him into the drawing-room. He had always loved it, always felt that it was his ideal of all that a room should be. The painted panelling, a delicate cream, softened and enriched by time, the gilt sconces which held candles, the great glass chandelier which the Rector's grandfather had brought from Venice, the delicate Aubusson carpet, and the one exquisite flower painting which hung above the great carved white marble mantelpiece had always appealed to him.

Now, he saw only Alicia, who stood waiting for him, her eyes full of kindness, her lips smiling a little.

The Rector said, "Well, Alicia, we've had our talk."

"Yes, Papa?"

"I shall leave you for a moment. Your mother is not down yet?"

"No, Papa."

"I will go to her." He turned as he reached the door, and smiling, said, "Belton will be coming in with the sherry in ten minutes."

The door closed and Flight caught Alicia's hands in his.

She said, "Tell me—what did Papa say?"

He grimaced as if he tasted something unpleasant. "Nothing very good from my point of view, and I like to think not from yours either, darling. It appears that you are a most important young woman, and must see what other suitable men exist in the world. You may think that you love me, but it might easily happen that when you meet the duke of this or the earl of the other, you would come to realise that the proprietor of a picture gallery in Bond Street is—unsuitable."

"Flight, my dear—don't be so bitter. Papa only wants to be fair to me, to both of us. This round of visits was planned long ago, and the stay in London with Uncle Herbert."

"How long will you be away?" he demanded.

"I have to be at Glenmere for the twelfth."

"Twelfth?" Flight said irritably. "What twelfth?"

"August, darling. I'm going to Uncle Mallingly's place in Scotland."

"Oh, grouse. You don't shoot, do you?"

"Of course I don't. Then I go to Rusmere, and on to Grandmama's, and then to stay with Aunt Geraldine at Luxton, and then to town. I shall be away about three months. Flight, don't look like that! It won't seem so long, and when I'm in town, think how often I can come to see you at the Gallery. We'll dine together, go to theatres . . ."

"What about this fellow Malcolm Brewster?"

"Malcolm Brewster! Did Papa speak about him? Dearest, have you ever seen him? I thought not," as Flight shook his head. "He's huge and red and has enormous ears. Don't let Malcolm Brewster worry you."

He sighed, but some of the strain had left his face; he looked less despondent and drew her to him, whispering, "Kiss me, Alicia!"

For a moment she hesitated. "I wonder if Papa would feel that we were keeping to our bargain?" Then she leaned forward and kissed him on the lips.

"You won't change?"

"You need not ask that, Flight."

"You'll try to see me every day until you leave?"

"Every day that it is possible."

"Ah . . . Oh, I am to be allowed to write to you, only I must not try to exercise undue influence.

74

How does one 'exercise undue influence', Alicia?"

She laid her arms round his neck. "I'm afraid you do, simply by being Flight Masters—only I shall keep that a secret from everyone but you."

That had been nearly a year ago. Alicia had gone away. The world had held its breath during the Munich conference, Chamberlain had been hailed as a saviour, been blamed for having allowed Czechoslovakia to be sacrificed, Hitler had increased his demands, and the Powers had shaken admonishing fingers and warned him that "This must really be the last time." Frances had heard her husband, her sons, and George Charlton discuss terms, hours of work in the factories, sitdown strikes, pledges and treaties, until she had stated firmly, "The next time politics are mentioned at this table I shall go to my own room and have my dinner on a tray! I mean it. Yes, indeed I do, Edward. I will not have my dining-room turned into an acrimonious debating society."

Chris said, "And she means it too! Pity you're not in Parliament, Mother!"

"Thank you, Chris," she returned, "I can find a better use for my time. Now please remember what I have said—all of you—yes, that includes you, George."

Flight overcame his first depression at being separated from Alicia; he wrote to her very often, and she replied at longer intervals. Her letters were affectionate, they recorded what she had done, where she had been, and the names of the people she had met. But they left Flight with a queer feeling of disappointment. Except for the beginning, "My dearest Flight", and the assurance at the end that she was always "his loving Alicia", they were, he felt, impersonal. There was no indication that she had met someone who attracted her, no hint that she realised that her father's decision had been very wise; it was evident that she was enjoying her visits, obvious that she was popular, but again and again Flight was conscious of a sense of frustration as he laid down her letters. When she went to London, and stayed in the huge house in Portland Place, she kept her promise, and came to see him in the Galleries many times. It seemed to him that the whole place lit up, that the colours in the pictures shone more brilliantly when she entered. He was bidden to dine at Portland Place, a singularly dull dinner, with the Earl of Rusmere and his brother Felix watching Flight with eyes like gimlets. He wondered if they hoped that he would use the wrong knife and fork, drink the water in his finger-bowl, or something of the kind. Lady Sophia was tolerant, even friendly. At Portland Place she seemed to have taken on an added dignity, if it were possible. The Earl said, as they sat after Alicia and her mother had left the table, "So you're the young feller who wants to marry 'Licia, eh?"

"I do, sir."

Felix, very tall, very thin, with a long scraggy

neck like an old bird's, said, "And does she want to marry you? Tee-hee, eh?"

The Earl said, "That 'ul do, Felix. She's a very wealthy gal, you know."

"So I was told by the Rector."

Again Felix interpolated. "That fact didn't make you less keen, eh? Tee-hee—eh?"

It occurred to Flight that this elderly gentleman was not quite sane; he registered a vow that when he married Alicia, one of her relations, at least, should never stay in his house—the Hon. Felix Sawley.

Again the Earl snapped, "Shut up, Felix! Well, apparently she wants to marry you. Had a talk with her about it last night. She'd had plenty of opportunities to marry other fellers, if she'd wanted to. MacInish was crazy about her, so was Donaldson, and Brewster . . ."

"Malcolm Brewster?" Felix asked. "He's been keeping Poppy Holman ever since he left school! Charlie Donaldson drinks—always has done— had d.t.s half a dozen times, to my certain knowledge; as for MacInish . . ."

His brother turned on him in a fury. "*Will* you hold your damned tongue, and let me speak? Blast it, you're like some gossiping old woman!" He turned back to Flight. "Sophia tells me you sell pictures. I'm interested in pictures. Come down to Rusmere some time and have a look at them. French mostly. You can keep yer English school, I'd not give yer a thank yer for them. Ricard

77

—know his stuff? Manet . . ."

His brother, who had recovered from the last rebuke, giggled. "That one in the Louvre— 'Olympia', eh? They used to say that Lara's wife, the dancer Olympia, believed that Manet called it after her. Wanted her husband to call him out. The fellow had been dead for years . . ."

Flight said, "Excuse me, sir, Madame Lara is a great friend of mine. Both she and her husband know far too much about pictures to make such an assertion. I shall be grateful if you will contradict that story should you ever hear it again." Then, turning back to Rusmere, he said, "You were saying, sir—about your collection?"

"I was," Rusmere agreed, and to his brother, "I hope that 'ul teach you to keep your mouth shut! Masters, you said that very well. I shall see that Lara hears about it when he's over next time. Come to Rusmere when you like, have a look round. I'll tell you one thing, 'Licia's damned lucky to get you. None of this family have any brain except meself! They'd not know a Degas from an Ingres if they met them in their soup. Lockwood's people are as bad, his old mother's as crazy as a March hare. Don't let 'em patronise you—and bring 'Licia down to earth. Pretty girl, nice girl, but spoiled! Now come on, and let's join the ladies. Felix, don't *talk*!"

The huge rooms, the vast expanses of shining parquet, the rugs which he felt might slide from under his feet at any moment, the heavy Victorian or spindle-legged gilt furniture, seemed un-friendly. He told Alicia as they stood looking out on to the lights of Portland Place, watching the taxis darting up and down the wide street, that he felt as if he was waiting to be let out of prison.

"But we've seen quite a lot of each other in town," she said.

"Not the same, angel. People, people, people everywhere. I want it like it was in the summer: you and me, the river, the banks slipping slowly past us, nearness. That's what I want—nearness!"

She laughed softly. "Flight, we shan't be able to be on the river much, tomorrow is the first of November."

"Then we'll find an empty cottage and build a fire and roast chestnuts and potatoes. Alicia, now you've finished wandering about, reviewing eligible young men, what is the verdict?"

"That there is only one man I want to marry, and if you will turn round and look in that particularly hideous mirror you will see who he is!"

They were formally engaged. The Rector inter-viewed Flight concerning his prospects; Lady Sophia was gracious, if slightly patronising. He was told that he must not attempt to press for an early wedding. There were so many relatives to consult, plans to be made regarding the wedding itself, Alicia's trousseau must be chosen with care, there were family jewels to be re-set.

"When can we be married, then?" Flight asked.

Lady Sophia looked slightly pained, and answered in what he had come to think of as her "patient" voice.

"Today is the first of February," she said. "Possibly we might be able to consider a wedding in early September. Yes, I think early September. You might spend your honeymoon in the South of France or even Italy, though I don't care for that idea very much. I feel that Mussolini is really behaving so disgracefully."

Flight said, "Well, we needn't call and see him."

Humour was not Sophia Lockwood's strong suit. "No, of course you would never do that," she agreed. "Sufficient if you sign the book at the Embassy. I can send a note to Lady Charles; she might ask you to dine there. Most hospitable, she and the Ambassador."

He told Alicia. She listened and said, "Yes, of course, that would be very nice."

"But on our honeymoon, darling! We don't want to go to big towns, we don't want to see lots of people; can't we find somewhere quiet and small, where we shall know no one at all?"

He heard constantly of new relations. There were distant cousins who lived in Rome; one of them had married a baron, who had a palace in Florence, there was "dear Margaret Classens" who had a villa near Nice, and "that delightful creature Edouard Predi" with his beautiful *appartement* in Venice. His heart sank as he heard strings of new names which were constantly being recorded on Lady Sophia's tablets—with exclamations as to how dreadful it would have been had they forgotten Edouard or Wilton, Margaret, or Maria and Baptiste who lived at Fiesole!

The winter was a hard one, and they had little opportunity to go out a great deal. Sometimes Alicia would come with Flight in his car, and with a sense of relief he would drive into the country, thankful to be alone with her. At the Rectory, even when he was bidden to dine there, he felt that they were allowed to be together only for periods judged sufficient by the Rector or Lady Sophia. At such times, when he took Alicia in his arms, feeling a sense of peace and content stealing over him, he would be conscious of a shock when she whispered. "Flight, dear, someone might come in!"

On such occasions he would return home chilled and despondent. He would wonder miserably if she really loved him; if some day she might feel a fraction of the passion for him which he had always felt for her.

On the day when he had taken her into the country and they stopped for tea at a little country inn called the "Wheatsheaf", he came home with his lips set into a hard thin line, which made Eleanor ask him what was wrong.

"Nothing," he said. "Nothing—or perhaps everything."

"Can't you talk to me?"

He shook his head. "I don't think so, thanks all the same."

In his own room he went back over the events of the afternoon. The little sitting-room at the inn, the bright fire, the brown teapot, and hot cakes, toast and home-made jam. He had said, "We might be in our own house! Will you always pour out tea for me when I come home?"

She had smiled. "I expect so."

He had moved closer to her as they sat on the old-fashioned sofa and slipped his arm round her. "We're going to be marvellously happy. Are you going to give me some lovely children, my sweet?"

"Yes—yes, of course," but he had heard a change in her tone.

He held her closer. "Adorable prude you are! I believe you feel shocked when I even mention such a thing."

"No, not really. After all, that is why people do get married; apart from the fact that they love each other and want to spend their lives together, isn't it?"

"Well"—he remembered that he had leaned forward and kissed her lips, a long, passionate kiss—"well, perhaps not entirely. I mean—oh, angel! you know as well as I do that two people who are desperately in love do want each other—physically?" His hand slipped down from her shoulder until he cupped his fingers round her breast, and felt it soft and tender through the thin wool of her sweater.

"Flight . . ." she said. "Flight, dear, don't!"

He remembered that he had laughed, laughed with pleasure because he felt that she longed to respond to his love-making, that she wanted his complete embraces.

"Lord! September—it's a devil of a long time to wait for you!"

Again she whispered, "Flight—please!"

He slipped his hand under the yellow sweater she wore, and moved it upwards until he felt her smooth skin. He said, "Alicia, tell me that you want to be in my arms, want to give me yourself completely, want this waiting to be over? Let's go back and tell them that we can't wait, that we must be married at once! Tell me that you're resentful, yes, resentful, that we have to live as we are doing, when there is so much loveliness, delight, and—fun, yes, fun . . ."

She sprang to her feet, as he remembered she had done before last summer in the meadow by the river.

"How dare you!' she said. "Never speak to me in that way again! It's abominable, Flight! If this is the way you expect to behave when we come out together, then—this is the last time. Love need not blind you to decency and respect, surely? Please take me home."

He faced her. He had felt cold, chilled, angry.

"Listen, Alicia," he said. "I called you a prude, laughingly, just now, but it's true. I'm an ordinary normal man. I love you desperately. I want you physically and I don't mind admitting it. I've done nothing wrong—touched your breast. What's that? Nothing? You resent it when I remind you that when we're married you'll have to let me sleep with you, make love to you. Good God! this long-drawn-out engagement is purgatory, and your father at least ought to know it. He's a man. I asked you to marry me last July, now I have to wait until September, when we are to be sent off to visit thousands of your relations. A delightful prospect! Can't you face facts? Can't you forget your conventional traditional upbringing, and love me sufficiently to give me a little peace and happiness?"

She had not answered, but had walked in silence to the door, and got into the waiting car. Flight followed her, and in silence they drove back to Baddock St. Mallory.

At the gate of the Rectory, Alicia said, "I'll walk up to the house."

"No, I'll drive. It's raining."

"Very well."

He got out and opened the door for her. "Can I come in?"

"I think not."

"Not even to say that I am sorry for my outburst?"

"I don't think that I can bear any more, Flight," she said, and he heard that her voice was quite steady.

"Very well, good night."

He drove back home and for the rest of the

evening sat alone in his room, miserable, hopeless. As the stable clock was striking three he finished a long letter to her, and rising early, left it at the Rectory.

4

EDWARD came down to breakfast on Sunday mornings wearing a tweed jacket, but formal, striped grey trousers and a black waistcoat. He had never insisted upon his family attending Sunday morning service; once they had left school he allowed them to decide for themselves. He admitted that he liked them to go to church, but he raised no objection if they preferred to stay at home, or if Christopher went to play golf.

"I, myself," Edward always said, "am not one of those people who voice that pleasant assertion that a man can worship God under his own hat, or out on the golf course, or playing tennis. I don't doubt that he *can*, my contention is that he never does! Therefore, I go to Sunday morning service."

On this particular Sunday morning Christopher was obviously dressed to play golf, Ann had not put in an appearance, Eleanor and her mother were evidently preparing to accompany Edward. Flight, looking ill and tired, came in when they had almost finished breakfast.

Frances said, "Flight, dear! you don't look well? Don't you *feel* well?"

"I didn't sleep much, Mother. I'm all right. No, just some toast, please."

Christopher said, "Coming to play golf?"

86

"I don't think so. I rather thought that I'd go to church."

His brother laughed. "That's right, keep on the sunny side of your future father-in-law! Make a good impression!"

Edward folded his *Observer* and sighed. "At the risk of annoying you, Frances, I must say that the more of us go to church today, the more we concentrate upon present events and ask for such help as may be given us, the better!" He tapped the folded newspaper. "Russia declares that she is released from any obligation to either France or England."

He turned and walked out of the room. No one spoke. Frances, because the full significance of the statement was not clear to her, Eleanor because the news came as a shock and filled her with apprehension, and Flight because, at the moment, he felt that what Russia did, or did not do, affected him very little, provided that everything might be well between himself and Alicia. Only Christopher whistled softly.

They walked through the garden to the beautiful old church. Edward scarcely spoke, only nodding to such people as greeted him. Frances laid her hand on his arm, and asked softly, "Is it very important, Edward?"

He said, "It's the orchestra going in to begin the overture."

Flight followed his father and mother into the pew, wondering, as he always did, why he didn't go in first, for his mother always sat next to his father, and Edward Masters, being a church-warden, had to be at the end of the pew, to be ready to assist either Wilberforce Cummins, Wilfred Horton or Jabez Britkerthorn in taking up the collection. He slithered past his mother's feet, and adopting a slightly crouching attitude, covered his face with his hands. Eleanor had entered by the vestry door and had taken her place at the organ.

Flight ended his rather nebulous petitions to the Almighty and sat upright. He longed to turn round so that he might see Alicia the moment she entered the church. By this time she must have read his letter, must realise how that scene yesterday had shattered him? Eleanor began to play something which he fancied was written by Bach. He liked Bach, there was something reasonable about him; he didn't carry you away on a great tidal wave of melodious sentiment; he didn't give you vague and unfinished problems with no real solution. He said, "Here, and here—and here—is the problem: Listen! and I will argue it out logically and beautifully for you."

The Rectory pew was still empty, late-comers were trickling into church, passing up the aisle unhurried, but with the intention of reaching their seats, and speaking a few private words to their Maker before the voices of the choir boys, chanting "Ar-men" as a response to some inaudible prayer, which only reached the congregation as a muffled murmur, should be heard from the vestry.

Lady Sophia entered. She moved with dignity, rather like a large swan on a smooth lake; Alicia followed her. Flight caught his breath sharply. How lovely she was! "My heart would awaken and beat had it lain for a century dead"; as well be dead now, here, if she were not prepared to forgive him! She knelt and covered her face with her hands. From the vestry came the murmur of the curate's voice. "Urra . . . erra . . . arah . . ." then "*Ar-men!*"

The little procession entered; everyone stood respectfully, while the newly washed choir boys, the stolid male members of the choir ceasing to be the tailor, the chemist, the draper's assistant, George Charlton's dispenser and Bernard Cummins, and becoming something only a little less important than the clergy themselves, followed. Then the Rev. Charles Wilkinson, the junior curate—for Lockwood had two—and lastly the Rector himself tall, splendid and ecclesiastical. Charles Wilkinson wore a hood, trimmed with rabbit fur; the Rector's was magnificent silk, scarlet and black.

Charles Wilkinson's voice began to intone, "Aye will arise end go to my fathah". . . . Flight allowed his attention to wander back to Alicia. He watched her, thankful that the Rectory pew was one row in advance of their own, and on the other side of the aisle. It was easy to assume interest in the tomb erected to Montacute Horton in 1754, to give concentrated attention to the hideous stained-glass window, where Mark, in bright blue, wrote at a desk which was obviously stained deal, whilst a lion, like an overgrown Pekinese, lay at his feet, staring at nothing in particular. In appearing to do both these things his eyes could constantly watch Alicia.

The atmosphere of the church soothed him. Not that the religious side had ever really touched him; he had been confirmed whilst he was at school, had hoped vaguely that the service might have a great influence on his life, and had been disappointed. He went at Christmas, and again at Easter with his family, to take Holy Communion, but except that he felt it to be something "good" that, too, did not affect him greatly. The quiet of the church, however, the beauty of the prayers—without paying much attention to their actual meaning—did affect him. He often thought that some Sunday he'd stay in town and go to Westminster or St. Paul's, he might even go to Farm Street or Brompton Oratory. He never did, but he often thought that he would like to. How much did all this mean to Alicia, he wondered? He had never discussed religion with her, and beyond once stating that she went to "early service once a month because papa like me to", she had never made any reference to her religious beliefs or exercises.

Flight, watching her now, wondered if he dared talk to her about her Faith? and if in doing so he might not come to some understanding of his own. He rarely thought about it much, and when he did, was conscious that he was puzzled. There were so many contradictions, so many illogicalities. Things were ticketed, this was "wrong", that was "right". Murder was wrong, fighting in battle was glorious; there were sets of small sins like saying "Not at home" when you didn't want to see someone who called; drunkenness, which, if it was convivial and carried out under proper circumstances, might be forgiven, even laughed about; then where did "lying and slandering" come in?

They were all repeating the Creed; Lady Sophia had made a slight curtsey (rather less, Flight judged, than she would have given had she been meeting the King or Queen), at the name of her Saviour, so had Alicia. Yet where was that remark in the New Testament, "At the name of Jesus every knee shall bow"? Strange . . . the Catholics believed in confession, absolution, and often the Rector had pointed out from the pulpit how wrong and foolish, and—"yes, I go so far as to maintain self-indulgent"—this practice was. But this morning, Wilkinson had intoned, "Hath given power and commandment to his ministers . . . to pronounce . . . being penitent . . . the absolution and remission of their sins." Flight frowned and looked back to Alicia. It was all too difficult.

Another stir, the congregation settled themselves comfortably; the Rector having knelt, praying, in his stall for a few moments, while the hymn was being sung, made his way to the pulpit.

Edward Masters pulled out his watch and studied it intently. Lady Sophia, on hearing her husband state, "The text this morning is taken from the Epistle to the Romans, parts of verses eighteen and nineteen, chapter twelve. 'Live peaceably with all men' and 'Vengeance is mine I will repay, saith the Lord'. Both of which are given as follows in the Revised Version—'Be at peace with all men', and 'Vengeance belongeth unto me, I will recompense, saith the Lord'," opened her Bible and found the texts herself, as if to prove conclusively that he was quoting correctly.

Frances whispered to Flight, "Oh! I do hope he isn't going to talk about politics?"

Flight smiled back at her and settled himself to listen, and, what was more important, to watch Alicia listening, at the same time.

The heavy rich voice filled the church, the Rector spoke smoothly and easily, he had a fund of quotations and used them effectively. When he had been preaching for twelve minutes Edward Masters again glanced at his watch, Sir Wilberforce Cummins did the same. Flight had long since lost the thread of the sermon, if indeed there was one to follow. He heard only a musical drone, rather like the sound of an organ, it was soothing and even pleasant. Alicia never moved, her eyes were fixed on her father's face. Flight watched her exquisite profile; at intervals words reached him. "Let not your hearts be troubled . . ." he remembered that he still had to get things straight with

Alicia, and that at the moment his heart was very troubled indeed. "The gateway of human liberation"—he hadn't bothered to listen properly to that bit! Those words—"Peace in our time ... none other that fighteth for us"—Lockwood was talking politics then? The voice had sunk to a slightly lower tone, "And now to God the Father ..." and there was the pleasant sound of people rising, stretching a little, picking up hymn-books and turning the leaves in obedience to Charles Wilkinson's announcement, "Hymn two hundred and twenty-four, omitting the second and third verses."

As he stooped to pick up the embroidered velvet collection bag, Edward whispered to his wife, "Nearly sixteen minutes! Too long!" The hymn ended with a long-drawn-out "Ar-men", Eleanor played something cheerful and innocuous, the choir and the clergy filed out, and the congregation began to leave the church.

Flight realised at this moment, when he would speak to Alicia, how his nervousness was mastering him. Frances looked at him sharply and said softly, "Flight, you're not feeling ill?"

He shook his head, and followed her down the aisle.

The churchyard, flooded with bright winter sunshine, was filled with people. The more important gathered in little groups, the more humble stood watching their betters with respect, and even admiration. Lady Sophia smiled and bowed, looking, Flight thought, rather like Queen Mary opening a new town hall or hospital.

"Good morning, Groves! Glad to see you about again . . . Mrs. Hanna, how is Martha? . . . Good, good! . . . Well, Frank, home from sea! Did you have a good voyage?" and so on. Her duty done, she turned and spoke to his mother, "Good morning, Mrs. Masters. How are you, Mr. Masters? Ah, Flight! You're looking tired; working too hard, eh?"

Alicia said, "Good morning"; then "Good morning, Flight."

He came closer to her and whispered, "Did you get my letter?"

She nodded. "My poor darling! Come for me after luncheon. We'll go into the country. I want to talk to you. Flight, don't worry! We won't allow things to—be spoiled."

Edward was dogmatic during luncheon, he carved the roast as if he had taken an acute dislike to it, and muttered, "Sixteen minutes! Giving us all a lot of dope, that's what it amounts to—dope!"

Frances said mildly, "Edward, dear, I thought that it was a very nice, reassuring, comforting sermon."

He snapped back, a thing which was unusual for him, "My dear, we don't want to be reassured or comforted; we need kicking into a state of reality. We need guts, not plasters!"

94

"Well, dear, I still think that it was a very nice sermon."

Edward turned to Flight. "What did you think?"

Flight smiled. "I didn't really listen, Father."

"Just as well. There again, that's the trouble with half you young people, you don't listen! You don't see! You moon! Dream! Well, one day you'll wake up, and it won't be so pleasant for you either."

"Edward, dear," Frances' voice was almost plaintive, "do eat your luncheon. It's such excellent beef, isn't it, Eleanor?"

"Excellent, Mother."

Flight scarcely knew whether he were eating beef or manna from heaven. Alicia had smiled, had said, "My poor darling!" had promised that "things" should not be spoiled for them. He was to spend the long afternoon with her, she would be her sweetest self, and he—he shied away from the recollection of yesterday—he would be wise and gentle and all that she wished him to be.

She came down the drive to the Rectory gates when he sounded his motor horn, gave him her hand, and, leaning forward, kissed him lightly. He said, "Where shall we go?" and she replied very quietly that they would drive back to the little inn, "where things went wrong yesterday, and where we are going to put them right today". He stared at her, wondering rather wildly what she meant; half-afraid, uncertain; then, restarting the car, he nodded, "All right!"

Back again in the little, rather dark sitting-room, Flight stirred the fire into a blaze, the landlady, pottering about, chattered contentedly. Alicia was charming to her, begged for some of the little cakes they had been given yesterday. Flight, with his arm on the mantelpiece, looked down and watched her. Only when the door closed and the woman had promised tea in half an hour's time did she look up at him.

She said, "Darling! I want you to let me talk to you, and if I seem stupid and rather foolish to make allowances; I lay awake trying to think all this out most of last night. Smoke, if you want to."

She waited until he had lit his cigarette, and then continued:

"You see, darling, I suppose that I have been brought up almost too carefully. I'm the only child, my father is a clergyman, my mother is strictly conventional. My father's mother has always been a woman of violent tempers, so has my mother's brother, Uncle Herbert."

Flight nodded. "So I gathered when I dined at Portland Place."

'They have always allowed their emotions to govern them completely. I have been brought up to distrust emotions—and yet—don't look at me all the time, Flight, please—I know that I am just as capable as either Uncle Herbert or my grand-mother of allowing my emotions to get the better of me. That day in the meadow, here yesterday, I

96

wasn't frightened of you, I was . . . I was frightened of myself. I want you to make love to me, I want to be married to you, but the other side of me says, 'Don't behave like some sex-ridden fool! Do retain your decency, pride, and the rest.' Flight, do you understand? Say that you do?"

He came and sat beside her, taking her hand in his, kissing it gently. "My sweetest, of course I understand! I'm grateful to you for telling me. But, Alicia, isn't there some half-way? Can't you sometimes forget that someone may come into the room, that when I kiss you it means something to me? There are times when you—you—freeze me, when I feel that you've flung a bucket of cold water over me."

He saw her fine eyebrows lift a little; some of the warmth had left her voice when she spoke. "You're dissatisfied?"

"Not when you are—yourself."

"But I've tried to explain what is—myself," she argued.

"Then if you can be yourself, what about me? Haven't I got any individuality, any right to my own set of emotions?"

"Not when you talk about going to bed with you, and how many children I am going to give you, and having—fun together!"

He leaned back, so that he could watch her face from a distance.

"My God!" he said, "and we're living in 1939!"

"Yes, and not in the unpleasantly robust days

of either the Restoration or the Hannoverians! I believe that, as St. Paul said, there are some things which should 'not be spoken of among you', and I still maintain that is right. Oh! you can call me a prude if you like, Flight! I will not run the risk of losing my sense of decency—even though I do love you—love you desperately."

"Do you? Do you really? I wonder, sometimes."

"You wouldn't wonder any longer, I suppose, if I told you to lock that door and—let you make love to me here and now?"

"I might," he said slowly, "I don't know."

"You are impossible!"

"You're not going to tell me to lock the door—are you?"

She got up and stood staring down at the crackling wood fire. Flight did not move, he wondered how they had reached this particular point in the argument—where it would end? He was numb, feeling nothing but a strange kind of speculative curiosity.

"I might say that," Alicia said, her eyes still watching the flames, "if I felt that it would really convince you that I love you? It wouldn't. Oh! for a few hours, days perhaps—after that the fact that I refused to let it happen all over again would make you dissatisfied, make you believe that I loved you no longer. And so it would go on, and it would lose all value, become a kind of secret habit, something furtive and unpleasant."

He said gently, "But, Alicia! I've never asked

you to let me make love to you, have I?"

"Not in so many words. You've railed against the fact that we are not to be married until September, you've—oh, let's leave it! Either you must accept me as I am, or you must break off everything and not see me again."

"I couldn't face that alternative," he said slowly, and something in his voice made her turn to him. He was sitting on the uncomfortable Victorian sofa, stooping forward, the lock of hair which she had smoothed back so often had fallen over his forehead; he looked miserable, crushed. Alicia came to him and knelt at his side, pushing back at the hair and pulling his head down on to her shoulder.

"Flight, darling!" she said softly, "don't look like that, it's all right! I swear that everything shall be all right."

"I couldn't face losing you," he said hoarsely. "I'll agree to anything, anything!"

"Darling! we're young—we've all our lives before us, surely we can wait a little longer?"

"Yes, yes, I will!"

Very gently she smoothed his hair, kissed him softly, and spoke to him quietly and soothingly. Her lips were smiling, her eyes kind, and yet in their depths was something like satisfaction. She had won her real victory over him, she had learned which was the most vulnerable place in his character. He could not even bear to contemplate losing her!

She had spoken truthfully when she told him that she had two sides to her character—and that one side she dreaded and feared. As a child she had seen her Uncle Herbert indulge in scenes that were terrifying to her, she had heard his voice raised in fury, had watched him storm through the rooms at Rusmere, picking up pieces of china and flinging them into the wide fireplaces.

She had heard whispered stories from her nurses and governesses, stories which they had believed were either unheard by her or not understood, concerning her Uncle Felix. Felix was "weak in the head"—"and if he is, he has no one but himself to blame". "My word! that was a scandal if you like . . ." and "They do say that her husband . . ." She had once heard her Uncle Mallingly talking to the Earl. They had not realised that Alicia was curled up on the window-seat. Mallingly had said, "You'd not think, to look at him now, that Felix was a damned good-looking fellow. Gad! how crazy the women were for him!" Herbert had returned. "How crazy he was for the women, the damned fool! Look at him now!"

Her father's mother too, the old Dowager, who lived at Callinton Manor, who still dyed her hair scarlet, who went to Monte Carlo every year and "lived at the tables". Alicia had heard her grandmother's maid say to her own nurse:

"At Monte she just lives at the tables! Old rip, that's what she is!"

Nurse had said, "Well, if all one hears is true . . ."

Jane Harlish had answered. "All that you hear *and* a good deal more, Mrs. Roberts! I could tell you things . . . there was that young Mr. Varley, f'r instance. And the Honourable Percy Newton. . . ."

Alicia had come to realise that she was being brought up strictly. Her parents were indulgent, she was petted and given more clothes than she could wear, she had one expensive governess after another, but when she asked when she could go to boarding-school, where Griselda Cummins and her sisters said they had such marvellous times, her father and mother made it quite clear that Alicia was to be educated at home.

Mercy Wilberforce said one day, "Lady Sophia, why don't you let Alicia come to Paris with us? It's heavenly! We go to the theatre, and the opera and—oh, it's marvellous!"

Lady Sophia smiled, her chilly tolerant smile, and said, "Oh, I don't think we want Alicia to go to Paris, Mercy!"

Certain subjects were never mentioned. People married and were going to have babies, but however well you knew them, you never referred to the fact. No ailments which occurred lower than the heart or lungs were referred to specifically. Possibly "a little gastric trouble" or, of course, such things as rheumatism, but nothing else.

Alicia accepted it and came to believe that the

101

"unpleasant things of life" must, by decent people, be ignored. Her mother had told her certain facts, told her very gently and sympathetically, but with such a wealth of extraneous detail that Alicia had been left wondering if bees and even flowers were as harmless and innocent as she had always supposed them to be? It was Mercy Wilberforce who had told her, bluntly and plainly, too plainly for Alicia's peace of mind; she had listened and gasped and said, "Mercy Mercy! you're making it all up? It can't be true!"

"If you'd come to Paris," Mercy replied, "you'd know that I'm only telling you half of what I could tell you. There was a girl at school who had an affair with a French officer. His sister used to write and ask her to stay with them, pretended that they were second cousins. She told me that it was only so that she and Georges could sleep together!"

Alicia said, "She must have been a perfectly beastly girl."

"No!" Mercy replied thoughtfully, "she was one of the nicest and certainly the cleverest girls we had there."

"But you don't think that it's *right?*"

Again Mercy considered. "I don't know about right. I suppose that it's—nature."

"Then I don't think I care very much for being natural," Alicia said.

Mercy laughed. "Darling! you said that exactly like Lady Sophia!"

That had been when she was eighteen, more

than four years ago. She had been taken to London, and Rusmere had given a coming-out ball for her; in return she had been asked to balls given by other people; she had danced, gone to theatres, and seen and heard a good deal that shocked her. Not only was she shocked at what she heard and saw, she was shocked when Mercy or Gwendoline or any of her other friends said, "My dear! what a time I had with Philip the other evening! He's simply dreadful! If Philip Gaunt had his way there'd not be a virgin left in London."

To which someone else had replied easily, "My dear, there aren't many."

Alicia hated to listen and yet she knew that she felt thrilled and excited when Gaunt asked her to sit out with him in a dim corner of the balcony. He leaned forward and stared into her face, saying, "I've never seen you look so pretty! You're quite lovely. Indeed, you are!"

He had laid his hand on her knee, she had felt his fingers slowly working up her skirt until he reached the top of her thin silk stocking and again she had experienced excitement, anticipation. Then, all that she had known asserted itself, all her upbringing, and she had pushed his hand away and said, "No, Mr. Gaunt! Do you hear? No!"

He had laughed and said, "It's all right, Alicia."

"It is not all right!" she returned, "and I don't like it."

She had risen and walked back to the ballroom, and had refused to dance with him again.

They had returned to Baddock St. Mallory and she had met Flight Masters and loved him. She liked his gentleness, his essential kindness, his love of beauty. He had asked her to marry him, and she felt that here was a man who loved her, who wouldn't want to impose his physical desires, who would have control and restraint. She knew that, in their hearts, both her father and mother were disappointed; they would have liked her to marry Malcolm Brewster or young Franklin, but they had been very sweet, and they both said that they liked Flight, and all had been well.

And Flight had proved to be very little different from those other men; he had wanted to slip his hands inside her dress, to fondle her, to whisper things about their future, which excited her even when they filled her with a faint sense of disgust. More than once, when he had caught her in his arms and kissed her, she had wanted to return his kisses with an ardour which equalled his own, and she had forced herself to push him away, with some excuse about "Belton might come in," or "Papa will be here in a moment . . ."

Now she had fought him, beaten him. She knew how sensitive he was, knew how completely he loved her. That threat that she might not see him again had crowned her victory. He lay now with his head on her shoulder, as if he were exhausted; she felt at once maternal, and passionately in love.

"Flight!" she whispered. "We've got all our

lives. I will make up to you for your goodness and patience, I promise, darling."

"Yes—I know, you're an angel to me."

"No, I just happen to love you, and that love is so precious."

For one instant he longed to spring up and shout, "That's bosh, and you know it! Damned silly bosh! For God's sake behave like a woman, not like some blasted heroine in an Edwardian novel!" but he felt too tired, and only sighed, saying, "I know, the most precious thing in the world."

They drove home through the gathering dusk, and Flight knew that she had forgiven him, and that life would flow smoothly and evenly again. That night the Rector asked him to have supper with them after evening service, and he tried to be bright and amusing, to listen intelligently to the Rector's carefully turned, rather stately sentences regarding the Government and this news from Russia.

When he left, Alicia threw on a cloak and walked with him down the drive. He slipped his hand in hers, and she felt the pressure of his fingers, thin, and rather cold.

"You're cold, darling?"

"No, not really."

"Happy?"

He laughed. "Silly question! I'm with you!"

They had kissed fondly and without emotion, and he had gone back to Little Manor to slip back into his old sense of depression.

Back at the Galleries on Monday he found a letter waiting for him, from Jules Matot. Jules was not optimistic concerning the war clouds, but he wanted Flight to come over to visit several places with him where he believed they might find bargains. He sat staring at the letter for a long time. It might be a good thing to go. Perhaps he and Alicia saw too much of each other; a separation might be good at this particular juncture? Pleasant, too, to see Jules again, to be in Paris, to meet Louis Lara and his incredible and adorable wife, Olympia.

He spoke to his father that evening when they dined at the flat. Edward glanced at his son. The fellow was too thin; looked fine-drawn. These damned silly long engagements were no good to an affectionate fellow like Flight. Lockwood and his wife with their preparations for a huge wedding, a gathering of the clans, making a blasted social affair of it all!

"I'm all for it. Rub up your French, possibly make money. Meet your old friends, and come back looking a good deal fitter than you do at this moment. You're too serious, my boy. You take things too much to heart. Worry, I shouldn't wonder? No, I'm all for it, and I'm certain that your mother will say the same."

Flight looked gratefully at his father. "Thanks, Dad. I've everything set at the Galleries, and Murchison is first-rate. As a matter of fact he knows far more about it than I do."

"Murchison is nearly fifty, you're twenty," Edward returned. "He may have gathered a devil of a lot of knowledge, but you've got something that cannot be *taught* you. I don't often pay compliments, particularly to my own children, though I may do to really good customers! But I believe in you, believe in you implicitly."

So Flight arranged to go to Paris, and knew that he felt a sense of relief. Alicia said, "I believe that you're glad to be going," and he tried to tell her that it wasn't that he wanted to leave her, but that—and then she stopped him and said quickly, "Darling! I do understand."

Eleanor packed for him—Eleanor always packed for him—and no one else ever contrived to do it half so well.

As she folded ties neatly, she said, "Does Alicia mind your going?"

"Well, we both mind being separated, but I shan't be away long. Only about three weeks. Chris was very decent, he said that he'd take her up to have a game of golf now and then. Alicia doesn't play badly, she only wants more practice."

"That was nice of Chris! But after all, most men would like to be seen with Alicia Lockwood, wouldn't they?"

"Rather! I'd say they would! You might see her sometimes, will you? And, I say, Eleanor, say nice things about me, won't you?"

"Could I say anything—truthfully—that wasn't nice?" she smiled.

107

Jules met him. Jules, who looked older and who seemed to Flight to be faintly "jumpy". Louis Lara, on the other hand, was in the highest spirits and drew plans of the Maginot Line all through dinner, with a fork, on the table-cloth. Olympia—large, lovely and slightly overblown—said, "Mon Dieu! do we 'ave to 'ave Maginot Line for all meal times? I am seek in my stomach of it! Be quiet, Louis, or talk of somesing else."

Jules said, "I remember my Julius Caesar—how apt it is at this time! This Hitler!—'He doth bestride this narrow world like a Colossus'—and we must creep about to 'find ourselves dishonourable graves'."

Louis said, "I also remember—'The Ides of March r-remember'."

Jules nodded. "This will, in my opinion, be a very critical period, this March."

Olympia screamed. "''Av I told you to *shut oop*. Fleet, I 'ave zis from morning until night, and if I don't pretend to snore, Louis will continue after we are in bed! Zis is my life. Olympia! I go to bed—and 'ave to listen to political discussions! A-ah, 'ow 'e 'as changed, zis Louis! I suppose zat 'e grows old? Poor old man!"

Flight had an immediate picture of how such a remark would have been received had it been possible that Olympia should have ever dined at the Rectory. He pushed the thought from him and felt disloyal.

The next day Jules seemed to have recovered his

spirits a little, he was like the man Flight had known before. He announced that he wished to take Flight to luncheon, "with the most charming woman in Paris—except our belovèd Olympia, that is to say."

She replied, "Ah, I know who this is you will veesit, Fleet. It is La Spero!"

Flight stared. "Do you know La Spero, Jules?"

"Fairly well—indeed, I might say very well."

"But she's wonderful! When I was in Paris before, I remember she was on tour in America, but I have seen her, she came to London last year. At—where was it?—the Ambassadors, I think. Yes, the Ambassadors."

"She wishes very much to make your acquaintance," Jules said, "and I promised to bring you."

Olympia said, "She 'as a magnificent chef, zees Spero!"

It struck Flight that perhaps Jules was in love with La Spero? She must be considerably older than he was, but, heaven knew, she was attractive enough to make most men go crazy about her. How old would she be? he wondered. She must be nearly fifty! Jules was a year older than he was—no, almost the same age. He looked at Jules with some respect. To be so young, and to be on such terms with the most fascinating French actress of her time.

They walked to the *appartement* where La Spero lived, and, as they drew near, Flight said,

"Jules, forgive me, but what—well, what terms are you on with La Spero?"

"The very best," Jules answered gaily.

"But, I mean—damn it, you know what I mean."

Jules threw back his head and laughed. "Oh, you dear, decent British fellows, what incredible minds you have! I know a great French actress, she tells me to ask you to luncheon, I admit that we are on good terms, so you think that I am in love with her."

Flight said stoutly, "I don't blame you if you are. She's a marvel!"

"You are at once the greatest romantics, and the greatest gossip-lovers in the world. Dear Flight! La Spero is my adored mother."

"Your mother?"

"She is Madame Matot, widow of another great French artist, after whom I am named. I never knew my father. He was murdered—six months, no seven months before I was born."

Flight whispered in horror, "Murdered?"

Jules nodded. "In the last war—murdered—by the Boche. That is why one day I shall be a soldier and fight against Germans. Now, here is my mother's *appartement*."

5

THE big room which they entered was empty. It was rather dark, the curtains were heavy and of a dark rich wine colour, a bright fire crackled in the polished steel grate. The scent of burning pine cones filled the air. The walls were panelled, and in the centre of each panel hung a picture; there were only four in the room. Flight stared at them, and Jules watched him, smiling gently.

Flight said, "That's a Rousseau, surely?"

"Indeed it is. That is a Poussin, and those two—two, mark you, my friend!—are by that divine man Giorgione. My mother is knowledgeable concerning pictures, to an extent. She once bought a Metsu which I disliked very much. I assured her that he was a German painter—she sold it the next day! Then, when I knew that it was on its way to America I told her the truth! But—let me give you a cocktail. My mother is late. She is always late for everything, except her rehearsals and the rise of the curtain."

Flight sipped his cocktail and let his eyes wander round the room.

"It's a beautiful room," he said softly; "beautiful!"

"She has great taste, my mother," Jules

admitted. "I believe that my father's taste was execrable, except in his work, which was superb. I honour his memory, but God forbid that I should ever wear his jewellery, except watches, which after all can remain hidden in my waistcoat pocket! Ah, here she is!"

Flight turned and saw Susanne Matot for the first time without the footlights between them. She was rather above medium height, with very soft, light-brown hair and eyes which were blue and friendly. She was wearing a good deal of make-up, but put on with exquisite care and restraint. Her clothes were obviously the very best and made in the latest mode. She looked, Flight thought, what she was, an immensely successful actress—but in addition, he felt, a woman one would like to know.

Jules kissed her affectionately, and she turned to Flight saying, "So you've brought your Englishman to see me, eh?"

She spoke with no trace of accent that Flight could detect, but at the same time he realised that to speak in French was more usual to her.

He answered her in French and she laughed, "How well he speaks, Jules! How do you come to speak so well?"

"I was at school, or rather I went, after I left school in England, to Chartres and Avignon; then for a short time I stayed with the priest at a little place called Matrec. He was very clever, an old man . . ."

112

La Spero interrupted him suddenly, "Yes, I know—and now what do you do?"

"I have a picture gallery, Madame. In Bond Street."

"Yes, yes—Jules told me—I remember now. You know the Laras, of course? I am very fond of them both; she has been so kind to me on many occasions. I wish that I could remember her when she was slim and young, and a great dancer."

She was talking very quickly, going from one subject to another. Flight frowned as he watched her, he thought, "What makes me imagine that she is 'running away' from that place I mentioned —Matrec?"

She asked him about the theatre. Did he like plays? Would he be in Paris long enough to come to her first night; it was due in a week's time. He would! That was splendid. Jules must arrange it with her manager, Regnault. He must come to her party on the stage afterwards. "That is if it has been a success! If not, then I shall come home and say that I have a headache."

The play? She gave him a brief sketch of it, amusing, and, Flight felt, slightly improper.

She shrugged her shoulders. "Not a good play, machine-made. But with plenty of doors, because it is comedy, and in comedy you must have at least five doors! Otherwise the situations cannot be brought about with the right amount of probability. That is the art of this type of comedy, to

113

make the highly improbable appear to be at least remotely possible."

They lunched, lightly and exquisitely. A *consomme*, a tiny strip of fish, *Écrevisses à l'Americaine*, and *coupes-aux-marrons*. La Spero, Flight noticed, ate very little except a special salad, which was served to her alone. They drank a white wine which was unfamiliar to him.

As they sat over their coffee he asked her if she was a Parisienne. She looked at him, her bright eyes shining with amusement.

"Shall I tell him, Jules?"

"Yes! tell him, Mama."

She said, her voice completely changed, "Why, lad, Ah'm noa mower French nor what thee is! Ah weer born i' Bricket's Farm, Crawdaale, i' t' West Riding o' Yorkshire. T' country as breeds handsome chaps, an' virtuous wimmen. Nah, tha knaws, eh?"

He stared, and stammered that "her imitation was wonderful."

"Nowt wonnerful abart it," she replied. "Yon't t' road Ah talked when Ah weer a little lass."

"But . . . how—I mean—I beg your pardon, I've always thought of you as a Frenchwoman?"

"It's a long story, I doubt if even Jules knows it all. I am a Frenchwoman, a woman takes the nationality of her husband." Then, as if she had talked too much, she rose and held out her hand. "I must go and rest. *Au revoir*, Mr. Masters, Jules must bring you again. And, Jules, remember

114

to speak to Regnault about the seats. Good-bye, darling."

She had gone, moving swiftly and yet without haste. The room felt empty. Jules looked at Flight and laughed.

"Well, what do you think of her?"

"What I thought before, multiplied by a hundred. She's marvellous!"

"That's true, you know, about being born in Yorkshire."

"Yes, but you say 'Yorkshire', she says, 'Yorksh'ur'."

That night he wrote to Alicia that he had lunched with La Spero and had found her charming. He did not refer to her ability to speak in the dialect of the West Riding, nor refer to the reason which enabled her to do so. He went on to tell her of the various appointments which he had made and the people he was going to visit the next day.

His days were full. He felt happy in Paris, even though there was a strange feeling that almost everyone was either "jumpy" like Jules, or in wild spirits like Louis Lara. Paris was still herself—there were already flowers being sold at the street corners, mimosa, and violets, their scent catching you as you passed and seeming to reassure you "Spring is coming, Spring is in the South now, soon she will reach Paris!"

The week passed. Jules explained that his mother was immersed in the final rehearsals and

115

that it was impossible for him to invite anyone to the house while they lasted.

"Either she is in the theatre all day and half the night, or she brings home someone who needs additional coaching in their part. We live in an atmosphere of theatre, lines, situations—arguments concerning this or that effect, the lighting—and so on. How my mother can support it I do not know."

Flight experienced a sense of excitement when he first saw the placards announcing the new play, *Faire le Bec*, with La Spero, and beneath the name, in smaller type, "Madame Susanne Matot". So she used her own name as well as the one which she had taken for the stage, he reflected. Madame Susanne Matot. He wondered what she had been called before she married? Was her name something quite ordinary, a name which would come more easily to the tongue of a North countryman than a Frenchman?

The night of the production he dressed slowly and with immense care. He was glad that he had brought tails, and could go in his full ceremonial clothes. That afternoon he had sent her an immense bouquet of red, white and blue flowers, with a note saying, *The colours of both your countries, both of which admire you. Flight.* At the shop they had protested that blue flowers were impossible.

"Monsieur, there *are* no blue flowers!"

"But there must be," he maintained. "I can think of many—cornflowers, forget-me-nots . . ."

and there he stuck, and the assistant said:

"Ah, you see, monsieur!"

"Then dye some white flowers blue," he said. "Only I must have those three colours."

There had been a long discussion with the owner of the shop, and finally some blue flowers which Flight had never seen before in his life were produced; they were small, but of a dark, deep blue. These should be mounted to make them as long in the stalk as the roses, and they complimented him upon the correctness of his taste. For La Spero!

"Ah! nothing would give her greater pleasure, for she is a great patriot," they told him. "If— 'they' should ever attempt to come here, you would find La Spero fighting at the barricades!"

"But they won't," Flight said, "there is the Maginot Line."

"Ah," they said again.

Jules said, "How correct you look! No one can make better evening clothes than the English. Your waistcoat is admirable. I am happy to be with you!"

Louis and Olympia drove them to the theatre. Flight thought that he had never seen any woman wear as much jewellery as Olympia wore and yet contrive to look so exquisite.

She said, "You admire my pretty toys? Louis gave them all to me. I had others—you remember, Louis?—the earrings which the Archduke gave me, and the exquisite bracelet from an even more important person?"

Louis nodded. "I remember!"

"But such is the fineness of my 'usband," Olympia continued, "that to see me vear zem was an agony to 'eem. I sold zem all, all! In re-turn Louis gave me all zese and many, many more. Each time we 'ave a quarrel—is it not so, darling?—'e rushes out and brings me back one of zese pretty toys. Zen, we are friends once more!"

Louis, holding her plump hand in his, said, "Lovers, my angel, not friends, please!"

The theatre was crowded. It appeared that Louis and his wife knew everyone. She sat in her box bowing, waving her hand; it seemed that she felt all Paris had come to see Olympia—Madame Lara—who had been born in a back street in Lyons and whose real name had been Sara Levine.

The play was an amusing and slightly improper trifle; Flight enjoyed it, threw back his head and shouted, as Jules said, "showing all his nice white English teeth". La Spero was delicious. That was the word which he felt fitted her—delicious—like something which is delightful to taste. She looked thirty, her voice had a quality of youth which was enchanting, and her movements were smooth, graceful and exact. It was evident that the audience adored her. A look, the least raising of an eyebrow, the hint of a smile, and they were in a state of extravagant delight.

When the play ended, she stood waiting to receive them on the stage. Olympia sailed towards her, embraced her fervently, with exaggerated affection, but when Flight heard her say, "Susanne, you are so *young*!" he knew that a real love existed between these women—so different, so far apart in everything except their mutual regard for each other. Louis bowed over her hand, murmured some compliment. Jules said, "Mama, I know how clever Louis is at saying the exactly right thing, but now I shall beat him. I shall just say the most charming compliment of all, which is also a great, profound truth—Mama, you were— *yourself*!" She turned to Flight, and made a gesture towards a table where his bouquet stood in a great cut-glass vase. "I liked your thought—thank you!"

The day before Flight left Paris he lunched with her for the last time. She was alone when he arrived, and greeted him warmly, saying, "Now, I shall give you a cocktail, because I must talk to you, and I should prefer to talk to you alone before Jules comes. We will talk in English, if you don't mind. Sit down, Mr. Masters. Tell me, you are going back to England?"

"Tomorrow, Madame."

"And you realise fully what is going to happen?"

"I don't quite understand you . . ."

"Tch! Don't be dull, Mr. Masters! There is going to be war—and soon. Here they talk of their Maginot Line. I have sufficient trust in the Maginot Line—not too much, but sufficient— but the danger is *here*, in the heart of France. Are you certain that it is not the same with you in

England? I know what we have here—traitors, blockheads, criminals—enough blackguards to outweigh the honest men. How far have your British half-hearted preparations advanced since 1937? Not very far! Oh, since Munich you have done something, but you were quite willing to be lulled to sleep to the tune of Chamberlain singing that lullaby, 'It means Peace in Our Time'. Your time! Adolf Hitler's time! Look at us here with our enforced forty-hour week, as against Germany's sixty-hour!

"I remember during the last war an Englishman said to me, in a tone of satisfaction—that satisfaction which in you British drives me to desperation—"We always send a boy to do a man's job, and by Gad, he contrives to do it!' This time you will be forced to send all the boys, and all the men, and there will still not be enough. Can you go home and *tell* people? Can you try, even in a limited way, to make people believe that this rat—this sewer rat—with his fat Italian bully standing behind him, is going to shatter the world—as we know it now? You have organisations in England, Territorials and so on, where men can at least get *some* military training. Will you try to persuade them to take that training?

"Don't go away with the belief that all France is rotten. Already there are people, and many of them, who are planning, devising, yes, plotting. But there are not enough of—us. Yes, *of us*! I am one of them; there are others you know who are

120

also—*of us*. Other people work like rats, gnawing away the structure on which civilisation is built. We work like moles, in the dark, tunnelling, planning. That smooth, overfat—she is so greedy—blessèd woman, Olympia, does she forget that she was born in the ghetto, and that her name is Sara Levine? Louis Lara, so gay, so light-hearted, but he, too, remembers what his people have suffered, and at whose hands. And—I, too—well, that's all part of my life—someday you shall hear it. No, there are people working on the right side, there are many—too many—working on the wrong. So, go home, Flight Masters, and talk! Tell them—try to wake them—to make them realists!"

She broke off and he saw that she was twisting her fingers together as if she suffered physical pain. He stared at her, wondering what promise he could give her, wondering how much he could do, trying to realise all that she had meant, to comprehend fully her urgency and sincerity. He said, "Madame Matot, I swear that I will do all that is possible—for me."

She held out her hand to him and he raised it to his lips. In some strange, inexplicable way he felt like a knight who has just received the accolade.

He said, "And Jules?"

Her eyes narrowed. "Jules will do his duty. Jules understands the danger fully."

Flight returned to England. His father had been right, he felt better, more certain of himself. He had been "running downhill", letting his nerves get the better of him; now he felt alive, awake, aware.

He was making plans, he would remember what Susanne Matot had said to him, he must do something practical. How much did she know? Was it possible that she belonged to some underground movement? A movement which included Lara and his wife? A movement which was based on the hatred which it was inevitable that the Jews must feel for their persecutors?

When he told Alicia, what would her reaction be to this warning? Would she listen and believe him, or had her father's conviction that there would be no war become an article of faith with her too?

A war. "The Ides of March." Today was the nineteenth of March. Nothing particularly startling had happened as yet. A war would mean separation from Alicia, possibly danger for her, danger for himself. March was to be a turning point, Louis had said. Flight frowned; if war came closer, whether Lockwood and his wife approved or not, he and Alicia would be married quickly.

He drove from Victoria to the flat in town; his father was there drinking tea and reading an evening paper. He looked up when Flight entered.

"Hello, my boy! Nice to see you back!"

"Nice to see you, Father. Everybody well?"

"Yes, first-rate. Have a cup of tea? Or care for a whisky-and-soda?"

"Whisky-and-soda, thanks."

They sat talking with their usual sense of good understanding. Edward told him that he looked better, and gave him various bits of home news. Eleanor and George talked of being married in the autumn. They'd miss Eleanor at Little Manor. Great girl, that!

"Now let's have your news, Flight."

Flight told of the etchings he had bought, quite a pleasant collection, and enough for a small exhibition. The artist wasn't very well-known, but Louis Lara thought highly of him, and predicted a great future for him—Pierre Lengale. Then his voice changed, he spoke more softly.

"Father, how do you think things are going?"

"Damned badly! Hear anything over there?"

"Yes, though I don't know how much of it was confidential." First he told of Louis' remark about the month of March, then of what Susanne Matot had said to him. Edward listened, only interpolating a word here and there, asking a brief question.

Flight ended his story and said, "That's all. What do you make of it?"

"They've got the wind up, and rightly. I wish to God that we had!"

"I'm going to get some kind of military training. Alicia's uncle, Rusmere, is something high up in the Territorials. He asked me to go and see his pictures. I'll go and see what he can do. I was in the OTC at school, you know. That may help."

Edward whistled. "Whew! you're taking it very seriously."

"I fancy if you'd heard Madame Matot talking you'd feel as I do."

"Possibly even without listening to Madame Matot I do feel as you do, but I'm too old to go and rush away to get military training, my boy."

"You don't disapprove?"

"I think if you'll take your mind back, Flight, you'll realise that I have very rarely objected to any of you doing anything which you could justify. I'm not going to begin now."

That evening he telephoned Alicia, and the sound of her voice made him long unspeakably to be with her again. Once in Paris, for a few hours he had wondered if he were a little in love with Susanne Matot? Now when he spoke to Alicia, heard her, "Darling, you're back!" he knew that nothing and no one mattered except Alicia.

"I'll be down tomorrow, my sweet."

"Tomorrow? When will you come to see me?"

"Let's see. I'll drive down with the Guv'nor; we ought to be there about tea-time. I'll come over immediately after tea."

"Lovely!"

That night Alicia slipped out after dinner, explaining that she had a headache and that the air might do it good.

Her father smiled tolerantly and said, "I suspect that it might be caused through excitement. The return of the wanderer, eh?"

Lady Sophia said, "Stanley, dear, don't tease her. You look as if your head was really bad, my darling. Wouldn't you be wiser to go to bed and take an aspirin?"

"I'd rather see what the air will do, Mama."

"Very well, wrap up and don't stay out too long."

Alicia walked down the long straight drive, then turned sharply to the right, which led through a shrubbery and into what was always called the "Home Wood", to differentiate between it and the big wood which lay at the back of the house. She walked quickly, and did not start when a voice said softly, "Hello, sweetest! You're late!"

A man stepped forward and, putting out his arms, caught her to him. She raised her hands and pushed him from her.

"No!" she said. "No, it's over, Chris! Flight's home—he'll be here tomorrow. Chris, I think we've been crazy, mad, these last two weeks."

The man's arms fell. "Damn and blast it!" he said. "What the devil does he want to come home just now for! Mad—of course we haven't been mad—we've been two sane, normal people, finding life a very excellent affair. Now he'll come home to hang about you like a moonstruck calf."

"We are engaged," Alicia reminded him.

"Listen," his hands were on her shoulders again, "listen, 'Licia! break it off! It's not too late. I'm making more money than he will make if he lives to be ninety. Let's get married. You like me really a great deal better than you do my brother, and in your heart you know it."

"No," she said, "that's just what I don't know, Chris. You're a very exciting person; you swept me off my feet. With Flight I can hold my own, I can get the better of Flight, make him feel ashamed or wretched. Frankly, if I had—well if I hadn't let you have your own way, you'd have walked off and I shouldn't have seen you again."

He laughed. "Come now, it wasn't all *my* way, was it? And so I take it that you didn't want me to—walk off?"

"No, I didn't. In a way I still don't want you to . . ."

"And as for making me feel wretched or ashamed, what have I got to be ashamed about, or wretched for that matter? I'm annoyed. I didn't want Flight to come home—yet—at all events. You're very lovely, you know, 'Licia! Marry me—yes, why not? I'd make you terribly happy."

"Perhaps. I'm not sure. No, Chris, nothing would make me break my engagement to Flight. I love him, really love him, as I should never be able to love you, never. And—oh, you'll laugh—I couldn't face the scandal and gossip. It would hurt Mama and Papa too badly."

He grumbled, "That's the side of you I can't understand. Last night, you were . . ."

She interrupted him. "I know, I wish that I didn't remember so clearly."

"Well, then—and tonight you're talking about fearing scandal and gossip! You're a mystery.

126

What would you do if I told Flight about us?"

Alicia's eyes met his; she saw the laughter in them, but her own were cool and steady.

"Flight would never believe you, and I imagine that he'd do his best to kill you."

"Melodramatic! And if he came and asked you, what then?"

"I should deny it, of course."

"You think that he'd take your word against mine?"

"Of course."

"'Pon my word, 'Licia, you're a bit of a bitch, aren't you?" He put his arm round her and tried to draw her closer. "Stay here for a little longer, 'Licia . . . the last time."

"No, Chris." She twisted away, freeing herself from his hold. "I'm going. Good night."

"Oh, go then, damn you! *Good* night."

Not that he was really angry—Chris Masters rarely lost his temper over anything—no one was sufficiently important to him. He had promised to give her some lessons in playing golf while Flight was away, promised out of the goodness of his heart. The girl was young, particularly attractive; it couldn't be a lot of fun being engaged to Flight, Chris fancied. Anyway, Flight had been very much pleased and had thanked him warmly. Well, he'd taken her to the golf course; she didn't play a bad game either, all she wanted was practice and she'd be definitely good. They'd driven there in his new Humber—nice car. Then one late afternoon he'd pulled up at the side of the road and kissed her. Everything began from there. He liked her, there had been moments when he wondered if he wasn't really in love with her. Perhaps he still was a little. There was something about her that got under your skin, you couldn't get her out of your system. He would marry her tomorrow, only he wasn't going to tag after her, whining that he was breaking his heart for her. He'd never done that with any woman, never!

And now she'd come and told him that everything was ended, that Flight was coming back, that she loved Flight tremendously, and had walked coolly out of his life—out of his arms too!—and said, "Good night"!

Chris laughed. The cool impertinence of it amused him. Next time they met she'd be as calm as if these past two weeks hadn't existed. She'd never be embarrassed or confused. Not Alicia! There was something to be said for breeding and upbringing, and all the rest of it, after all. He lit a cigarette, stuck his hands in his pockets and walked back home.

His mother said, "Chris, Flight is coming down with your father tomorrow."

He said, "Really? That's good. Nice to see him again. Does Alicia know?"

"I expect so. But telephone and tell her if you like, Chris."

He said, "Well, just in case Flight hasn't let her know."

"Might he speak to Miss Lockwood? Yes." Ah, here was Miss Lockwood!

"Hello, Alicia! This is Chris speaking. We've had word from Flight that he'll be home tomorrow. . . . Oh, he telephoned to you earlier? That's good. We thought perhaps you didn't know. . . . Good! He's coming over to see you? My mother sends her love to you. *Good* night, 'Licia, *good* night!" When he walked back into the drawing-room, his mother said, "What did Alicia say? You look so amused, Chris."

In the green drawing-room at the Rectory, Flight sat talking to the Rector and Lady Sophia. Alicia had shown a warmth in her greeting which had made him feel secure and confident. She had laid her cheek against his and said, "How good to have you home, Flight, dear!"

"You missed me?"

"I'm not really myself with you away." Then, with sudden intensity, "I need you, I mean that, really *need* you."

He tried to tell her what he had heard in Paris; she listened, and when he ended his recital said, "But why should those people know more about the possibilities of war than we do here?"

"Maybe because they see more clearly, more realistically."

"I wonder . . ."

"They're better haters, Alicia. They know what invasion means—we don't."

129

"But surely no one can invade them with their Maginot Line?"

"I met many people who didn't think that salvation lay by the way of the Maginot Line, Alicia."

Now he told his story again in the drawing-room, and the Rector laid his well-kept finger-tips together and listened in grave silence. Lady Sophia said calmly that the French had always been scaremongers, she could recall incident after incident to prove it.

"And what is your own reaction, Flight?" Lockwood asked.

"That is what I want to discuss with you, sir. I want to get some military training. I was in the OTC at school, and I believe that Lord Rusmere has considerable influence in the Territorials. He asked me, when I met him in town, to go and see his collection of pictures. I felt that this might be an opportunity, and I could discuss the possibilities of getting training and a commission with him."

"Really! You feel convinced, then? On the word of a few French people—one of them an actress, and therefore excitable—as indeed I find most French people are . . ."

For a moment Flight longed to say, "But she is not, she's a hard-headed Yorkshire woman!" But he remained silent and the Rector's voice flowed on, ". . . and a few other people, all artists, or following some artistic bent. I'm afraid, Flight, that I don't allow *myself* to be influenced so easily.

Why should March be the crucial month? Today is the twenty-first; so far the month has been uneventful."

Flight licked his lips, his mouth felt dry. "Hitler occupied the port and district surrounding Memel in Lithuania yesterday," he said. "He won't stop there, he wants Danzig incorporated with Germany. He won't go on merely talking, making demands and sending notes—then what happens?"

Lockwood answered calmly. "If Poland is attacked, Britain will go to her aid."

"Which means war?" Flight demanded. His face was white, his hand shaking, he knew that his voice was not quite steady; the sight of this dignified, well-dressed man, unmoved, and confident that his own ideas were correct, raised a kind of fury in him.

"My dear boy, remember that there is still British diplomacy!"

"I wish that I did not remember it, sir."

"Tut, tut! I don't like to hear you speak in that way."

"Troops are being poured into Slovakia. What does that mean except an attack on Poland?"

Lady Sophia held up her hand—a very fine hand—white, thin and exquisitely kept. "I think that we will change the subject. After all, we know, *can* know, so little. Far better to leave this speculation to wiser heads than ours. Of one thing I am certain: I have no doubts that whatever events may

131

come to pass the country which we all, I hope and believe, love so dearly will do her duty, completely and bravely. Now, Alicia, will you play something, dear?"

Flight sprang to his feet. "Forgive me, Lady Sophia! If war comes—and no one hopes more than I do that it may not come—will you and the Rector consent to Alicia and me being married immediately?"

Her voice was even, and very cold, as she answered, "I think that decision may safely be left until—war does come, Flight. Now, Alicia, dear! Yes, Chopin—delightful!"

Three days later, in reply to his letter, Rusmere telegraphed:

Yes come along car meeting the 5.46 on Thursday. Rusmere.

Flight found him in his library, a huge gloomy room, where white marble busts of dead-and-gone statesmen seemed to shiver against the dark walls. The air was thick with cigar smoke; a Great Dane rose and walked towards Flight, stared at him with bloodshot eyes, then returned to its master and flung itself down, emitting a long-drawn sigh as if the effort had exhausted it.

Rusmere said, "Glad ter see you! Now what's all this bosh Lockwood writes to me about your visit to France having unsettled you? You've not been going gay with some French tart, have you?"

132

Again Flight told his story. The little dried-up nobleman wriggled in his great winged armchair, grunting from time to time.

"Ugh!" he said at last. "And now we've given a guarantee to Poland! We're going to dish out these guarantees right and left, I suppose. By God, I'll bet that Hitler roars over them! He'll press harder for his road and rail business through Pomorze. Wants to carve up Poland as he did Czechoslovakia. He's got factories at Pilsen and Brno—they're working fullsteam. Tell Stanley Lockwood he's a blasted ass—always was, always will be! Sitting there with blinkers on, blinkers he put on his own eyes with his own fat hands! Well, what d'you want to do?"

Again Flight told him. He listened, nodded, grunted, "Leave that to me. Wish that you could get twenty thousand other fellers to feel as you do. I doubt if, for the sake of one just man, the Lord is going to make any great effort to save the City—but it shows willing, yes, it shows willing! Now have a drink, and then I'll show you some pictures that *are* pictures. Put in special lighting so's I can see 'em any time, day or night. Had a German over to install it—that's funny! Chap called Schnellier. It's good, I will say that."

Flight found that he liked the little Earl. He was shrewd, his speech was blunt and frequently coarse; but he loved his pictures, his etchings and his fine drawings—and, what was more, he understood them.

133

He stood before them, rising and falling on his toes, moving his head this way and that to get the best possible view, murmuring, "Lovely, lovely! Look at that brush-work. It's not brush-work at all, it's a bloody miracle in paint." He never mentioned the price which he had paid or recounted the magnificent offers which had been made to him for his paintings; he was content to love and admire them, and he was ready to realise that in Flight Masters he had met someone who felt as he did.

Felix joined them at dinner, and immediately Rusmere changed. He was the irritable old man he had been at Portland Place, snarling and snapping. Flight thought, "Why does he let his brother live here? It's so obvious that they hate each other."

The following afternoon Rusmere said to Flight, "When you get back, go into Mexfield. That's your county town, eh?"

"Seven miles from Baddock St. Mallory, sir."

"Right! Go there and see Colonel Carteret, old buddy of mine—Mike Carteret. I've talked to him on the telephone about you, he'll arrange things quickly. Mention my name. He lives at a place called Longlands Close. Better telephone for an appointment. He's all right. Bit of a fool, but a decent fool. I've a respect for Mike Carteret."

Carteret saw Flight the following morning. He was a tall, gaunt man, with a drooping red moustache. His manner was melancholy in the extreme. He said, "Want a commission, eh?

134

Rusmere says that you ought to get one quickly, says you're highly intelligent. What the deuce does he mean by that, d'you imagine? In the OTC? Better than nothing. Well, let's see what can be done."

Flight flung himself into his training. Night after night he drove to Mexfield, where he drilled, marched, studied and tried to equip himself for a commission. From time to time Carteret visited the barracks and nodded to him, saying, "How'y'r getting along?" Then, without waiting for a reply, he would ask the officer who was giving the lecture, "How's he getting on? Good! Push him at it, make him work!"

At Easter he went into camp at Bifford, and on Good Friday heard that Italy had annexed Albania, the day before Britain had signed the Anglo-Polish Pact. He was back home again, travelling up and down to the Galleries every day and working at his military training practically every evening, when, on April 28th, they heard that Hitler had annulled the German-Polish Non-aggression Pact. Edward Masters said that it was common knowledge in the City that Germany was sending large forces into East Prussia by sea.

Flight said, "Looks as if the orchestra was really tuning up, Father!"

"The only question is, when will the conductor lift his baton, my boy?"

Flight's commission came through on May 1st. Chris listened tolerantly to the news, and asked if

Flight were going to "dress up" and show himself to Alicia.

His brother was stung into asking if Chris himself didn't think that a uniform might suit him.

Chris replied that he wasn't going to be rushed into anything.

"You might be," Flight answered.

On May 18th the Conscription Bill passed its third reading, even though both Labour and Liberals had opposed it.

The following evening Flight was dining at the Rectory. Before dinner he sat with Alicia in her sitting-room and holding her hand in his, said, "Well, that's practically an admission that—it's coming quickly."

"Oh, my darling . . . !"

"Will you marry me, Alicia? Let's take what we can of happiness together. Promise me that you will, promise me."

"I promise," she said, and putting her arms round his neck, to his astonishment she began to cry. Not easy tears, but long-drawn-out sobs which shook her body as it pressed against his own.

"Alicia, darling, don't—don't! We may have quite a long time together—only"—he tried to laugh—"it's better to be on the safe side."

Slowly her sobs subsided, she dried her eyes, and said gravely, "Flight, I'm not really the nice person you imagine; if you really knew me, you wouldn't even like me. I've all sorts and kinds of faults, but I promise that I'll try to be all you wish me to be."

"I wish you to be your own adorable self," he told her.

That evening Lockwood seemed to Flight to be even more unctuous than ever, Lady Sophia more firmly and coldly assured of Britain's ability to avert war without losing one iota of her own self-respect.

"This Bill—conscription," Flight hazarded—"how does that strike you?"

The Rector answered, "It bears out a contention which I believe to be sound, that to ensure Peace one should prepare for War. This is what the Government is doing. A Ministry of Supply, Munitions—call it what you will—this Bill, factories working their hardest; labour unrest, all forgotten in this great common cause. We have every reason to be proud of our beloved country and of the ministers who govern her."

His wife, delicately dissecting a piece of chicken, said, without raising her eyes, "Ex-*actly!*"

Feeling slightly sick, Flight said, "Oh, I forgot to tell you, my sister Ann is engaged."

Alicia exclaimed, "Ann—but she's a baby, Flight!"

"Eighteen, and they both seem very happy about it. It will be in *The Times* tomorrow. She's going to marry Claverley."

Lady Sophia put down her knife and fork and repeated, "Claverley! Sholto Claverley?"

Alicia said, "Flight, dear, how marvellous! When did this happen?"

"Unofficially, when he came to luncheon and talked to my father some time ago. He's a nice fellow, isn't he? I liked him a lot."

"What does the Duke say?"

"Apparently he's delighted. Claverley has driven Ann over to see him today. They're going to be married in a month. Quite quietly, here at Baddock St. Mallory."

Lady Sophia said coldly, "In a month! I wonder what all Claverley's relations will think. It will be a terrible rush."

The Rector agreed. "Terrible!", as if to arrange a wedding so quickly was an offence against all decency and social laws. Flight wished that he had refrained from telling them until he had made his own proposal; he ought to have spoken of his own wedding first, and then used the argument that Ann and Claverley were to be married quickly to bolster up his own request.

His eyes met Alicia's across the table. She smiled as if to encourage him. He drew a deep breath, then said, "Which brings me to what I want to say. As you know, I am convinced that this country will go to war, and I want you to allow Alicia and me to be married quickly—say next month. There's no reason why we shouldn't be married on the same day as my sister and Claverley. Will you please consent to this?"

"On the same day!" the Rector boomed. "My

good boy! Do you know how many people St. Mark's holds? I can tell you. Barely—barely—two hundred and twenty, not, of course, including the clergy and choir. Impossible! Why, my dear, how many invitations have we sent out alone?"

"Three hundred and seventy-four, and there are still another fifty to be sent, Stanley."

"I suppose that Claverley will want a certain number of guests? Why, it would be impossible, completely impossible. No, no, wiser to let matters remain as we have arranged. After all"—with a tolerant smile—"the church may be *spiritually* open to all, but the walls are not elastic. No one can, to use a homely expression, cram a quart into a pint pot!"

"But let me say this . . ." Flight began, but Alicia stopped him.

"Let me speak, Flight. Mama, Papa—Flight and I have already had a very long engagement. It hasn't been easy, because we are very much in love. Flight has been angelic always. Now he believes this war is coming soon. He's done everything he can to prepare himself for what he thinks will be his duty. He'll go out to fight. Very well—if he does, then he is going out as my husband. Nothing is going to prevent that. If we cannot get all these relations—for most of whom we none of us really care tuppence—into the church, then Flight and I will go into Mexfield and be married at the Registrar's Office."

Her mother said, "Alicia! I am surprised—

more, I am deeply hurt—that my daughter should speak in such a way. I refuse to discuss it."

Again Flight tried to speak. Again Alicia said, "No, Flight, leave this to me. Mama, I mean what I say. Flight told me that he loved me nearly a year ago—not quite so long—but we've waited long enough. Papa, may we be married with Lord Claverley and Ann? Or shall Flight go into Mexfield in the morning and give notice of our wedding there?"

Lockwood, his face scarlet, almost spluttered. "Alicia, I entirely refuse to allow you to speak in this manner. It is most improper, most! Your mother and I must discuss it fully, and at length."

"Flight, I'll telephone to you in the morning, dear," Alicia said. "Then we'll make our own arrangements. I'm not a child, Papa. It's my wedding, it's my happiness. Flight, I'll come with you to the door. I don't feel that any of us will enjoy the remainder of this dinner."

6

HE kissed her good night, whispering, "God, I'm proud of you!—and grateful to you, my dearest!"

She answered confidently, "We shall win. I'll telephone you in the morning."

He went home with a greater sense of security than he had ever felt before. It seemed that in some miraculous way Alicia saw clearly what lay before them, that she realised that her happiness would lie with him and that she was determined not to jeopardise it through lack of courage.

He found that Ann and Claverley had returned and were eating a late dinner. They were both in the highest spirits; it appeared that the Duke had been charming, was having various pieces of jewellery re-set immediately for Ann, and that he had thanked God, in a most pious manner, that Sholto had the good sense to choose a girl with straight legs, a straight back, a decent skin and small wrists and ankles.

Chris said, "You're looking very set up with yourself, Flight. Not often you look so aggressively cheerful."

"Not often I have such good reason to look aggressively cheerful," he returned. "Mother,

141

what do you think about having a double wedding?"

Ann shouted, "A double wedding? Marvellous! What headlines for the Press! Grocer's son and daughter marry into the aristocracy!"

"And in the p-picture p-papers," Claverley added. "They'll all wonder which is the Duke and the Earl of Rusmere, and immediately s-spot your father as the Duke, and—oh, I d-don't know who they'll decide is old Rusmere. Both he and m-my father always look like tramps."

Flight told his story, explained why he and Alicia wished to be married soon and what she had suggested should her parents prove unamenable.

Frances Masters said, "Oh, I don't think that I should like that very much, Flight. I've only been to one wedding in a Registrar's and it was such a dreary business. No clergyman—only an old man who I am certain took snuff. Oh no, a church wedding is so pretty. Isn't it, Edward?"

"It's a question, it appears, of the guests, Mother, apparently. The church only holds two hundred and twenty people. The Lockwoods have already invited nearly four hundred."

"Flight, dear, what masses of cruets and silver salts-and-peppers you're going to have!"

"I'm going to send him a bearskin, complete with head, over which I've been t-tripping for years. And in an additional b-burst of generosity, I s-shall throw in a roll-top desk of hideous design which the tenants g-gave me when I was twenty-

142

one," Claverley told them.

Edward Masters listened, smiled, then said, "The question as I see it is, are you both willing to face an uncomfortably packed church, or do all these somewhat extraneous people—many of them totally unknown to you, mean a great deal?"

"They don't mean a damn to either Claverly or I," Ann said.

Claverley murmured, "Claverley or me, darling, not I."

"Pedantic idiot!"

"And Alicia is carrying on the battle single-handed. Gallant girl! Well, wait until the morning when she telephones," Edward advised.

Eleanor followed Flight up to his room when they went to bed. He took her hand and pulled her into his room. She sat down on the edge of his bed, smiling contentedly. "I'm so glad, Flight, dear!"

"So am I. Glad! That's not nearly strong enough. If you'd heard Alicia, she was wonderful. She was so calm, so direct. Oh, Eleanor, she's a wonderful person!"

"It doesn't really take a very wonderful person to want to marry you and be happy with you, my dear. You're quite a nice man, you know."

The door opened and Chris entered. He frowned when he saw Eleanor, then said quickly. "I say, Flight, let me have a razor-blade, will you? I've run short and I want to be off early."

"Of course. I'll find some for you."

Chris lounged against the tallboy and flicked his

cigarette-ash on the carpet, grinning when Eleanor said, "Chris, dear, there is an ash-tray!" and answering, "Good for the moth. So you're going to hurry up the wedding, eh? Because you're afraid of this war arriving suddenly?"

"Something like that."

"That the only reason?"

Flight swung round and said abruptly, "What the devil do you mean by that, Chris?"

"Good Lord, what's the matter with the fellow? What could I mean?"

"I didn't like your tone much."

"Don't be so damned touchy! You're in love with Alicia, aren't you?"

"Naturally, but . . ."

"Don't be so blasted prudish! We aren't children, are we? Not even Eleanor here."

Eleanor said, "I'm afraid that I agree with Flight, Chris. I don't like this conversation very much."

"Sorry—very sorry. I'll get along. Thanks for the razor-blades. Good night."

While they were at breakfast the following morning, Chris, who had not left so early after all, answered the telephone. He came back and said:

"It's Alicia—wants to speak to Flight. Very starchy, your young woman this morning, Flight!"

"Chris, dear," his mother said reprovingly, "perhaps she's worried."

They heard Flight's voice, eager, anxious, speaking.

Alicia said, "It's all right, darling! It was a struggle, but I won. Now I'm having breakfast on a tray in bed. Mama has been in to see me, she looks pained but resigned. Papa and she have been drawing up notices to send to everyone we've invited, except a special few, explaining that the church is small, and that it's to be a double wedding. The fact that Ann is going to marry Claverley does appear to make it slightly more bearable. Papa is driving down to the printer's at Mexfield immediately."

Breathlessly Flight said, "Ann and Claverley want to fix it for the twentieth of June."

She answered, "You and I want it fixed for the twentieth of June, never mind Lord Claverley and Ann. Tell them I said so! Come and see me this afternoon about four, darling. Good-bye."

During the weeks which followed Flight knew that he had never been so happy. Alicia seemed to have come to a realisation of her love for him; she was tender, affectionate, and always ready to spend long hours with him. Where previously she had often pleaded that Lady Sophia wished her to go calling, or that she must spend a week-end here, or two days there, now she refused to leave home. Neither did she like him to be away from Baddock St. Mallory, and he made the daily journey to London, conscious that he was not only anxious to make it, but happy in making it, since it pleased Alicia.

When he left her in the evening she always said,

"Tomorrow—I shall see you tomorrow?"

Only once was he obliged to remain in town for two days, when an important business meeting made it imperative.

He grumbled to Chris the evening before. Flight had never been on really intimate terms with his brother; there were times when he didn't even think that he liked him much, but this evening Chris was sympathetic and kindly.

"Yes, I suppose it is a bore," Chris agreed. "You see Alicia every evening, do you?"

"Why, yes—that is, ever since the date of the wedding was settled."

"And it really is imperative that you stay in town for these two evenings? Can't you wriggle out of one at least?"

"It's difficult. You see, I shall be away on my honeymoon for a month, and both Clintock and old Evans are important clients. Either of them could do me a whole lot of good, or harm, for that matter, if they wanted to. No, I don't see the slightest chance of getting away. I'm dining with Clintock at his dreary club and with Evans at the Savoy. If I know him, he'll sit there drinking until they fling us out."

"Umph! Too bad! I've got to go to Raisley for a match. It's all right for me; this war scare has played the devil with business. Wish to God it was settled one way or the other! Well, if I should catch a glimpse of Alicia as I go through—which isn't likely—I'll assure her that you're not just playing truant."

"Thanks, Chris."

Old Clintock was more of a bore than usual, but he had a proposal to take the Galleries for a month for a particularly distinguished exhibition, which would enhance their prestige, and leave Flight a very pleasant margin of profit. The following morning he telephoned to Alicia.

"You'll be back tonight?" she asked.

"I can't, I wish that I could. I've got to meet Evans at eight—I shan't get away before eleven. I know the fellow! The evening after, sweet, I'll be with you."

"I wish that you could have come back tonight, Flight."

"Not more than I do. But I've got my living to earn, y'know."

"Yes—very well. Good-bye, darling."

Then, just as he was in his bath, preparatory to dressing to go and meet Josiah Evans, Wilkinson knocked on the bathroom door and said, "Telegram, Mr. Flight."

He had cursed, wrapped himself in a towel and opened the door, standing to read it while the water made little pools round his feet.

Regret illness prevents keeping appointment writing Evans.

"Right!" he shouted. "I'm going up to Baddock, Wilkinson. Back in the morning. Or no, I'll lunch in town, and come here before I drive back tomorrow. Telephone the garage, will you? I want the car filled and brought round. Tell them to look at the oil."

He dressed rapidly, flinging things into his small suitcase; he was waiting for the car when it came round. Old Wilkinson watched him drive away, then went back to the kitchen.

"That's love, that is!" he said to his wife. "Mr. Flight gorne tearing off like a mad fellow! Ten minutes ago 'e was standing wrapped in a bath towel dripping all over the bathroom tiles. Now he's orf ter Baddock an' 'is young lady."

His wife replied, "Then there'll only be the Master fer dinner, eh, 'Erb?"

"That's so. Mr. Chris is orf somewhere, bin playing golf, I b'lieve."

Flight drove well. He prided himself that he could get the last ounce of speed possible and yet do no harm to the car. Now he sped out of London, and his heart was singing as he saw the long, wide black road stretching before him. This was where he could open up, where the car could eat up the miles. Half past seven—with luck he could be home by half past eight. He'd cut dinner, tell his mother that he'd eaten in town. Then a quick wash, and round to the Rectory—and Alicia.

That was what really mattered, to see her, talk to her, press his lips to hers and know that she was glad that he had come to her. The rest—the gathering clouds, the continual giving of guarantees, the

148

arguments of Stalin that it was necessary for his country's safety for him to occupy Lithuania, Latvia and Estonia. The protestations of the British Government, the growing mistrust of Stalin's policy and aims—these things were too big, they were all part of some great piece of dangerous machinery which had been set in motion. He was driving to Alicia; with her his fears and apprehensions would vanish like dew under the bright morning sunshine.

Here was the big hill which led to Bilford, change down—up and up—the top was reached; he changed gear neatly and silently, and raced along the long level road which led to Baddock.

Eleanor was alone when he came in, she looked up. "Flight, dear! I thought that you were in town."

He laughed. "It's pretty obvious that you were wrong."

"Nothing the matter?"

"Only old Josiah Evans got a bilious attack or a touch of gout, and had to put off the appointment."

"You've had dinner?"

"Well, yes—no, not really. I don't want anything, I'm going round to see Alicia. If you like to be an angel, tell them to leave me some sandwiches and a drink. I'll have them when I come back. There, I must go and wash. See you later, eh?"

She heard him race up the stairs, and smiled indulgently. He was so young, so very much in love, and how much happier he seemed than he had been during the first months of his engagement to Alicia. Dear Flight! in three weeks' time he and his beloved Alicia would be married. Ann, with her usual impetuosity, had said, "Eleanor, why not a triple wedding?"

She had shaken her head. "Sweet of you, darling Ann, but George and I are going to be married very quietly early one morning in September, and we're going to have very, very few people there. Your wedding, even Flight's, is different." She laughed. "You're marrying 'Very Important People'."

"Poof! Don't be a snob, Eleanor!"

"I'm not, I'm stating facts. Sholto is important, so—in a different way, I suppose—is Alicia. No, I don't want a big wedding, darling. It isn't the kind of thing that George and I enjoy. We're not terribly social."

Ann sighed. "I should have liked to be married at St. Margaret's, with Sholto's troopers and people for a guard of honour. He said that he'd die of fright. The King and Queen are sending him a present, think of that! He heard yesterday. I believe that he is rather thrilled, though he won't admit it."

There was Flight, clattering down the stairs and racing off to the Rectory. He had told her that whilst the Rector and Lady Sophia were still adopting a slightly resigned attitude about the wedding and never missing an opportunity of pointing out how very difficult the change of dates had made everything, they were not continuing to argue about it. He had said, "A patient and Christian-like acceptance"—that was their line. He added, "I can bear it."

The butler told him that dinner was over. Would he go in and see the Rector and Lady Sophia? —they were in the drawing-room. Miss Alicia had gone out after dinner for a stroll. She had complained of one of her headaches. "In so far as I know, sir, she went down the drive."

Flight said, "That's all right. I'll find her. I'll bring her back quite soon, Belton."

"I don't think as Miss Alicia was expecting you, sir."

"No, this is just a piece of unexpected good luck. Thanks, Belton!"

"Thank *you*, sir."

Down the drive to the gates. They were closed. Alicia wouldn't have gone walking down the high road, she always said that she hated it, hated the "'ammer, 'ammer, 'ammer on the 'ard 'igh road". He turned and went into the Home Wood. Halting, he whistled the first four notes of the Westminster chimes—their own signal to each other. There was no reply, no sound. He walked on for another fifty yards and fancied that he heard a movement. Again he whistled, and a third time. Someone was moving, crashing away through the bushes, running madly. Flight called, "Alicia! Alicia!" in an agony of fear, and heard her call back to him.

"Flight—Flight!"

He tore through the trees and saw her standing, leaning against a silver birch, her dress showing white and ghostly in the half-light. Somewhere on the high road he heard a car starting up, the roar of the engine increased, then, as the car moved away, there was silence again.

"What is it?" he asked, frantic with anxiety. "Alicia, darling! Tell me!"

She stared at him almost vacantly. "I don't know. I was walking here, I had a headache. There was a man here—a tramp, perhaps. I don't know. He asked me for money. I told him that I had none."

"A tramp?" Flight repeated. "He's driven off in a car, darling."

"Has he?" She still seemed vague, looked at him with eyes which scarcely appeared to recognise him. "Then he tried to take my necklace. Look!" He saw that her cloak lay on the ground, and that her dress was torn a little. She had been wearing a flower of some kind, which lay crushed and broken. She said, "He's gone."

Flight caught her to him, watching her white face intently.

"You're all right, Alicia, tell me that you're all right?"

"Yes, I'm all right. I'm safe, Flight—dear Flight!"

Then she slipped quietly from his clasp and slid to the ground. He knelt beside her, rubbing her cold hands, trying to gather her cloak up so that he might lay it over her. He kept whispering, "Alicia, Alicia, wake up, darling, wake up! I'm here, it's all right!"

Her eyes opened, she sighed and said his name, then told him that she was better, adding, "Take me home, Flight, please take me home."

He helped her to her feet, and together, Alicia leaning her weight on his arm, made their way back to the Rectory. Belton opened the door to them, and the wide shaft of bright light rushed out, dispelling the soft dusk of the evening.

"Miss Alicia—Mr. Masters—what has . . ."

Flight said, "Call Lady Sophia, will you? Someone must help Miss Alicia to her room; she's ill."

Alicia said protestingly, "No, no! Take me into the drawing-room. I shall be all right. I don't want to go to my room. Flight, please!"

Lying back in one of the big chairs, while the Rector gave her brandy and Lady Sophia watched Flight as if she felt that he was responsible for her daughter's indisposition, Flight wiped his forehead and tried to recover his self-control.

Speaking slowly, Alicia said, "I went into the Home Wood . . . a man came along. He came from the opposite direction. I think that he was a tramp. I told you that I thought he was a tramp, didn't I, Flight?"

Flight nodded. "I don't think that he was. He drove away in a car."

"Did you hear a car drive up at first, darling?" Lockwood asked.

Alicia said that she didn't remember. She didn't think that she had heard anything—no, she was certain that she had heard nothing. The man seemed to appear—just like that—appear suddenly. He asked for money.

"I told you that, Flight, didn't I?"

"Yes, darling, yes."

"His voice, my dear—can you recall it?" her father asked.

No, she only fancied that it was a rough voice —yes, rough—uneducated.

"And then . . ."

"Then he tried to—to snatch this chain, and tore my dress a little. I showed you, Flight, didn't I? Then I heard Flight's whistle and called to him, and the tramp ran away. That's all I know."

She was taken to her room, whilst Lockwood, for once shaken out of his usual calm urbanity, debated with Flight as to what was to be done.

Flight said, "I did hear a car drive away. It was getting dark in the wood. Either the man is a dangerous lunatic or a car thief. We ought to get on to the police."

Lockwood hesitated. "What made him come into the wood at all?"

"Heaven only knows! The fact remains that he should be traced and caught."

The Rector seemed unwilling, and when Lady Sophia came down to report that she had given

154

Alicia a luminal, and that she was drowsy already, she supported him.

"There is no good to be served by making all kinds of enquiries. Alicia—and thank God for it—assures me that this creature exercised . . ." she paused, evidently sought for a sufficiently innocuous phrase, then continued—"no physical violence. To make the police come into this is only going to create a great deal of *talk*. There will be exaggerated stories, incredible rumours, and so on. No, our darling is safe, she has suffered . . ." again that pause, "no grievous physical harm. Let it rest at that."

"Only," the Rector said gravely, "Alicia must understand that she must not walk in the Home Wood again unaccompanied."

Flight's nerves felt like over-tight fiddle-strings, they quivered at every word; he listened to the smooth pronouncement, then threw back his head and laughed immoderately. He knew that Lady Sophia and Lockwood watched him uneasily. His laughter increased. They both spoke to him— soothingly, even kindly—his sides ached, his eyes smarted, his throat was giving him definite pain. Lady Sophia said, "Stanley, I think a brandy-and-soda might do him good."

Finally he gasped out, "And that's all that we're going to do, eh?"

"What is—all we are going to do, my boy?"

"Tell Alicia—not to walk—there alone— again."

155

"That at least will prevent a recurrence of this unfortunate incident."

Flight said, "You swear that she's all right?"

"By this time I imagine that she is sound asleep."

"Then I'll go. I'm a bit shaken. Sorry if I made a fool of myself!"

"No, no!"—the Rector's hand was on his shoulder. "I say in all sincerity that I see the hand of the Almighty in this sudden visit of yours, so unexpected. The Divinity which 'shapes our ends' was at work tonight."

His wife agreed. "Indeed, yes. We have a great deal to be thankful for."

As he walked home, Flight muttered coarsely, "Divinity that shapes our ends! I'd shape that bastard's end for him if I could lay my hands on him, the dirty swine!"

He said nothing to either his mother or Eleanor, but tried to eat the sandwiches which had been left for him, and found them dry in his mouth. He drank a whisky-and-soda thirstily and listened to what his mother had to say about the wedding

". . . and at last, I admit, I said quite sharply, 'Really, Lady Sophia, this is the wedding of my daughter and my son, and I intend that the reception shall be given here. My husband has made arrangements for a very large marquee, and this is his unalterable decision.' She stared at me, then said in that short manner of hers, 'Very well. I am sure that I don't know what my husband will say.' I nearly told her that whatever he said would not have the slightest effect on *my* husband, but I didn't, and the matter ended."

Eleanor said reflectively, "How difficult all these things are—being born, and married and buried. All so complicated."

"We make them complicated," Flight said. "It's our own silly fault . . ."

Ann interrupted. "You can't include being born in that list. No one wants any fuss about being born."

"Native women go into the bush, have their baby, then walk on," he insisted.

"Native women," she retorted, "don't live our artificial lives, don't diet, or dance half the night, or play tennis or a dozen other things."

Their mother said placidly, "Think of the time when women wore stays and had eighteen-inch waists. What's that?"

Ann said, "Listen! Whoever's arriving at this time of night?"

A moment later Chris walked in. "Hello, everyone! I decided to drive back from Raisley. No, thanks, Mother, I had dinner at the club-house —rotten dinner too. Hello, Flight! I thought that you were kept in town by old Evans."

"The old blighter put me off, so I tore down here."

"Good." He poured himself out a drink. "Seen Alicia? Good. Glad to see you?"

"I think so very glad. How did your match go?"

157

"I was in the same position as you—my opponent didn't turn up—sent a message that he's sprained his wrist. Damned annoying!"

Eleanor asked, "Who were you playing, Chris?"

"You don't know him; he's not a member of Raisley. Chap I know in the City."

"And he was coming all the way from town to play a match with you? He must be keen," Ann said.

"He is keen, my child, very keen. Well, I've got to be off in the morning; I'll just put the car away. Good night, Mother. Good night, everyone."

They heard him start the car. Flight uttered a smothered exclamation.

Eleanor said, "What is it, Flight?"

He said, "Nothing. Very characteristic sound a Humber makes when it starts, doesn't it?"

Ann preened herself slightly. "Sholto is giving me a Rolls two-seater."

"Heaven help the pedestrians!" Eleanor said.

"I think that they're right," Alicia said. "The police are so heavy handed, and they drag things out so. I'm still convinced that the man was a tramp, Flight, dear, and don't let's talk about it any more. It was all hateful and very frightening."

Flight said, "I discovered one thing. The car I heard drive away was a Humber. I'd recognise that sound anywhere, just as I'd recognise the sound of a Standard. I didn't recognise at the moment, but late that night Chris came home from Raisley, and

158

when he started up his bus to take her round to the garage it came back to me. It was a Humber. That swine was no tramp, Alicia!"

She caught his hand. "You didn't speak to Chris about—that affair?"

"No, darling, not to anyone. I promised that I wouldn't."

"Then let's forget all about it! I don't ever want to think of it again. I want to believe that it was some kind of a nightmare, that can't ever, ever happen again."

"I still wish that we could have traced him."

Alicia still held his hand tightly. "Flight, don't! What good would it do? Papa was right, no good could have been served by tracing this brute . . ."

"It might have stopped him frightening girls again."

"Flight, promise me that you won't begin making enquiries yourself. I ask you to promise. Once you began, the police might hear of it. I should have to give evidence and be questioned—I couldn't stand it. On the eve of my wedding —please, darling, please!"

Flight promised, repeated his promise again and again. Poor Alicia, he realised what a dreadful impression this business had made on her. She was imaginative, and it must have occurred to her, as it had done to him, what might have happened had he not come back from town, had he taken the high road instead of going through the wood, had old Evans not been ill, had the car broken down—a hundred possibilities came to his mind. At night he would wake and imagine that he was dining at the Savoy with Evans, that he had broken down on the road—one thing after another—until he lay sweating and shivering. The night before the wedding Flight and Sholto dined in London with Chris and George Charlton; they had planned that it should be a real "stag" party, that they would eat wonderful food, and drink just a little more than was good for them. Instead, the gaiety fizzled out like a damp squib, and Flight found himself discussing Stalin's aims and how far they would agree with Adolf Hitler's.

Sholto, the freckles showing very plainly on his rather snub nose, said, "Frankly, it's m-my belief that Flight and I are j-just getting our respective weddings through in t-time."

Chris asked, "In time for what, exactly?"

"In t-time to watch the pot boil over. We've got too many commitments, and we shan't have sufficient c-capital to pay the debts we've contracted. Or rather, the bills we have backed. That's what we've done—backed bills right and left."

"Well, whatever happens we always manage to come out on top in the end," Chris said.

"Possibly," Charlton agreed, his voice very crisp; "it's the interval before the end that is so damned unpleasant—and dangerous."

"And this," Chris spoke dramatically, "is a gay party before a wedding; and you're droning on about something that may never happen! Good

God! can't you forget this Hitler-cum-Stalin nonsense?"

"If it were indeed n-nonsense," Sholto agreed, "we could and w-would forget it. It isn't, my good fellow, and the sooner you all get used to accepting that as a fact, the less will be the s-shock when the whole thing boils over, or blows up, or whatever you like to call it."

No, it was not a gay dinner. No one except Chris even had one glass too many, and even Chris was painfully sober. Flight thought what a hateful week it had been; the house turned upside down, long tables in the billiard room, displaying presents. Ann looked at them with him, said, "Ours —Sholto's and mine—are more expensive, but yours and Alicia's are in better taste, I think."

"If they are neither Alicia nor I can take credit for that. Once we come back from our honeymoon we're going to do a spot of weeding-out. No one wants eleven silver inkstands and neither do they want ten card tables even if they do come from Finnigans, and Aspreys!"

Ann was the least disturbed of them all, Flight thought. Dressmakers might plead for fittings, photographers beg for sittings—Ann was unmoved. She looked at the exquisite wristwatch which Sholto had given her, and said calmly, "I can spare you ten minutes" or "twenty minutes", and nothing would move her. She insisted upon shutting herself into her own room with Sholto, and allowed no one to disturb them.

Frances said mildly, "But, darling, there are so many things to attend to! So many people to write and thank. Surely you can do without these long talks? After all, you've got the rest of your lives!"

"We shall be married then," Ann said. "We're engaged now and I mean to make the most of my engagement. After Wednesday, Sholto won't be able to say, 'Darling, how heavenly when we're married!' That will be over."

Alicia was more tractable. The years of training had not been wasted, Lady Sophia reflected. Ann Masters might go tearing over the countryside with Claverley in a car, or galloping for miles on the mare he had given her, while he rode beside her; Alicia realised the importance of the occasion, and stood for hours while dresses were fitted, obediently wrote charming little notes thanking people for their presents and good wishes. Once, when she said in Ann's hearing that she felt tired, adding that she had been writing notes of thanks all the afternoon, Ann stared at her.

"But why?" she asked.

"You have to thank people."

"Get a secretary! If she has any intelligence she needn't make them all the same—these notes. That's what I'm doing. Anyway, how can you even sound sincere writing to thank someone for a set of asparagus forks? I didn't know what they were, neither did Sholto! He thought they were some kind of obstetric instrument!"

No, he'd be thankful when it was all over. The

162

whole business seemed more than a little foolish. Dressing up in tight, uncomfortable clothes, standing about under a bell made of flowers, shaking hands and smirking. He scarcely slept, and dropped into a sound sleep just as it seemed Wilkinson woke him, and said, "The best of luck, sir, on this most important day!—and it's time you were moving. The car's ordered for half past nine."

Flight groaned. "Thanks, Wilkinson. Oh, Lord! I'm so sleepy!" He drank tea thirstily, he bathed and dressed, Wilkinson packed his bags, and Chris entered, bawling, "Ding-dong, ding-dong, we gallop along," doing the trilling, chromatic part with great fervour. "For-or-or, it is —my wed-ed-eding morning!"

Flight said, "Oh, dear Lord, this is too much!"

Rusmere's enormous Rolls called for them; Sholto was sitting well back, crouched against the cushions as if he were a criminal escaping from justice. His friend, "Batty" Brentworth, sat stiffly upright beside him.

Sholto greeted Flight, in a voice which seemed to hold nothing but acute misery. "Good luck, Flight!"

Automatically Flight replied, "Same to you, thank you."

He had said nothing, he felt, but "Thank you" to people who wished him "Good luck", ever since he woke.

Brentworth said, "Ah yes, good luck, Masters!"

163

Flight muttered, "Same to you—damn it—I mean, thanks!"

The drive to Baddock seemed endless; from time to time Chris or Brentworth uttered a brief sentence, and either Sholto or Flight replied equally briefly.

"Ah, we're nearly there!" Chris exclaimed.

Sholto appeared suddenly galvanised into life. He said, with some bitterness, "I believed that I wanted to see Ann m-more than anything or any-one in the w-world, now I know that I don't really care whether I s-see her again or not! I w-wish we'd been married in a Registry Office."

Flight said, "It's not Registry Office—it's Registrar's Office—and I wish we had too."

Brentworth added, speaking in an informative manner, "I once heard a fellow in the Brigade say exactly the same thing. I was his best man. He got over it all right. Told me so. The minute he saw her coming into church."

"You'll both be all right when you've had a glass of bubbly," Chris told them.

He wasn't looking so bright himself, Flight thought. All that "ding dong" business had evaporated as they drove out of London. Chris looked less healthy than was usual with him. He had a rather high colour, but this morning he looked a bit pasty. His eyes were a trifle bloodshot; perhaps he'd had one or two extra drinks before he went to bed.

The car turned in at the gates. Flight saw the

164

huge marquee, nudged Sholto and said, "Look at that?"

Brentworth said, "Looks like a circus!"

"That's what it is, we're the p-performing elephants!"

Not a particularly good joke, but he and Flight laughed hysterically.

Chris said, "Pull yourselves together, for God's sake!"

They entered the house with the gait and expressions of funeral mutes. Edward Masters met them, shook hands gravely, and motioned them to follow him into the library.

"You've got to stay in here," he told Sholto. "It appears that if you so much as catch sight of Ann before she comes into church, all kinds of dire and dreadful things will happen!" He turned to Brentworth. "You're his best man, eh? Then see that he stays here until you get the word."

"Very good, sir."

Miserably they drank champagne, and when Brentworth said, "That's a good wine," both Flight and Sholto glared at him.

He proceeded to stuff chicken sandwiches into his mouth. "Have some, they are good," he said.

Sholto said wearily, "Oh, do shut up, Batty!"

"Sorry, old man."

"I know that you don't mean to be a bore, b-but you are being a bore, in f-fact a damned bore. Chuntering on about food and drink . . ."

Flight added with some heat, "And drink and food . . ."

"And never imagining for a moment that possibly we should l-like to have a little peace and quiet. You've only g-got to flirt with the bridesmaids —we've got to g-get married."

"Yes, indeed we have," Flight agreed, "and it's a serious matter."

Then Edward Masters came in and said, "Now, if you'll all move off to the church. Take a car if you want to, but the walk—it's only five minutes —might do you good."

As men condemned to execution, Sholto and Flight, followed by their "best men", walked in silence from the room.

They passed through what appeared to be crowds of well-dressed people, again and again they were stopped to receive good wishes, to have their hands shaken, to listen to comments on the good fortune which was theirs in having such a beautiful day.

As they entered the churchyard gate, Flight said to Sholto, "It's queer, isn't it, that we've got to go through all this flim-flammery to make it legal to share the same bed with girls we love, eh?" Sholto grunted. "It's—barbarous, but it's also the tribute-money which Society extracts from us. Gosh, I wish it were over!"

For hours they stood, it seemed, at the side of the altar rails. They watched the church fill, heard the subdued sound of voices, and the music rose

166

from the organ, where an organist sat, who had been imported for the occasion in order that Eleanor might enjoy the festivities. Nothing seemed to happen, Flight felt that they might conceivably stand there for the rest of their lives. The Duke shuffled into a front pew with an enormous woman dressed in purple satin. "That's my Aunt Adelaide," Sholto whispered. The choir, even more meticulously washed than on a Sunday morning, entered. The senior curate followed—the Rector in his red and black hood—and behind him a thin man with curly hair thinning on the top of his head, with lawn sleeves and a very wide stole.

Sholto said, "That's my uncle, Bishop of Camtingly."

Flight whispered back, "You're well represented."

The senior curate announced that they would sing the first hymn on the sheet provided. The organ roared suddenly, the choir boys and the male voices blared out into "The Voice that breathed o'er Eden."

Brentworth said, "They're coming! Your girl's first, Sholto. Turn round!"

Flight turned too. Ann was half-way up the aisle, her hand on her father's arm. Flight thought that he saw the flutter of his mother's handkerchief. Of course, women invariably cried at weddings! A bridesmaid arranged Ann's train. Sholto moved to her side, his ears looked scarlet. Chris said, "Now you, Flight!"

Flight thought, "I believe old Chris is sickening for jaundice, he looks awful!" Then he saw Alicia, accompanied by the Earl of Rusmere, who looked old and shabby; Flight was certain that his morning coat smelt of moth-ball, and Alicia—she was advancing towards him, tall and lovely. "'My heart would awaken and beat . . .' I'll be good to you, don't worry, I'll make you happy! Alicia, Alicia, Alicia."

Chris said, "Move up; stand next to her."

The Bishop advancing, Lockwood at his side, but moving one pace to the rear. Flight wondered how they learned these moves. "One pace to the —rear!" He instructed his men like that when they were drilling. When would he be able to see Alicia? He thought that her eyes had met his for a moment when he moved to stand beside her. Now he was giving Sholto his cue. Sholto was repeating: "S-sholto William Archibald Purvis take . . ."

Ann mumbled shockingly; he couldn't hear a word. He intended to speak up for everyone to hear.

He tried to say, "I, Flight Melton, take . . ." but no sound came except a strange whistling of his breath. Alicia spoke softly, but he could hear every word, "Alicia Geraldine Sophia . . ."

Then the Bishop took one pace to the rear and gave the Rector a chance to say a few lines. After that they sat down on chairs with red velvet cushions and listened while the Bishop told them their duty to each other and to the world in general, and hoped that they would come to church regularly—or words to that effect—and live sober lives, and be happy ever after.

After that they all marched into the vestry, while the choir sang another hymn, "All earthly joys transcending", and crowds of people pushed in after them; people kissed each other and shook hands and signed the register, and Sholto whispered, "You were right. This is a register, the other is a Registrar, go up to the top of the class!"

Flight was standing face to face with Alicia; his hands shook a little; she looked pale but smiled at him, and whispered, "Flight—it's over!"

He kissed her, gently, his heart very full, wondering in a sudden excess of humility why this glorious creature should have been content to marry him?

"As the best man and brother of the bridegroom," Chris said, "don't I have the privilege of kissing the bride?"

Alicia smiled. "No! the chief bridesmaid, I think; not the bride!"

The remainder of the day was hot and dull and tedious. He sat beside Alicia and listened to speeches, he raised his glass to drink a toast and she whispered, "No, not this one, they're toasting you!" He subsided, feeling that he'd made a fool of himself, and was encouraged when later he saw Sholto do exactly the same thing—in fact he laughed more loudly than he should have done.

Suddenly, Alicia and Ann, Lady Sophia and his

mother, and a whole covey of bridesmaids, disappeared into the house, and Chris said, "If you don't want to travel to London in your glad rags, you'd better come and change."

Wilkinson was standing in his bedroom, fussing about. "Very nice, Mr. Flight! Every word came over as clear as a bell—lovely! Oh indeed yes, I heard you. So did the wife. Said to me, 'I'd know Mr. Flight's voice anywhere.' Brown shoes, yes —I'll take this other stuff down to be pressed later. Nice suit, this, very 'doggy', festive without being too much so. Nothink like a nice broken overcheck. Keys, passport, change, notecase—nice case that; Miss Alicia give you that, I'll bet. I should say Mrs. Flight Masters, shouldn't I, be rights? Beautiful links; also present from the bride, eh? Studs are in your case. All set, ship-shape and Bristol fashion. Good luck!"

He rattled down the wide, shallow stairs; again people greeted him. "Flight, my dear boy, be happy!" "Good luck, my boy. All the best." Ann's voice, higher, and with a lovely fresh youthful quality, "Do we meet in Paris as we come back? Let's!" The Rector's deep tones, "God bless you both, my boy!" and Lady Sophia, "Take care of my darling girl." The Duke, tall and thin, but still contriving to seem flabby, shaking his hand, "Glad to see you and your wife any time—in the family now, eh?" Felix Sawley whispering something inaudible behind his hand into Flight's ear and Rusmere shoving him away, with a snarling, "Shut up, you dirty old so-and-so! Good luck, me boy! Lovely girl! Find some decent pictures on yer travels." Sholto shouting, "Ann, we'll l-lose the connection!" Down the steps—confetti—what a mess for the gardeners to clean up in the morning! His own voice saying, "Make a bolt for it, Alicia, it sticks like blazes this confounded stuff!"

Voices—"Goodbye-byes; good luck, good luck"—fading away as the car moved off. Alicia sitting beside him. He slid his hand along to meet hers, and held it tightly.

"Whew!" he said, "I'd not go through it again, sweetness, even for you."

Part Two

1

TO wake in Paris, to lie with half-closed eyes in a huge bed with long pale blue silk curtains, to blink lazily at the sunshine which came dancing in, spattering on the carpet; to turn and find Alicia lying asleep at his side and realise that it was all true—and not some lovely but fantastic dream!

He sighed—how terrible if it had all been a dream—and if, after rubbing his eyes, he had found himself in his own room at Little Manor or in his bedroom at the flat, with Wilkinson offering him a cup of tea, saying, "Close on eight, Mr. Flight!"

There was Alicia, his wife since yesterday, sleeping quietly, one hand outflung on the coverlet. He raised himself very gently so that he could watch her face more easily. Lovely, tranquil. He fancied that he detected the shadow of a smile on her lips. Tomorrow they would go South, watch the country change, until at last they were on the shore of Lake Como. Together—he had never realised what a wonderful word it was—together they would spend long, warm, dreamy hours, lying on the smooth slope which led to the lake itself, or moving slowly over its blue waters.

Alicia's eyes opened, she stared at him, a little

puzzled frown puckering her smooth forehead; then her eyes were wide, her lips parted in a smile, and she said, "Flight—darling! It's all—true!"

He said, "Did you think that it might have been a dream? I did."

"Yesterday—all those people, the heat and noise, those endless speeches, that was a nightmare. Aren't you going to kiss me good morning? This is a bad beginning, isn't it? Your very first morning and you only lie there and stare me out of countenance!"

"It's your own fault, you shouldn't be so adorable."

"Pouf! Excuses!"

Paris didn't satisfy him, somehow. There was an increase in that "jumpiness" he had noticed when he came there early in March. Louis and Olympia were away; indeed, Flight wondered if Alicia were, as yet, ready to meet them; Jules was in America, and La Spero also on tour in that country. He spent a great deal of money buying Alicia soap and scent and incredibly fine silk stockings—himself, shirts at Sulka's. They ate delicious, if over-elaborate meals, went to the Casino and saw some exceedingly pretty women, and, to his astonishment, the sight of complete nudity did not appear to shock Alicia in the least.

She watched these women and whispered to Flight, "They're quite lovely! People who are really beautiful ought to go without clothes often for the sake of the rest of humanity!"

He whispered back, "Remember, if I agree with you, that I consider you the most beautiful woman in the whole world!"

It was something of a relief to join their train, the huge transcontinental monster which made the journey right to Istanbul, and was never more than one minute behind time at the end of the journey. They slept—and woke to find themselves out of France; the whole contour of the countryside had changed. True, the houses standing in their fields of corn and *polenta* were less trim; they stood at the open window watching the towering mountains, the rushing rivers and streams, the stationmasters in their shabby suits, but always wearing magnificent red velvet-topped caps; even the first sight of huge dun-coloured oxen plodding their way along dusty roads was exciting and capable of holding their complete attention.

Their first Italian meal on the train, with *pasta*, served with tomato sauce, slices of veal of a paper thinness, little marrows, and diminutive carrots, fruit and many kinds of cheese. The waiter beamed on them, saying, in a kind of contented singsong:

"*Bella Milano Bella Paese Gor-rgonzola Emen-thal Parmigiano, formaggio crema!*" he chanted. "All ver' mooch good!"

Alicia, looking round at their fellow travellers, said, "These people aren't all Italians, are they?"

Flight shook his head. "Germans, I imagine."

"So many of them—do they all come abroad for their holidays? I thought that they were allowed to bring so little money out of Germany?"

"I don't know; now that the Axis is accepted, perhaps there is some agreement."

"I always heard that the Italians traditionally were our friends and Allies?"

"So did a good many other people. Alicia, don't let's bother our heads about Italian or German politics. Let's forget everything except that we're together, making our way to a land which is—again, never mind its politics—lovely, and incredibly romantic."

It was the waiter himself who forced their minds back to the present conditions. As the last of the thick-necked men and heavy-hipped women left the dining-car, leaving only Flight and Alicia dawdling over their coffee, the black-haired little waiter stared after the solid, retreating forms. His full lips curled, his shoulders lifted, he made as if he would spit on the thick carpet, and contented himself with doing so in excellent pantomime.

"*Porci!*" he said.

Flight said, "*Tedesci?*"

The waiter lifted his shoulders still higher, and answered, "*Per me è lo stesso.*"

Flight did not continue his questions. The little waiter gave them the bill, received his tip with a smile which showed all his splendid teeth, and they returned to their carriage.

At Como Alicia said, "Now our honeymoon really begins!"

They lazed away their time; the gardens of the

Villa d'Este were sufficiently large and certainly sufficiently attractive to offer them exercise and beauty. Each day they resolved to visit this place or that, and each evening found them assuring each other "Well, there is always tomorrow." With a supreme effort they visited the Villa Carlotta, and each was relieved to find that the other disliked, with considerable intensity, the "Cupid and Psyche" of Canova.

Flight said one morning that his conscience was pricking him, that he was in Italy, that he was a picture dealer, and that he had not attempted to look for anything which he could buy and take back to England.

"The trouble is," he said, "that in watching you I forget that there can be any pictures worth looking at! But come to Milan with me, darling; we can be back in time to bathe before dinner."

Milan was terribly hot. The streets were crowded, it was almost impossible to push your way through the Galleria, and here again were Germans—Germans who shoved and pushed and behaved as if they were the lords of creation.

"I'm taking you to one of the most famous galleries in the world," he told Alicia. "You've heard of Sir Max Gollantz? Well, these Galleries are owned by his son. I've wanted to meet him for years—a great character, I believe."

They entered the magnificent building and saw the long Gallery stretching away before them. Flight, Alicia thought, changed as he entered. His rather dreamy, almost indolent manner fell from him; he looked eager, alert, his eyes were shining with excitement. A tall young man came forward, and asked if he could help them? Flight, returning for a moment to his slightly diffident manner, asked if Signor Gollantz was in the building?

The young man replied in carefully correct English that he regretted deeply that Signor Gollantz was, at the moment, in England.

"It might be that you would care to speak with Signor Maroni?"

Flight never forgot the first sight he had of Maroni. He was short, with dark curly hair and a face like a sophisticated cherub; his skin was perfect, his eyes large, and shaded by lashes which looked over-long for a man. His clothes were of an unbelievable elegance. A double-breasted white silk jacket, trousers of the same silk, and a pale blue shirt with a blue-and-white spotted tie, which Alicia told Flight later "Really screamed Burlington Arcade at you!" His socks matched his shirt, his shoes were white buckskin with brown strappings. He wore two beautifully fresh cornflowers in his buttonhole.

He advanced towards them, smiling and saying, "At sair-vice alvays please! Maroni Guido—in the distance—no, excuse—absence, of my master, the great collector Gollantz, I am his unworthy sekkon-in-commando!"

Flight explained the reason for his visit. Maroni eyed him curiously. He bowed over Alicia's hand

and as he bent his head to brush it with his lips, she caught a whiff of expensive scent.

Turning to Flight he asked, "You arre from—please? Ah, London! You are, per'aps Eengleesh?"

Again Flight explained, adding that he was a friend of Louis Lara's. Maroni's face became wreathed in smiles. "Louis is my blood brother. For so many years we have been—what do you say?—bloodies?"

Very gravely Flight said, "Buddies, I think!"

"Thank you! I am a leetle excited to meet again Eenglish people. I have a grreat love for Eenglish, instructed by one who is a model—Emmanuel Gollantz. To know heem is to know all that is best in the character of Eenglishmen. Now, I shall show you pictures. Zis way, if you do-an mind!"

He beckoned to a man in uniform, who came with them, and at Maroni's orders held the pictures—such as were not actually hung—in the best light.

"Surely," Flight said, "that's a Solario? You remember his 'Virgin with the green Cushion', Alicia, in the Louvre?"

Maroni shook his head. "I veesh I could say, 'Right you arre again!' but eet is not so! I bought zees and carried it home, as warriors return in triumph. I cried 'Emmanuel, Emmanuel! I have found a Solario!' I remember he looked at it for a long time—in silence you understand, signora—then, smiling a leetle, he said, 'Guido *mio*, you have bought a very charming picture and I like it!' I had tears in my eyes. It was not a Solario! But"—and his voice lost its melancholy—"it is a pretty picture."

"So pretty," Flight said, "that unless it is too costly, I am going to buy it." He bent forward to examine the picture more closely and drew back. "It is sold? The red ticket!"

Guido's teeth showed again as he smiled and whispered, "All sings in zees gallery are sold! All, all!" He dropped his voice to a confidential whisper and came nearer to them both. "It is possible zat people come here to whom I do not veesh to sell. Zey have money, very much. They come marching in here . . . promp, promp, like soldiers. Zey look at sings, pick up china and glass, and say 'Zees I shell hev' or 'Zees to buy I veesh'. I say 'Million regrets, signor, zat is sold! Watch zee little teeket, here eet is! Alas, how sad!'

"One time, a big fat porco got mad, fur-i-oos. He demanded 'Please to say, ees everysing in zees place sold?' I bowed—like so—I escorted heem into a salon vere ve keep zee rubbish-*sfaciujme!* 'Buy what you veesh,' I said." He was overtaken with a fit of laughter and when it passed he had to wipe his eyes. "*Finalmente* he—zees peeg, saw a 'orrible painting. Eet was bought with what Emmanuel says alvays 'Lotter yunk'. Peeg esk 'By who is zees painted?' 'Ow vould I know, except 'e vas a bastardo artisto? I say 'Please, a moment vhile I examine the teekit. My memory ees so bad. I find zee teekit and say 'Now I shall read vat is written 'ere! Attention! Sabastiano Lucioni call-ed Sabastiano del Piombo. Il anno—1527. Now, mistaire, you know as mooch as vat I do.' 'E bought it, vent avay smiling; in hees mind existed the idea zat Maroni is one goddam fool! 'Ow 'appy I vas! And not even a leetle lie on my soul, for I promised only to read vat vas on zee teekit."

But he could be grave too, this little Italian, and Flight found something almost touching in the way he handled delicate china, glass and old jewels.

"There is so much," Flight said, "I could spend days here! I must be wise, commercial. I still want the Solario—yes, even if it isn't a Solario. And that drawing for a cupid's head—who? Romanino, yes! And this tiny Calcar. That must be all. Thank you, Signor Maroni."

"Now, you veel take caffé? Or maybe cold beer? I know all Eenglish *gusti*—'tastes', yes, tastes. Even, per'aps Veeski-sodda? In the room of my master and patron. Please enter."

Alicia asked for tea and Flight for beer; Guido beamed at them and assured them that the tea would be English of "the tippo consumed by the late Earl Grrey, vich our friend, a Signor Jeckson, who has a palace in Piccadeelie, sends each month to my master. Per'haps you know 'im?"

When he trotted off to give his orders, swearing that he had been instructed in the art of tea-making by someone to whom he referred as "La Forbez", Alicia said, "Flight, what a darling little man!

Can't we ask him to dine? I'm sure he's got a car and could drive over."

Flight stared at her. Was this his Alicia, brought up to regard all tradesmen as slightly beyond the pale of the Lockwoods, Rusmeres, and the rest?

He said, "If you want to; he's an entertaining chap."

When he returned, followed by an elderly woman in a very neat black dress and white apron, Alicia cried, "Oh, what perfect china!"

Maroni said, "Small compliment we alvays pay. Vhen Madame Lara veesits us, tea is ser-ved in Sèvres; for La diva Alfano—Capo da Monte; for you, Signora Mastaires, Rocking-ham, the Eenglish type! Vith zee glass eet is zee same—Bohemian, in the days ven ve entertained the Tedesci; forr you Bris-tol!"

Alicia glanced at Flight, raising her eyebrows and tilting her head towards Maroni. Flight laughed and said, "It's your invitation."

She coloured a little, then said, "Signor Maroni, my husband and I want you to dine with us. Can you dine this evening or is the notice too short? Have you a car, or shall we send one for you? We're at the Villa d'Este."

Maroni rose and bowed profoundly, saying, "An honour most surprising and pleasing! I am happier zen I can possibly assure you of being. My 'eart is beating fast with delight. Madame, do you veesh tails-coat and vite vaistcoat, or short deenair jecket and bleck, please?" He added modestly, "In

184

my position it is necessary zat I hev both. You understand?"

Flight said, "Oh, dinner jacket, eh, Alicia?"

"Certainly." But there was a trace of disappointment in his voice, and he added, "I am not presumuoso—but I hev been assured zat in tails I am a great ornament! I do not vear bleck, I vear blue mezzanotte obtained by Emmanuel for me from Mistaire Drummond Mill in Brad-ford."

Alicia said quickly, "Flight, it's our first guest! Our first dinner-party—because, Signor Maroni, we are on our honeymoon and we didn't want to meet a whole lot of people. . . but you're different, and—well, I think we should make a festival of it! You will both wear tails and white waistcoats, if you please."

Again Maroni bowed and said, "Your pleasure, signora, is my 'eart's joy! I hev a car, given to me by my patron, Emmanuel. A Lancia of great beauty and fastness." He laughed. "As you say in English, 'she is a beetch to go!'"

Flight thought that he had never known Alicia to be so charming as she was that night when they met Maroni for dinner. He had said that in dress-clothes he was an ornament, and Flight admitted that he had rarely seen such magnificence. His clothes fitted him perfectly, his patent boots gleamed like polished jet, his shirt, waistcoat and collar were all made of *piqué* of exactly the same pattern. Even his gold watch, which he wore without a chain, was the thinnest Flight had ever seen.

185

His links and studs were of a restrained but quite definite magnificence.

Flight said, "You make me look positively unkempt, Signor Maroni!"

To which he replied, "I believe that to look dusty, untidy, and to vear old clothes is one of the correctest signs of an Eenglish gent, no? Only my master does not look so—but 'is brodder Beel, his good friend Geelbet, both men of great distinctness, they are disastri! To me it ees evident zat you, Meestair Mastaires, are a very 'igh up gent!"

Flight grinned and said, "I accept the compliment."

When they sat down to dinner Alicia said, "Flight! we want champagne. This is my first dinner-party, and we've got to do everything properly."

"You are married recently?" Maroni asked. "'Ow scharming eet is, sis marr-i-age. Indeed you must be 'appy, for you look so beautiful. I said to myself ven you 'ad gone, 'Zere goes a beautiful lady—the grace of Venus, the visdom of Cleopatra, the charm of Ariadne, the wit of Ninon, end,'" he paused impressively, "'the chic of the Ducessa de Vindsor!'"

Flight said, "There you are, Alicia! no one can say fairer than that!"

"Are all you Italians so charming, Signor Maroni?" she asked,

He ceased to smile. "All—*Dio mio*, no! Many

are peegs, many are blockheads, several are criminals. Oh, they're scharming men and vimmen, but
Italy has ceased to *t'ink*." He said the word with
great care. "Many years of Fascismo hev robbed
zem of zee ability to do so, also wiz zee
'and in zee 'and of Fascismo walks—*pigrizia—
indolenza*—what is zee vord?"

"Laziness?" Alicia hazarded.

"Laziness—zank you, signora! What a qvick-
ness of mind, she 'as! Eet is today we eat, so maybe
we don't go 'ungry tomorrow. If ve do, zen it's too
damn bad. But ve won't. Zat is 'ow zey t'ink. Ve
vonce upon von time 'ad a leader," he spoke softly,
"now we 'ave two, and von is much strongaire zan
ze ozzer. Von ees Beeg Boss, ze ozzer is dirty
bastardo dog, saying 'Oh yes, please, Mr. 'ouse-
painter man, gled to do vat you'd like mostly, good
morning!' It is a metter vicht begins to make it
necessary to vomit!"

Later, when they sat in a secluded corner of the
wide terrace, looking over the lake, with the mountains towering above and the bright lights of the
town of Como sparkling and glittering, he talked to
them gravely. His voice was pitched very low, he
leaned forward and often glanced round to make
certain that no one was overhearing what he said.

"Zees Axis—oh! you vill pardon me if I tell you
zat your country might 'ave done better in zee
Ambassador vot you sent. No, I doan mean zee one
'oo is alvays 'ere in Rome. I mean special envoy of
Government of Briteesh nation. I 'ave learned long

187

time since, you can be 'igh 'at—you know 'igh'
—American, eet is. Not 'igh *silk* 'at, you understand? 'Igh 'at of zee mind, yes?—zees you may be
vith duke, earl, count, gent'elman, not vith a men
who 'as what you call—manufactured himself.
Understand, please? Our leader is a self-
manufactured men.

"'Owever, zees Axis is made. No von cares a
damn of two pennies!" He smiled at Alicia. "You
vith your great quickness, signora, veel note—I
'ope with pleasure—'ow many phrases of Eenglish
I speak with readiness? Zen 'Ouse-painter says,
'Cam on, bloody—no, vait, buddie—cam on, ve
veel milk all Jews!' All right. Vhy? 'Ere in Italy ve
don't 'ave so many; ven ve'ave zey are rich, good
peoples. Cheritable, patrons of opera, well-kept
peoples, be'ave very well. Vhy persecute?"

"Did you?" Alicia asked.

"Italians as one people—no. Dirty lickers of spit
for Fascismo zink 'Good morning, fine morning,
persecute a few Jews, and get fine job for reward
from zee Boss!' Ozzers say, 'I doan care to mix up
in dirty mess, so I doan do nossing, zen I doan get
in bozzer any road'. Ozzers—the best—say, 'Zis is
all damn wrong! Eff Jews are my friends, zen zey
remain my friends. Zey doan change because 'Itler
scream "dirty peeg Jew"! Zet doan mak' zem dirty
peeg Jew, eh?'." He ticked off on his well-kept
fingers the three classes which he had cited. "First
classe—rrotten peegs! Secondo classe—not
strong, not ver' brave, but not too bad! Szird

classe—good! but not enough in Italy; numbers were too small. Remember zat not many Jews were really persecuted. I, myself, doan know one single case vere a Jew was killed or tortured—not one; but small nastinesses, pin-prickings, additional taxes, veesits to the Municipio, qvestions, 'Now your fader's name, and place of borning? Now your muzzer—yes? So! Feefty cento per cento Jew. Not good! Good morning.' To people of refinement, or established position, culture, zees remarks are not nice. Per example; my master, of an uprightness that is incredible, has left Milano, left his splendid business for zee reason zat—or for one of zee reasons zat—'e is 'alf Jew. 'Ees son, Simon, 'oo I love viz my 'ole 'eart, ees twenty-five per cent. But 'ere in Milano, 'e vas not vanted at the school. Imagine that for yourself, signora! My master vas alvays forced to bear some *leetle* pin-prickins—so, 'e went back to Eengland, and 'ere is poor Guido left viz a broken, empty life until Emmanuel vill rreturn. And zen, as your song says—somevere zee sun veel be shining! Eet vill be shining in the Galleries of great Gollantz. Eet vill be shining in zee fait'ful 'eart of Guido Maroni."

"And—war, Maroni?" Flight asked. "Will Italy go to war?"

Guido sighed profoundly. "I believe zat zere vill be war. I do not believe zat Italy ess so imbecile as to join in eet. Maybe some boys in bleck, and dirty, shirts may cry '*Guerra, guerra!*' but not such as are vise. Eef zey do," he spoke with great sincerity,

189

"zen eet vill be because the gods vish to destroy zem, and so first make zem mad. Now, signora, it grows late. I hev talked too much, I have wearied you? I have not said all I veeshed, to tell you of Emmanuel, of his beautiful vife—La Forbez, the singer . . ."

"Where is she, signor, in England?" Alicia asked.

Guido answered gravely, "She is wiz God and His saints, signora. She died. And the 'eart of Emmanuel died also, except for the love which 'e 'as for 'is son and poor Guido. I hev not told you 'ow 'e found an undoubted Raphael—and donated eet to your Gallery of the Nation in London? I recall zat your Keeng—Giorgio—send 'im a ver' nice letter, saying: 'Thank you so much, it is awfully decent of you!' Or somezing of zat kind in really Eenglish language, which I know so well. But"—he slipped his hand into the inside pocket of his coat and pulled out a blue leather case—"I placed ziss in my pocket. To my mind came the idea 'Guido, old fruit, you will ruin the fitting of that coat!' I replied, 'Oh, go burning hell! For a beautiful lady I will ruin tventy such coats!' So, for a little ricordo of our meeting, of your vedding voyage, your *luma di miele*, and a token of the love and admiration of Guido—please accept!"

He handed the case to her with a flourish. Alicia opened it and found a necklace and a pair of long ear-rings, set in antique and very beautiful gold. She said impulsively, "Oh, but how exquisite!

190

Guido, are they really for me? Oh, Guido, thank you!"

He beamed at her. "But of course for you, unless the signor objects? Had my master been 'ere, of course, 'e would 'ave given you precious carpets from Persia, golden vases and drinking cups, fine china, and possibly a chandelier of the glass from Vater-ford; and entertained you as princes entertain ozzer princes. For me, even to attempt to do zis vould be wrong—you understand?" Turning to Flight, he offered him a small gold box, saying, "Louis Fourteen of France. Nice leetle piece. For zee snuff, zee pen nib, zee stud and so on and so on."

Flight turned the pretty thing over in his palm. "It's charming, but, my friend, you're too generous! We ought to give you presents for the wonderful way you've talked to us."

"Your signora," Guido said, "'as already given to me a gift of great value. Two times she has said my name, 'Guido'. I am 'appy! 'Ow long do you stay 'ere, please?"

"Three more days, Guido."

He spread his hands wide in a gesture of humility.

"Ah! zen you veel not veesh to spend one 'alf of a day in Milano so zat Guido might offer some hospitality. You understand, I live in the *appartement* of my master—as I did ven 'e was 'ere. 'E told me ven 'e vent avay, 'To do me a pleasure, use eet as your own'." He added pensively, "The cook is a

191

cordon bleu, I do not vesh you to imagine zat my patron is an anchorite, for all his seriousness; in fact in many ways sybarite might describe him better."

"The day after tomorrow," Alicia said firmly, "we shall call for you at the Galleries at half past twelve."

When he had gone, driving his Lancia with great skill away from the Villa, Flight slipped his arm through Alicia's and said, "Enjoyed your dinner-party, darling?"

"I think that little man is entrancing! His devotion to this man Emmanuel, his thought for other people, his queer little conceits which are so childish as to be almost pathetic—oh, he's charming!"

"Yet, when I first saw him coming towards us, I felt a little nervous that you—well, might not care much for meeting him," Flight said.

She drew him to a seat the side of the path and sat down. "Listen! I want to talk to you. You don't really know me, darling. You know Alicia Lockwood, who has been sheltered and protected all her life, who is more than inclined to be intolerant and narrow, and—yes, a snob. Then I met you and fell in love with you—for I am dreadfully in love with you, Flight!"

He leaned forward and kissed her. "So am I, dearest, with you."

"Don't interrupt!" she admonished. "Well, I suddenly began to grow up. No, not exactly grow

192

up but to grow *out*. I realised that I wasn't the completely well-behaved, conventional person I had believed. I can say this to you now, frankly; it was too difficult before. Once or twice when you wanted to make love to me—you remember—I knew that I wanted to be made love to, wanted it very, very desperately. Almost frighteningly. I suppose"—she faltered, was silent for a moment, then continued—"I suppose while you were away in France, I really grew up? Began to understand that there is nothing so particularly meritorious in allowing oneself forcibly to suppress all evidences of physical hunger, as it were. I knew that I was hungry; hungry for your lovemaking, your kisses. I wanted you as you wanted me. Does it sound horribly materialistic to say that during—that time—I began to understand, and to be glad that I did understand what being your wife would mean?"

He said gently, "How did you come to realise it?"

She answered quickly. "I don't know, I can't tell you. I can only assure you that I did. When you came back I was not only glad that you had come home, but I was thankful—as well. Thankful, because I knew that as well as loving me—and wanting to be with me—you could satisfy *all* of me—mental, physical—everything!"

"And do I?"

The urgency of her reply surprised him. "Don't tell me that you find me cold!"

193

He laughed contentedly. "I've no intention of telling you anything of the kind," he said.

"Then," Alicia went on, "with that, I think, came a sort of—I don't know what to call it—a sort of mental 'loosening-up'. I felt that one was an idiot to live a completely restricted life, that it wasn't possible, that the only pleasant, friendly, kindly people must automatically be those in 'our set'. You know, at first, when we wanted to be engaged, it was only the fact that your father is in *wholesale* grocery on a very large scale, that made it possible for Papa and Mama to consent! That fact, and also that you had chosen a more or less artistic career. Do you know that in spite—yes, in spite—of the fact that I was passionately in love with you, in those days I understood completely how they felt about it.

"I loved you. That was something stronger than any feeling about 'social scales'. You were all that mattered. That fact made everything else sink into insignificance. Then when you came to dine at Portland Place, Uncle Herbert told Mama that he liked you. Apparently you'd said something after we left the table that delighted him? He said, 'I'll tell you this, Sophia, and Alicia can listen, we're damned lucky to get him in the family! Your husband's old harridan of a mother is as nearly batty as doesn't matter a curse; Felix is half-witted and getting worse. None of us have any brains, except myself, and I'm too lazy to use them! I wish that he could have Rusmere when I go—he can't,

194

but I shall do every damn thing I can to help him to make money. I'll leave him pictures worth a mint o' money someday. You snaffle him, Alicia!' That was Uncle Herbert's opinion of you, and of course Mama went home and told Papa, and the balance swung over to your side.

"Of course," she laughed, "Ann's engagement to Claverley was another help!"

"I don't really seem to have made much of an impression off my own personal bat, do I?" Flight said. "But what's all this got to do with Maroni?"

"Oh! it all fits in. I'm going to enjoy everything, Flight! I'm determined that from now, people I like I shall see often, if it's possible. Things I like I shall do—when I like—and so often as I like. I don't want to go back to that placid, well-run, completely 'ordered' life ever again. I've got my life to live, and I'm going to live it and get every bit of experience and enjoyment possible out of it."

"But I thought," he said humorously, "that you had given your life into my keeping? I fancied that that was among those odd things you promised?"

"Only so long as you give me an equal hold over yours! Oh! I don't mean that I want ever, ever, ever to be unfaithful to you, or even have silly flirtations—I don't. But I want to give myself a chance to develop, all of me. I don't even mind taking risks . . ."

"Risks?" he asked, "what kind of risks?"

"Did I say risks? Oh! I don't know—we all take risks sometimes. I took one when we were

195

engaged. I took a risk when I allowed myself to be carried off to pay a round of visits without you—I might have met someone else, and I should have been miserable if I had done, darling, believe me. We both took a risk in asking Guido to come to dine! He might have been quite awful—picked his teeth or eaten with his knife or something!"

"What would you have done if he had eaten with his knife?"

"Eaten with my own, I hope," she said.

"Only," she said after a long silence, "don't be too nice to me! I mean, don't give in to me in everything, Flight. Never go away and leave me for too long, never let me imagine that you're growing tired of me—I couldn't bear it. I'm not really sufficiently good for you, darling. You'd better beat me at regular intervals, I think, or give me a black eye!"

"You little silly! Not good enough? I remember you once said that before, and although it's very flattering to my vanity, my sound common sense tells me it's the most appalling rubbish!"

"Suppose—just suppose," she said, "that some-one, anyone, ever came to you with stories about me, telling you—oh, I don't know—that I'd taken dope, or drank in secret or—or lived with other men before I married you. What would you do?"

"Well, that's not difficult! I should try to knock their teeth down their throat, or else murder them. This is a silly conversation, darling, I don't like it a great deal."

"Wouldn't you come to me to ask if I could deny it?"

"My God! I hope not! Alicia, do let us drop this rubbish, please."

"But I want to *know*?"

He rose and held out his hand. "Angel, you do know already. All this 'What should I do,' and 'What would you say' is morbid nonsense. Come and take one walk down to the lake before we turn in."

Two days later they went into Milan and called at the Gollantz Galleries for Guido. He came, elegant in palest grey, with a lavender tie, his smile was all-embracing. Together they drove to a large block of flats, turned into a courtyard, where a fountain sent up a delicate jet of water which fell tinkling into a wide marble bowl, where gold and silver fish were swimming.

They ascended in a gilded lift like a small drawing-room, Alicia thought. Guido ushered them in, saying, "In the absence of my master, permit me to ask you to accept a welcome. Ah!"—to the man-servant who waited on them—"the Signor and Signora have come?"

"They are waiting, Signor Guido."

Alicia and Flight followed him into a very long, cool room where striped blinds were lowered to keep out the midday sun. There was a pleasant dimness about the place, a dimness which obscured nothing, but only softened everything. A great fireplace, beautifully carved, filled with

197

flowering plants; a very large grand piano, brocade-covered chairs and sofas, a hint of gold shining from the frames of pictures, the glass of china in a large cabinet. Flowers standing on every table except one—where a very slim man stood, reflectively shaking cocktails.

He looked up and said, "Hello, Guido! you don't mind this liberty, I hope?"

"I am thankful to you, Paolo," Guido assured him, and made the necessary introductions. The slim man was Paolo Mancini; seated on a deep sofa was his wife, Iva Alfano, dark, beautiful, and magnificently dressed. A small grey-haired man who came forward was a Mr. Gilbert.

Iva Alfano said, "God made Gillee to be His own accompanist, but in His goodness He allowed him to come to earth to help singers. Am I not right?"

Her husband said, "You couldn't be more right."

Cocktails were served, and Flight, sipping his, thought, "I bet any money this man's English, for all his Italian name."

The beautiful woman refused a cocktail. "My damned voice," she said with a lovely smile; "I am a victim because I seeng."

Gilbert said, "Iva, *cara*! sing for us now. I happen to know what Guido has ordered for luncheon and you will certainly not be able to sing afterwards."

"Oh!" she cried, like a spoiled child. But she rose and went to the piano and played her own accompaniment, "So that poor Gillee shall not lose his nice cocktail, as I have to do." She laughed, "My arrt—alvays my arrt!"

Her husband said, "She means art, not heart, Mrs. Masters."

As she ran her fingers up and down the keyboard, Alfano said, "Dear Paolo, shut your mouse, if you please!"

She sang. What the words were Flight did not know, he was only conscious that the long quiet room was filled with sounds like precious stones, each jewel more lovely than the last. Or like that fountain which he had seen when they entered the courtyard, a bright jet of water, the drops catching the sun's rays, dancing, leaping and at last subsiding, so gently that it did not seem possible that it had ceased to play.

Guido sat with clasped hands, his eyes seemed suffused with unshed tears. The tall, slim man stood perfectly still, watching his wife, and when she ended Gilbert walked to the piano and leaning forward struck a note—Flight fancied that it was G sharp—saying, "Ah, Iva, what an improvement! That is if improvement were possible. That was magnificent!"

She shrugged her shoulders. "Well enough. I never enjoy singing at this piano. I am always too conscious of La Forbez."

Gilbert laid his hand lightly on her shoulder, "You're wrong, Iva! She was purely a concert artist—the greatest, perhaps, in the world. You are an operatic artist, remember that. Juliet would have been wild in her admiration for you, as you were in yours for her."

Luncheon was announced. Guido sprang to his feet saying, "Oh, *Dio mio!* I am so nairvous! At first I t'ought zat eet must be ross beef an' Yarkshire pudding, an' maybe plom pudding efter. Zen I zink—No! in Eenglish proverb, 'Better for chef zee devil w'at he know, then rosbif w'at he don't know!' *Ecco* . . ."

Never had Alicia seen so many and so varied kinds of *hors d'œuvres*; they seemed to appear in relays, some recognisable, others complete mysteries to her. She watched Alfano eating with tremendous gusto, and wondered how on earth she managed to keep her figure? No one refrained from commenting on the food, when the risotto Milanese served with white truffles followed the *hors d'œuvres*.

Alfano said, "These are from Piedmont, the best in Italy."

Her husband added, "They are costly, these truffles."

She retorted, "Guido can afford it!" and they all shouted with laughter.

"How they eat," Alicia thought. "They eat with such relish, like children at a party. If this luncheon continues much longer I shall have to plead lack of appetite."

Guido said, "This trout, it was sent up on a *rapido* this morning."

Iva added, "Garda trout is the best in Italy. This mayonnaise is very good. Smooth. My cook never gets it like this—it is silk, silk. Give me some more, please."

Paolo added, "The price of trout is against it, to my frugal mind."

"Then don't eat it," his wife admonished. "Leave it for me, I shall dispose of eet all."

A few moments later she was peering at a dish which was offered her, and announcing with delight, "My favourite dish—*Rognone Trifolato!*"

Guido beamed at her, then, turning to Alicia, explained, "A simple dish, but of character. It contains veal kidney. Sees ees stewed in burro; *anche* tom-atoes, peperoni. For us—but neffer for honoured Eengleesh guests—*con aglio*; w'at you call gar-rlic. Zen is added a leetle Marsala vino. You like eet?"

White wine, red wine, wine which was still, and like limpid gold, wine which frothed and sparkled, all appeared. More food, a great wooden dish which carried a dozen types of cheese; a smooth, foaming sweet which they called *Zabaglione* in which again she detected the flavour of wine. Great plates of fruit, laid on bright green fig leaves; and at last, to her relief, they moved from the table back to the drawing-room and drank coffee—black, strong, and a little bitter. There were more liqueurs ready to be served than she had ever seen in her life.

Iva Alfano sighed, "I hev eaten too much. I

201

am—what is eet?—gorged, like snakes after they eat."

Mancini said, "Later I shall take you walking in the Park, Iva."

"Neffer! I shell tell you, signora! once, long ago, my 'usband took me for a walk. Forr zees walk I 'ad special shoes—*Dio mio!* of a weight, of a thickness, of a discomfort. We walked—neffer hev I known such agony! At last I sat by the side of zee road, vhile 'e went to find a *carrozza* to take me 'ome. To Brescia it vas, Paolo, you remember? Neffer 'ave I walked since. Instead I do exercises in my bathroom, and 'ave massage."

Never once was the war or the possibility of war mentioned. Only once when Emmanuel's name was spoken, Guido sighed deeply, and said, "Imachine, zees fine man, a private soldier! it is impossible!"

Mancini said, "If war comes that's what I shall be, being British."

"You're British, Mr. Mancini?"

He nodded. "So is my wife. Through her marriage to me, of course."

Alfano almost shouted, "Paolo! I'ave forbidden you to mention any war! I prromise zere be no war, not in Italy anyway. I may be Breetish vomman, but I 'ave not lost my brain, yes? No war! I, Alfano, tell you."

As they drove back to Como, Flight said, "I say, did you ever eat such a meal? Do you suppose they eat like that every day?"

202

"It nearly killed me! I feel that I shall never eat again. But what nice people! I'm sure there is a story about them all? I wish that I knew."

On the boat crossing to Folkestone the next day Flight bought the evening papers. Alicia watched his face as he read. She felt that some of the sunshine had died away from it, he looked older, graver—almost sombre.

2

THE flat which they had taken was not ready for them, would not be ready until the end of August; until that time they would live at Little Manor. Lady Sophia had tried to persuade Alicia that the Rectory was more suitable.

"Darling! it really is larger and so many of your own things are there."

Alicia shook her head. "Little Manor is better for Flight, Mama. Neither you nor Papa get on really very well with him; he's always shy and rather 'prickly' when he is with you. Far better let us stay with his people."

They had gone there the day after they arrived back in London. Frances greeted them with great warmth, said how well they both looked, and was enchanted with the gifts which they had brought for her.

She sat smiling at them as they drank tea in her drawing-room.

"Ann and Sholto decided after all to stay for another week. They are delighted with the bathing, with the South of France altogether. She wants him to take a villa there. Chris—ah! here's news. Chris has gone to America. No, not for always, of course; he'll be away for six weeks or so. Then he wants his own flat in town. I quite see his

204

point too. He's busy, he has interests there, friends, and he can always come down here when he wants to. At first your father was—not against it, but a little dubious—but he is always so reasonable, isn't he, Flight?"

"No one more so, dear."

"So finally he gave in, and I must say he was most generous about it. We're going to give up the flat in town. The Wilkinsons are growing—well, elderly—they've saved, and want to retire, and perhaps take a little hotel somewhere in the country. Chris will take most of the furniture. Oh! it's all worked out very well, but"—she sighed—"we're going to be lonely without you all. Eleanor's going to be married in September; you and Alicia will be in town, so will Chris, and Ann—it seems that Ann can have her choice of half a dozen houses."

Flight said, "Now, darling, don't wallow in sentiment! You know that when you have us all married you'll be very satisfied."

"My dear! only if I am certain that you're all happy."

Flight took up his work again, and several times a week went off to Mexfield to drill and receive additional instruction; to drill other people and generally make himself proficient in a profession which he felt he might be called upon to practice in the not-too-far distant future.

He talked about the gathering clouds very seldom. He had realised that in doing so he distressed

Alicia, and, in some degree, his mother; only to his father, when they sat together in the library, did he open his heart, and together they would pore over maps and try to discover the inner significance of the new events, these demands and threats which appeared to increase every day.

During the weeks that followed he felt that he lived two distinct lives. One with Alicia, and all that concerned her and their mutual happiness, a life, which, to Flight Masters, seemed the most perfect he had ever imagined. Daily his love for her grew and strengthened, and again he thought of the quiet, star-lit evening on the shore of Lake Como, when she had tried to explain herself to him. In every way she satisfied him. To be with her, to listen to her voice, soothed and tranquillised him. He worshipped her beauty, her air of "fineness", her poise. He delighted in the fact that she returned his passion, fully and completely.

With each day his belief in the unavoidability of war became stronger. Watching Alicia's lovely face, listening to her voice, walking, talking with her, fear sometimes overtook him. War meant separation from Alicia; war meant danger, destruction; war might mean the end of their life together. In London he heard men talk of sending their wives to America until the danger was past. Vaguely he wondered if he ought to take Alicia to America, wondered, for brief seconds, if he might not be able to work out there, and so remain with her?

Old Rusmere wandered into the Gallery one afternoon, strolled round, trailing a badly-rolled umbrella behind him, grunted at the pictures he disliked, bought one which took his fancy, and finally joined Flight in his office. He sat down, dropping his disreputable hat and equally shabby umbrella on the floor.

"Got a drink?" he asked. "Good! Any ice? Better still. I'll have a whisky-and-soda. Thanks. Now, whatcher going ter do about Alicia when this damned business starts?"

"You think that it will start soon?"

Rusmere nodded. "Must do. Can't go on for ever listening to Hitler giving assurances. 'Just this little bit, and I won't ask for any more'. He's making a blasted laughing-stock of us all!"

Flight poured himself out a glass of soda water.

The Earl barked, "That damned stuff 'ul give you wind!"

Flight shook his head. "No, it won't, sir. I wondered—I mean I have heard fellows talk about sending their wives to America. What do you think about it?"

"Sendin' 'em alone?"

"I don't know. I thought that if I could take her over I might do some work there. Pictures sell well out there, don't they?"

"Ugh! And miss the curtain going up, or the pan boiling over, or the lid being whipped off hell. Well, yer can if yer *like*. Hope it won't look as bad as it sounds, that's all!"

"Bad?" Flight said. "Bad—how 'bad'?"

The old man cocked his head on one side, and laid his finger to the side of his nose. He looked like some cunning old bird—a bird with dusty, shabby plumage.

"Yer know what people are! I know what I should think, even if I kept my mouth shut and didn't say it. 'Where the devil's Flight Masters?' 'He's selling pictures in America.' 'Oh, *I* see!' That's what I mean by bad."

Flight's hands clenched. "You don't think that I'd try to get out of it, if it came to a showdown, do you?"

"I think that when a man's in love he's liable to do all kinds of things, and find not the slightest difficulty in justifying himself—to himself. No, you wouldn't consciously funk it; subconsciously, I'm not so sure. I'd be careful if I were you. Send Alicia by all means—if she'll go."

His other life was one which he shared with his father, with men he knew, who talked, speculated, argued about the war as a foregone conclusion.

At Mexfield, Colonel Carteret said to him, "Just a word, Masters. I'm pleased with you. You've got the makings of a good officer. I don't say a brilliant one, but a good 'un. We're lamentably short of them too. That's why you can add another pip to the two you've got. Shan't have long to wait now."

"When d'you think, sir?"

Carteret tugged at his melancholy moustache. "Oh, about a month!" He gave his queer, neighing

208

laugh. "No long summer holiday for you, my boy. Well, congratulations."

"Thank you, sir."

About a month—and this was August the twenty-first. Two days later the German-Soviet Pact was signed. That evening his father said, "Well, there are precious few countries we haven't given guarantees to; he's bound to be able to drag us in somewhere or other."

He spoke in a voice curiously dull and expressionless.

"A close agreement. If either are attacked by a third the other will give no help to the attacker. I wonder they didn't use the word—aggressor. There's a good deal more to it than that! Between them they have Europe and the Balkans carved up nicely. Poland will be next, and Russia will want a cut at Finland. By God, Flight, it's coming close!" He shivered, and Flight saw that his face looked pinched.

They discussed the possibility of sending Alicia and Frances Masters to America. Edward said, "No use asking Eleanor, she'd never leave George. And I don't blame her."

That evening after dinner Edward lit a cigar with care, and adopting a manner of great ease and unconcern said, "Francy, m' dear, Flight and I have been talking. Yes, Alicia, listen to this, it concerns you as well."

Eleanor asked, half smiling, "And not me, Father?"

He appeared to be suddenly at a loss and said testily, "Why, yes, dear, of course! Concerns all of you, eh, Flight? Well, I'm not a scaremonger, but things look very black—very black indeed—and I'm worried, and so is Flight. We both—he and I—know men who are sending their wives and children to America, and we thought that—well, we thought that . . ."

Frances said, "You *thought*, Edward. That's exactly what you *didn't* do."

"My dear . . ."

"If you imagine that because there is going to be a war, that I intend to run away and leave my husband, my home, my children—no really, Edward! You do surprise me, you do really!"

Eleanor said calmly, with a trace of amusement in her tone, "Father, you didn't really think that I should go?"

Her father, taken off his guard, answered, "No, frankly, Eleanor, I didn't!"

"But," his wife said, her pretty face scarlet with annoyance, "you and Flight had the effrontery to assume that although Eleanor would not go, either Alicia or I might be willing to do so? Thank you very much! Both of you! Well, Alicia, dear, we know what our respective husbands think of us, don't we?"

Flight took Alicia's hand in his. "Listen, angel. It wasn't that either my father or I thought that you'd want to go. It was probably because we knew that it must inevitably be a time of anxiety; and, selfishly perhaps, we thought that if you were out of England we might be spared some additional worry. Can't you see that?"

Eagerly Masters said, "Ex-*actly*, ex-*actly*!"

"Did you evolve this marvellous plan unaided?" Alicia asked. She smiled at him tolerantly, affectionately, as she might have done at a foolish child who had done something outrageous.

"As a matter of fact, your own uncle approved of the idea."

"Uncle Herbert, or Felix? Oh, Herbert! His brain must be going as weak as his brother's. Flight, don't be so silly! To begin with, if there were a war, I shouldn't be with you anyway, because you'd have to go overseas, I imagine. I should have to work at something or other."

He flushed at her tone and said, "What if I say that you've got to go?"

She laughed. "Darling, don't be so inane! Shall I play something for you all?"

"Do, dear. No, Edward, I refuse to discuss it. I am deeply hurt, more hurt than I really care to admit. Yes, Alicia, something pleasant, and tranquil, nothing"—with sudden sharpness—"about sailing over oceans or any nonsense of that kind. To imagine that I should ... well, really, Edward!"

That night Alicia was very tender towards him. She took him in her arms, and held him closely, saying, "My poor Flight, you mustn't allow yourself to get into panics like that. Whatever comes, we'll face it. If you have to go away"—he felt her arms tighten round him suddenly—"then I shall wait here—not in America—for you to come home again." He heard her laugh softly, as if she tried to break the strain. "Your poor little mother! Like an angry little bantam hen!"

He whispered, "Darling, it's all a ghastly nightmare! Germany mobilised, and Poland delaying their mobilisation at the request of Britain and France. What does it all mean? What can it all mean?"

Those last few dreadful weeks, Flight felt that the great monster had gathered speed and was now rushing forward down an incline. No power could stop it, nothing was sufficiently strong to change its course.

Ann was home, shrugging her shoulders and saying that if Claverley had to go with his regiment, she would turn one of his huge houses into a hospital. Only Flight fancied that, at times, her voice took on a quality which was shrill and touched with hysteria. Claverley, so burnt by the southern sun that his freckles showed no longer, rushed about from one estate to another, "setting his house in order," he said.

Eleanor had grown more silent, and returned home one morning to say, at breakfast time, that she and George had been married that morning in Longford, where George had a surgery, which apparently qualified him for residence. She looked placid, but her face was pale, and when Flight asked if they were not going to have a honeymoon, she shook her head and answered, "When it is all over—not until, Flight, dear."

On September the second Flight received a letter from Jules. *Keep a watch for me, we shall meet, I feel this in my bones. Louis has joined the Army, so have I.* The next morning they heard that England and France had declared war on Germany. Protests, arguments, threats were at an end. Poland was being overrun, and by the time her agony was over, and she lay wounded to death, invaded both by Russia and Germany, Flight had sailed with the Expeditionary Force for France.

Claverley had gone two days before. Chris had cabled that he was on his way home; old Dr. Charlton had left his comfortable hotel in Harrogate and had come back to Baddock to take over the practice from his son, who was joining as a medical officer and going out immediately.

Ann said, "Strange, isn't it? Alicia, you, Eleanor, and I have all got husbands—brand new husbands and yet we haven't one among the lot of us!"

Edward snapped, "Cheap paradoxes don't get us anywhere, Ann."

The Rector seemed to take it as a personal affront that England had not sent a larger force. "Pitifully small," he said. "We know the difficulties. I am the last to underestimate them, but what does it amount to? A handful of men, a few of the Royal Air Force. I am afraid that our French friends will take this as a very sad disappointment."

"If we haven't got 'em, we can't send 'em!" Edward barked.

Chris, returning, asked why we didn't retaliate against German attacks on Polish airfields? "Why didn't the French do something?" he demanded.

"Over there," he told them, "they call it a 'phoney war'."

"Let them keep their criticisms to themselves," Claverley answered, "until they're in it. Then they can talk."

Ann came off the best. Claverley was on the Staff, and kept arriving for odd nights, or days, from time to time. He was obviously harassed and worried, nervy and short-tempered. Only when they were alone together did he lose his sense of being over-tightly strung, and sit beside her talking, with the same old stammer, about trivial ordinary things.

Eleanor was driving old Charlton round the country. George's own driver had gone with his master. She kept the books, helped with the dispensing. Her father-in-law said, "Ah, you're a grand girl, Eleanor! George will be proud of you, as I am."

The autumn passed. Alicia watched the brilliant sunsets and wondered where Flight was—if he were in danger? Once Chris came and stood beside her, and said, "I'll give you a penny for them, 'Licia?"

"Not a particularly generous offer," she said.

"You must know quite well what I'm thinking. The same as Ann thinks, and Eleanor." Then, abruptly, "When are you going to join the Army, Chris?"

"When the Great 'I-Ams' think that the work I am doing ceases to be of National Importance. Food stocks might easily win this war, my dear."

"And of course you're making a great deal of money?"

He grinned. "I don't believe that you like me very much—and yet—you did at one time. Well, well, we can't all be bloody little heroes!"

"One day," she said, "I shall kill you."

He laughed outright. "Not you, m'dear, not you!"

On December the fourteenth he came home and told them that he was going. His father, more cheerful through the news of the *Graf von Spee*, clapped him on the shoulder.

"We'll manage at Clark Square! Good lad! You'll see that this sinking of their confounded pocket battleship is the turning of the tide."

"Now I'm going," his son said, "it's as good as over, eh?"

Edward said the same thing when, on May 10, 1940, Winston Churchill became Prime Minister and set up a Ministry of Aircraft Production.

"Now we shall see," he said, beaming at them all. "Chamberlain's an old man, a tired man. Churchill's a bulldog. Speaks out! Only offers blood, toil, tears and sweat. Not unlike Garibaldi, remember? Hitler's launched his attack, has he? Herr Hitler's going to learn his lesson, and a very nasty one it is going to be too."

From that time Alicia felt that always names, names, words, odd phrases rang in her mind, day and night: Louvain, Namur, the Scheldt, Amiens, Abbeville. The break-through, encirclement, armoured divisions. Then Flight, Flight—it seemed as if his very name were an omen of ill-fortune!

His letters came irregularly; he hinted vague things, half-statements which she never fully understood. Only when he wrote of his constant thought of her, his love for her, did she completely understand him.

Claverley rushed to Baddock from London for two hours; Ann carried him off to her room and they emerged, looking bright-eyed but, in some queer indefinable way, fearful.

Finding Frances alone, they came and stood near her. Claverley said, "Tell your mother, Ann."

Ann said, "Mother, I'm going to have a baby. Do you think that's nice? I don't believe that Sholto's certain."

Frances laid down the sock she was knitting. "My darling child, when?"

"Unless I'm all wrong in my reckoning—December. I'm delighted."

Sholto licked his dry lips and said, "Y-yes, I am d-delighted. Of course I am, only this isn't the n-nicest time to p-plan to have babies."

His wife returned, "You unnatural brute. You

216

can't behave as if it were all my fault! Now, be fair!" But she smiled at him and his face looked less pinched.

The weeks which followed were like a frightful dream, so horrible that it seemed they must be distorted, not real. Alicia said to Ann, "It can't all be true! It must be a mistake. The Maginot Line, the Germans closing in, and only the Dunkirk bridgehead left for us to escape. Ann, what does it mean? No letters. I've not heard from Flight for ten days. I'm afraid . . . dreadfully afraid!"

That fateful June the sixteenth, and Reynaud and his Government replaced by Pétain and Weygand. The fighting on the part of the French was to cease. Mrs. Noakes said to Edward, as he went through the lodge-gates that morning, "And it was 'im, sir—this Weygand, or whatever 'e calls 'isself—that a bit back was saying as 'e was satisfied! I sed ter Noakes at the time I sed, 'Satisfied, is 'e, well it's mor'n what I am!'"

Dunkirk—and the miracle of the incredible effort of the British seamen, of the tugs, motor craft and "little boats". A sense of pride was everywhere, pride tinged with apprehension. Men were being saved—men were being lost. A military collapse of France, refugees crowding soldiers off the roads, German 'planes roaring overhead. And the Casualty Lists. The war coming home to everyone. Names which were familiar, too familiar. Sholto Claverley left lying on the beach at Dunkirk, a bullet through his throat, Flight

217

Masters missing; Noakes' elder son believed to be a prisoner; Philip Gaunt killed; Lists—long, long lists; and the equipment of those who were saved, missing, and only to be replaced by a costly and wholehearted effort. They must go back, the men who had been saved. Soon, as soon as they could be given clothes to wear, arms to carry. Go back! Noakes stood twisting his hands together talking to Edward—Edward, who looked older, more frail, who had lost something of the gallant walk of Major Masters.

"It's a blow, sir. A good boy. The best of sons. 'Is muther is all ter bits. An' fer you, sir, sad noos. Miss Ann's 'usband—an' Mr. Flight. But it says 'missin', about Mr. Flight, sir. While theer's life theer's ope. Mustn't ferget that, must we?"

"No, we mustn't forget that," Edward said. "My wife will come along to see Mrs. Noakes very soon. She's not quite able to face it as yet."

Edward walked back to the house. Words flitted through his mind: "your house shall be left unto you desolate". He knew that he was limping, limping as he had not done for years. He thought, "I'm maimed, maimed that's why. Flight— missing! Presently it will be 'missing, believed killed'. Those two poor children! My poor Ann, her baby coming, with no father to welcome it. God, it's hard!" For a moment he had it in his heart to hate Christopher, who was still training for the RAF at Bufood. Ann met him in the hall. She was very pale but she slipped her hand through his

218

arm and said, "I'd like to come and talk to you, Daddy."

"Yes, my dear. Sure that you feel up to it?"

"Daddy, I'm whipcord and wire. Don't get worried about me. I'm going to have Sholto's baby, and he'll be fit and healthy and do a real job of work when he grows up. You see, Sholto and I discussed all this, we knew that it *might* happen, it had to be faced. I've heard from his father, he wants to open Alcaster as a hospital. I'm going to run it for him. Oh, with proper trained supervision, of course! I shall be able to work for quite a long time yet—I've got to. There isn't anything else to do." She opened her hands in a gesture of dismissal, and Edward saw that both her palms were scarred with reddish-blue marks.

"Ann, what's that?" He pointed to them.

"Those? Nothing. It's where I dig my nails in when I don't want to let people know what's in my mind. They don't really hurt."

Alicia scarcely left her room. She said to Eleanor, "Oh, I know that I'm being selfish, that I ought to remember that for me there is a faint gleam of hope, while for Ann there is none at all. I can't help it. It's just the way I'm made. Flight was everything, everything! My lover, my husband—even my saviour. I tried to explain to him when we were on our honeymoon. He didn't understand. Flight never could understand the carnal side of anyone's nature."

219

Eleanor said, "Carnal? I don't understand what you mean, dear?"

Alicia shrugged her shoulders, "No, you couldn't, you're too like him."

Eleanor made no comment, she only said, "You must fight things out in your own way. We—Mother and Ann and I—all understand."

"I must work. I shall go to the flat in town; I can find work there. One of the Women's Services, but I mustn't go abroad"—she spoke almost in a whisper—"in case Flight comes back!"

Her father came to see her, spoke soothingly and even beautifully.

She turned on him furiously.

"Papa, don't come here with 'plasters', they're no use! How can you sit there saying 'Let not your heart be troubled'! My heart is troubled. How can it be anything else? I've lived with Flight sufficiently long to know something of where we —where Britain—stands today. Edward Masters has talked to me, even Uncle Herbert when he came to see me. Our men lying on the beach at Dunkirk—German pilots brought down in France by *our* men, are being repatriated by that unspeakable Vichy Government! The whole world, except ourselves, believes that we're beaten. No, Papa! don't come here to give me soothing medicine. I don't want to forget, so long as I remember I shall work harder. I'm going to London next week."

He stared at her. Was it possible that this was his dutiful, obedient daughter, Alicia?

He said, "To London? What are you going to do there? I consider that the matter must be given serious thought. It is inevitable that if Germany does attack us here in . . ."

She interrupted him, "In 'this precious stone set in a silver sea'. Yes, go on, Papa."

"It is inevitable that London will be the first objective."

"And what if it is? The King and Queen haven't run away from London yet!"

"Alicia, my dear! I deplore this spirit. The name of your mother's second cousin's son, Hector Bartlett, is among the missing. It is in *The Times* this morning. We *all* have to face troubles, loss; it is almost part of our national heritage. Surely your place is with your mother and myself, here in Baddock St. Mallory?"

"My place," she persisted, "is where I can do the most useful work. I never knew Hector Bartlett, I don't think you did either. I'm sorry that any young man is missing; for one reason, we can't afford to lose them. But I have to work out"—she smiled sourly—"my own salvation. Don't try to stop me, Papa! I'll come over and talk to you both before I go. I'll tell you my plans as far as I know them."

Ann left for Alcaster, Eleanor lived at the flat-fronted Georgian house in the main street with old Dr. Charlton; Alicia went to London, and took with her Deborah Miller, who had been her nurse, and had later slipped into being her personal maid.

She was a stout woman of forty-five, with bright, dark eyes and a fresh complexion. Her will was inflexible.

She listened to what Alicia said concerning going to London, and her comment was "Drat it! I've never liked the place, never!"

Alicia smiled. "But you're not asked to go there, Deb."

The elder woman grumbled. "Not axed, indeed! You know as well as what I do, that if you go I shall go too. Some nasty poky London flat, and all the work ter do. Oh, yes! there'll be no keeping there in staff, not now, there won't. They'll be wanted for munitions. I shall have the lot to do. Nice prospect, an' me rising forty-six. Tut, tut!"

"But I haven't asked you to come, Deb."

"Then we'll tak' it as I've axed mself, shall we? I know where my duty lies, Miss 'Licia! I'd better get packed. Are you takin' all them wedding presents? That 'ul meaning cleaning silver from morn while night, if you do." She laughed. "Deborah Alice Miller's war work! Cleaning silver salvers an' coffee-pots!"

Alicia said, "No, we'll leave them here. Someday, perhaps, if . . ."

Deborah came closer and laid her hand on the girl's arm. "Hark ter me!" she said, "I'm not so green as I'm cabbage luking, my dear. It's such as—as him, that comes through anything. Not the energetic, tearing-about sort, but the quiet, dreamy ones. Comes a time when things is all agin them that they wake up. And when they wake up—my word! It's God help anyone who tries ter stop 'em! Mark my words, Miss 'Licia!"

Frances Masters opened a workroom, pressed into service every woman in Baddock St. Mallory who could sew or knit, and a good many who could do neither. They adopted two crews of mine-sweepers; they sent off innumerable parcels, and when Lady Sophia, visiting the workroom, glanced in some dismay at Elizabeth Fotherly, who had been known as "weak in the head ever since she was born", Frances nodded, "Yes, I know, but we've discovered that her real mission in life is to pack parcels. Elizabeth, show Lady Sophia those parcels you have ready for the *Mermaid*."

Lady Sophia said, "Beautifully done, Elizabeth, quite beautifully!"

Elizabeth beamed and nodded, and said, "D'yer knaw wot I pack 'em in, yer ladyship?"

"What is it, unbleached cotton?"

"Naw—Luv—that's what they're wrapped in—luv! Mrs. Masters gie me the tip. And t' string is—what did yer say t' string was, missus?"

Frances said, "Now, Elizabeth, *think*!"

"Eh, I got it! Bands o' faith an' 'ope. That's right, eh, missus?"

"Really! it's a charming idea, Mrs. Masters. They want me to become Commandant of the hospital which is being opened at the Cummins'. I wish that I could persuade Alicia to come back to help me. It will be a tremendous work,

223

tremendous! She tells me that she is working on—or in—I never know which is correct, a mobile canteen. She's joined some organisation called The Women's Regiment of Service. The Rector is frankly against it. Alicia has changed very greatly . . ."

Frances said briskly, "Well, she's been through enough to make that understandable, hasn't she?"

Lady Sophia sighed, "Possibly! Possibly!"

At night, when she sat talking to Edward, Frances said, "I thought that she might have wanted to join our workroom. I was so relieved! She's going to be Commandant at the new hospital at Wilberforce Cummins'."

Edward said piously, "God help the wretched nurses and patients! Never mind, Francy, she'll come out of this with decorations, which is more than you'll get m'dear!" He went on to talk of the new idea which was occupying the minds of older men, a Home Guard. He and Cummins had talked it over going up to town by train; for he no longer used the car unless it was imperative. Cummins was all for it. The Lord Lieutenant had given the idea his blessing, the Government approved, but could promise no equipment at the moment. Edward told her that in some places the arms of the new Guard consisted of bill-hooks and scythes. He added, "As they fought in the Monmouth rebellion at Sedgemoor. Well! they'll fight with them again if they have to!"

They rarely spoke of Flight—or Claverley.

224

Once Edward met a man in town, a friend of Wilfred Horton's, who had come back wounded from Dunkirk. He had seen Flight, they had exchanged a word as they passed. "Just a very brief meeting," he said. "You'll understand one didn't stop to chat at that time." He had seen Claverley too. "By rights, he should have been with the Staff, but he was tearing about in twenty places at once. And, curiously enough—I knew him quite well —when I spoke to him he didn't stammer." But usually they did not speak of either Flight or Claverley. Chris was commissioned—he was not to be a pilot—but was on the administrative side.

"He'll be good at that," Edward said.

Francy nodded. "Yes, yet, in some ways I wish that he had *wanted* to be a pilot, Edward. I'm sure that I'm wrong but—oh, I don't know! He's young enough, he's strong, he never seemed to have any nerves to speak of. Perhaps losing Flight has made me—ungenerous."

Edward said, soothingly, "No, no! never ungenerous. We can't judge, we mustn't judge. People have to make their own decisions, decide where they will be most useful. Probably in his case that was decided for him."

Edward flung himself into the organisation of the Home Guard, he worked at Clark Square all day, and every evening he was out drilling, planning, going round the countryside begging arms from people he knew. It had its funny side, he told Wilfred Horton. "We've got everything from

225

double-barrelled sporting-guns, breech loaders, damme! we've even got a couple of old flint-lock horse pistols! But the men are keen, that's the main thing. The rest will come, the rest has got to come."

He had lost weight, his leg bothered him; he resented the fact that he was barred from taking part in some of the exercises, felt that the men might feel that he was shirking. Frances watched him, and at last protested.

"Edward! flesh and blood cannot stand it! Day after day, night after night! It's too much. You'll make yourself ill, get pneumonia, then I shall have to nurse you and neglect my own work at the depot."

He laughed at her fears at first, but later, after the opening of the Battle of Britain, he agreed that he was trying to do too much.

"I've been training a fellow at Clark Square," he told her. "Nice lad, lost one foot in an accident when he was run over as a child—Frank Tiller. Remember old William Tiller, who used to be invoice clerk? His son. Been with us since he left school; he's nearly thirty. He'll run the place when I'm not there, and he'll run it very well, believe me!"

"God never closes one door but He opens another," Frances said fervently, if with a certain obscurity.

Alicia in London, living in the flat which was to have been her home with Flight, wearing a uniform which did not become her particularly, learnt what bombardment meant. From August the eighth to the end of October she faced the dangers, the horrors and the terror. All through the Battle of Britain she, and women like her, took their part. She knew what it was to be dirty, unwashed, to have her nostrils assailed by smells which were sickening, and her eyes offended by sights which were incredible. She was cold, soaked to the skin, aching with weariness, and often when she had a moment to think, terribly afraid. She went on, as the rest of the women did, doing their duty, trying to laugh and make rather feeble jokes about Hitler's attacks, and, in common with the rest of the world, she felt her heart swell with pride as she watched the spirit of the people rise higher and higher with every bombardment.

Not only in London. Between the long months from September to May, stories came in from all parts of the country, stories which were often fantastic in their magnificence. She was drafted on special duty, to Portsmouth, Southampton, Birmingham and to Newcastle; she returned to report that the spirit which existed in London, existed too in the other cities that she had visited.

"They call us 'The Monstrous Regiment of Women'," she told the grey-faced Commandant when she reported on her return.

"So we are—we're 'monstrous' because we're born of something gigantic, incredibly huge, colossal, terrifying! Now, Masters! go home and get some sleep, we've got a big job on tonight. East Ham, Dockland. You'll go down with No. 17 canteen, take Macmillan, Gorridge and Maitland with you."

"Very good, ma'am."

"They'll be over early, there's a moon. Get off not later than five."

"Yes, ma'am."

On the ninth of December Ann's twins were born. She lay in a wing at Alcaster which was apart from the hospital, while the Duke sat biting his nails in the gloomy library, which also served them as a dining-room.

She had continued her work until the doctor had forbidden it. The men were noticing her condition.

Ann flashed back, "What if they are! I know they are. One of them said to me the other day "My missus 'as just 'ad 'ers. She's come through a treat. Good luck, ma'am, hope as you do!'"

He shook his head. "It's not only that. You're on your feet too much, expending too much energy. No! stop this work until it's all over."

The last Inspection she made, she spoke to all the patients, made no attempt to conceal why, she said, "My last Inspection for a time, boys! Only remember—any wickedness on your part will be duly reported to me! I shan't forget, I'll deal with you when I come back! Be good, boys, all of you; concentrate on getting well."

228

A voice called out, "Aye, an' when we do, they'll send uz back!"

She answered, "And why the devil not? Unless you want us to be over-run by Nazis?" She pronounced the word as Churchill did—Narzis—and the men laughed. "If we are, those chaps who have got wives or girls—well—just lie there and remember what it will mean! You, Ike Berman, you and yours won't find it a picnic!"

The little curly-headed Jew from the East End said comically, "Nah, ma'am! don't pick on me, they can't send me back ter leuke fer me leg wot I left somewhere over theer, can they?"

She said, "Sorry, Berman! I forgot." But the rest of the long ward roared with laughter as Berman did himself.

When she had gone, whilst every man said, as she passed, "Good luck, ma'am!" and the Matron listened with a face which was mercifully expressionless for she felt that the whole thing was "highly irregular", Berman said to Jock MacInnes, "Think of it! w'en this y'ear biby is born, if it's a boy it 'ul be a ruddy Juke!"

The Scotsman answered, "Aye, Ah'd not wunner."

"I'm a Communist," Berman continued, "out-and-outer. My motter is, 'Workers o' the world unite, you 'ave nothink ter lose but yer chains.' But—I like that gurl. She's ar'right!"

"Chalky" White in the bed at his other side said, "Oh, shut up abart yer bloody motter! Could

229

Stalin 'ave done wot ole Winston's done? No! There'll allus be poor, an' allus be rich, an' as long as the rich be'aves theersevles, well let 'em alone. Yet livin' in a toffs' 'ouse, being treated like wot a toff is . . ."

The Scot said, "Aye, mair or less, yon's the truth."

Berman protested, "Nah, nah, china, we've all got a right ter our perishin' opinions, ain't we? I don't say as 'ow I wish the toffs any atchual 'arm, but I remain yours truly, Ike Berman, Communist."

Daylight was breaking when Sir Newton Fosset came into the library. The Duke raised his pallid face and said, "Well?"

Fosset smiled. "When you remember that Lady Claverley is only nineteen, that she has been through a grave bereavement and has worked . . ."

Alcaster snapped, "Oh, get on, man! get on, for God's sake!"

Fosset continued unmoved, "As I say, has worked at considerable pressure, and has now given birth to twin boys—each weighing approximately five pounds each—I regard this confinement as something nearly approaching a miracle. My congratulations!"

"And my daughter?"

"Would like to see you—not more than three minutes, please."

Alcaster tore up the stairs as he had not done for years. Frances Masters opened the door to him, her finger on her lip. "Sshush!" she breathed.

Ann said, "Hello, 'Grandpapa', we've managed a litter! Tell my mother which one you'd like us to keep, will you? Yes, look at them. They're completely hideous! I'm going to sleep. Are you pleased?"

He bent and kissed her, whispering, "My brave Ann . . ."

Her eyes were very heavy, but she whispered back, "My clever Sholto!"

At eleven that morning, having obtained due permission, the butler—the only remaining man-servant except the Duke's valet, who was imposs-ibly short-sighted and suffered from arthritis—carried champagne and dry biscuits round the wards. The Duke himself explained the reason for this celebration. "I shall be obliged if you will drink the health of Lady Claverley and her two—her two sons. Thank you."

Berman, sipping his wine, said, "Blimy! it ain't 'arf good, tickles yer nose a bit, eh?"

The Scot nodded, "Aye, Bairman, mon, ye mind me o' an old song. You—a Communist! Supping champagne, drinking healths, an' what will ye, to aristocrats! The worrds, if memory sairves me reit, run this way, 'An' they drink the booze she sends them, but her shame they can't forgie.' Yer mind the song, Chalky, eh?"

Berman replied, "Oh, stow it! Fancy that little gurl . . . twins! Whatcher know abart it!"

3

RAIN! Well, rain didn't matter, it would flatten the sea. All to the good. He had been down to the water's edge, had shoved and pushed some of his men into the boats, had tried to make jokes and felt that they were particularly poor, even for him, and he was no comedian. Now he was running back again, because Allen had stopped one in the leg, and could only hobble along. He waved to the boats as they moved away, shouted, "Good luck!" and laughed, because in this hell of a noise no one could hear anything. How he hated noise. He mustn't think about it, but he kept remembering how he loathed it. Bang—whizz—crash—tons of coals being unloaded—a whole convoy of carts filled with bricks spilling them out all at once.

Once he stopped running and stared up at the sky, yelling at the top of his voice, "Oh, stop that bloody row, for God's sake!" then laughed again, because, of course, the Jerries couldn't hear, and if they could they'd not stop.

He found Allen, a big west-country lad, patient and uncomplaining.

"Hurt badly?" Flight asked.

"Noa, surr, doan 'urrt soa badly, surr."

"Come on, then! Here, give me a hand with him.

Up you go, my lad. I might make this trip with you; you're about the last of our lot."

Going down to the water again someone ran past him, a smallish man, a "Brass Hat", holding a packet in his hand, shouting, "Here, this has to go to UK!" It was Sholto. He reached the water, thrust the packet out to a man who was in one of the boats, wading in knee-deep; then, shaking himself like a dog, came running back.

Flight bawled, "Sholto-o-o!"

The "Brass Hat" checked, waved, then tripped, as the sand and pebbles round him were thrown up by a burst of fire. He scrambled up, then fell forward.

Flight said, "Here, hold on, Allen, that's my brother-in-law."

He reached him, yelled his name, turned him over and saw that where his throat had been there was nothing but a great, thick plaster of bloody tubes and flesh. He pulled the scarlet-banded cap over the face and went back to Allen and the other soldier. "Dead," Flight said, "come on!"

A boat was waiting, so small as to be like a cockle-shell on the water. A girl, wearing blue trousers and a wet pink shirt which clung to her, showing her small young breasts. She said, "I can manage two."

Flight said, "You're alone?"

She grinned and looked like an impertinent boy. "I've obviously got no one with me. Come on, heave him in! I want to be off. You coming?"

Flight shook his head.

"Not room."

She said, "We'd manage—come on."

"No, good night!"

"Good night, sweetheart!" she called.

He laughed. "Sweet dreams, angel-face."

Dusk was falling. Flight knew that he was terribly tired; he felt suddenly lost and alone. A tall man, with a bristling chin and sore-looking eyes, walked beside him. He said in a mumbling voice, "I estimate that nearly four thousand have gone."

"And the rest . . . ?"

"I dunno. Getting dark. Can't use flares. Oh, blast these bloody Huns!"

The roar overhead swelled. The whole world was being shattered by the tumult. The tall man shouted, "Get down, you fool! Get down!" and Flight flung himself down. They lay there together while it seemed that hell was let loose overhead. He did not know how long they lay there, he lost all consciousness, he fancied later, that something hit him on the head. When he opened his eyes night had come, and he felt as if someone had struck a penknife into his thigh. He put out his hand to see if the other man were still there, felt the cloth of his tunic and whispered, "Here, we ought to move, you know, and quick!"

The man did not move. Flight shook him gently and said, "Here, you, wake up. Come on, let's move!"

He moved his hand upwards until he reached the

face, it was cold. The fellow was dead.

He had never felt so lonely, so abandoned in his life; he thought that he must be the only man left alive in a world of dead, a world which held death wherever you turned; Death was inevitable. Sholto was dead, the man who had spoken to him was dead. Was it possible that he too was dead and didn't realise it yet? He pinched his leg, taking up a piece of flesh in his finger and thumb, nipping it hard. No, he couldn't be dead, because he felt the pain. He remembered once at school a fellow used to pinch you, a big fellow with a pair of eyes like boiled gooseberries. What the devil was his name? —something very fanciful—Claude, Algernon, Aubrey? Damn, he couldn't remember.

He began to talk to himself, moving his lips, but making no sound.

"Where do we go from here? North, South, East or West?"

"East or West, Home is best."

"Bloody fool! You can't get home. Got to go somewhere. The Jerries will come out presently. The idea of a prison camp isn't funny. Get a move on. Not the roads. Oh, not those ghastly roads! Can't face that. Come on!"

"I'm so tired—terribly tired, my leg hurts."

"Mor'n your leg 'ul hurt if Jerry gets you, my lad. C'm on!"

Slowly he began to crawl up the beach, first going carefully through the dead man's haversack. Tin of emergency rations, two bits of water-logged chocolate, and a water-bottle. With difficulty he transferred them to his pocket and slung the bottle over his shoulder. Then he began to move. Slowly, painfully slowly, he crawled. He had no thought except to get away. He did not think of Alicia, of his father and mother, of Ann's grief at Sholto's death; he had only one thought—to get away, to hide somewhere where the Germans could not find him.

For hours, it seemed, he crawled. He was off the beach now, creeping through high, coarse grass, grass which pricked through his trouser legs, and stung his face. Once he slipped and rolled into a dyke where there was water. He scrambled out and pulled himself up a bank on the farther side. He was in a field, the largest field in the whole world, miles and miles of it. With the sensation of being remarkably clear-headed and sensible, he thought, "At the present rate of progress, if, as I assume, this field is a thousand miles wide, I shall reach the end of it sometime the year after next; that will be Anno Domini or the Year of Our Lord, 1941." Then he wondered if that were correct; what was this year?—1939 or 1940? He whispered to this idiotic Flight Masters, "Oh, dry up, you silly . . ." using a word which he could never remember using before in his whole life.

Then, with awful suddenness, he felt himself touching stones and falling, down, down into pitch-black darkness. He reached the bottom and must have lain there for a long time, for when he came to himself, he stared up at a patch of grey sky, and felt rain drops falling on his face. He found that he was in a cellar, a cellar which was all that was left, except ruined walls, of a little farmhouse. The roof had gone, everything had gone, except this cellar.

His leg hurt and he twisted round to try to find out the extent of the damage. It was difficult to get to his thigh, and the blood had clotted on his trousers, and the cloth had stuck to the wound. Better leave the damned thing alone. His hands were caked with dirt and he crawled to a little puddle and dabbed them in the water, drying them on his tunic. He nibbled the chocolate and heard himself laugh—it struck him as strange to hear himself laugh—"Same old NAAFI chocolate," he said. It struck him as irresistibly funny, and he rolled about convulsed with mirth.

Then came hours, days, years, when as darkness fell again he set himself to crawl out of the cellar. He moved slowly and very carefully, testing each stone before he held on to it. His leg was on fire now, not only where someone had stuck a pen-knife, but for the whole length of the limb. At last he reached the earth again and lay panting like an exhausted dog on the ground, his mouth half open, his breath whistling as it came. A long way off he heard the dull pounding of guns. He began to crawl in the opposite direction.

He lost count of days. Only at long intervals did he remember incidents clearly; once a dog came and pushed its wet nose into his face as he slept, then nuzzled into his pocket and took what remained of his chocolate. He stirred, and it rushed away. He moved immediately and swam over a little river, congratulating himself that water destroyed the scent. He had read that in a book years ago, a book with a dark blue cloth cover. Once he heard the tramp of feet and rolled into a ditch, lying there among the nettles and brambles. Voices, harsh, guttural, speaking German, but a dialect of which he only understood one word in ten. He slept a great deal and on waking said, "Flight, I regret to tell you that you are very ill." He answered himself, "I know that, you silly fool. I am very ill."

Nothing mattered any longer. If he were caught, all right; if he died, it was still all right. If only he could sleep in a bed once again, for one night. That was when he suddenly hit his head, hard, against a wall. He had managed to limp along, his hands and knees were bruised and cut to ribbons. The night was very dark, there were no stars. His head hurt. He rubbed it stupidly, and remembered that where there was a wall, in all probability there would be a door. "Find it," he whispered to Flight Masters. "Good dog, find it."

He found the door, moving slowly, his hands against the rough stone of the wall. Not a complete door, a half-door. He put his head inside. The place was warm, stuffily and yet pleasantly warm. Someone was breathing heavily. He hesitated, sniffed again. The place was a cow-byre, and the breathing came from the beasts within. He fumbled for the latch, found it, swung the door open and went in, closing it behind him.

Moving cautiously he felt the soft, smooth flanks of a cow. Going farther, an empty stall; hay was on the floor. He flung himself down—and slept.

He woke to the sound of milk squirting into a metal pail, hearing a voice say in French, "There, be easy, my dear, be easy." He stirred, and his leg hurt so badly that he had to clap his hand over his mouth to prevent himself crying out. A voice called, "Who is there? Answer, or I shall shoot!" but it was an old voice, a woman's voice, and he did not feel afraid.

He called back, "Madame, I am 'Malbrouck', I am not dead, I have returned from the war." He wondered why on earth he had said that, and felt pleased that he had spoken in French.

He heard the bucket set down, heard footsteps on the paving stones, and a head appeared, through a haze, the head of an old woman wearing a print cap, who stared at him, and called softly upon God for protection.

She whispered, "Who are you?"

He said, "Malbrouck—returned from the war. Indeed, madame, I have come a very long way. I am ill."

The head disappeared. There was silence, and he drifted away until he was conscious of being moved, of a voice making strange noises, whimpering like a hungry puppy. He said, "*Pauvre chien—il ne faut pas battre,*" and then realised that he, himself, was making the whining noise. When next he woke he was lying in a little attic room in a bed, his uniform had gone, one leg was wrapped in bandages, his hands were bandaged too. The head, the old face, the pring cap, seemed to hang above him.

The thin old voice said, "Ah, monsieur, can you tell me who you are?"

He licked his dry lips and said, "I told you, Madam—my name is Malbrouck."

She shook her head, "Your papers say—Flayeit Maistaires?"

"That is my name when there is no war. I am English. Thank you for this pleasant bed."

"But—Malbrouck?" she asked.

He felt very tired and answered irritably, "One must have a name, it is as good as any other," and went to sleep again.

He knew that he drank soup, rather thin soup, but good; he drank milk, and whimpered again when they were washing and dressing his leg. He was very weak. Then, one morning, when he woke up, he found his mind clear and though his leg still hurt, he was able to dislike the pain, not merely to accept it as something unavoidable.

He said cheerfully, "Good morning, Madame," when she brought him some milk and a piece of bread.

She said, "It is time, now that your mind is clear, for you to tell us something about yourself. My son, Pierre, is here, and must speak with you."

Flight replied gravely, "The pleasure will be entirely mine, Madame."

Pierre entered. He wore shabby peasant's clothes of faded blue, his hair was cut very short, and he held an unbelievably old hat in his hands. He bowed to Flight and came forward.

His face was thin and craggy, his eyes light-grey and very intelligent. His teeth were excellent. He began to ask questions, and Flight told him all that he could remember. He added, "All this you can verify if you will find my papers. They are in my uniform pocket."

Pierre answered gravely, "I have satisfied myself on these points. I am able to read a little English." He smiled and said, "'Ow-do-you do, good morning, 'ow is your aunt?"

Flight answered, "Magnificent! Now please tell me about yourself?"

Pierre explained that he was a doctor. He had lived with his mother—his father being dead—in the little neighbouring town of Matrec.

Flight exclaimed, "But I know this town. I studied French with the priest there, Father Moussines. Tell me, is he still there?"

The Frenchman's jaw hardened, his eyes looked like flints.

"No. That good man—like many others—is not there any longer. But I continue, monsieur. My mother has always liked to have this small farm, where she came in the summer-time; in winter, Jacques and his wife looked after it. Jacques is still here, his wife is not. We came here to live, you will understand, completely as peasants. After June the fourteenth, we realised that we must stay here. We have sufficient money hidden—with your papers, monsieur—in a secret place in this house. Our name is Peloux. When I add that my mother's name is Lea, and that before her marriage to my father she was Mademoiselle Wernecke, you may realise at least one of our present difficulties. Yes?"

"She came from . . . ?"

"Alsace, monsieur."

Flight nodded, then asked, "Tell me, Monsieur Pierre, what day is today?"

"It is June the thirtieth. On June the fourteenth the enemy entered Paris. On the sixteenth the new Government—Pétain-Weygand—asked for peace; and on June the twenty-first, at Compiègne—you remember Compiègne, perhaps, as a historic place in 1918?—the armistice was signed—yes, monsieur, in the same railway carriage." He laughed unpleasantly. "Who shall say that the Germans have no sense of humour? Four days later another armistice was signed, with Mussolini and his Fascists. Now, monsieur, you have the Story of France, up to date."

"And the Germans hold France?"

"They believe so, monsieur. They are stupid people."

"I don't follow you."

Pierre stood up, and set the chair on which he had been sitting back against the wall. He looked down at Flight and said, "Possibly you will. You are welcome here, welcome to what we have. Your name is François Pascal. You are a distant cousin of my father's, you speak a little, very bad, English; you are a commercial traveller. Your age is twenty-one years. You never wished to fight—if the truth must be told, you suffer from a slight affliction of the liver—it is white. You escaped here and were wounded in escaping. You have strange ideas. You believe that Germany has a 'mission'. That France is—finished! I shall prepare your dossier, you will commit it to memory. My friend, Max Brevet, will take a photograph of you. It will be no better and no worse than the usual photograph on Government documents. Your home is in Paris—in a humble yet clean *appartement* in Rue Lepic, fifteen."

"It's all rather confusing," Flight said. "Perhaps I am being more stupid than usual. Are you arranging to help me to escape to England?"

Pierre raised his shoulders, his eyebrows, his hands. "Alas, monsieur, I am not God! I cannot do impossibilities. I am paying you a great compliment. I am assuming that you are a patriot and a man of honour. Now, sleep—I shall come again."

He lay there in the little attic which was terribly hot, for it was immediately under the roof; there was not a great deal of air and somewhere—he

243

sniffed—apples were stored. With the smell of those apples the remembrance of his own home came rushing back to him. How often had he savoured that smell as he went up to the attic at home? With that came the thought of Alicia, his wife, his beautiful wife. Had she heard that he was dead: did she believe it, or had they posted him as missing? Here he was, lying in a little French farmhouse in the country, not far from Matrec —Matrec, he remembered, was south-east of Paris. No—east-south-east. About a hundred and fifty kilometres from that city. He had listened to instructions regarding his identity; a dossier was being prepared—not a word about helping him to escape. There in England, Alicia was waiting for news of him; with the lack of it, slowly coming to believe that he was either dead or a prisoner in German hands.

He clenched his hands tightly. The thought was intolerable. Somehow he must get in touch with her. He couldn't allow her to go on suffering, constantly imagining terrible disasters which might have overtaken him. His thoughts went racing back to those days that they had spent together in Italy; he remembered her love, her tenderness, her desire to be everything to him, her determination that their love should be quite perfect and complete. Now she was waiting for news of him, and he lay here, helpless, unable to send her any message, impotent to do anything to alleviate her distress and anxiety.

He lay there thinking of them all. His energetic, kindly father; his mother—Alicia had said that she was like a "little Bantam hen" that night when he and his father had ventured to suggest that she and Alicia should go to America. Eleanor—where was George? Had he gone overseas? Was he still alive? And Ann—gallant little Ann? And Chris. Not that he had ever got on well with Chris, they'd never "mixed", somehow. Now, where were they all? What was happening in England? How many of the boats from Dunkirk had got home again? That girl in blue slacks and a soaking-wet pink shirt, she had called, "Good night, sweetheart!" and he had replied "Sweet dreams, angel face!" Had she got safely home with her two soldiers?

On and on, his brain twisting and turning and always coming back to Alicia. To speculations concerning her, endeavouring to make plans, fantastic, impossible plans, to get a message back to her in England.

It was growing dusk when Pierre Peloux returned, bringing with him a slim, clean-shaven young man, wearing cheap, rather flashy clothes.

Pierre said, "This is Father Maurice, he has come to talk to you."

The man shook hands, and Pierre pulled up a chair for him.

Flight said, "I beg your pardon, did you say this gentleman was a priest?"

Pierre nodded. "Indeed, yes. He has a very large parish, a very scattered parish. Tonight he is not

Father Maurice, he is—Nicholas Maria Laliche, of Lyons. He travels in—what is it?"

The other man said gravely, "Articles of hygiene, for the toilet—such as baths, water-closets, bidets, and so on. Also, I have a very strong line in holders of hygienic paper—one, even, which plays a delightful tune when the paper is torn off—charming, decorated with birds and flowers in exquisite colours."

Flight stared and said, "Please forgive me if I am dull. One moment I am told that you are a priest. The next that you are Monsieur Laliche."

The two others glanced at each other and smiled. Pierre said, "Tell him, Father, if you please."

"You are a British soldier, monsieur, an officer. We imagine that you were wounded at Dunkirk and escaped. How, we do not know precisely. When you arrived here and were found sleeping in the cow-house, it was impossible for you to give any information. Now you are better. Soon you will be well again. What do you wish to do? Speak frankly."

"I wish to let my wife know that I am alive. After that, I want to get back to England, rejoin my regiment and go on fighting," Flight said.

"And if I assure you that—at this moment —neither of these two things is possible, and that even to attempt either of them might mean not only danger but death . . ."

Pierre growled, "A most unpleasant death, too."

246

". . . to people who have helped you, saved your life, what then?"

"Then," Flight said, "then, my God, my wife will break her heart!"

The priest, who in some mysterious fashion, despite his abominable clothes, contrived to sound and even look like a priest still, said, "My son, no! Hearts do not break, believe me. Men and women suffer terribly, almost unbearably, but their hearts do not break. Today the whole world is suffering. It is for all of us to make the decision. Shall we take the road which is only wide enough for one, and that one, oneself? Or shall we take a wider road which has room for many, where we may walk shoulder to shoulder with our comrades? Tell me—if we give you papers, permits, and forged visas, and tell you that you may go and try to find your way back to England—what chance will you have? Within twenty-four hours you would be facing a German Enquiry Officer, and within another twelve, either be on your way to Germany or facing a firing squad. How will this help your wife, your family, your country?"

"You swear to me that this is true, Father?" Flight's voice was hoarse with anxiety.

"I swear it! Remember that the Germans may be masters here, but with each day they grow more and more highly nervous. The fact that you managed to get through was a miracle. Also you were going from the coast, not towards it. Did you ever know an officer of the name of Huff?—no, what was the name, Pierre?"

"H-ooh," Pierre said, "H-ooh Wilson. We looked after him for a time, a few days. He was not hurt, only exhausted. He decided to make his escape. He left a place near here five days ago. He was shot in Paris two days ago. We heard this afternoon. God rest his soul."

"And if I stay here? Shall I ever be able to communicate with my wife?"

It was Pierre who answered. "Monsieur, tides turn when they are ready to turn. Nothing anyone can do can make them turn one moment sooner than they are destined to do. Who knows? In a year, two years—how can we, any of us, make predictions. We can only work . . ."

Flight frowned. "Work?" he repeated. "Work like moles, eh?"

Pierre said sharply, "Who put those words into your mouth?"

"A woman, a woman I know in Paris. A well-known woman."

Again he saw the quick exchange of glances between the two men.

Pierre asked, "It may be that I know her. A well-known modiste?"

"No."

"Ah, perhaps I am wrong—an artist. She sings remarkably well?"

"I have never heard her sing, monsieur."

"Her home might not be very distant from Rue Royale?"

"Not farther than you could walk in comfort," Flight replied.

"Her daughter . . ."

"I do not know of any daughter."

"I am stupid. A son—who at one time wished to follow the profession of his father, eh?"

"I have a great friend who wished to follow his father's profession. His father was, I have heard, a great actor. He was following an artistic career, until he entered the Army."

Pierre and the priest both laughed. It seemed to Flight that they laughed with a certain sense of relief. They began to talk to him, speaking rapidly, never halting for a moment until the whole story was laid before him. Only once did the priest hold up his hand, admonishing silence, and say, "We are trusting you implicitly, Monsieur."

Flight answered, "Believe me, you can, completely, Father. I have made my decision."

Certain phrases which they used remained imprinted on his memory.

"'. . . called it a war of nerves. That is what we are waging now, a war of nerves.' 'The underground network—the "moles" are at work, night and day.' 'Danger is a great incentive to intelligence.' 'We promise nothing, the end maybe an ignominious death at the hands of barbarians'."

Flight listened, knew that his blood ran quicker for what he heard, and at last he stretched out his hand.

"I make a bargain with you," he said, "I will

work with you, and for you, I have only, after all, taken up my place under another banner, the banner of one of Britain's allies; you can trust me. I, on the other hand, shall give you the address of my wife, and you will swear to me that at the first possible opportunity, you will let her know that I am alive. Is that a bargain?"

They shook his hand gravely and promised. He lay back on his pillow and wiped the sweat from his face. "Pooh," he said, "how stupid to feel still weak, like pulp."

But as the days passed, strength came back to him. He was able to hobble down the stairs, even to help a little in the house and little farmyard. He spoke nothing but French, was addressed only as François or Pascal. Once, as he walked a short distance along the road, a man he did not know accosted him and said, "Your name, monsieur?" He answered without hesitation that his name was François Pascal.

"Your habitation?"

"Paris—but I am staying with my aunt, Madame Peloux."

"Your profession?"

"I am a commercial traveller in office equipment—pencils, paper, ink, and such things, you understand."

"Are you always lame?"

"Since I fell off my bicycle, monsieur."

He told them of the encounter when he returned to the farmyard. Pierre and Jacques both smacked their knees and shouted with laughter.

"That was old Lucien. Bravo, François! He is a fox, this Lucien."

Later in the evening the man himself entered. He was grim, with a mouth which drooped at the corners; he needed a shave very badly, and his clothes were extremely dirty.

He jerked a grimy thumb in Flight's direction, and said, "He'll do. Let him work. He's ready." He turned his fiery little eyes on Flight and said, "Maurice says that you speak German, yes?"

"A little."

"I, also. Give me your opinion of the Germans —briefly—in German."

Flight hesitated for a moment, then said, "'*Der civiliserte Wilde ist der Schlimmste aller Wilden!*' Will that do?"

The man flung up his hands. "And with a complete French accent he speaks, making even their horrible language tolerable. *Mon brave*, you shall begin!"

He never forgot going out on his first enterprise. He was told that it was small, not particularly dangerous, but that it was necessary. There was a small wood, five kilometres away. In this wood, the Germans believed that the "moles" were meeting. They had been informed by old Lucien that the meeting would take place, so far as he could ascertain, about half past eleven. They must arrive to find that the moles had vanished. Underground, where you will, but—vanished. There must be,

251

nevertheless, the remains of their meeting-place.

As he limped over the fields in the half-light, he knew that he felt like a schoolboy, going in to bat in an important school match for the first time. He carried some scraps of old newspapers, a few sticks of burnt wood and wood-ashes, in a bag. He had never given greater attention to any work in his life as he did to tramping down the grass, laying the sticks in what he felt to be artistic disorder, and scattering the ash round them. He stood back, surveyed his handiwork and smiled in satisfaction. Then, making off over the fields by another route from that by which he had come, he reached the farmhouse again.

That was his first work for the "moles".

Pierre asked one day, "How does it go, that leg?"

"Better, I scarcely limp at all."

"Good, but don't forget how to do it, it might be useful."

He was never quite happy, but there were times when he was almost content. Only when he remembered Alicia, her lack of all knowledge of him, did his spirits fall, and he would allow depression to sweep over him. News dribbled through. Stories of the Battle of Britain, and his heart sank. He felt physically sick at the thought of what might have happened to Alicia, to his mother and father, to his sisters. They heard of the Tripartite Pact—Germany, Italy, and Japan—of the fighting in Africa. There were times when Flight knew that a sense of foreboding gripped him. Could it be that Germany and Italy, that these yellow-faced Japs, were right, and that superiority of arms on land carried more weight than seapower? Always it was Pierre and the priest who rallied his spirits. He was entrusted with more difficult and dangerous work. There was a man who came and went, called Shaff, a smallish man who always carried a cheap battered portmanteau, who moved rapidly and silently. He had gone once with Shaff and given him some assistance in the top of an empty barn where the other set up a receiving set, and then sat back on his haunches, listening intently, like a small, eager watch-dog.

He never stayed long, but disappeared as he had come, silently and swiftly. There was a whisper that Germany was about to attack Russia; the news had filtered through, Shaff told them, from Washington.

Pierre said, "So! 'When thieves fall out . . .' Wait, watch, we shall see!"

There was the terrible time when Harry Wilmot, an Englishman who had joined them, was caught and taken to Paris. He managed to escape, when they had all given him up for dead, and when they asked him how he had got away, he said in French, but with a magnificent English accent:

"I complained that I disliked my cell—it was damp, you understand. I was not a soldier, I was a civilian. I asked them to allow me, kindly, to send a telegram to my ambassador. They stared, but they

253

were impressed. They tried to get information from, me. I refused to say anything until I was moved to quarters suited to my dignity. I was moved to HQ, at the Crillon. The colonel who interviewed me was distressed that I had been in discomfort. I said, 'Dear fellow, indeed it was damned uncomfortable! You, as a gentleman, can understand the feelings of another gentleman.' That night I sat talking to him for a long time, he was disgustingly drunk. I made him believe that I was also. I pushed him under a sofa—they have magnificent sofas at the Hotel Crillon—and walked out wearing his greatcoat and cap; yes, and his sword. I also had a good many of his papers. As I went out I said to the sentry, 'Watch that pig Englishman, he is drunk; he'll sleep for hours. I shall be back immediately.' My German is good, far better than that of François. It was all too easy."

Through the long winter they worked. Often they were half-frozen with cold, almost dead from hunger, but whenever any of them penetrated into the towns, even into a small place like Matrec, they were conscious of the "war of nerves" telling upon the Germans.

Some of it was mere "cut-throat" work, running swiftly, with socks pulled on over thin shoes, leaping suddenly, and as suddenly disappearing into the darkness; leaving a man lying in the snow or on the ice-covered road. Some of it was spectacular, as when Flight was caught and questioned, and finally taken to the German headquarters at

Melun. He kept protesting that he was only trying to visit his uncle at Orleans, and that he had samples there which he must try to sell.

They examined his papers, bent their shaved heads over them, pointing out this and that, with stubby fingers which ended in highly manicured nails. They asked if he spoke any German, and he assented eagerly that he did. Again they whispered, and asked if he could interpret. They had an interpreter, but twice his German had proved unreliable.

Flight replied that while his German, he regretted, was with a French accent spoken, he was anxious to be helpful, because he a "Mission" believed the Germans to have.

A man was brought in. He stood between two bullet-headed fellows in grey uniforms, his mouth was bleeding at one corner, and one ear was puffed. The officer ordered the two soldiers to stand outside the door. He turned to Flight and ordered him to ask him certain questions in French. First the man's name, place of residence, and trade.

Flight asked. The man answered in the argot which was used all round the district of Matrec. Flight spoke to him again in the same dialect.

The German frowned. "That is not French."

Flight smiled disarmingly, with considerable charm. "I, Kommandant, am of a cunning. I speak in his own dialect. Hideous, is it not?"

"*Ach!* It is all hideous. Continue."

Flight said, "What were you doing hanging

255

round this place? It is my belief that you are a 'mole'."

The man did not bat an eyelid, but when he answered his voice was steadier. "So humble as scarcely to be called by this name. I was doing no harm, I swear it, this time."

So it went on, until Flight turned to the officer, and shrugging his shoulders, said, "The man is a half-wit. I can make nothing of him. He says that he was catching moles—imagine it!"

"Moles in winter, when the ground iron resembles?"

"That, Kommandant, is why I maintain that he is a half-wit."

Tempers were short. Two German officers had disappeared the night before and a sentry had been badly mauled; the officer himself wanted to get away to see a charming, if unpatriotic, lady in Melun; he was late already and he had his doubts as to her complete devotion to him. He had watched Colonel von Kraptz ride off in the direction of Melun half an hour ago.

He howled to the soldiers to take the man with the cut lip away, and send him on his road with a kick to hasten him. He turned on Flight, and yelled that he was a dumbhead, with no knowledge of the so-beautiful German language, that he had better take care or he might find himself in trouble.

Flight spread his hands wide and murmured humbly, "Trouble abounds."

The German roared, "What is that?"

"*Paternoster du singe*," Flight said.

"You'll have need to say your prayers. Coming here as an interpreter. Get out, get out!" and he caught Flight a clout over the head which sent him reeling through the door. As he leaned against the wall, half sick and dizzy with the pain, Flight watched him rush out and fling himself into a waiting car.

Three days later, Flight discovered the house at Melun where the beautiful but frail lady lived. Again the German visited her, taking with him a roll of fine silk, which his friend, Haltzmann, had brought him when they looted a secret store of some pusillanimous French merchant at Alençon. The miserly creature had hidden all his best stock, but they had found it. The German laid it beside him on the seat and patted it with satisfaction. He had explained to the lady—Rose was her name, she had often mocked him very sweetly for his inability to say it correctly—that his respect for her was such that he would never stoop to offer her money, he preferred to bring her valuable gifts. He entered the house, knocking in the manner which they had agreed upon as a signal, and made his way up the stairs, thinking, "*Ach*, my feet are cold. It will be good to get these boots off." In her room, filled with so many really charming things which he had brought her—for he had taste, and prided himself upon it—a woman was waiting. Not Rose, a stranger.

She was delightful to the eye, young and slim,

with an oval face and short curling hair. She wore a peignoir of pale blue silk. He had brought Rose that silk, he remembered.

She spoke German, though haltingly. "Herr Kommandant, my cousin has had to go to Paris. An order from the colonel, you understand . . ."

"The devil take the colonel," he thought, "he always wanted Rose."

"I am not Rose, I have not her charm, her beauty"—she was delightfully modest—"but for so long I have watched and admired you. Is it forward of me to say that there have been times when I was jealous of my cousin?"

He flung back his head and laughed, "Haw-haw! Forward, no! You're as pretty a bird as Rose. Look, take the present which I brought for her. I'm a very generous fellow, you understand . . ."

How she laughed for joy at the silk. Her voice was soothing, deeper than her cousin's, fuller, richer. A voice to quicken a man's pulse.

He sat down and pushed off his tight boots, sighing, "That's better! Now, come and kiss me—what's your name? Something pretty, eh?"

"Ivy," she said, "Ivy clings to the strong walls, so I cling to the strong, beautiful officer."

She laid her arms round his neck, she held him closely. By Thunder, the girl was passionate!

He laughed. "Gently, gently—time enough for that! Here, not so tightly, you'll throttle me, Ivy . . ."

258

Her voice, deeper than ever, said, "Yes—that's me—Ivy, clinging to the old garden wall. Don't clout people over the head so lightly again. They don't like it, and don't . . ."

He sagged in his chair, only his stockinged feet still twitched.

A shabby-looking fellow came out of the house. He looked like a modest kind of tradesman. His face was pale and looked sore, blotched. He grinned at the Kommandant's driver, and pointed to the window of the upstairs room.

"You'll have a long wait," he said. "I know that Ivy. I've watched her twist herself round people—they can't get away. She'll give him supper. And wine! Whew! Some people are lucky."

"Not me, sitting here in the cold. Supper? It's only six o'clock now."

The man said indifferently, "Well, I heard her order it from old Madame Dupont. For two, she said, at half past eight. Good night!"

He strolled away, and it was not until midnight that the driver of the car, growing weary, ventured to enter the house and enquire for the Kommandant. They found him dead, lying without his boots, and covered with a peignoir of pale blue silk.

Flight, sitting dressed in his peasant's clothes by the wood fire at the farm, rubbed his cheeks and grumbled, "That last lot of grease-paint, it's not so

259

good as the Leichner we found, it makes your face smart most damnably."

Madame Peloux called them to the table to take their soup. She watched Flight as he came, and said, "François, you're growing too thin."

Pierre laughed. "Yes, he's got a figure like a slim girl, eh?"

4

STORIES reached them, thanks to Shaff and his hidden radio sets. They heard the level, unmoved voices of announcers from London, they heard of disasters, and as he listened Flight would shake his head like a dog who seeks to dislodge something which stings and bites his ear. News from Africa changed; they whispered together of Cunningham and Wavell, of the closing pincers, and old Mère Peloux chuckled and said, "Ah, Foch taught them that move in the game—last time, do you remember?"

They learned of the invasion of Sicily and heard through "the grape vine" of captured British Generals, taken to imprisonment in Italy. Later, Father Maurice, wearing the clothes and carrying the correct papers of an engine driver, named Henri Chienet, returned from what he called "a tour in search of ill health" and reported that the Generals had got away; that in Italy, too, there were people who were—moles.

Pierre said, "Italians will never work underground, they are children, always anxious to show their clever exploits."

Then the priest rebuked him, saying, "I have seen. In the midst of that welter of villainy, treachery, self-seeking and chicanery, there are not

261

only five just men, but thousands of just men. They are fighting, suffering and dying—as we are here, Pierre."

Flight listening to them as they talked, always speaking quietly—for that was a lesson which they had all learnt—thought how hard they had all become, how impervious to pain, danger, and —yes, even to brutality. The news that some ghastly cruelty had been perpetrated no longer roused them to white-hot fury, rather it left them cold, even in a curious way satisfied, for here was a reason, here was something tangible, here was a further crime that they might avenge.

He, himself, had killed them, killed them in cold blood; had tricked them into situations where they were in his power. He felt nothing when he killed, it was either kill or be killed, and if they killed you, your death was usually prolonged and unspeakable. Life—Death—those were the two things which moved the whole world. Death not only in the fields of battle, but Death which lurked in the shadows of narrow streets, which waited behind the wide trunks of old trees, which might lie hidden inside tins of food, where a hole no larger than a pin-point had been made so that death waited in the contents.

How, he wondered, were they—such as survived—going to find a place again in an ordered civilised life? He tried to picture himself, leaving a well-ordered comfortable flat, after a morning bath and a properly-laid breakfast, driving down to the

Galleries—always supposing there was anything left of them after the bombardment—wearing neat, well-brushed clothes, waving good-bye to Alicia. . . .

Always when he got so far in his line of thought he stopped, his mind shied away from her, and yet the thoughts came back, insisting that he should attend to them. Alicia. . . .

He had not seen her since the end of September 1939—and now, it was January 1941. Where was she, was she still alive, or had she been left dead during one of the enemy attacks? Did she think of him, had she ever heard anything except that notice that Flight Masters was reported missing at Dunkirk? How long did the War Office allow a man to remain posted as "missing", when did they change that to "missing, believed killed"? And when that notice appeared, what would she do? She was young, beautiful, she wanted love—what if she married again! He pushed the thought from him, violently. His Alicia—never! She'd wait, hope against hope, and one day a message would come, sent over in some tiny fishing smack, delivered to some fishermen on the coast of Cornwall or Devon, perhaps. "Flight Masters safe". Flight Masters! He had almost ceased to think of himself by that name, he had almost come to believe that he was indeed François Pascal, a young French commercial traveller in "office equipment".

When he shaved, which was no more often than

was necessary, unless the part he was playing demanded it, he stared at his face in the small spotted mirror which hung in the kitchen. Often he frowned, because the face which stared back at him was so unlike the face he remembered.

Thin—well, he'd always been thin; lines, tiny, thread-like, at the corners of his eyes, brought there by screwing them up in order to see more clearly in a dim light. So much of his life was spent in a dim light. The bridge of his nose, shining white through the skin, heavy furrows graved at the corners of his mouth, the mouth itself tight-lipped and hard, his chin jutting a little, aggressive, and—yes, cruel.

He said to Pierre once, "Since I came here, do you find me changed?"

"Changed, *mon ami*? Of course! We are all changed. Once we were quite nice people, now . . ."

"Yes, now?"

"We are not nice people any longer—except perhaps Maurice—but we are damned useful people. So—what matter."

The winter passed. Again the chestnut trees bore fat, sticky buds, and in the sheltered places Flight watched the bright yellow of the celandine showing, smelled violets as he went through the woods, and glimpsed the pale softness of an early primrose. Birds fluttered, absorbed in their courting, their love-making, and—later—in building their nests. Madame Peloux grew anxious concern-

264

ing her chickens, and recounted the varying behaviour of her sitting hens. How this one possessed a devotion which was a model of maternity, how that one was "just a modern mother, forever wishing to race round the farmyard, and only remembering her eggs at the last moment".

Maurice, leaning over the gate at the farmyard, watching the distant woods, the grass which was changing from the cold grey-green of winter to the brighter hue of spring, hearing the songs of mating birds, and the distant lowing of "Lisette", who resented it that her calf should have been taken from her and fed from a bucket, turned to Flight and said softly:

"'*Et expecto resurrectionem mortuorum*' when one watches all this. It is logical, isn't it?"

Flight started. "My thoughts were a long way off, Father. I don't know, I've never thought much about religion. Somehow I don't feel that it had much place in—what we're doing. Religion should, surely, make for peace and kindness—gentle things."

Maurice sighed, "I know—but He said, 'I come not to bring peace, but a sword . . .' and surely if men of their own free will light a fire which, left alone, will consume the world, it is the duty of sane men to put it out?"

He smiled.

Flight thought, "What a wonderful smile he has, this man."

Maurice continued, "I am not very clever. After

265

all, it is not strictly necessary for a priest to have extensive education. True, he must know sufficient to satisfy his superiors, but that is not really a great deal. I was never very clever at the seminary. Thick-headed, you understand, François. I was diligent, but—I never made great or rapid progress. I was assistant priest at Matrec, with the old priest—God rest his soul! Ah, he was clever. Oh, the books he read—not merely kept on his shelves to impress the bishop. He told me, 'Maurice, my son, God will give you a sufficiency. You will not be asked to take a great place in the Army of God, but merely to be a good soldier of the line. It may be that one day you will be given a "stripe". Be content to make the most of your sufficiency.' That is what I try to do, François."

Flight nodded. "I should say that you've got several stripes, Father."

Two days later he disappeared, he had gone on one of his long journeys, this time in the direction of Paris. He went as Nicholas Marie Laliche, wearing his outrageous clothes, and with a packet of evil-smelling cigarettes in his pocket.

The night before he left, Pierre and he sat together, talking in whispers, drawing maps on odd bits of paper and burning them in the wood fire after they had studied them. About midnight, the priest put one of the maps into an inside pocket in the lining of his check waistcoat, and rose. He shook hands with them all, and Madame Peloux pulled down his head and kissed his forehead.

266

He smiled at them—at Pierre, Flight, old Jacques, and Shaff, who happened to be there that night, then raising his hand said, "*Dominus vobiscum.*"

Old Jacques, who professed himself a man of logic, and therefore an atheist; Shaff—who could swear more surprisingly in five languages than any man Flight had ever heard; and Pierre who prided himself upon being harder and less sympathetic than iron, answered:

"*Et cum spiritu tuo.*" And he opened the door and was gone.

Shaff said, "It's two to one on his getting through."

Pierre shook his head. "Two to one against his getting through."

A week later and they had no word. Men came who might have met him on the road; all the "moles" knew Maurice, whether as a priest, as Nicholas, as Henri, or as a filthy old man called Père Rappel; only one had seen him and spoken with him.

After ten days Pierre grew anxious, and after a fortnight allowed his anxiety to become evident to everyone. He went off on long tours, he came back exhausted, to fling himself down and toss in restless sleep. Old Jacques, opening a grimy hand, showed Flight a little medal of white metal, gleaming and bright against his rough palm. He whispered, "St. Christopher, he protects travellers. Not that I believe in all this religion and priest-

267

craft—but there might be something in it, and so to be on the safe side I ask St. Christopher to keep his eye on Maurice."

Three weeks passed. They had continued their own work, they had been out into the countryside, they had, as Shaff said, "Blazed various trails of various intensity". They scarcely spoke of Maurice now.

One morning, as Pierre came in from milking Lisette, he watched an old man coming along the road with a small cart drawn by a diminutive donkey. He didn't know the man, did not recognise his face—and didn't like it. The cart drew nearer and Pierre called, "Hello, old one, from where do you come?"

The man stopped, and Pierre saw that he had a small load of wood on the cart. He said, "I want to sell this small load of wood. I need the money."

Pierre asked, "Where do you come from, then?"

"Many kilometres away. Here, look!" He pulled out of his pocket a greasy piece of paper. Pierre read the name which was written on it, it meant nothing to him; he turned it over in his fingers and found on the other side a rough drawing of a mole.

He handed it back and said, "All right, I'll buy your wood. What do you want for it?"

"Fifty francs."

Pierre said, "There you are—though it is too much. Unload it round in the yard, beside the cow-shed. I am going to breakfast."

The old man took his cart into the yard, and as

they ate their bread and drank their coffee out of basins, they could hear him unloading.

Flight said, "He's a long time stacking that wood!" Then, as a knock came to the door, "Ah, he's finished."

Pierre opened the door. The man pointed to the neatly stacked wood.

Pierre asked, "Is that all?"

The man nodded. "Don't leave the wood there —it is too valuable."

He walked off, and Pierre came back to the table, frowning. "I don't know him, don't like his face. *Dieu!* I'm going to have a look at his load. Come on, François."

Shaff lit a cigarette and said, "You're getting jumpy, my friend."

Together they went out. The wood was neatly stacked; for what it was, it was good enough wood. Pierre said, "Looks like sawn-up planks to me."

Flight stooped and picked up a piece, turning it over in his hands. "Look," he said, "Pierre—look! There . . ." and he pointed to some letters.

Together they bent their heads over it, and with their fingers traced out the words, *Gott— trunkener Mensch.* They stared at each other, their eyes wide, and by a common impulse, began to fling aside the wood, searching—they dared not say for what.

At last they found it. A sack which must at some time have held coal. It was heavy, unwieldly, clumsy. Flight cut the string which bound the neck, and flung down his knife with a scream of horror. His fingers had touched the short hair of a man's head.

His face ghastly, Pierre said, "Help me to carry it into the barn."

There, crouching on the ground, while the sun's rays filtered into the dim place, each beam filled with dancing motes, they found what was left of the priest. He was dressed only in his coarse underclothes, even the little chain with its cheap medal had gone from his neck. Pierre pulled out his red cotton handkerchief and covered the face.

He stood up and held his hands against the small of his back.

"Fetch Shaff," he said, "we'll bury him here, at once. Bring a sheet, there are spades here."

Together they dug the grave, and in it placed the body, rolled in a clean, coarse sheet. Flight knew that again and again he had to wipe his eyes with the back of his hand, pretending that it was sweat that ran into them and not tears which flowed from them. Pierre, his face like grey granite, never spoke; Shaff muttered between his teeth. Suddenly Flight stared and said, "The man who brought the wood. We can catch him, question him, bring him back."

Pierre shook his head. "We have found nothing."

Shaff grunted, "That's wise—they'll be here. There, it's finished. Some dust over the earth

—that block and wood, there—bring it, François! And the saw—get to work sawing wood, just here, as if your life depended on it. No use trying to get away, they may be watching in the fields. Everything hidden, Pierre?"

"Everything."

"Go and warn your mother and Jacques."

Together he and Flight sawed wood. The sawdust fell on the grave and hid the traces of newly disturbed earth. Flight shivered.

"Caught cold?" Shaff asked.

"No, no. The sweat's pouring off me." Then, after a moment's pause, "Shaff, don't either of you care?"

"About Maurice? Too much to go and undo what he's tried to do, and lost his life doing. It won't give him any satisfaction, poor devil, to know that we laid his body out on the kitchen table, washed it, and got killed through paying extra and unnecessary attention to what is only— clay."

"It seems pretty awful," Flight said.

"Oh, get on with your work!"

They came a few hours later. About twenty of them, well-clothed, with shining black boots and belts, with revolvers and machine-guns. Flight heard their voices in the kitchen and started to join Pierre.

Shaff said, "Stay where you are, you don't know that anything is wrong. Get on with your work, will you?"

271

Presently Pierre came out. Two troopers were with him. He walked across the yard and called, "Hi, both of you, you're wanted!"

Shaff called back, "The devil we are! We're busy. What is it?"

"The Germans, to interrogate you."

They walked out, and the trooper on Pierre's right motioned them to come into the kitchen. Jacques stood, looking more stupid than Flight had imagined it possible for a man to look.

Madame Peloux sat near the small wood fire, her hands folded on a blue checked handkerchief. An officer sat at the table, papers before him.

"Which of you is Georges Jean Schaffer?"

Shaff said, "I am. I am, sir, a traveller in articles of hygiene . . ."

"I can read that for myself. What are you doing here?"

Then followed a long, and Flight had to admit, amusing story of how he had, or rather his firm had, installed a new toilet, named—as the officer might verify for himself if he cared to look— "Piquante". These people had never paid for it, and as business was slack, Shaff was taking his holiday out "in kind".

"Is this true?" the officer demanded of Madame Peloux.

She nodded, "Very true, monsieur."

"And you?"—to Flight. And he recited his story, watching the man check his statements by the papers which lay before him.

He turned to Pierre, "You bought some wood this morning?"

"Yes, Herr Kommandant."

"Only wood?"

Pierre frowned. "Only wood? I do not understand you. Only a small load."

"Who did you buy it from?"

"An old man with a donkey-cart. I gave him fifty francs for it."

"Who unloaded it?"

"He did, Herr Kommandant. I went to have my breakfast. I was hungry."

"Where is the wood at the moment?"

"In the yard where he left it. I have not touched it, I have been busy with other matters."

"You have not touched it, eh?"

"Not yet. We were going to do it this afternoon; we are busy making a fresh wood pile now. These two"—pointing to Shaff and Flight—"were sawing wood when you arrived. That is so, eh?" he asked one of the troopers. The man nodded.

"Ah! We will see this wood! Show us where it is. Yes, bring them all."

They stood round the small pile of wood. The officer was frankly puzzled. He ordered one of the troopers to unstack the pile, the man did so, flinging the pieces right and left until the flagstones of the yard were reached and laid bare.

Then, "Show him a piece of the wood. What kind of wood is this, would you say?"

Pierre examined it closely, still frowning, then said, "Deal."

"Yes, yes, but this is not firewood, surely?"

"Anything that is wood is firewood in these days, Herr Kommandant."

"Would you not give it as your opinion that this wood for planks has been intended?"

"I could not say, Herr Kommandant."

The German stared at him. It was obvious that he was mystified by the whole matter. He said, briefly, "Search! Make them show you everything."

He marched back to the kitchen, motioning Shaff to come with him, and stating that he wanted coffee. The house had an abundance of coffee, and good coffee at that, but Madame sighed and explained that they had only "substitute", and that not very good. Shaff whispered, "I have a little wine, Herr Kommandant. Given to me by a lady who was a friend of a German officer, for whom I was able to do a small service."

"Bring it, and quickly."

He brought it, uncorked it with ceremony; more, he brought some of his samples, and particularly extolled the virtues of the bracket for holding toilet-paper, which played a tune as pieces were torn off. The German was entranced, his features, at first set in rigid lines, relaxed, he even whispered to Shaff a joke of such salaciousness that it took the other all his time to bawl a laugh.

He bowed and said, "It is too much presumption

to offer this toy to the Herr Kommandant as a gift? It has given you amusement, you find pleasure in it—it is not for me to retain it, then."

The German said pleasantly, "You bastards of French can be open-handed when it suits you, most of you are tight-fisted. And liars, as all the world knows." He narrowed his eyes and poured himself out some more wine. He made no attempt to offer any to Shaff. "Listen, tell me, did that pigdog find nothing in the wood?"

Shaff answered, "As Americans say, 'Find no nigger in the wood pile.' No, he found nothing —could not, for he had not touched it. Ah, he is a man to work, that one! All the morning, François and I have been standing there sawing wood. My back aches! No, he touched nothing, for we could see from the open door of the barn. More wine, Herr Kommandant?"

The troopers came back and reported that they had found nothing.

Pierre said, "For a favour—for what do they search, Herr Kommandant?"

"For what? Never mind for what? Someone is going to suffer because you did not find anything. What do you imagine that we might have found?"

Pierre shook his head. "I have not a great deal of imagination."

They went away, taking with them half a dozen hens and the little calf. They would have taken Lisette, but she was out in the far pasture, happily unconscious of her offspring's fate. Madame

Peloux cried a little. The officer said, "Tell the old sow to stop her snivelling. Where is the cow? If you have a calf, there must be a cow?"

Pierre said sulkily, "That is why she weeps. The cow is dead, the calf is all we have left."

The other roared. "All you have left. All that you have *not* left, for I have it!"

That night they sat round the table, their voices even lower than usual. "It is time for you to move, Shaff," Pierre said. "They are bound to find out, sooner or later, and it is better that you move on. François, you too, then Jacques and I and my mother will continue here. There is plenty of work for you, François. Maurice was to have gone to Paris"—he shivered—"how far he got, who knows? You will leave for Paris tonight. You once told me that you knew a certain lady there, the one, you will recall, who is not a modiste, neither is she a singer, eh? Find her, she will be able to use you better than we can here. It is possible that we have all been here too long? So watch, François, I shall show you a road. Not the road which Maurice took, but another. There are your papers, they are in order, the others—your British passport, cards and the rest, are hidden. One day perhaps you may come back for them. Take very little with you. You ought to start in an hour."

No word of that burial in the barn, no regrets for Maurice, no direct reference made to his death, until, as Flight was ready to leave, when Jacques

276

shook his hand and said, "You see, I was right. I wasted time talking to St. Christopher. Bah, this religion! *Bonne chance!*" Shaff, too, shook his hand and said that they might meet again.

Madame Peloux took his face between her hands and kissed him, whispering, "*Mon pauvre—mon pauvre!*"

Pierre came with him to the door and pressed a packet of cigarettes into his hand. "Now, Mole," he said, "you have a reason to dig harder than ever. He was attached to you, this Maurice." Watching him, Flight saw that there were tears in his eyes.

Then began his long journey. He had memorised the map which Pierre had given to him, he had learned to make his way by the stars at night, and how to lie hidden in secret places during the day. He stole eggs from hens' nests and ate them raw; he pulled up some new potatoes and they sustained him for half a day. Once he got a day's work on a farm and was given a good meal and a bed for the night as payment. Everywhere he found ruined farms, depleted stocks, the cattle —such as were left—were obviously the least valuable of the herd; hens, frightened by many pursuits, fled at the sight of a man. The peasants working in the fields looked depressed, sulky, resentful. When he passed through a town, he saw that the shops were empty, shutters closed, and the inhabitants fearful of every face they did not know. The Germans alone looked well fed, and even they had lost something of their assurance; only the

277

officers swaggered and pushed lesser folk off the pavement, shouted and bawled orders.

That morning he had helped an old woman to chop some wood. She was old and feeble, and told him a long story of her two sons who had been killed, of a daughter sent to Germany to work, adding, "Ah, such a beautiful girl, now working like a slave for some fat frau!" Flight wondered, but said nothing. He offered to chop her wood in exchange for a piece of bread and a mouthful of coffee substitute. She accepted his offer readily enough, and he whitewashed her hen-house, where half a dozen scraggy old hens sat in depressed attitudes. When he left she gave him five francs and a pair of shoes which had belonged to one of her sons.

That night he went into a café and ordered a glass of thin beer and a small roll. As he sat eating and drinking, making it last as long as possible because it was pleasant to sit on a chair and listen to people talking, he realised that several men were watching him closely.

Presently one of them came over to him and said abruptly, "Why did you, please, choose this café, monsieur?"

Fight smiled and said, "Because I was tired, because also it was open, and because it was the first one at which I arrived."

"You're a stranger here?"

"Yes, I make a voyage through the country."

"Your business is . . ."

278

He said, studiedly offhand, "My business? I have none at the moment. I like the country, I like to study the animal life of the fields—the rabbits, hares, the birds, the badgers, stoats, the hard-working moles. These things interest me, monsieur!"

With apparent irrelevance, the man said, "Have you heard that Germany has attacked Russia—on a very wide front?"

Flight managed to hide his surprise and said, lightly enough, "So? I did not know, but, then, I never read the journals."

The man said, "Neither do we here. That Churcheel speaks well. He is magnificent, this man!"

Flight, his voice very low, said, "So *we* think, monsieur."

There was no comment, no explanations were made, none were needed. Flight thought that a common danger quickened men's minds, sharpened men's brains, made them observe and come more rapidly to just conclusions. He finished his beer and found himself talking—not, perhaps, very freely, but without that pretence that "France was finished, the Government was in Vichy, Germany was the overlord of the whole earth!"

They were mostly small tradesmen. One, they told him, was the Mayor, or had held that position before the Occupation; now to be the Mayor only meant additional danger and the chance that you might be made the scapegoat for any misdemeanour, whoever committed it. One man laughed; very subdued, but a laugh all the same. "Not all—jem an' 'ooney—that is what they say in England," he said.

They spoke quietly of what was happening in the world; of the Battle of Britain, of the *Luftwaffe* in Sicily, of the raider *Bismarck*, and of the sinking of the battle-cruiser *Hood*. "But now they fight with a fully prepared nation," said one old man, with a face like well-tanned leather. "There, factories are working. *Mon Dieu*, how they work. True they have had good fortune, they have had Allies who were ready and willing to make sacrifices. *Mes amis*, watch—this day, June 22, 1941—is the beginning of the end!" He was still speaking when the door opened and two men entered, both ordering beer; the old man made no sign that he had seen them enter, but continued, his voice unchanged, "The end," he said, "for unless it is possible for these English to devise some plan by which they can outwit the power of Germany's great land force—and how can they?—then as I say—the end must come."

One of the men drinking his beer said, "Be careful if you talk of military matters, monsieur."

The old man cupped his hand round his ear and said, "Pardon?"

Another man said, "He is terribly deaf, the old one, that is why he always shouts."

They finished their drinks and went out. There was desultory conversation. Then the talk began again. Flight listened, astonished to find out how much they knew. He had thought that at the farmhouse they were fairly well informed, thanks to Shaff's radio set, but these men appeared to know practically as much as they did.

". . . the Iraq oilfield is what he wants, what he must have, if"—the old man was saying, when again the door opened, and he continued, "if you are to have a beast which is fit for hard work. Grass—and he is blown out; hay—well, that's all right—but corn, corn, that is the secret."

The man who had entered held a stick in his hand and tapped his way to a table, where he sat down and, turning his eyes, seemed to seek the direction of the bar. Flight went over to him and said, "Can I help you?"

The man stared a foot to the right of his questioner's face, and answered, "That is kind of you. Perhaps you noticed that I am blind? Yes, I will have a beer, thank you."

A man at the other table said, "You're new to these parts?"

"Yes, I am making my way to my sister—Madame Rombert—you may know her? She married the chemist, Paul Rombert."

They knew the chemist, but they did not know that his wife was expecting her brother, they had heard that he was in hospital at Amiens.

The blind man nodded, "He was, monsieur, until ten days ago. He was wounded in Paris when an explosion occurred. There had been some trouble and punishments were deemed to be necessary. I was there—there I left my sight. There were"—he lowered his voice—"twenty-five French people left dead, some of them small children. It was the punishment judged right for the death of a German major."

Flight heard the low murmur from the little group of men. Like the growl of a furious beast, he thought—dangerous and ugly.

The blind man asked, very humbly and modestly, if he might be allowed to come and sit nearer to them. "When one lives in the dark," he said, "and one has not become accustomed to darkness, it is good to be near other human beings. You permit?"

A huge red-haired man, with hands like hams, brought him over. His eyes were filled with tears and his movements with the blind man were very gentle. "Sit there," he said, "you are with friends."

In a whispering voice, as if he were almost afraid to speak, he told them of things which he had seen and heard; terrible things which made them clench their hands and wipe the sweat from their sunburnt foreheads. They began to talk of their plans, their hopes and fears. One man said that he was in daily communication with his son. "We have a cipher," he said, "on the radio. I have a little set hidden in my cellar. Ah, he is a clever one, that little set. Look, I shall show you the cipher . . ."

He was fumbling in an inside pocket, when

Flight leaned over the table and placed a cigarette between the blind man's lips. "A light?" he said, and as he spoke, flashed before the man's eyes, the glare of a small electric torch. For one brief second the eyes quivered, then steadied again, and the blind man said, "I cannot find the match . . ."

Flight sat down, his hand covering the cipher which the Frenchman had laid on the table. He said, panting a little as if he had been running, "He's not blind, he's—he's an Informer, an Agent!"

The man said, his voice shaking a little, "Monsieur, this is madness! I, an Agent, an Informer! Messieurs, you have listened to what I have said, do I sound like one? Messieurs, you are being not only foolish, but wicked!"

The red-headed man rose. "We'll find out," he said. "Walk out through that door at the back—march!"

"But I cannot see—I tell you that I am blind" —his voice rose, a huge hand was clapped over his face, he was propelled into a room at the back of the shop. The old man with the face like leather rose and followed them, walking slowly, apparently unconcerned. "Continue to talk," he said as he went. "If anyone wants me—I have gone to the closet."

A thin, nervous man said, "It promises to be a hot summer, monsieur. That was very smart of you."

Flight replied, "I have noticed how much hotter

283

the sun has become in the last few days. It was nothing. I saw his eyes flicker. I had my misgivings concerning him."

"They will, no doubt, be settled shortly. We should have a crop that is not too bad, under the circumstances."

They continued to talk. Not one of them appeared to be in the least concerned, their voices were even; the proprietor of the place rose from time to time to supply his customers' needs when they required more beer. Half an hour passed, when the door opened and two troopers entered.

"Has a blind man been here?"

A man answered, "Blind man? What blind man?"

"Making his way to the house of his sister, Madame Rombert."

"I have never heard that Madame Rombert has a blind brother."

"Never mind what you have heard—has he been here?"

Several of them answered, "Not to my knowledge. I have not seen him."

"The Mayor has been here all the evening, ask him!"

"Where is the Mayor?"

"At the moment he is in the closet."

The door opened and the leather-faced man came in, fumbling with the buttons of his trousers. He said, "Well, and what decision have you come to? A good cross, or pure-bred? What pays the

. . ." He stopped and stared at the two soldiers. "Anything wrong?"

"They're looking for a blind man, the brother of Madame Rombert."

"He's not here, my friends. I should look for him at his sister's." He stopped and frowned, asking, "Since when did Mathilde Rombert have a blind brother? This is news to me, and I know the family."

The two men went behind the bar and looked under the counter. The proprietor said, "Whoever he was, he won't be behind my bar, I'd attend to that." Everyone laughed.

They peered into the room at the back. It was pitch dark, and they were obviously not anxious to go farther. Someone called out, "The Mayor has pushed him down the closet!" and there was more laughter.

The soldiers scowled, and as they left, one called over his shoulder:

"You'll laugh on the wrong sides of your ugly faces, some of you!"

Ten minutes later the huge red-headed man came back and sat down. "Ah, a beer, immediately! It is hard work guiding a blind man in the dark."

"Where is he, Aristo?" the Mayor whispered.

"Resting—resting. He wanted a long rest. His nerves were in a shocking state! Well, I drink to—your flash-light, monsieur."

285

5

HE was making fair progress, but he was growing very tired, the constant sense of being on the look out, the vigilance, even when he slept, Flight thought that his ears were open. He slept very lightly, though he was dog-tired. Again and again he was warned not to keep to the road which he had taken, but to go to the right, or to the left, through a wood, or to follow the course of a stream.

His thoughts began, he felt, to take a definite shape, and this frightened him, because he feared that they might divert his mind from his plan of reaching Paris. They seemed to walk beside him sometimes slowly and heavily, at others hurrying, walking so fast that they outstripped him. He tried to think, gravely, in a business-like way, of his Gallery in Bond Street. Once he was back he would have it repainted, the walls hung with a very soft buff—which was really neither buff nor yellow, but a combination of both. He might even be forced to have the material dyed specially for him—well, that could be done. The carpet would want renewing, it had been down a long time; and even when he left—when *had* he last seen it—in September 1939—nearly two years ago, it had been showing signs of wear then. It must be very shabby by now.

The Gallery, shining with new paint and softly coloured walls. Rusmere might lend him some of his French pictures? He could obtain others and have a French exhibition, "By kind permission of the Earl of Rusmere". They'd have a rather formal but very friendly opening. Cocktails, tea, coffee, and tiny sandwiches. Alicia would be there, wearing . . .

It was at this point that he began to be afraid. Thoughts of Alicia disturbed him too badly. He could half-close his eyes, as he lay hidden during the hot bright days waiting for the evening, and see her so plainly. Alicia greeting people, "How nice to see you," and, "It is really a charming exhibition, yes!" That was all right, it was when the other thoughts intruded that the pain and fear began. London—air raids on eighty-two nights out of eighty-five—intensive bombing—fear of invasion. "A possible invasion". Danger everywhere, impending danger, present danger. Directed against women and children, old people and cripples. Alicia believing him dead. Heartbroken, driven frantic through lack of news. He clenched his hands, the sweat standing on his face, running down into his mouth, tasting salt on his lips.

Wherever his thoughts ran, they always reached Alicia. They might begin with his father, with Hitler, with the Russian front, but they always ended in the same away. He never escaped from them. When he began to walk in the cool evening, through the soft half-light, treading softly but, remembering Pierre's instructions, never furtively, those thoughts moved along at his side. Sometimes he actually stopped, and hoped that the thoughts would move forward alone and leave him, but when he began to walk again, he always caught them up, and again they fell into step beside him.

Sometimes he would repeat, as a kind of litany, all Pierre's instructions. They had been given to him in the very early days when he had first begun to hobble about in the farmhouse.

Never move furtively. Make as little noise as possible, but never appear to be afraid of being seen. Never run, unless as a last resort. Never adopt an affectation which you are not certain that you can maintain. Never use an assumed voice. Shun wigs, false beards and such things. Always remember your name and all particulars that you have learned. How often had he repeated them over and over, those and many more. Small things, points which were apparently so unimportant and yet upon the observance of them might depend not only your life, but the life of your friends.

Maurice had said to him once, "It is not a bad thing to whistle. It keeps up your spirits, and makes other people believe that you have not an anxiety in the world; but—my friend, be careful what it is that you whistle."

That was what he forgot to remember.

He was travelling by day, walking along a narrow and very dusty lane. The sun was high, the sky cloudless, and the hedgerows were white with dust. He felt better. Paris was drawing nearer, and for the first time he remembered Susanne Matot in a concrete fashion, recalling her not only as a name, but as a woman he had known, a woman who had charmed him and talked to him, in a long, quiet room with wine-coloured curtains.

A room that looked out on the white expanse of the Champs Elysées. A woman who had acted so beautifully that she had made an indifferent French comedy seem entrancing. A woman who, when all was said and done, was English like himself. He was going to see her. With each step Paris drew nearer—the golden towers of Notre Dame, the bridges spanning the river; the Madeleine, the Vendôme Column, the flowers at the street corners, the newspaper kiosks—everything that went to make up—Paris. He began to whistle. He whistled a song of Mistinguett's about Paris—a gay, rioting kind of song; he whistled "Roll out the barrel" and was so pleased with it that he whistled it through twice; he whistled "September" and "Thanks for the memory"—this, very sentimentally and long drawn-out. He remembered a record he had of that song, sung by Greta Keller; and on the other side, another song he had liked, "These foolish things remind me of you". He remembered another song and grinned because it seemed applicable to himself on that bright morning in June, "The best things in life are free!"

He sat down by the side of the road, took a piece of bread and a bit of rather stale cheese from his pocket and began to eat it. It might be stale, the bread might be—and was undoubtedly—very dry, but it tasted good, and in the grass he found some sorrel leaves and munched them too; they were crisp and cold and faintly acid.

Suddenly from behind him came a voice, and turning he found himself staring into the face of a man who stood behind him, a man wearing a service cap, very high in the front, with a rimless eyeglass screwed into one of his pale blue eyes.

The voice said, "Allow me to wish you a very good morning, Mr. Whistler! Where is your dog? In the song, is it not correct, it is 'The whistler and his dog', yes?"

For a split second he was on the point of answering, "Who the devil are you?" when he remembered, and said in French, "I do not understand," and rising to his feet watched the man with the eyeglass. With him were two German soldiers.

The officer smiled, not too pleasantly. "How do you come these English songs to know so well?"

Flight said, "Please?" for the officer continued to speak English.

He spoke again, this time in guttural French. "These English songs. How is it that you know them?"

"English? No, American," Flight said.

"You speak English?"

"Spik Eensleesh?" Flight smiled engagingly.

"Oh, yes—ver' mooch. 'Ow do you do! Good nite! Yes, no?"

The other said, "You can't make a fool of me. Stay where you are." Then to his men, "Take him along!"

They made him march between them, while the officer walked in front and as he walked, he whistled a new song which Flight had never heard, and which he felt, had the circumstances been more favourable, he would have liked very much indeed. As it was, his mind was twisting and turning. He was cursing himself for a fool. He had every opportunity of making a survey of the officer. He was tall, very slim, with a beautiful waist and broad shoulders; his legs were very long, his hips narrow, his hair—what there was of it, for it was cropped very short—was fair and inclined to wave where it had grown a little. Altogether, Flight thought, he was a pleasant-looking fellow, and when he turned and took a long look at his prisoner, Flight saw that in spite of his rimless eyeglass, his face was intelligent and fairly good-humoured. Only the small pouting mouth betrayed him.

They reached the barracks, a small place— evidently a place either for rest or special exercises.

The officer halted, coming to a standstill like a machine when the brake is applied suddenly. "Bring him to my room!"

Flight's eyes, trained to observe, decided that this good-looking German with the full, pouting mouth was probably the officer-in-charge. He might have a couple of lieutenants under him, not more. The place didn't hold, he judged, more than a couple of hundred men. He was pushed into a room—half office, half bedroom. A smell of expensive scent hung about the place. At the farther end of the room, which was fairly large, stood a bed—a good, very comfortable French bed, covered with a magnificent embroidered shawl. The pillows were both in silk covers of pale blue silk. Two colour prints, their subjects being of bedroom interior, with women showing a good deal of lace-trimmed peignoirs, and gallants in wigs and satin "small clothes", palpably lost in admiration.

Flight looked, noted and thought, "Loot! So that's his choice, is it?"

The officer was removing his tunic and his batman handed him a velvet jacket, much frogged, and also a huge silver and gilt cigarette-box. He stretched, yawned and said, "Search him!"

One of the soldiers placed his papers and odds and ends on the desk. The officer turned them over disdainfully with an over-manicured finger.

"Nothing else?"

"Nothing, sir."

"Go! Wait outside. I will interrogate him."

Heels clicked, and like a pair of mechanical figures they went out.

"You too, Fritz, get out! Oh, give me a drink first." He spoke for the first time to Flight, "Would you like me to offer you a drink?"

"You are too kind, sir!"

"Give him one, too." He laughed. "Amusing to think of my offering you a drink, eh? Cognac and seltz, eh?"

"I shall be grateful, sir."

They were left alone. The young man removed his eyeglass, polished it with immense care. Flight wondered if he didn't see just as well without it?

"And now"—he referred to the papers—"you are François Pascal. You are twenty-three. Born in 1918. As I was myself. A fateful year for the world—to unthinking people; fateful for the Fatherland, to thinking persons—possibly more fateful for other nations, eh?"

"It may be possible."

"A traveller in office equipment." He picked up a pencil which lay on his desk and offered it to Flight. "What would you have charged for that before the war—for a dozen?"

The pencil was octagonal, green, bearing the words *Venus—made in England 2B.*

Flight shook his head. "This is a line that I have never sold," he said. "I imagine—it is a good pencil—possibly, to retail, at five francs? To sell wholesale"—he weighed the pencil in his hand and frowned.

The other watched him with silent amusement. Suddenly he put out his hand and took the pencil, laying it down carefully.

"Now," he said briskly. "Let us stop play-acting. You act very well, but I have seen you

293

before. Oh, yes! I well remember you in London. You are an art dealer in Bond Street. You showed an exhibition of drawings by Leonardo da Vinci. Very admirable it was, too."

"Not quite correct," Flight said. "A *picture* dealer. Other forms of Art I leave to antique dealers—Gollantz, for example."

"And is it indiscreet to ask what you are doing wandering about France, calling yourself François Pascal?"

Flight bowed. "Most indiscreet, sir."

"Ah!" The small full mouth hardened. "And yet it will save us both trouble if you tell me."

"I regret it is impossible."

"Then"—briskly—"I shall be forced to believe the worst."

"In a censorious world, that is not unusual, is it?"

"Possibly not . . ."

"And yet," Flight said reflectively, "it is a provincial trait." He was enjoying himself. The chair in which he sat was comfortable, the brandy and soda excellent; he even found pleasure in the conversation. If he were really caught, if this was the ending to it all, well—he could at least extract what enjoyment he might from the incident. He had rarely felt more free from care than he did at this moment.

The blue eyes opposite to him narrowed in annoyance.

"One scarcely calls Berlin provincial."

"To be provincial," Flight replied, enjoying the ease with which stilted phrases came to him, "is a matter of mentality, not geography. You agree, surely?"

The officer rose, he bowed stiffly. "My name is von Ludbach." He added, "Baron von Ludbach."

Flight also rose and said, "Mine is Percival Melton of the Melton Galleries, Bond Street, London."

"That I knew already. I never forget either faces or names. It has escaped your memory that I bought a small etching from you, of a street in London, by one Joseph Pennell. I have the receipt still at home. The paper is blue, with lettering in a darker shade."

Flight thought. "Some of our old paper. How useful that it was not the new lot, with my own name added."

Von Ludbach waved his hand towards the colour prints. "What do you imagine is the value of those?" he asked.

"Am I being asked to give a valuation? I usually ask a fee."

"*Usually*, you are not a prisoner," the other returned.

"You're right." Flight examined the prints. They were good, but not outstandingly so. Slewing his eyes round so that he could catch sight of the other's face, he tried to estimate how much he really knew. The face was attentive, the lips pursed a little, but he did not appear to understand clearly what Flight was looking for, or to show any great knowledge of the prints themselves.

He hazarded, "I fancy that they have been cut?"

"Cut? They have not been touched. That is how I—found them, just as they are now."

Flight returned to his chair and gave a short and carefully incorrect account of the prints. He declared that they had been printed in Paris, and added a brief summary of the artist's career and works. From time to time the German jotted down notes in a small, blue leather-covered book which he produced from a drawer. He nodded and appeared to show every satisfaction.

"When the world is normal once more," Flight said, "I will willingly offer you—let's see—twenty guineas for each of those."

Again the amount was jotted down. Von Ludbach looked up smiling. "When the world is normal again, my friend, you will be in no position to offer twenty pence for anything! Remember that, will you?"

Quite unexpectedly, he called for the soldiers to re-enter. He ordered them to take the prisoner away and bring him back again in two hours' time. "You can give him something to eat," he added.

His eyeglass caught the light and gleamed, harshly, as he looked at Flight. "They won't hurt you. Later, I wish to see you again. I shall have a proposition to make to you."

If the soldiers did not treat him with much civility, at least they did not ill-treat him; he was put into a small room which was empty except for a table and chair, he was given a plate of coarse and very greasy stew, with a hunk of bread and some thin, substitute coffee. That eaten, he folded his arms on the table and wondered what fate held in store for him.

To his surprise he was not unduly frightened. Vaguely he wondered if people always felt like this when they were liable to face a firing squad at any moment? He didn't trust that smiling face with the "petted" mouth and the blue eyes. The fellow was what he would describe as a "nasty bit of work". Though exactly why he was "nasty", Flight would have been hard put to say. He went to the small barred window and looked out. Before him stretched a wide expanse of fields; almost flat country which continued to the skyline. There would be precious few places in which to hide, even if he contrived to get away; and as the window was barely a foot square, escape in that direction would be almost impossible. The door was an ordinary enough one, made of wood. The key did not appear to be anything except the average type. The floor was of wooden planks. He peered out of the window again and discovered that the whole building was raised above the ground to a height of possibly eighteen inches. His spirits rose again. Provided they gave him time, escape might lie below the floor-boards.

Later the soldiers came for him and took him again to the room of von Ludbach. The captain was still wearing his velvet frogged smoking-jacket, to which he had now added a pair of trousers, heavily braided down the seams to match. Round his neck was a wide white collar of Byronic pattern, and a large flowing silk tie of canary yellow.

He nodded towards the chair. Flight sat down and eyed the immense box of cigarettes. The captain pushed it towards him and dismissed the soldiers. He lit Flight's cigarette and his own. Then, leaning back, his elegant legs crossed in a negligent manner, swinging a beautifully-shod foot, he announced, "I am about to make a bargain with you, Melton."

Flight thought, "Damn it! I've just learnt to think of myself as Pascal! Now I'm Percival—a name I've always disliked—Melton."

"I admit that such a statement is unusual. Among people of your own class—tradesmen—it would be unusual; coming from me, Baron von Ludbach, an officer in the Army of the Reich, it is astonishing. Pray give me your complete attention. Help yourself to cigarettes, if it will serve to hold your attention on what I am about to say. I should wish you to regard this as confidential."

Flight drew a long stream of smoke into his lungs, expelled it, and answered, "As one gentleman to another, you may rely on me."

The small full mouth pursed suddenly, then von Ludbach continued. He was on work of National Importance, he explained. One which had been given to him by a person of such importance that in all probability there was only one person greater in the whole of the civilised world. This personage, it appeared, was a collector of Art in many forms; particularly was his taste inclined towards pictures, but only such as were of real and great value.

"It may be," von Ludbach smirked suddenly, "that in my great anxiety to please this great personage, I over-rated my knowledge of the Art to which he is devoted. Naturally, as a man of taste and education, I know what is good. That is understood. But when by several works of Art, all good, I am confronted, I admit that my judgement is not faultless. Good—let it be acknowledged, as witness these *objets d'art* here in my room." He waved his hand, indicating the contents of the room.

His work was to search for Beauty. The phrase pleased him and he repeated it several times. "The search for Beauty, Beauty which will enhance the treasure-troves of the Fatherland, Beauty which will enable the people of Germany to enjoy even more fully the beauty of the world's Great Masters. I have been sent to search for Beauty!"

Flight, taking a second cigarette, for they were excellent, murmured, "A profound and exquisite thought."

The French, he told Flight, had proved themselves to be the same selfish, hoarding, greedy wretches that they had been down the ages. Instead of throwing open their doors, instead of allowing the conquerors to select the best of what they had, so parsimonious were they, that they had hidden these treasures in cellars, had buried them in their gardens! Von Ludbach raised his hands to heaven as if appealing against such baseness. It was his proud duty to find, discover, and select these works of Art; the majority to be sent to museums, galleries, and so on in Germany. A few—the most exclusive and beautiful—were to be laid aside for the private enjoyment of that splendid connoisseur, that master of taste—his Patron.

"Not of necessity the largest," he explained. "It does not matter if the picture is quite small, the importance lies in the fact that it must be of a complete uniqueness. You understand me?"

Again he referred to his lack of what he called "specialist's or tradesmen's taste". Take, for example, what happened two days ago. He had found two pictures by Watteau—he pronounced it "Vatto"—and admitted that had his life depended upon it, he could not have said which was the better.

"Naturally, my mind has been devoted to other and possibly greater issues," he explained.

Now Melton was his prisoner, he had the power of life and death in his hands. There was no doubt that Melton was a spy, he was willing to take the risk, he would have no opportunity of spying here. If he tried to do so—he gave a spirited and amusing imitation of a man being hanged. When he went on his "voyages of discovery" in search of Beauty he proposed to take Melton with him. Melton would give his knowledge, his experience, in exchange for his life, yes? He would be kindly treated, fed, and given a good bed on which to lie.

"And when you have finished with me?" Flight asked, taking his third cigarette and lighting with a gold automatic lighter which lay on the desk.

Von Ludbach shrugged his shoulders. "That will depend. It might even be possible that my illustrious Patron might see fit to employ you in his own home. To arrange, to catalogue. If not—it is difficult to say . . ."

"Oh, I agree, very difficult. Well, Baron, this all sounds most interesting, but how can I go with you, an important officer, wearing these clothes? They are all I have. I do not even possess a suit of pyjamas."

"That will be arranged for. First, I must have your assurance, your word, your sacred promise that you will take the best—and only the best?"

With his brain racing like a steamer's screw out of water, Flight was thinking rapidly. Somewhere, in his sub-conscious mind, an idea was evolving, a plan being formulated. He frowned, tapped with his fingers on the desk top, then said, "I promise to take the best and only the best."

"Your word of honour?"

"My word of honour."

"I shall not always require you. There are times when a gentleman company does not desire, you understand. On such days you will be able to go through the small collection which I have already made—ha, ha!—you will not find the taste of von Ludbach too bad, I fancy. These in due time I shall take to Paris, where to the home of my Patron they will be despatched. Tomorrow we shall a beginning make, no?"

"I am all anxiety to begin."

The white, manicured hand was waved again. "I give you leave to ask for what you want. We are generous, we wish to make everything smooth and as pleasant as possible. These swine of French refuse this to completely understand. I doubt sometimes even if the Vichy Government altogether comprehends. The inevitable must be bowed to. Germany has been destined through the ages the Mother of Nations to become. Once the world understands this fact—for fact it is—then we shall live in peace again under the beneficent rule of our beloved Leader."

Earnestly, Flight said, "Baron, you must convince me. You have shaken me, I admit—conviction will come more slowly."

The Baron rose and laid his plump hand on Flight's shoulder. He said in a curiously gentle voice, "My friend, you are terribly thin . . ."

The days went past. Flight had been measured by the tailor attached to the detachment. He now had several very good suits, two of which bore the label of well-known Parisian tailors. He had shoes of elegant cut, silk socks, ties in plenty—several of which were from Sulka's—his shirts were made of expensive silk although the embroidered monograms on the left breast were none of them the same, two were surmounted by coronets. He sat night after night with von Ludbach and slowly told him many things. He said that he began to realise that these Frenchmen in the underground movement were actually hindering the cause of Peace rather than assisting it. Von Ludbach examined his notes and asked questions regarding a number of people. "There is a priest. He has many disguises, but he is a priest all the same," he said. "The name is Maurice. Do you know anything of his whereabouts, Melton?"

Flight hesitated, pinched his lower lip between his finger and thumb, then answered, "He is not a priest. He is really 'Chienot'. He is in Paris, or was, until a short time ago. I met him on the road, he was travelling with an old man who had a donkey cart."

"*Ach*, so!" Again notes were made; in a red-covered book this time.

"And another—with a terrible name—Shot, no, Schaft . . ."

"You don't mean Shaff?"

"That is the name."

"He is in Italy, somewhere near Palma."

Again the gold pencil recorded the facts.

So it went on. Very rarely did Flight admit that he knew nothing of this person or that. His memory was incredible, his facts precise and useful.

Day after day they visited the old houses in the district, and there Flight saw another side of the German's character. The smoothness, the smile, vanished; and in its place there stood an overbearing, implacable servant of the Third Reich. The eyes narrowed, the whole figure grew still and unyielding, the jaw looked as if there was iron lying beneath the fresh, well-shaved skin.

He saw doors broken down, locks smashed under the heel of soldiers' boots, he saw old ladies dragged away from some room which they would have protected, watched loved possessions flung hither and thither, while women wailed and men bit their lips to keep back the words which rose to them. The soldiers dragged out everything which might be of value. Furs, old lace, silver, china and glass were all piled on the tables before von Ludbach, who delicately and thoughtfully went through them.

"Jewels!" he would shout suddenly, raising his eyes from a piece of lace which, apparently, had been absorbing his attention completely. "Jewels! You have some, don't lie! This lace, this glass and silver—though there must be more silver than these miserable pieces—where are the jewels?"

"Many," some old man would stammer, "have already been taken."

"You accuse the German Army of robbery? They have taken them—so! Show me your

304

receipts! I am a German officer, I know that no German ever takes anything, however small, however worthless, without either paying for it or giving a receipt." He would turn to Flight and say in German, "What incredible liars these French swine are, no?"

From whatever was found, he would select what pleased him, making his sergeant—who wrote with difficulty and spelt everything incorrectly—give receipts on odd bits of paper, on which von Ludbach scrawled his name. Sometimes he would fling a piece of old brocade, a piece of silk or lace, to one of his soldiers, saying, "Send that back to your wife, to prove that the Army is not wasting its time."

Flight watching the faces of the French, saw pain, astonishment, fear. But always, in addition, a dreadful, cold hatred. To see their treasures, kept so carefully, laid away among sweet-smelling herbs, dragged from their drawers and chests, was something horrible to them, something which stank of violation.

Once when von Ludbach held a pair of beautifully embroidered sheets in his hands, smiling as he felt their smooth softness, an old lady cried, "Monsieur, do not take those, I beg you. Leave those . . ."

The single eyeglass swung round in the well-shaven face, the small mouth smiled, "Why particularly not these, Madame?"

The old lady twisted her thin hands together,

she was shaking as she spoke. "My mother lay in them when she was prepared for her burial, and—last year they covered my son, when he, too, died."

"And you want them," said von Ludbach very gently, "to cover you too, Madame, when you die? Is this so?"

She nodded, making a pathetic attempt to smile as if to excuse her weakness, whispering, "Yes, monsieur, yes!"

He crumpled the sheets into a bundle and flung them to a soldier. "Too bad," he said, "you'll have to lie in another pair. I want these—and not to cover dead bodies, either."

When it came to the pictures, a few of which were still hanging on the walls, though the best had to be searched for—in cellars, hidden in lofts, behind huge wardrobes, even under floor-boards, he would beckon to Flight.

"You see, how just the Germans are?" he would explain to the French. "We even bring a tradesman who buys and sells pictures, to see which are good and which are worthless. So—kindly observe, you really get a valuation for nothing."

It had not taken Flight long to discover that the Baron's knowledge of pictures was remarkably slight. Names he could reel off by the score, he even had some idea as to what style of picture the various great painters had produced, but anything more complicated left him completely at sea. He had some elementary knowledge of German and

Dutch painters, even less of the English school; but of French and Italian painters—with the exception of da Vinci and Tintoretto—he knew nothing. He would watch Flight examining a picture, his pink face assuming—so Flight always thought—the expression of a child who admires, but cannot comprehend, what its elders are doing.

At first, there was a risk, and Flight knew it. What if the German did really know more than he admitted? What if he were tricking his prisoner into making mistakes; far more, what if he realised that this "tradesman" was tricking him?

Flight insisted upon having a book for his receipts, one of which was given to the owner of the picture, the other he retained. At night when he, as he said, "made up his books", and von Ludbach laughed and said, "Ah, the old tricks of the shopkeeper die hard!" Flight made out a third receipt, which he retained and hid away in the lining of the very fine hideskin suitcase which von Ludbach had given him.

"It is a very beautiful case," he said when he gave it to Flight, "but I prefer to give no presents at all if they are not of an excellence." The fact that the case was stamped, as were the remaining silver fittings, with the initials "F. DE B." and surmounted by a coronet, did not detract from von Ludbach's pleasure in making such a magnificent gift.

Slowly, as Flight grew more certain of himself, he found a considerable amount of amusement in this inspection of pictures. Once when they visited a very old château, he stood before a particularly ugly painting of an old man, inscribing something on a sheet of parchment. The colour was poor, but the background was dark, and relieved by small patterns in dull gold. He turned sharply to the owner and asked in French who was the artist? The Frenchman, his eyes filled with cold hate, answered that he did not know. No one in particular; he had the picture from his great-uncle.

"And where did he live, this great-uncle?" Flight asked.

"Near Strasbourg, monsieur."

"A-ah! And you do not value the picture highly?"

"I do not consider that it merits great admiration."

Flight laughed and called von Ludbach over to him, drawing him nearer to the picture. He whispered, "Look—if you please! How incisive the work, and yet how sweet. Observe the background, which holds something of the best Italian workmanship. These French, they make one laugh! 'It does not merit admiration.'"

Von Ludbach swung backwards and forwards on his toes. "The style to me is familiar—familiar—and yet I am unable to give a name—tch, how foolish of me!"

Flight whispered, "You remember in Dresden —yes, a portrait of two ambassadors? Another of the English King, Henry the Eighth? Holbein."

He rejected a fairly good Rigaud and, examining the pictures which had been unearthed in the cellar, found a small Boucher, which he carefully cut out of its frame, and, being alone, hid it between his own waistcoat and shirt. It was so obviously good. The subject, a woman reclining, showed so much of her lovely figure that he felt certain if he did not take it some German would. The ugly painting of the old gentleman was carried in triumph to the waiting car. Von Ludbach kept repeating, "A Holbein . . . what joy for my dear Patron! A Holbein!"

He began to realise that the owners of the various châteaus eyed him curiously. He mentioned the fact to von Ludbach, who smiled affably and said, "These French pigs, they all have the minds of shopkeepers! They are surprised at the efficiency of the Germans who bring a shopkeeper to beat them at their own game."

One afternoon, when von Ludbach was devoting considerable time to sorting out the best of some moderately good tapestries, he sent Flight with the owner of the château to look at pictures. The man was old and very thin, he looked as if he might be made of white paper. His manner was cold and resigned. He showed Flight what he had, saying, "Not very many—and not even very good, monsieur."

"Any German pictures?"

The thin lips curved into a sneer. *"L'école allemande est médiocre dans l'histoire de l'art—as* you, being a connoisseur, know well, monsieur."

Flight stooped to examine an old chest, the whole place was very dusty. He made marks in the dust with his finger-tips saying, "This place wants dusting. It is filthy—look!" Very rapidly he wrote, "Men are not always what they seem," then quickly sat down and moved, as if he watched a picture on the opposite wall, moving slightly from side to side, until he was certain that the words were obliterated.

Slowly they began to trust him. They were clever, they spoke to him in the same cold voices, their lips were as tightly compressed, but more than once he went back to the camp with frameless pictures lying under his waistcoat, pictures which were hidden immediately in the lining of his aristocratic suitcase.

Once when he had left as worthless, or "indifferent copies", an Ingres, two beautiful little Watteaus, and a very fine David, shrugging his shoulders and assuring von Ludbach that this bore out his contention that the French had no real individual taste, but merely bought what dealers told them to buy, von Ludbach replied, with his usual charm of manner, "You should understand that—eh, my shopkeeper?"

An old man, gross, with a huge nose shot with tiny purple veins, said, "Kommandant, your assistant has taught me a great deal, and I am grateful. Would you allow me to present to him—a gift, you understand—a copy which my aunt made of a Dutch flower painting?"

Flight said, "I believe that the old beggar is being rude."

"Possibly not, they have no sense of fine manners. You may take it if you like. It cannot be worth anything or no Frenchman would give it away. Yes, accept it."

The picture was very bad. It was small, about eighteen inches by twelve, the painting was crude, the colouring poor and muddy. It was signed with elaborate care, in red paint, *Louise Meriville*.

Von Ludbach laughed. "And what are you going to give me, monsieur?"

The old man shrugged his shoulders. "There is nothing left of sufficient value to give you, Kommandant."

That night, with his door locked—for the concession had been granted to him that he might lock his own door, being warned, "There is always a guard at the end of the passage, remember!"— Flight examined the picture again. He turned it over and over. There was nothing of interest on either front or back. Carefully he took the picture from its frame and there lay a second picture—a woman's head and shoulders. A beautiful woman, beautifully painted. It was grimed, but through the dirt he could see the brilliant colours and delicate treatment of the dress, the fine hands, the loving attention that had been given to every detail. He sat back on his heels, holding the picture almost tenderly, from time to time wetting the tip of a finger and rubbing gently so that some new colour might blaze out. He turned it over. There on a small, age-stained piece of paper was written, *François Clouet—Madeleine de Mèdicis*. And below it a more modern script, *Our thanks. We understand.*

6

LIFE, Flight reflected, was not altogether unpleasant. He had been wrong when he assumed that von Ludbach had other junior officers serving under him. The man was alone, and, what was more, he did not like being alone. At first Flight wrote him down as a fairly intelligent, in a limited fashion, very ordinary, overbearing young German; then slowly his opinion changed. There was something definitely unpleasant about the fellow. He was too fond of laying his white, plump hand on your shoulder, and leaving it there. He had a trick of staring at you with his blue eyes half-closed, as if he tried to sum you up correctly, and failed to do so completely.

Other things Flight noticed. Amongst them that half a dozen of the soldiers were of a recognisable type, they had high-pitched voices, and giggled inanely. One was von Ludbach's own servant. Flight saw him displaying some fine silk underwear to his friends, and when he ventured to say to von Ludbach, "D'you think that servant of yours is completely honest? He's got some remarkably luxurious underwear for a private soldier!" the other stared at him, then said, "Fritz? honest as the day! I gave them to him. His own smelt so unpleasant. I must have servants who conform to my somewhat fastidious sense of cleanliness."

Then one day Fritz was sent to Paris, and did not return. Von Ludbach asked Flight if he would care to take on his work?

Flight said, "What—be your batman? Not particularly, why?"

"Fritz has gone and I hate soldiers who breathe heavily, who smell, who have dirty hands . . ."

"Find one who has been taught to breathe properly! See that he takes baths and washes his hands . . ."

Von Ludbach twisted his shoulders irritably. "Oh, you are obtuse!"

He began to ask Flight into his room to dine; the food was good, for he had discovered an old chef in a large house near by, and as he said, "requisitioned" him. The old man hated the Germans and made no attempt to conceal his dislike, but he was too fine an artist not to cook to the very best of his ability, and the best of his ability was very good indeed.

They were excellent dinners in the small dining-room which led off von Ludbach's bedroom and office. On the walls hung some of the less revolting pictures over which Flight had gone into raptures. Von Ludbach admired particularly an astonishingly good, and astonishingly gross, copy of a Rubens, concerning which he made remarks from time to time of a very frank and personal nature.

He drank a good deal of the French wines which he had found in cellars, and at such times became

314

expansive at first, then sentimental, and later offensive. Flight had learnt to watch the development of all three phases. He had an excellent memory and had invented a cipher for himself, an elaboration of one which Pierre had taught him. In this he wrote many facts relating to the German Army, to life in Germany, the characters of men who bore great names in that country, and of the ultimate aims of the "Great Leader".

From the first stage the German passed to one in which he sank into a slightly drunken melancholy, giving vent to long-drawn and, to Flight, completely artificial sighs.

"The life of an officer in a post such as mine, an officer who is recognised as being destined for very high positions, is often very lonely. What friends can I make here? I am sufficiently broad-minded to recognise that you were forced to fight on the side of the British. I loathe the British, I distrust them, I despise them—yet, I could make a friend of you. Friendship is a glorious thing, real, true, lasting friendship. Don't you agree, Per-ci-val?"

Flight, astonished at his own bluntness, for all his life he had disliked wounding the susceptibilities of anyone, however little he cared for them, said, "Our friendship wouldn't last long. We belong to different worlds—they'll be even more different when this war ends."

He pressed gifts on Flight, immense silver cigarette-boxes, a large ring with a fine engraved stone set in it, a heavy gold bangle, a beautiful ivory knife and so forth. Flight always refused, saying, "What use are they to me? People will only think that I have looted them."

"Why do you say like that . . ." he imitated Flight's inflection, 'they will think that *I* have looted them'?"

"Because that is what they will think."

"And who are 'they'?"

"Your friends—or for that matter, possibly mine, if I ever get back to them."

"Back to them and your nice picture shop in London! You dare to talk to me, to Baron von Ludbach! I could have you shot as a spy at any hour—do you know that? I have the power of Life and Death! It is part of the godlike quality given to every German Officer of the Third Reich. You imagine, little pig tradesman, that because I condescend to eat with you sometimes, because I . . ." and a great deal more in the same strain, until finally he would shout, "Go! get out of my sight! It may be that tomorrow morning you will be dead mutton."

Flight would walk out quietly and shut himself in his room, and wonder where it was all going to end.

The next day von Ludbach would sulk, sulk in a dignified, aloof way, addressing Flight rather less cordially than he would have done his servant; making heavy-handed remarks about his dislike of the British, and commenting upon how badly matters were going for them in the war. Then

316

towards evening he would send for Flight, and offer him cigarettes and wine, invite him to dinner, and stare at him mournfully in silence.

Once he sighed deeply and said, "I am very unhappy!"

"Why should you be unhappy?" Flight asked. "You've got everything you want—you're free to go where you wish."

The other shook his head, "*Ach*, no! I am bound by invisible chains."

"Break them, then!"

Again that long-drawn gusty sigh, and the scent of toothpaste was wafted across the table to where Flight sat. Von Ludbach was very clean, always bathing, and using boxes and boxes of expensive talcum and good French scents—he preferred Chanel's "Russian Leather".

"Alas, there are some chains, chains of fine, light gold which one could never have it in one's heart to break."

Piously Flight ejaculated, "Good God!"

Von Ludbach sighed deeply, then said in a tone of beautiful patience and tolerance, "You don't understand. Why should you? What do you learn of the good and the beautiful in your cold island."

Flight said shortly, "I doubt if it's any colder than your own country."

"I was thinking of mental things, of a mental atmosphere. You are a cold people, cold because you fear experiences, dread knowledge. The finer, more subtle sides of life are unknown to you. In

317

Germany, that great strong, kindly mother of nations, love of beauty, courage, the joy of youth are cultivated, taught as part of the magnificent system under which our people live and prosper."

One night he was drunk. He carried his drink badly, though he could drink a good deal without it showing on him; then suddenly, without warning, you knew that he was drunk.

This particular evening he asked Flight if he cared for reading.

"When I can get anything to read, yes."

He rose and went, swaying, to a cupboard, returning with half a dozen paper-covered volumes which he laid on the table.

"I have books here for you to read," he said. "They are amusing. I have heard my great Patron speak of them all with admiration. Take them, and have pleasant dreams."

Flight lay on his bed and opened the first of the paperbound books. He read a couple of pages, frowning, then closed the book and took up another. They were all the same—crude, intolerably stupid, coarse—and revolting. Flight returned them the next day.

Von Ludbach looked up eagerly. "*Ach!* you have read them?"

"I read some of those when I was fourteen. My father found them and gave me the only hiding I ever had from him. I've grown out of thinking them even amusing now."

"But surely they . . ."

318

"If you meant me to read them as if I were taking an aphrodisiac, it didn't work!"

Von Ludbach shivered. "My dear Percival, how crudely you put things. I have always said that you and your nation have no sense of delicacy."

Flight experienced suddenly a feeling of desperate hate. He was no prude, neither was he ignorant of life in its less conventional demonstrations. He had known men of every type; types which did not conform to his own, but for whom he had a liking and respect because he felt that, no matter what was the way of life which they had chosen to follow, they were honest with themselves, and they observed a decent reticence concerning themselves.

Now watching this exquisite, well-washed, slightly scented German, he felt as if he were in close proximity to a snake which was doing its best to inject the poison which it carried into his veins. He longed to drive his fist into the well-shaved face, even if in doing so he would sign his own death warrant.

As he spoke, he realised that his breath was coming in gasps, that his whole body was shaking.

"Delicacy!" he repeated, "I don't pretend to have any. I'm a typical British bully. I hit people when they annoy me. Hit them hard or kick them even harder. Oh, I know that you have 'the power of Life and Death'—well, I don't give a damn! I'm sick of all your hints, and sighs and nonsense. It's not even a real sentiment. It's fake, d'you hear,

319

fake. It's part of your system, that is an elaborate fake too. You're cheap sensationalists, tasters, samplers! I've done wrong to take your meals, your presents, in allowing myself to smoke your cigarettes. I've let myself down badly. But I have the grace to feel ashamed of myself at least. You stand there with your mouth lolling open, and admiration—yes, blast it, *admiration* in your stupid face because I am daring to tell you what I think of you!

"I don't really mind being called a tradesman, a shopkeeper commercially minded; I don't really give a damn if you think that the British are *effete*, and finished and utterly brainless. I don't care, d'you understand? It doesn't matter to me because it's not true! Get that, it's not true! But when you insult my 'shopkeeper's' intelligence by giving me your trashy pornographic books to read, when you try to get sentimental and look unutterable things—and you only succeed in looking damned silly incidentally—I won't stand for it!

"If I have any more of your hints and nonsense I'll give you the finest hiding you've ever had in your life—and if you have me shot the next morning, all right, I'll console myself with the thought that mine hasn't been a wasted life! And while I'm on this subject, I don't like being called 'Per-ci-val' as if the name, which I've never liked, was something good to eat. Now remember all that—or I'll rip the hide off you, I'll only just-not-kill you, you nasty stinking sensation-monger."

320

He met von Ludbach's eyes, they were filled with admiration, his whole expression showed deep and intense interest. Flight felt, suddenly, rather like a balloon which has been unexpectedly pricked.

He said sharply, "Well?"

Von Ludbach drew a deep breath. His voice when he spoke was charged with deep feeling.

"I have never admired you so much. What a magnificent person you are! Caring nothing for death or danger . . ."

Flight said, "Don't be so infernally silly. I care a great deal about death, I don't want to die in the least and I loathe danger in any form, believe me."

"Ah, but that challenge which you flung out! Your indictment of the German system, the magnificent air with which you uttered those harsh words. They were untrue, that is the fault of the lies which have been instilled into your minds by the enemies of the Fatherland. Believe me, we are generous, we Germans. We never fear to recognise courage when we meet it. It may be founded on error, but such is the fineness of our intelligence that we recognise it, we admire it. Oh, you are so convinced in the righteousness of what you say and feel, so brave, so strong—so—so admirable!"

Flight almost stamped with rage. Here he had insulted the fellow, called him every opprobrious name to which he could lay his tongue, and he had only succeeded in calling down upon himself a sentimental eulogy which would have done credit to a schoolgirl.

He said miserably, "Oh, I give it up!"

Back in his own room, seated on the reasonably comfortable chair which von Ludbach had given him—saying as he did so, "We cannot allow that you return to say that the Germans are people without kindness, so!"

Flight reviewed the position. What were they, these people? With their veneer of culture, their vaunted love of beauty and knowledge, their philosophy and yet still in many ways retaining the mentality of stupid and abnormal children. Nasty little children, whispering, furtive children. Even their pride of race, their aims and political amibtions might be disregarded when it came to the gratification of their lusts and desires.

How sick he was of it all! He had been here four months. It was now October, days were growing shorter, and over the flat fields thin wisps of mist trailed in the evenings and early mornings. The summer had gone, and before him stretched the long, dreary winter. A winter either to be spent in the warmth of von Ludbach's friendship, or in the chill of his dislike and the danger of his possible revenge. A pretty prospect!

He had examined the floor-boards of his room, had even dislodged two of them, but beneath lay tightly-packed rubble through which he could not hope to force his way. Then there were his pictures. Those pictures which he hoped to deliver in Paris, to some place of safety. His private receipts too, he had kept them with such care; one day they should be handed to authorities who would trace those pictures, even those that held but little value. He could not escape, leaving behind all that he had saved, and he most certainly could not hope to tramp over the country carrying a large and expensive suitcase.

They had taken his money and papers from him, though the money had been returned. There was not a great deal of it, not more than the equivalent of two or three pounds. His papers, made out in the name of François Pascal, they still held.

He heard himself say, "If only I could get home!" and started taking himself to task, thinking, "My God! this won't do if I start talking to myself! I shall go batty if I do that."

During the days which followed von Ludbach was like a lamb, indeed he showed something of a lamb's timidity when he spoke to Flight. He asked him in a tentative way if he would dine, adding, "Is there anything particularly you would like to eat? I have thought that you looked pale during these last few days."

After dinner, during which he talked nervously about trivial, rather silly things, he said, "I wondered if you would care to play cards? It is not easy with two players only, but if you could suggest a game . . ."

Flight said crossly, for this humility embarrassed him, "I don't know of any game for two players except 'Beggar My Neighbour'."

Von Ludbach answered, "Would it amuse you to play that?"

"No, of course it wouldn't!"

One day the German said, his voice sentimental, "Today is my birthday!"

"Many happy returns of it."

"I have had a letter from my Patron. It is so like him to recall these little matters. On my last birthday he gave me a great Venetian flask filled with Chanel's scent."

Flight said rudely, "If that's a hint, I've nothing to give you."

"And yet there is much that you might give me, if you wished. Your trust, your friendship, your confidences, your hopes and fears . . ."

"I've not much hope stuck in this dump and I've no fears that anything much worse can happen to me," Flight said.

The other man sighed, "I am foolish to be so sensitive, I admit it. All my life it has been a fault of mine. My great Patron has said to me so often, 'Amadeus . . .'"

Flight said, "He said *what?*"

"Amadeus, that is my first name, I am Amadeus Siegfried Wolff Eitel von Ludbach." He glanced at Flight and said almost shyly, "All my friends call me Amadeus. I should like you to use that name when we are alone, perhaps."

"Oh well—I don't know."

"I call you Per-ci-val!"

"I know you do, I wish you wouldn't."

The German rose, and stood looking down at Flight. He said, "I am offering you friendship. True friendship is no mean gift. It enriches the giver and the receiver, it . . . ."

Flight interrupted, "It blesses him that gives and him that takes, go on, I know that part."

"Indeed it does," eagerly. "To have my honest, warm-hearted, generous friendship treated as something to be held at arm's length, to be looked upon with suspicion is terrible to me. It makes me unhappy. Indeed it does."

Flight scowled at him in silence, he thought, "Unhappy, not you! You're loving this act! Imagining me as a kind of brute beast and yourself as a shrinking sensitive plant. You damned piece of affectation, you unhealthy lout."

He was growing to hate him, knew that sometimes he tried to plan some way by which he could kill him, imagined that he could feel the soft flesh of that thick, smooth throat giving way under his strong fingers, see those blue eyes bulge and bulge, until they could bulge no more. The feeling frightened him. Again and again he thought, "Papers, I must have papers! I can't move until I have them."

It was late in October when the idea came to him. The room was hot and very stuffy, von Ludbach was sulkily reading a month-old paper which had been sent to him from Germany, the reading of which appeared to give him considerable satisfaction.

Flight said, "Today is my birthday—a sad one for me, spent as a prisoner. Oh, dear!"

The paper was lowered, von Ludbach almost bounced out of his chair.

"Oh, what can I give you as a present? Let it be something really nice. It will make me so happy!"

Flight said, "Ah, Amadeus, you're too good to me and I'm not nearly nice enough to you."

"O-o-oh!" The long-drawn-out sound was ludicrous in Flight's ears. Like an old spinster being shown a new baby, he thought. "Tell me what you want, Per-ci-val?"

He said, "Let me talk to you. I want to talk seriously. Suppose that you were moved from here? We've pretty well combed the countryside, and it is obvious that they are not going to keep anyone of your attainments in this backwater for ever."

"Possibly not . . . it is improbable."

"If you were moved, do you realise that I have no papers whatever. What would happen to me? Has that struck you? No?"—with simulated anger— "No, you have never given it a thought. I should be left—here . . ."

"I should take you with me, Per-ci-val!"

"What if that were impossible? Or what if you had to go quickly and I had to join you somewhere, what should I do?"

Von Ludbach struck his forehead with his hand, not very hard, but the gesture was effective. "I had not thought, but now I shall think. This shall be my birthday present to you. What papers would you wish to have?"

Flight considered then said, "But you can't get papers here!"

The German nodded. "Oh! but yes, excellent papers. That corporal of mine, he is a perfect artist. He will make them according to my orders. He has made many in his time. He has a small but excellent printing press. It is a beautiful thing. Now you shall see how efficiently we do such things. What shall they be?"

"Let me have my old ones made out to François Pascal."

"Oh!" He was disappointed; he pulled open a drawer in his desk and produced the papers, turning them over critically. "They are not badly done. Who made them? You don't know?"—the voice was sharper. "Then who gave them to you?"

Flight thought, "Here it comes! The old Hun bully. Three minutes ago you were a twittering old maid, all gush and girlishness, now you're back running true to form." He said, "They were sent to me, I was to meet a man at a café in the village of Matrec. The sign was, 'This beer is damned flat!' The proprietor said, 'Sorry! let me give you another glass.' How plainly it all comes back to me! Later he handed me the papers wrapped in *Le Soir*. Are you satisfied?"

Apparently he wasn't, for he pushed them back, closed the drawer and looked up smiling, saying, "We'll think about it. No! you must have a really nice present."

He smiled and nodded, and disappeared into the other room, returning with an immense ring, one of the most vulgar pieces of jewellery Flight had ever seen. Heavy gold, much decorated and twisted, and set in the gold a large diamond. He had returned to his timidity, and held it out to Flight, smiling shyly.

"I should like you to have this. May I put it on your finger?"

Flight wriggled uneasily. "It's very kind of you, but honestly, I'd rather have my papers."

"You shall have them later, but let me give you this, *please*."

"Very well, thank you."

He slipped the ring on Flight's outstretched finger, then gazed at him and sighed deeply. Flight twisted the ring round and examined it.

He said, "It's a very valuable ring, isn't it?"

"I got it in Rouen, from the best jeweller there. It was the finest he had. It is very heavy, solid gold and the stone is real. I made him give me a guarantee to that effect."

Flight nodded. "What did he ask you for it?"

Von Ludbach laughed. "Dear Per-ci-val, I gave him one of our army receipts."

That night as he undressed. Flight looked at the

328

ring again and murmured, "Well, stock's as good as money, I suppose."

The place hummed with excitement. Every soldier was cleaning boots, belts and equipment; passages were scrubbed, windows cleaned, and the chef driven frantic by the number of orders issued to him.

Flight asked the corporal what was happening, adding, "Is Hitler coming to hold an inspection?"

The corporal looked slightly shocked and then leaned nearer to Flight's ear. "*He* is coming!" he whispered "and he is the friend of the Baron!"

"He—Hitler?"

"No, no!" he made a movement indicating a large stomach. "He!" Again he made the same gesture.

When Flight met von Ludbach, he found him completely changed. Gone was the timidity, the anxiety to please, the humility and the soft voice. Instead, he was stiff as a ramrod, his uniform spotless and beautifully brushed, his very eyeglass appeared to gleam with a new lustre.

"Melton!" he said sharply. "Tonight I entertain one of the Leaders of the Fatherland, the man who is probably responsible more than any other for the historic victory which we shall shortly over the Allies gain. The man who is the brains and mentality behind the glorious *Luftwaffe*, the man who . . ."

Flight said, "It's all right! I know who it is. How

does it affect me?"

Von Ludbach stared at him, his face a pink mask of insolence.

"It affects you in this, that I order you to wait at table. He is most sensitive to noise, to clumsiness, to coarse hands and so on. Also," he dropped his voice, "it is necessary that such conversation as he is sufficiently gracious to hold, must be confidential kept. Soldiers—talk."

"So do shopkeepers . . ."

The little pouting mouth smiled. "But you have no one with whom to talk, my friend!"

"I know nothing about waiting at table . . ."

"At least you can fill wine glasses, remove plates and hand them to someone who is waiting to carry them away. Come, come, surely you can realise that I am doing you a great honour?" His voice was less abrupt.

Flight felt a spasm of amusement, it sounded almost "winning".

"All right. D'you want me to dress like a waiter?"

"No, no! only to wear your very nicest suit. The dark blue one, I think. And now let us arrange the dining-room, and see that everything is as charming as may be."

Flowers were brought; a soldier had driven miles to find some château where a few still bloomed; fine linen—that pair of linen sheets which the old lady had begged so hard to keep—rugs were unpacked from cases, pieces of brocade, cushions covered in silk and satin—the two rooms were transformed.

Von Ludbach surveyed them, nodding his satisfaction. "How well it looks! My gracious friend will be pleased. He loves passionately all Beauty!"

Flight said, "It looks like a whore's boudoir to me!"

The other lifted a shoulder pettishly. "How coarse you English are!"

Flight protested. "Well, I've got most damnable stomachache. It might be appendicitis," he added hopefully.

"Now don't go and be ill!" von Ludbach said crossly, "just when I really need you. It's probably indigestion. Go and ask the cook to give you some bi-carbonate of soda in hot water."

"But I'm not allowed in the kitchen . . ."

"Damnation! I order you to go."

In the warm kitchen, filled with savoury smells, the old chef was bustling about; despite the fact that he was not allowed in the kitchen Flight frequently wandered there and talked to the old fellow, who was full of odd stories, recollections of the great people who had visited the hotel where he had once worked in Paris, their particular fads and fancies.

Flight said, "I've been sent to ask for a dose of bi-carbonate of soda, it's for indigestion."

Old Emil blinked his heavy-lidded eyes. "Have you got indigestion?"

"No . . ."

"Then you don't want bi-carbonate?"

"No . . ."

"What the devil do you want, Eengleesh?"

"Something that will look like it, so that I can talk to you while I drink it. Something hot . . ."

The heavy wrinkled eyelid descended slowly. "Hot water—and something in it. Am I correct in thinking that a little rum might do good?"

"You are indeed!"

He stood with the steaming glass in his hand, grumbling from time to time in a loud protesting voice, that Emil had made it far too hot, and keeping up an undercurrent of talk in a lower key. Very briefly he told of a famous and historic occasion when a lady, beloved by a certain king, entertained another lady who hoped to attain the same high honour, "or dishonour, as you choose to look at it!" Flight commented. How the second lady, visiting the first and being notoriously greedy, was given sweets which were delicious, but which contained a certain medicine, tasteless but powerful. She ate voraciously, was seized with dreadful griping pains, followed by certain symptoms which made it quite impossible for her to remain long in the Royal Presence.

Flight said, "It's a quaint story, *mon brave*, eh?"

The chef grinned broadly. "Did she die?"

"No, she was only supremely uncomfortable for twenty-four hours."

Emil frowned. "But why not—sweets to make

332

—someone die? This would be meritorious! I know of such a medicine."

"No, no!" Flight said, adding loudly, "How hot you have made this damned stuff. What an old fool you are. No, no—to incapacitate, that will be sufficient. I have dreadful pains now, be sure that the orderly who carries away the dishes will also have dreadful pains tomorrow . . ."

"Tomorrow? Tonight! This stuff is a rapid worker. Yes, I will do it. Don't eat any of the exquisite sweets which I shall prepare. Drink that bi-carbonate. . . . You great baby! It's not too hot!"

Von Ludbach grumbled when he got back. "You've been a devil of a time!"

Flight replied, "I'm feeling damned ill. Can't think what it is." He gave various symptoms which were present, many of them of an exceedingly unpleasant and private nature, adding, "I believe it's something I've eaten. What did I have yesterday?"

By seven the table was laid. There were two great branching silver candlesticks, finely chased and bearing the arms of a historic French house, there were silver dishes for holding salted almonds, shaped as delicate shells; the table silver was of the finest, even the knives had beautiful silver handles and long narrow pointed blades. The tablecloth was heavy with lace, the napkins smooth, shining and embroidered at the corners with intertwined initials, surmounted by a ducal coronet.

333

Von Ludbach gave his instructions twenty times. "You, Melton, will stand here. Klaus and Stoffer will hand the dishes to you through the door; Klaus will hand them, Stoffer will carry them away.

After the fifth time Flight said, "All right, Amadeus, I've got it all in my head now."

The German wheeled round, his face scarlet. "Don't dare to call me that when—my Patron is here. I'll—I'll have you shot if you do!"

"You yourself asked me to call you— Amadeus," Flight protested.

"That was different—this evening, should I ask you a question you will answer, 'Yes, my Kommandant,' or, 'No, my Kommandant.' Understand?"

"And if—he asks me a question, what do I call—him?"

Von Ludbach smiled loftily. "He won't even notice that you are there!"

At half past seven, a huge covered Mercédès-Benz, followed by two smaller cars containing luggage, drew up at the door of the barracks. By craning his neck at his own small window, Flight could watch the descent of the arrivals. He could hear orders being shouted, hear the tramp of feet, the rattle of arms; four stockmen in dark uniforms with shining black belts descended from the smaller cars, they stood stiffly at attention, while from the Mercédès issued a figure slightly above medium height, enormously stout, wrapped in a heavy sable coat, the collar of which was turned up so that the face was almost invisible.

The troopers marched off in charge of the sergeant, the sable coat disappeared into the building with von Ludbach walking at its side.

Ten minutes later, the corporal opened Flight's door. "You're wanted!" he said, then grinning suddenly, added, "What a sight he is! Be sure that you don't laugh. You're to mix cocktails."

Flight followed him down the long passage and knocking, was told to enter. Von Ludbach stood by the fireplace, while lounging in an armchair sat one of the most extraordinary looking men Flight had ever seen. The huge gross body was dressed in a light-coloured uniform, a palish blue; a wide scarlet and black sash extended from shoulder to waist, and on the left breast were at least five rows of medal ribbons. Very bright, new-looking ribbons. Flight felt that they were renewed very often. The face above the stiff collar was large, and at first sight seemed the face of an overgrown child, of particularly good temper. The cheeks were full and heavily roughed; the eyebrows were plucked and carefully outlined, the eyelashes painted with mascara, so that they stuck out stiffly. The wide, full-lipped mouth was artificially reddened. It looked moist, as if lipstick had been applied quite recently.

It was only when he looked more closely that he realised that the face bore no actual likeness to a good-tempered child. The heavy lids lifted to show eyes which were flint-like, the nose was fleshy and had a spreading base, with wide nostrils, the mouth—the mouth was horrible—relentless and indulgent.

Von Ludbach said, "Cocktails, Melton!"

"Yes, my Kommandant."

"What have you?"

Flight said, "Clover Club, Diplomat, Dubonnet, Gloom Raiser, London Cocktail, Pink Lady, Alexander, and Chinese Cocktail. Also, my Kommandant, Martini and Manhattan cocktails."

Von Ludbach turned to his guest. "Marshal—which shall it be?"

A voice surprisingly light and high-pitched for the man's size, answered, "I don't like some of the names of his damned cocktails. London—pah! Alexander—that puppy! Chinese—the swine! Have those names changed—and immediately!" He spoke directly to Flight. "There is one called—Between the Sheets, do you know that?"

"Indeed, Marshal, I do—gin, cointreau, barcardi and ice."

"Correct!" He smiled at von Ludbach. "Amusing, eh? Between the Sheets! I shall have a Pink Lady."

Flight mixed and handed it on a silver salver. As the stout man took his, he noticed the many rings which adorned the plump fingers; saw, too, the varnished nails, painted blood-red.

The Marshal sipped. "Very good—where did you find him?"

"He is an English prisoner, Excellency. I caught him walking along the road, whistling, one morning."

"Humph! We might do worse than take him to Berlin and set him up in a bar. A small, ve-ry exclusive bar, eh?" He finished his drink, held out the empty glass to Flight and said, "Another—you English pig!"

"The same again, Excellency?" Flight asked.

"I'll try this Gloom Raiser of yours. Heaven knows, the British should need to drink these all day and every day! God be thanked, we have no gloom to need raising! Eh, Amadeus?" He gave a high, whinnying laugh, like a horse.

Dinner was served, and Flight handed plates, removed dishes, and wondered where the Marshal put all the food that he ate, all the wine that he drank. He ate messily, spilling sauce on the cloth, leaving trails of grease at the corners of his big mouth; by the end of the meal his napkin was filthy. He unhooked his collar, he was sweating on the forehead and neck, his make-up ruined.

They talked in low voices, and once the big man put out his hand and gently pinched von Ludbach's ear. That gentleman gave a slight squeal, and the Marshal said tolerantly, "Now, now! that didn't hurt you?"

"It startled me!" The same coy tone that Flight knew, set his teeth on edge.

"Pooh!" The fat white hand with the blood-red nails patted the thinner one of von Ludbach. "You feed well, here, eh? Ve-ry well. That last sauce was excellent. Let me have the recipe before I go. My chef is good, but lacks imagination. I shall probably take the one from Foyot's when I leave Paris. Paris . . . By God! I ought to be there now, but I wanted to catch a glimpse of you, my dear."

"Such an honour you pay me, Excellency! I am very conscious of it."

"I must leave early in the morning. And listen, Amadeus, I don't want anyone to know that I have been here. *No one*, you understand, *no one*. My troopers and drivers know better than to open their mouths when I tell them to keep 'em shut. See that your men here do the same! You understand what I say, eh, English pig?"

"Perfectly, Excellency."

He jerked his head in Flight's direction and asked, as if Flight were not even present, "Is he—in so far as any of them can be—a gentleman?"

"He is a picture dealer named Melton, has a Gallery in Bond Street. I have used him to assist me in the estimation of the value of certain pictures. Ah!" he clapped his hands with pleasure, "I have found you a real jewel. At first this man was dubious, but later he agreed with me. A Holbein! think of it, in the best manner! The value must be tremendous."

"I don't care for them a great deal—prefer

something with a touch of femininity to it. However, it ought to fetch a good price. Is it packed?"

"Everything is packed in strong cases, with the greatest care."

"Good! you have done very well, very well. Ah, what have we here? Dee-licious sweets! Pink, pale green—a charming colour, *café-au-lait*, and white. And how good! You don't eat sweets, Amadeus, no? All the more for me. Here, English pig—have a sweet."

Flight bowed. "I thank your Excellency, you are too kind, but I dare not eat sweets, I have not been very well."

Von Ludbach said, "Indigestion."

The Marshal, stuffing another sweet in his capacious mouth, said, "Constipation, I suppose. All Englishmen suffer from it."

The room was growing terribly hot. The air was heavy with the smoke of Turkish cigarettes and food, the faces of both men glistened with sweat. Flight felt an overpowering longing for air. There they sat, drinking the wine which they had stolen, eating food which they had snatched from the people to whom it rightfully belonged, the table covered with the loot which they had taken, silver which had been handed down from generation to generation. Even the walls were hung with tapestries worked by French fingers destined originally to beautify French houses.

The Marshal said, "No more sweets? Damn that Englishman, can't he see the dish is empty? Your discipline's very slack, Amadeus."

Flight sped to the other room, to refill the little silver dishes. Schoffer was leaning against the wall, his face pallid, his hands pressed to his stomach. As Flight drew nearer, he groaned faintly.

"What's wrong?"

Schoffer opened heavy, tortured eyes. "*Himmel!* I'm very ill."

"You've been eating something!"

"Only one or two bits that were left on the plates, I swear. And one or two of those sweets. O-o-oh!"

Flight said, "Better get out or they'll hear you. Go on, I'll manage."

He returned with the sweets. Von Ludbach asked sharply, "Who were you speaking to, Melton?"

"Schoffer, Kommandant. He's ill. I told him to go along, I can manage."

"Really ill, or shamming?"

"Really ill, I think, sir. Stomach pains—like I had this morning."

The Marshal, stuffing sweets, said, "That 'ul do, we don't want to hear about your disgusting inside! Shut up about it."

He stood leaning against the door, for the heat of the room had tired him. Something was going to happen. He was certain of it, almost certain what it was going to be. It was so faint a hope that he scarcely dared to think of it as a possibility. He saw that the two men were deep in some whispered conversation and slipped into the other room. Moving very softly he reached the desk, laid his hand on the drawer where von Ludbach had put his papers. It slid open, there they were, and lying beside them a thick roll of notes wound round by a rubber band. Silently he transferred them both to his inner pocket, then bearing an ancient bottle of fine brandy he went back to the dining-room.

The Marshal said, "W'a-er-got-there?"

Von Ludbach, with a trace of his old girlishness, said, "A bottle of very special brandy. The old man almost cried when I took it. I remembered you liked good brandy—don't you?"—with intense anxiety.

"Cerr-ly like it. No big glasses? Pig Englishman! Don't you know that civilised people drink ou-err tulip glasses—for fine brandy?"

"I was about to bring them. They are warming, Excellency!"

He was about to raise the beautiful bulging glass to his lips, when he set it down hastily, rose unsteadily to his feet, and muttering something to von Ludbach hurried from the room.

Von Ludbach said, "You have done very well, Melton. His Excellency is pleased. How charming he is—and what an intellect. A very great man . . ."

"And, of course, obviously a gentleman," Flight said.

The Marshal returned. He was slightly more

sober, but seemed shaken.

He sat down and began a whispered conversation with his host, whose face assumed an expression of grave anxiety.

"Drink your brandy, it may do you good," Von Ludbach said tenderly.

The Marshal clapped both hands over his stomach, threw back his head and emitted a noise like a dog howling at the moon. Sweat glistened on his huge face, his lips were rolled back over his teeth, his face was the colour of putty. Even the ruined traces of his make-up had faded.

"My God!" he groaned. "I'm ill—I'm in agony. What is it?"

Flight said, "That's how Schoffer was, how I was this morning."

The Marshal rolled a bloodshot eye. "Pains—here?" He patted his huge stomach. "Sickness—and—er—all the rest of it? Whew—whew!"

"Precisely, Excellency!"

"O-oh! Amadeus, this is terrible! Dreadful! Cramp in the stomach."

Flight offered more brandy, then pushed forward a dish of gleamingly white sweets saying, "Excuse me, Excellency, these are peppermint—peppermint creams. Peppermint does help—that kind of pain."

He gasped, grabbed half a dozen and pushed them into his mouth, muttering, "I b'lieve the damned Englishman is right. Whew—there's another spasm coming. I can't stand this. I tell you it's agony."

"The doctor . . ." Flight murmured.

Von Ludbach said, "Bring him."

The writhing Marshal yelled, "No! keep the Englishman here. I may need him. He's no fool. Go and bring the doctor yourself, Amadeus."

Flight tiptoed into the other room, brought back a clean napkin and a large bottle of eau-de-Cologne. He dabbed it on the Marshal's sweating forehead, he fanned him gently with the damp cloth, he offered him more peppermint creams. The bloodshot eyes rolled, the groans seemed to ebb and flow, the Marshal muttered, "Stay here—I'm ill. Oh—my head—I'm going to be sick." He was exceedingly sick.

7

FLIGHT said, when the worst was over—for the Marshal abandoned himself completely to his physical weakness, in addition to making a noise which was like a train entering a tunnel—"Let me help you to lie down, sir."

"No, not yet. Help me along the corridor. Wait for me."

"Of course, Excellency."

His brain was working very fast, things were going to work out somehow for him. This gross fat German trusted him; in a strange animal fashion he was grateful, for when matters had been at their worst, when Flight had held the great heavy head, he had muttered, "I shall n' forr-et."

And again, leaning on Flight's arm as he staggered back to the bedroom, "Whew! I'm glad y'here, glad."

Flight lowered him on to the good, well-sprung French bed, unfastened his tight tunic, undid the top buttons of his equally tight trousers, removed his fine, well-polished boots. The great head rolled from side to side on the pillow. The mouth hung slackly open.

"D'you really think peppermint helps?"

"I have always heard that it did, Excellency."

"S've I! Gi'me some more."

He again crammed the sweets into his mouth, grunting as he did so.

The doctor arrived, following in the wake of the elegant von Ludbach. He was a heavily-built, tousled-headed young man, who spoke with an accent so broadly Bavarian that it was difficult to understand him. He was evidently so impressed with the importance of his patient that nervousness rendered him almost inarticulate.

They undressed the huge body and laid it between the fine sheets.

The doctor said, "Corporal Schoffer is suffering in the same manner . . ."

The Marshal groaned. "Blast his guts."

Flight said gently, "I was ill in exactly the same way this morning . . ."

Another groan and, "Don't let's hear any more about your damned stomach. We've heard nothing else all the evening. O-o-oh! That was awful . . ."

"I a medicine shall prepare, the stomach to soothe and quieten . . ."

"Prepare it quickly—it's my b'lief that I'm dying."

"No—no—no!" soothingly, as if he were speaking to a child. "In twenty-four hours—light food—milk perhaps—milk puddings . . ."

The Marshal bellowed like a wounded bull. "Twenty-four hours! I must be in Paris by morning. What time is it?"

The doctor drew out a great silver watch like a

turnip. "The time is now five and twenty minutes to two."

"I must be in Paris by eight o'clock. How long will it take to get to Paris—two hours? I must leave at six, not a moment later. Very much depends on it. English pig, more peppermints. I b'lieve they assist me."

The doctor said, "I do not advise sweetmeats . . ."

"Mind your damned business, you fool!"

Flight bent over the writhing body. "I ventured, since you find that they relieve you, Excellency, to instruct the chef to make some more—stronger, more peppermint."

"S'right! This fellow's got more sense than the lot of . . . Whew . . . er—AH!"

Flight did not add that when he gave the order, that he and the cook had clung together, rocking with silent laughter, unable to speak, weakly wiping their eyes on the backs of their hands.

It was two o'clock when the Marshal, being helped back to bed by the pale and anxious von Ludbach and Flight, collapsed and murmured, "I cannot go to Paris. Oh—no, it is impossible! There are papers—important—which must be delivered."

Von Ludbach whispered, "Shall I telephone to Paris?"

"I've told you, you blockheaded effeminate fool, that I do not wish anyone to know where I am. I don't want telephone operators, clerks, a hundred and one people discussing my business. .... Give me some brandy, Englishman!"

"Then shall I go to Paris and explain?"

The heavy head rolled weakly from side to side. "And leave your post, your men? God save me from these fools!"

The doctor hazarded, "The sergeant could go perhaps?"

Flight clenched his hands. It was coming, closer and closer. What—he still did not know clearly? Something—coming like the hooves of galloping horses, coming nearer and nearer.

The Marshal continued. "It must be someone who will not comment arouse. Someone who can be trusted not to talk. Remember, the story of my illness must never get out, never be talked of. It is too—too undignified!"

He closed his eyes, and two large tears forced themselves under the lids. Flight wiped them away. The man was actually weeping because his precious dignity was endangered. What an incredible people.

Flight whispered, "Excellency, might I venture to suggest—can I not go for you? I have papers —made out in another name; who will take notice of me? I am too unimportant. I swear that I will deliver your papers, I swear that on my word of honour."

"But you're a prisoner—and Englishmen have no honour."

"Very good, Excellency."

He lay quiet, only moving at intervals to clutch his stomach, only uttering long-drawn-out groans. His face was clay-coloured, his breath came short and rapidly.

He said, whispering, "I'm convinced that I'm dying—don't deny it!"

"No, no—ah, in Paris we could find a specialist, a professor."

"Impossible . . ."

"Nothing is impossible when such things as the very life of Germany are at stake," Flight said, and felt a certain pleasure at his grandiloquence.

"A-a-ah! But you would like me to die!"

"Indeed no, Excellency. I can admire a man without subscribing to his beliefs. There, eat some more peppermints."

"That is true—ah, these are much stronger, they feel warm in my throat. I wonder . . . ?" he said more loudly. "All—leave the room. Stay here, Englishman. All others—go!"

Flight caught the venomous glance which von Ludbach gave him as he passed through the door, and returned to the suffering Marshal.

"Where are your papers? In that drawer?"—as Flight indicated the drawer in the desk from which he had abstracted the papers. "Get them! I suppose that ass has left it unlocked?" Flight went through the movements of taking papers from the drawer, standing so that his body blocked the line of vision. "You've got them? Now, on that table, a leather case—blue leather, with gold letters. That's it. In the inner pocket of my tunic are two letters, both addressed to—ladies of my acquaintance. Got them? Oh, Lord, it's coming on again! O-o-ow! Wipe my face. I'm dying. My poor wife! Our unfortunate leader! For, as the world knows, I am the brains of the Fatherland. Listen—deliver the contents of the leather case to the Head-quarters—the Crillon. To General von Leibstruk. Explain to him what has happened—don't give details—nothing undignified. The doctor fears—fears . . ."

Flight said, "Appendicitis, Excellency?"

"Exactly! He is to send his own doctor—at once. He can return in the car which takes you. Then deliver those two letters—say as little as possible —merely present my warm greetings. I am delayed."

He lay back, panting, and repeated that he was dying, and shed several tears at the thought of his "belovèd wife" and her subsequent grief.

"And then? What do I do then?"

"Oh, it may be that General von Leibstruk can use you as an interpreter. When I come—if I live, you understand—I myself may be able to use you. There—is that clear? Oh, this terrible pain. Give me some more peppermint sweets. Whew! More eau-de-Cologne—ah!"

"Excellency, forgive me, but I must have more than this . . ."

"Money, you mean. In your country all men think only of money, eh?"

"No, Excellency, but a line written by you —signed by you—that will carry me anywhere. Otherwise—the General may imagine that I had stolen the papers, the—excuse me—two ladies may . . ."

"You are right. Later, I believe that I shall take you with me. You have intelligence, I recognised it at once. Yes, I shall find you a good position. Find my card-case—blue leather with gold borders. A pencil—no, a pen is better. Now, lift me up a little. Oh, the pain. *Ach!* what I suffer for the beloved Fatherland. Whew!"

He wrote in a hand which was strangely lacking, Flight thought, in either character or education. *I rely on this man. Give him what help he needs. H. G.*

Flight laid him down and slipped the cards into his waistcoat pocket.

"Those cards," said the Marshal, "would open the gates of heaven itself to you. Ah! oh, I feel that they will shortly open for me to enter."

The doctor and the scowling von Ludbach were readmitted, orders were given for the Marshal's car to be ready immediately. The time was now half past two. If the General were still asleep when Flight arrived, he was to be wakened, the doctor was to leave Paris immediately.

"Otherwise he may be too late!" sighed the Marshal. "Too late!"

Flight said, "Excellency, courage, the doctor will be with you by seven o'clock this morning. I

350

beg to take my leave of you."

He walked out, his last impressions being of von Ludbach's white, furious face; of his whisper, like a melodramatic snake, "Betrayer, Judas!" and of the Marshal, the "Brains of the Fatherland", being violently sick into a bowl painted with flowers, which had once belonged to a Queen of France.

The car was waiting. Even in the dim light of a lantern, Flight could see how the varnish gleamed, how the silver fittings shone, how rich and deep were the cushions. The driver sat like a smallish, thick statue, stolid, impersonal, immaculate. A black uniformed trooper stood at the door, and as Flight came out, he moved to one side to allow old Emil to put in a splendid cowhide bag, bearing initials and a coronet above them.

The trooper said, "Is that His Excellency's?"

Emil grunted. "How should I know? I was told to put it in the car. It's not mine, be certain of that."

The trooper spoke to Flight. His voice was cold, without either expression or friendliness. "I understand that you are to be taken to Paris. Have you arms? Let me see!" Deftly the strong hands ran over Flight's body, the voice grunted, "No! Good. Understand, any attempt at—what would be very foolish—I am armed, even if you are not. Get in—no, no, in the front, where I can watch you. This bag . . ."

Flight answered, "The Marshal wishes me to deliver it—to a certain house in Paris."

351

"Is it locked?"

"I don't know—how should I? Oh! can't we start? I have to send a doctor back from Paris, quickly." He flung the deepest anxiety into his voice.

"Get in!"

Just as the engine was warming up, a head appeared at the window of the car, a furious, pink face was pushed forward so that it almost touched Flight's, a single eyeglass glared at him.

"I shall never forget. After my goodness to you—to usurp my place. Pah! you filthy English, how I loathe you all."

Flight said, "Sorry, Amadeus. I didn't want to hold his head."

"*Ach!*" The face disappeared in the darkness, the car moved forward.

The driver sat stiffly upright, the guard behind leaned forward, his arms folded on the back of the seat in which Flight was, his breath came heavily and evenly, it smelt of beer. Beer and vinegar.

He spoke to the driver. "Do you suppose that he is really ill?"

"God knows! Over-eating again, as at Sedan."

"No one's supposed to know that he is here."

"That is understandable."

"The brains of the *Luftwaffe*. God in heaven!"

The driver said, "How much German do you understand, prisoner?"

Flight answered, "A sufficiency."

"Ah!" The talking ceased, they drove on in silence.

The guard took out a packet of cigarettes, and offered one to the driver. They both laughed and commented upon what the Marshal might be expected to say if he saw them. The driver said, "Here, prisoner, have one!"

With one hand the driver offered an automatic lighter, and the spurt of bright flame illumined his face as he lit Flight's cigarette. The driver was Shaff. His face was expressionless. He extinguished the light. Flight thanked him.

He sat there, trying to understand it all. What was Shaff doing here? Were both he and the guard anti-Nazis, were they both "moles"? What were they going to do? Would they try to wreck the car? Refuse to take him to Paris, where he might rid himself of those precious pictures, give his carefully-gathered information?

He said to Shaff, "Been driving the Marshal long?"

"What's that got to do with you?"

"I was thinking that it must be a responsible kind of a job, that's all."

"You thought right. Satisfied?"

The guard laughed and Shaff added, "Sticking their noses where they aren't wanted. What the hell has it to do with him?"

The sky was beginning to change to grey as they entered Paris. They drove through the quiet streets, where only at long intervals a shadowy

353

figure passed, hugging the wall of the house, or a couple of German officers in their long coats walked smartly—almost too smartly—their feet ringing on the pavements. Behind the blinds of a few houses lights were burning, shining blue through the black-out curtains. An almost unbearable wave of homesickness swept over Flight. He was driving into Paris, and he longed, passionately, wildly,to be driving into London. Was London looking like this? Were all the lights out? Were people moving about furtively, except for the soldiers who were patrolling the streets? How much of London was left standing? The places he knew—his Galleries, Clark Court, Buckingham Palace? The Germans had told him that it was "battered flat" and that the King was so injured that he would never walk again. They had told him too that "Vestmeenster" was in ruins, and that King's Cross Station, which they appeared to regard as a great and noble national monument, was only a mass of stones and rubble.

Then, as always, thoughts of Alicia forced themselves into his mind. Where was she, what was she doing? Had she perhaps been injured, as they said the King had been? He felt his hands clench and knew that the palms were wet.

Shaff said, "Headquarters?"

The guard answered, "Headquarters!"

Flight saw that the clock on the dashboard showed the time to be a quarter to five. How still the city was! Mistinguett's rowdy, joyous song rang through his head. Nothing very rowdy or joyous about this deathly-quiet city, these silent streets, those darkened windows. He thought, "It's too still, too silent! It's dangerously still, frighteningly quiet. Like the countryside before a storm, when even the leaves cease to move—then comes a little, savage wind and stirs them into life, and then—the storm breaks!"

They were moving noiselessly along the Avenue des Champs Elysées, passing shops he knew well. There he had bought scent for Alicia; on the other side was a jeweller's, where she had bought him a pair of cuff links; now, the Place de la Concorde, here was the Crillon, where they had stayed for the first night of their honeymoon, in a room with long, pale blue silk curtains, and a carpet with bunches of flowers scattered over its surface. There was a clatter of arms, the car stopped, the guard got out, and began a conversation with a huge man who emerged from a lodge near the entrance.

Without turning Shaff said, "Surprised to see me? I'll tell you about it sometime. I'm going great guns! He's a fool that Marshal—a bloody, cunning fool! Russia's getting it in the neck though—bad show. Don't worry though—we're not beaten yet —or ever, for that matter."

"Any news of Pierre? Madame Peloux, Jacques?"

"Pierre's in the south. The others are all right."

"Good!—*au revoir.*"

The door swung open, Flight climbed out, carrying his bag. The guard said, "Can't take that into the General's room with you. Leave it here. They'll look after it for you." He shouted to one of the sergeants. "Here! look after this bag, it belongs to the Marshal." He added, "It's locked."

Upstairs in an immense room which Flight thought must have been used for banquets and receptions, a pale-faced young man sat at a desk. His eyes were heavy for want of sleep, his hair was ruffled, he yawned.

The guard saluted. "A messenger for General von Leibstruk, sir."

"The General is still asleep."

"It is from the Marshal, sir. Important. The messenger has papers and particulars which must be given to the General alone. Those were the orders."

"The Marshal was expected here early this morning . . ."

"His Excellency has been detained, sir."

"Who is this messenger? Where are your papers?" The mists of sleep were being dispelled, the eyes brightened a little; he passed his hands over his rough hair to reduce it to some kind of order.

"He's a prisoner, sir. Sent by the Marshal. He has his papers." Then to Flight, "Produce your papers immediately!"

He examined them, frowning. "You're French? I don't understand . . . ?"

"I have instructions to report fully to the General, sir."

"What's that you're holding in your hand?" The voice was suddenly sharp.

Flight opened his hand and disclosed the roll of notes.

"Money? Where did you get that?"

"His Excellency gave it to me, sir."

"What for?"

"Reasons concerning which I shall be grateful if you will allow me to keep silent. It is not for me, I am merely to disburse it."

The young officer rose, stretched, and yawned again. He sighed deeply, and twitching down the front of his tunic, set his belt straight.

"I'll see the General. Watch this fellow. I don't know that I trust him."

"Yes, sir."

Alone, the man came nearer to Flight, and whispered, "You've got a lot of money there, my friend."

Flight said, "Do you want some of it?"

"It's always useful."

Flight stripped off a few notes, folded them small and gave them to him. "If you want any more," he said, "just open your mouth—quickly."

The fellow glanced round, then speaking very rapidly said, "I work with Schultz, the driver. We've a radio set in the car now—receiving set. That road we came along this morning—it will be all right for us to return, after that . . . it will be unpleasant for the next heavy touring car that makes the trip. I'm a Jew from Munich—he's—I forget!"

Flight asked, "Many of you in the suite of the Marshal?"

"Only us two. If you want a place in Paris . . . top floor . . . Madame Gagè . . . 12 Rue Feydeau. Mention . . . Jacob Rappe. . . ."

More notes changed hands, neither of their faces betrayed the slightest hint of emotion. Flight said, "And this man, Schultz?"

"He's a deep one. A dangerous one—for them. He arrived one evening, helping in the Marshal's driver, who had been set on by some French 'moles' and was almost dead. So Schultz said. The Marshal—he takes unaccountable fancies to people, that one!—was pleased because Schultz mended his portable radio. The one in the Mercédès. He also improved something in the wiring—I know nothing of these things. He is an expert driver, he was taken on in the place of the other fellow. You understand, the Marshal is glad to change his drivers fairly frequently. Schultz won't be with him long, but—long enough for what Schultz wants."

"What does Schultz want?"

"Something that he will get!" the other replied, laying a stubby forefinger against his nose.

The door opened, and a very tall, exceedingly handsome man of about thirty-five entered. He

358

was fair, his skin was clear, his eyes large and wide open. He walked forward with the air of a man used to authority. The young officer followed. The guard and Flight stood to attention.

"This the man?" the General asked, pointing to Flight.

"Sent by the Marshal, sir."

"Deliver your messages!" the General ordered.

Flight hesitated.

"What is it? You heard me, didn't you?"

"Sir, respectfully, I mention that the Marshal gave me certain orders of a very private nature to deliver to you. In your presence—alone."

The other laughed. "What are you, an assassin?"

Flight drew from his waistcoat the card which had been given to him. He handed it to the General, saying with such hauteur as he could achieve:

"This is my credential, sir."

The other studied the card, returned it, saying, "Your pardon!" Then to the two men who were standing near, "Wait outside. I suppose he is not armed?"

"No, sir. I myself searched him."

"Good—wait!"

Slowly Flight told his story. That it did not adhere strictly to the truth did not disturb him. The Marshal had been taken ill, so had a soldier, also, Flight added modestly, he had himself. Suffering untold agonies, the Marshal had shown the greatest fortitude, he had actually shed tears when the doctor assured him that he must not travel. His devotion to duty! . . .

The General tapped with a pencil on the desk top and said, "Yes—go on—go on!"

Because he had wished no one to know that he had broken his journey, for reasons which no doubt the General would appreciate, though they had not been communicated, he had chosen a poor French prisoner—in the person of François Pascal. There were also two letters which were to be delivered, with due secrecy, in Paris.

"To women?"

Flight bowed. "I believe so—also a cowhide bag, which is locked."

The other said, "I don't want to know anything about them. Pah! Now, where are these papers?"

Flight produced them. He had scanned them quickly in the lavatory before he left the German barracks, the salient points were safe in his memory, very pleasing points to remember, they were too. He handed over the beautiful leather case with its decorative gold corners and monogram. The General raised it to his nose, sniffed it and said again, "Pah!" Drawing out the papers he began to read. Without raising his eyes he said to Flight, "Sit down. You can smoke if you wish. There are cigarettes in that box."

For what seemed to Flight to be a very long time, he read on, the only sound in the huge room was the rustling of the documents as he turned them over, once only he whistled softly. Then laid them down and said, thoughtfully, "What is the date?"

"November the tenth, sir."

"Um—No-vem-ber the tenth," he repeated slowly. "Ah well—nearing the end of another year, eh? Two years of war! How many more I wonder?"

Flight ventured, "Your Leader says . . ."

"I know. What does Churchill say? Well, the first part of your duty is done. Now—what next?"

"His Excellency wishes you to send your own doctor back to him at once, sir. He was most emphatic on that point. *At once!*"

"What's he got, stomachache? Well, there's plenty of room for it! Very well, let's get the doctor sent off." His manner was pleasant, even friendly; he smiled as he leaned forward and touched the electric bell on his desk. He gave his order crisply, and added, "Bring some coffee! Strong—for two." Then as the door closed said, "You can do with a cup I don't doubt? And then? . . . oh! you have these two letters and the bag to deliver. No, you can have a car. I'll arrange for that. And then . . . ?"

"I presume that I return to you, sir, into custody."

"What the devil can I do with you?"

"The Marshal hinted that he might use me as an interpreter when he arrived here, sir."

The good-looking young man stretched his arms above his head. "I shan't be here," he said.

"I'm leaving today for Africa." He laughed. "For Africa. To join Rommel. I suppose I ought not to tell you that, eh? What the hell does it matter! If I ever get there—I shan't be there long. You see, I'm not von Leibstruk! He's sleeping off a heavy night —he took over from me this morning, officially. They couldn't wake him. I'm Eitel Stromburg, and they don't like me—much. This"—tapping the blue leather case—"will be a nice little—what do they say? 'cup of tea' for my respected—or possibly not so respected—colleague when he wakes! I don't care much—François Whatever your name is—and I suspect that it's not your name at all! I'm finished, done with." He raised his hand in the Nazi salute and said, with considerable dramatic force, "Heil! or Hail!—it really doesn't matter either—we who are about to die salute you! I think that I'm just a little crazy. So, Herr François, do what you like! If you can slip away— well, slip! I can't—if I did I should only be caught and—dealt with."

The coffee was brought, and he sat stirring it slowly, meditatively. "Queer!" he said, as if he spoke to himself, "How much one believed. One believed everything. Ideals, hopes, faith, trust—were all there. Now, after two years, these things have vanished into thin air."

Flight said, "Perhaps there'll be another chance—in Africa?"

The other wrinkled his nose in derision. "There aren't 'other chances' in the Third Reich," he said.

362

"They are expensive luxuries, which cannot be afforded. They can't afford to put you against a wall and shoot you. People begin to whisper that there is dissension, differences of opinion, so there are provided, aeroplanes that don't land—where they are scheduled to land. Bullets which don't hit the mark for which they are supposed to be intended. These things are regretted; beautiful letters are written, eulogies composed about the man who didn't carry out all that he was told to do. The man who had not sufficient imagination to invent a new type of rubber truncheon, a fresh means for extracting information, the man who was too squeamish to stand by, listen and watch. So it goes on! . . ." Again he rang the bell, and gave the order that a car should be placed at the disposal of the emissary of His Excellency the Marshal. He unlocked a drawer, saying again as if he talked to himself, "These must be cleared out ready for my successor." Then to Flight, "D'you want any money? It's no use to me. Better take this, I've more than I need. Yes, please! Is it too early to offer you a drink? I have some real Scottish whisky. Oh, yes—eat, drink and be merry . . ."

He moved over to a cabinet, produced glasses and a bottle, searched again for a syphon of soda water. Flight watched him. Did he actually mean that he was being sent out, ostensibly to Africa, but in reality—to die, to crash in some hideous death, shattered to pieces on the side of some snow-covered mountain, in the waters of a great lake, in the Mediterranean, even in the desert sand? Were these things planned, coldly and deliberately, by this man's superiors?

He came back, carrying two glasses, saying conversationally, "I like Scottish whisky-and-soda, don't you? I like Scotland I used to go there to shoot sometimes. Not far from Aberdeen. Aberdeen, the granite city; how pretty it looks when the sun comes out after the rain and shines on all the bits of—what is it?—some kind of chips of stone in the granite? It looks like a city set with diamonds. In Yorkshire too, I've shot—over the moors. Those wonderful moors! I went to school in England, near Whitby. My mother was English. You'd have liked her, she was a fine person. Fine —you know what I mean? No base metal there. What are you really? I suppose I ought not to ask that because if I knew there might still be some threads of duty left hanging about, and habits take a lot of breaking. The habits of a lifetime. I'm thirty-six. My promotion has been rapid in the extreme. My descent will be equally rapid, believe me! Hello, it's eight o'clock! I leave at ten. Well —think of me tonight, 'Jove's planet rising slowly over Africa.' I don't know if I've got that right? Goodbye, and in using your wits remember you're using them against fellows who are far more cunning than you are."

Flight stammered, "I hope that—after all you're wrong—that . . ."

"Thanks, I'm not wrong. Look here, if you like,

slip up to my room and have a wash and a shave. I've got a lot to do here. Yes, that's all right, my man will show you. Poor devil, he'll have to come with me. Well, good-bye—the best of luck, and remember, whatever happens—the game is still playing."

He was escorted by a stolid-looking soldier-servant to a bedroom, suitcases, uniform cases were scattered about, ready strapped for the journey. The stolid servant showed him the bathroom, uttering only grunts as he indicated where everything was kept. Flight wondered if he had any idea what lay before him? If he guessed that once they boarded that 'plane it was improbable that they would ever reach the ground again alive. Eitel Stromburg, this soldier-servant, the pilot, the navigator—possibly others—were they all to share the same fate? He shivered. The whole business was so cold-blooded, so matter of fact, so calmly bestial.

In the solitude of the splendid bathroom, he drew out the two letters which the Marshal had given to him. Carefully he opened the envelopes by holding them over the steaming bath tap, extracted the letters, tore them in small pieces, and threw them into the water closet. At least he could cause a little additional annoyance to the fat exaltedness. He felt sick, revengeful, bitter. The empty envelopes he put back in his inner pocket.

Then, shaved and washed, he descended the stairs, retrieved his bag, and entered the waiting car, giving the driver the first of the two addresses.

The first was a fine *appartement* house near the Faubourg St. Honoré. He examined the name plates and found that of "Madame de Ravillac". He mounted the wide stairs, heavily carpeted. He rang, a maid opened the door. The kind of maid he disliked, too smart, too be-capped and be-aproned, her face too pert. "Madame is still in bed."

That was to be regretted, for he had urgent business with Madame. Business which concerned a person of the greatest importance. Need he say more?

She went away, returning with the message that Madame would see him, and ushered him into a *salon*, crowded with fine furniture, good rugs, and some magnificent china. Flight glanced round, assessing the probable value. More loot—more handsome presents—more generous gifts from the open-handed German.

Madame entered. She was small, very fair, her complexion was completely artificial, her eyes bright and acquisitive.

She said, "Yes, monsieur—what did you wish to see me about?"

He tiptoed over to the door and opened it carefully, peering out into the corridor. Then closing it again, returned to where she stood. She was nervous already, her fingers were twisting the lace of her *peignoir*.

"Yes, monsieur?"

He drew out the empty envelope and held it up for her inspection.

"The writing is familiar, Madame?"

"Yes, give me the letter . . ."

"Madame, there is no letter. No letter was possible. Too dangerous. Here is a card, given to me as a credential by the Marshal. Look!"

"Yes, yes?" She was shaking a little, her voice was not quite steady.

"The message is this, 'Go immediately, to delay is dangerous'."

"Go, go! But where—where?"

"His Excellency did not say, he apparently imagined that you knew."

"But—where is His Excellency? Surely he said more than that—I must know? Tell me immediately! Cecile!" she called, and again, "Cecile, immediately my bags must be packed. Now, tell me . . ."

Flight said gravely, "Madame, I grieve to tell you that His Excellency is gravely ill. He sent me to you. When I left he could scarcely speak . . ."

"You mean that he is dying?" She clutched his arm with a hand like a bird's claw. An over-manicured bird's claw, Flight thought.

He bowed his head. "Madame, His Excellency is in the Hands of God . . . he is very, very ill."

"Did he send me money?"

"I regret, Madame, that he was beyond thinking of such things."

She became suddenly practical. Calling again for

367

Cecile, muttering, "I must go, they hate me—the others hate me!" Then to Flight, "Go! you can do no good here, I don't need you here. Yes, quickly."

He went, descended the stairs again, and as he went he heard her shrieking some message into the telephone.

He re-entered the car. "Now, to deliver the Marshal's bag. For which I must get a receipt, eh?"

The driver grunted. "It is always wiser."

"Then, 12 Rue Feydeau."

He climbed to the top floor of the tall house, lugging the bag with him.

An old woman opened the door and asked what he wanted. Flight smiled, and told her that he came from one Rappe. She opened the door wider and admitted him and his beautiful bag.

"Rappe said, Madame, that you would keep this for me until I called for it. Believe me, it is important, but it contains nothing in the least dangerous." He stripped off several notes and watched her eyes widen with surprise as she noticed the value of them. "When I come for the bag, I will give you as much again. My name is François Pascal."

She nodded. "It will be safe, I promise that. You know my name?"

"Yes, Madame, your name is Gagé, Rappe told me."

"That is one of them at least." She smiled, showing indifferent teeth.

"Good day, Madame. Many thanks."

He smiled as he ran down the stairs. Everything was shaping well, and soon he would be able to make his way to the house of Madame Matot, to meet Jules again, to hide there perhaps, until the hue and cry was over; for he was certain that the Marshal would search for him. He must be very, very careful.

"Now," he told the driver. "My last visit is to a street off here called Rue des Graves. The number is seven."

A mean street with tall, modern houses divided into flats. A street where the inhabitants appeared to be of every class; there was a tall, thin man dressed in an ultra-respectable style, carrying a small black bag; there was a stout woman, probably the wife of an artisan, with her shopping basket; then again, two women wearing incredibly high heels and cheap but effective clothes, standing together indulging in a discussion which sounded acrimonious; a big nigger, who might have been a boxer, lounged past them and flung them a word over his shoulder. Not a particularly pleasant neighbourhood.

The driver said, "Here is seven."

Flight got out. "Don't wait for me," he said. "I shall walk back to Headquarters. No, it is all right, believe me. I shall report in due course."

Again he showed his precious card. The driver whistled softly, nodded and drove away. Flight glanced at the address on the envelope—

Mademoiselle Jamais. He grinned. "That's all right so far as I am concerned."

The place smelt stuffy, the carpet on the stairs was stained and dusty; as he mounted them, a door opened and a woman peered out at him as he passed. On the door of the topmost flat a card was pinned with thumb-tacks, it was a cheap card and bore the name, "Mademoiselle Louise Jamais".

He knocked, and after a slight delay the door swung open. A very tall, heavily-built woman asked what he wanted.

"Mademoiselle Louise Jamais?"

She nodded. "Well?"

"May I come in? I have a message for you from a friend."

She jerked her head backwards to indicate that he might enter.

Flight saw that she was wearing a very large, shabby dressing-gown and leather slippers down at heel. He didn't like the place. There was something curious and sinister about the woman. He followed her into the untidy, slovenly room, where the remains of a breakfast was cluttering the table. She sat down, planting her big hands on her knees, and stared at him. "Come on!" she said, "let me hear this message."

Flight said, "It is from the Marshal."

"Yes—and . . . ?"

He wished desperately that he had not been such a quixotic fool as to tear up the letters unread.

What could the Marshal, that fat, luxury-loving creature have to do with a place like this? He pulled out his box of cigarettes, took one, and held it up to Mademoiselle Jamais.

"Have one?" he said. She nodded. He took one out and threw it over the table to her. She caught it, but not before Flight had seen the automatic movement which brought her knees together. He lit his cigarette, and leaning forward, offered a light, saying, "So you're not a woman, eh?"

"Who said that I was?"

"Mademoiselle Louise Jamais . . ."

"I'm a variety artist, a female impersonator. That's why my hair is short. You can probably still see my make-up? I wear wigs. I am probably the best female impersonator in Paris . . . Poof! Paris! In Europe, in the world. And you—what are you?"

The last question was asked in a voice which was cold with heavy fury.

"I am the bearer of a message from the Marshal . . ."

"So you say. What proof have you?"

Flight produced the envelope. The man turned it over, sniffed it, and laid it on the table. "Stolen, I presume."

"You'd be wrong. Look at this . . ." and again he offered his card for inspection.

"Forged! What's your name? François Pascal. Umph! And the message?"

It came as a shock—like a blow between the

eyes—to Flight, that he had concocted no message, and that he was at a loss as to what to say. He glanced round the room, wondering if he dared make a bolt for it? The window would be very high; to clatter down the stairs with this fellow in his wake would be to rouse everyone in the building.

The man said, "Come on—give me the message."

He said, "Wait a moment! How do I know that what you tell me is true? There's a woman's name on the front door, when I came in you didn't deny that you were a woman. I've got to be careful. How much money does the Marshal generally give you?" That was a shot in the dark, but it might land somewhere.

"Depends on what he wants . . ."

"The usual . . ."

"Depends on how much he needs."

"Could you get a little more than usual this time? How much more?"

"I might manage an ounce . . ."

"The powder?" That again was a shot in the dark.

"Of course, d'you suppose I get it by the bottle, idiot."

"Five thousand, eh?"

"Six—can't do it for less."

"Whew! It's a lot of money, my friend. Still, those are my orders. Let's have it."

The man rose and gathered his shabby dressing-gown around him. As he walked across the room, Flight noticed that his gait was curiously woman-ish, not particularly natural either, but as if he had learnt it after years of training. He said, "I'd like to see your act."

"It's damned good, my act. My clothes are magnificent." He was busy unlocking a small cupboard. Once he looked round at Flight, his eyes narrowed. Then he returned to the table, his whole, rather coarse, face expressing satisfied cunning. He laid two packets on the table.

"Where is the Marshal?"

"He will be in Paris, in all probability, tomorrow. At the most distant day, the day following."

"What are you going to do with this stuff?"

"Give it to him when he arrives, of course."

"What's the hurry if he won't be here until tomorrow?"

Flight shrugged his shoulders. "You know what the Marshal is, don't you? Anyway, those were my orders."

The man opened the two packets, both contained fine white powder.

He said, "Make your choice. You know it when you see it, don't you?"

"I'm—not very certain—let me see . . ."

"Not very certain!" The man bellowed suddenly, "Not very certain and you're supposed to be in the employ of the Marshal. Not very certain, you damned fool . . . one is table salt the other is camphorated chalk. You wanted cocaine. Or pretended that you did. You stinking spy, you, you blasted agent, what are you? French underground? We'll see. No, don't move, we'll talk this out."

8

THE man tipped his chair backwards and sat there, tilting backwards and forwards, staring at Flight, his face expressionless and stolid. Once or twice he sucked his teeth noisily, but otherwise remained silent.

Flight found him singularly unattractive. His face was heavy, and there were distinct traces of last night's make-up still lurking in the folds of his heavy chin and neck. Years ago he might have been good-looking, but those years were long past. He looked what he was—a fifth-rate variety artist, well on the down-grade, and possessed of neither intelligence nor imagination, though probably of certain grosser characteristics, which Flight did not doubt were developed to a high extent.

He spoke at last. "Smart of you to spot me, eh?"

Flight knocked the ash off his cigarette lightly on to the dusty floor.

"Not very! I'm not been a 'tec for nothing all these years."

"Where?"

"That is my business, monsieur."

The heavy face grew even heavier, the man appeared to brood over what Flight had said. "There's a devil of a lot that's going to be *my* business before I've done with you. A 'tec! And you don't know salt and camphorated chalk from 'snow'? D'you know Madame Ravillac by any chance?"

Apparently unmoved, Flight answered, "Very well indeed."

"Know her address?"

"I know what *was* her address. You won't find her there now."

The man rose, lifted his chair and set it down with a bang, as if he had arrived at some conclusion. He glared at Flight, but behind the rather theatrical expression, his eyes were puzzled. He was like a stupid bull, Flight thought, trying to give the impression of clever cunning.

He said, "I'm going after this! Let me have your papers."

"Certainly not! Don't talk such blasted nonsense."

The glare died, the expression of uncertainty achieved the upper hand.

"Well, anyway, I'm going out—and you're staying here until I come back. There's nothing to find. I'm not such a fool as to leave things lying about. There's no telephone either. Come into the other room while I dress." The inner room was in a state of wild disorder, a half-drawn curtain gave a glimpse of many female stage dresses, all rather dirty and shabby. There were a number of shoes with high heels standing against the wall. Over a chair was flung a creased brown suit and a soiled shirt. The man began to pull on the shirt, and as his head emerged, he nodded towards the dresses.

"Wonderful stage wardrobe. The Marshal himself gave me some of them when he first came to Paris. Some of them belonged to Max Larrière—you've heard of him, eh?"

Flight had never heard the man's name before, but he only smiled and said, "You forget that I am a Parisian, monsieur!"

The other dipped the corner of a grimy towel into a basin, full of water, on which grey soap-scum floated, and applied it delicately to his mouth, nose and eyes. He peered at himself in the glass and the reflection appeared to satisfy him. He pulled on his trousers, added a pair of brilliant socks with holes in the toes, a pair of very long, narrow brown shoes, and finally a collar, tie and waistcoat. He picked up his jacket, dusted it with his dilapidated hair-brush, which he then applied to his own head.

"Now!" he said briskly, "you'll stay here, my clever friend. The door will be locked—everything else is locked. I'm getting to the bottom of this—I don't like it at all. We'll see what headquarters have to say about you."

Flight said, "Look here, you're making an infernal fool of yourself. You've seen my credentials from the Marshal, you've seen his handwriting on that envelope. You'll only get rapped over the knuckles, I can promise you that."

The man shook his head. "I like to make certain. I'm not called 'Honest la Blanche' for nothing, I'm not."

"'La Blanche' isn't your real name any more than 'Jamais' is."

"I didn't say that it was. Stay there, nose about as much as you like, there's nothing—where you can find it, Monsieur Detective."

He walked out. Flight heard him pass through the outer room and go out of the front door, locking it behind him. He sat very still on the rickety bedroom chair, surveyed the litter of dirty, shoddy clothes round him, and whistled softly.

It would have been useless to attempt to hold him back, he was a big powerful fellow, even though he might be flabby; he had probably eaten his rolls and drunk his coffee this morning. Flight was uncomfortably conscious that he had eaten nothing since six o'clock the previous evening. By the time this fellow, La Blanche, arrived at the Embassy, Stromburg might well have gone, on his way to Rommel in Africa. Stromburg was under some sort of a cloud, the fact that they had been closeted alone together would certainly not prejudice anyone in Flight's favour.

Again Flight whistled, and then murmured softly, "I am undoubtedly in a nasty spot. Catch me ever being too scrupulous to read a man's letters again. I'll read every damned word. If I'd done that I shouldn't be in this jam now. I wonder what that fat lump of conceit really did want? I'll never know now."

He got up and began to make a careful search of the rooms. "La Blanche" was right, he found nothing. Nothing except dirt and disorder, filth and stuffy-smelling clothes. In the big cupboard in the outer room were a few bits of food lying on greasy plates; some ham curling at the edges, a tin of milk half-empty, and the heel of a small loaf of bread. He wondered if he ought to try to eat, but his stomach turned at the thought. Under the bed, among rolls of dusty fluff, was a small black tin box. It was locked, but after breaking a pair of rusty nail scissors Flight managed to open it. He found some fading photographs of "Mademoiselle Jamais" wearing tremendous hats and very low-cut dresses which exposed what were obviously false bosoms; half a dozen "dirty postcards", some old letters written on mauve paper with a large scarlet "M" embossed in the corner, several rolls of notes of considerable value, and two packets of white powder. So this was where "La Blanche" kept his stock.

He went back to the kitchen and compared the powder which he had found, with the camphorated chalk and the fine table salt. With great care he mixed them all together, and then redistributed them in their original packets. He returned two to the cupboard and shut the others away in the tin box. "A war of nerves!" he murmured.

He went to the window—the prospect was not encouraging. The top floor of a tall house, with no sign of balconies to break a fall, and no sign either of a fire-escape. The window in the stuffy bedroom opened on to a steep slope of grey slates which terminated in the gutter which ran round the house. The window was a dormer window, jutting out of the main roof. Flight stood back and rubbed his chin reflectively.

He examined the bed. It was large, sagging in the middle, made of what had once been black lacquered iron, with brass knobs—two of which were missing. He pushed it near the window, then removed the sad-coloured sheets and began to tear them into strips. He worked swiftly but without undue haste. He plaited the strips into a rope, tested it with his hands, pulled down the corners of his mouth as if he doubted its strength, then fastened it securely to the rail of the bed. The other end he hung out of the window. Then removing his shoes, he grasped the rope with both hands and slid through the open window.

The first sensation was one of complete lack of faith in the strength of the sheets; the second was one of no longer possessing any stomach, the third was that he was most certainly going to have a run for his money. Dangling on the rope, he looked upwards. The dormer window jutted out from the roof—once he could reach it, straddle across its apex, he could scramble to the top of the main roof and work his way along. Hand over hand he climbed, until he reached the gutter. He tested it with his hand, and, still holding the rope, levered himself up and up. He grasped the side of the window, slid out his other hand to clutch the slightly overhanging roof, levered himself again, and felt the gutter behind him this time, his toes pressing hard against it.

Again a greater effort, and he was seated with his legs dangling over the apex of the little dormer, looking down into the distant street where people marched like pigmies.

He recovered his breath, and slowly and painfully wriggled round so that he turned away from the edge of the roof itself. The top was not more than three feet away. Again he pulled and strained, this time without even the somewhat doubtful comfort of having the rope to protect him if he slipped. Again and again, until he found himself —feeling that every one of his toes was dislocated through the pressure which he had put on them —astride the topmost part of the grey slate roof.

Working himself along with his hands, as if he were riding some kind of hobby-horse, Flight moved slowly forward. Once a slate gave way under his foot and went crashing down into the street far below.

He heard himself say, "Oh, dear! I hope no one's hurt," then continued his progress. He reached the end of the house; the next one was several feet lower, and he swung himself down, falling in a confused heap, his hands clutching wildly. This roof was easier; he decided that he preferred tiles to slates. He passed a large water-tank and leaned gratefully against it to rest for a moment or two. He had no plans; he could not, most certainly, go crawling over the roofs of Paris for ever, he would have to descend somewhere. He continued his journey, realising that his hands were cut, bleeding a little, and filthy dirty.

The third house had a parapet. His heart warmed to whoever had been the architect. He slipped down the roof until he reached it, and lay pressed against it, his heart beating furiously. He peered over the edge; below him was another house, a house with a roof in which was set a huge skylight. The difference in height between it and the roof where he lay was possibly fifteen feet. Again no fire-escape, but as he wriggled along he found an iron drain-pipe fixed to the wall; it reached to the ground, but on its way it passed close to the roof where the wide, partially-open skylight was.

Drawing a deep breath, he leaned over the parapet and tested the pipe with his hands. It was quite firmly fixed. Again he levered himself into a sitting position, and carefully flung one leg over the parapet. He slid it down the iron, holding himself firm, the other leg followed, and he began to descend, inch by inch. Sweat poured from him; it ran into his eyes so that he had to blink to clear them, his mouth tasted sour and dry. Time had ceased to exist. How often had he read of descents being made easily and light-heartedly by a pipe such as this? Thieves, escaping lovers, naughty schoolboys. He muttered savagely, "Lies— damned lies! I'd like to see them try it, that's all!"

The pipe was moving under his hands; a piece of

projecting iron which should have held it to the wall had worked loose, and as his foot slid past it, he felt his sock rip and the iron cut deeply into his foot.

The pipe swung loose; he twisted his head to see how far he was from the roof, he judged it to be about ten feet. As the pipe tilted, he let go his hold and dropped on to the roof below. There he lay in a crumpled heap, the breath driven out of his body, his foot bleeding copiously, his hands spread, nerveless, filthy and covered with blood. Cautiously he moved his legs and arms to reassure himself that he had broken no bones; he stared about him. The skylight was open about a foot. Slowly he crawled towards it and peered down.

He could see what appeared to be part of a studio. He saw a section of carpet, a large chair, and a moment later the figure of a man. He drew back and lay on his side, scarcely daring to breathe. Below he heard the sound of something being dragged across the floor, and presently a man's head appeared through the opening in the skylight.

Flight stared at him, he stared back at Flight.

Neither spoke, each regarding the other in silence.

Flight saw a large face which terminated in a small pointed brown beard. A delicate nose, which surmounted a mouth which was generous and which at the moment twitched a little at the corners; the eyes, with great pouches of flesh beneath them, danced with amusement.

A soft voice enquired, "Did you make that abominable noise?"

"I'm afraid so . . ."

"Do you want to come in? If so, why not come to the door?"

"Because I came over the roofs . . ."

"Ah! Eccentric, but no doubt explicable. Come in, won't you?"

Flight thought that he might have been inviting him in for a drink after being at a theatre together. He said, "I'm very dirty and my foot is bleeding."

"Oh, I can't have you bleeding over my carpet! Wait a minute."

The head disappeared, there was the sound of a heavy body descending, and a few seconds later of someone mounting, with difficulty, a chair. A hand, large, well-kept and very smooth, stretched out and handed Flight a clean table-napkin, saying, "Wrap that round your foot, then come along."

With difficulty Flight wrapped the napkin round his foot and crawled along to the skylight, which the man opened more widely to admit him.

He descended from the chair and held out his hand, saying, "There you are! Lord, you are in a mess! We might do worse than follow Mr. Dick's advice to Miss Trotwood regarding her nephew. Come on, sit down. Let's look at that foot."

With surprising activity for such a stout person —for he was one of the heaviest men Flight had ever seen—he hurried away, returning with a basin and warm water, drawing a roll of clean bandage from his pocket.

As he worked on the foot he kept uttering small exclamations and detached phrases.

"Oh, nasty! That's better—smarting? Can't be helped. Very dirty. Roofs in Paris no better, I suppose, than in London. Tut, tut—there, round once more—that's got it! All shipshape, eh?"

He carried away the basin and bandages, while Flight surveyed the room where he had arrived so surprisingly. It was very large, with two big windows curtained in shabby but fine brocade; a long narrow table, polished until the old wood gleamed softly, ran down the centre of the room; a great sofa, piled with cushions, stood against the wall opposite to the window. A big open fireplace where a small fire burnt was at the farther end, and near the sofa stood a kind of desk, on which lay what Flight recognised as a plate in process of being engraved.

The man came back, seated himself in a large armchair with wings, puffed out his cheeks, and said, "And now—do you want to talk, or remain silent? Just as you like."

Flight said, "I feel that I owe you an explanation. I was making a getaway."

"I had the impression that you were going for the milk," the other commented, and shook with silent mirth so that his whole body quivered.

"It may not be particularly safe for anyone to find me here."

"I can always say that you've come to clean the windows, and cut your foot by sticking it through a pane of glass—there are none broken, but we can rectify that. Let me first tell you about myself. There is nothing I enjoy so much as talking about myself, it is a passion with me! First, I'll give you a drink . . . what is the time? Nearly twelve o'clock. We'll have a pernod and seltz. Yes?"

As he bustled about, Flight noticed that his movements were particularly swift and exact; his hands moved quickly and without hesitation. He knew exactly what he needed, where to find everything, and how to use it. He brought back the glasses and set them on a beautiful little table, then lowered himself into his chair again, smiling like a beneficent Buddha.

He said, "Now my story. I tell it to everyone. Some people believe it, some do not. That is immaterial to me. I *like* it. My name is Moses Goldstein, and I call myself Maurice Gold. Why do I call myself that? Because I like the name Maurice, and because all is not gold that glitters, and at times I glitter profusely! Scintillate might be a better word. I am an engraver by profession. Many people do not regard my work as having great merit, I myself consider it—remarkable. I am not in the least interested in the war or matters political. I dislike the Germans because I was born a Jew, because I consider their food heavy and much too rich—without that light richness, you understand, of French cooking. They are overbearing—but so

386

I am myself—frequently. Their voices are inartistic, their virtues non-existent. The English I dislike, because their food is the best in the world, and they take a pride in ruining it by their cooking; they are hypocritical, and idealistic to the extent of shutting their eyes to whatever they dislike, and swearing that it does not exist. A childish people, saved only by a sort of unreasoning and courageous determination. They say with pride, 'We always win the last battle,' and that is their excuse for all the mistakes they make."

He took another sip of his drink. "It's not bad, is it? Prewar, of course. The French have decided long ago what a Frenchman should be, and are determined to develop along those lines only. Their cooking is superb, their women almost as charming as they themselves believe, their men are so provincial that they still believe that it is *épatant* to have a mistress, even if they really don't want her and she bores them to extinction. Their art is deplorable—once it was admirable. Their music pitiful. The *décor* in their theatres is not good. They are as self-satisfied as the English, but less hypocritical and more genuinely amusing.

"That is why I live among them. I was born in Hackney, educated at a Board school—they are called council schools in these days. I was a very charming-looking person when I was about eighteen. I studied art—heaven help me! One of the teachers was a well-known R.A.—of course I learnt nothing. I came to Paris and studied at the studio of one Pinchon—who showed me that my true bent was engraving. I have a very light, firm and steady hand. There one day I met the Duc and Duchesse de Villontelle. Immensely rich, childless, and possessed of perfect taste. The long and short of it was, they adopted me, and when they both died they left me everything which was not strictly entailed. There is my story. How do you like it?"

"It is most interesting . . ."

"Then I am satisfied. You are under no obligation to believe it unless you wish. If you prefer to believe that I made my money—and I have a great deal—from my engravings, from selling tripe, or by forging banknotes, you are at perfect liberty to do so. Now another drink, and I will give orders regarding luncheon. My man waits, his wife cooks. It is a mistake to believe that only men can cook. Women need training, but they can be trained, as you shall see." He leaned forward and rang a small silver bell which stood on the table. It was answered by a thin, dark man wearing an immaculate striped jacket and dark trousers.

His master said, "My compliments to madame. I have a guest. I suggest that she prepares some clear soup, the *poulet sauté à la crême*, and possibly a sweet omelette to follow. A simple meal, you understand. And the wine—shall I say Cheval Blanc the 1911? Yes. And, Passepartout, another pernod for monsieur and for me." As the door closed Gold said, "I call him Passepartout after the

388

famous servant in *Round the World in Eighty Days*. Now have you had time to concoct a story, O Scheherazade?"

Flight said, "Honestly, I have had so many names that I never know which one to choose. My real name is Flight . . ."

Gold said, "After your exploit this morning this is an excellent choice."

"It's my real name . . ." Flight began, but the other calmly held up his hand, saying:

"Please go on, I am enthralled."

Flight told as much of his story as he deemed fit, including the story of his escape from the dirty flat and the reason for his having to make it. Gold listened, nodding from time to time. Flight wondered how much he believed.

When the story was ended, he said, "Ah, I don't blame you for not reading the fat creature's letters! Other people's letters are so dull. If they promised to be amusing, well of course one would read them. I should have no scruples." He laid his fingertips together. "Now, for the sake of argument, we will assume that this story is true—more or less. This being so, what do you plan to do? Collect this bag of yours? Well, Passepartout shall go for that. I suggest that you take a bath while that admirable servant of mine tries to clean up your clothes a little and finds you another pair of socks. I have some rather pleasant socks, make your own choice."

"You are most kind . . ."

389

"First, if you will wash your hands, we will have luncheon."

They enjoyed a most beautiful luncheon, perfectly served and admirably cooked. The china, cutlery and glass were all, so far as Flight could judge, perfect of their kind. He estimated that with prices as they were in Paris, Gold must be a very rich man.

He ate with appetite, never hesitating to praise the food, the wine, or the furniture in the room where they sat. "That is a beautiful piece," he might say, waving his hand in the direction of a cabinet or occasional table. "My taste is always admirable. I often wonder where I get it from. My own home, I remember, was filled with monstrosities of all kinds."

He appeared to have travelled greatly, for he talked of America, of Africa and Australia as if he knew them all well. "The Americans," he said, "are like their own slang—completely beyond understanding to strangers. Once you learn them and their language they are engagingly simple and most entertaining—except when they tell stories about 'shaggy dogs', which I have never understood, and my sense of humour is most highly developed."

Later, after what he termed a "discreet interval for digestion", he took Flight into his bedroom, and showed him a bathroom which was staggering in its restrained magnificence. Marble steps led down to the bath, taps gleamed, the shelves were filled with silver-topped bottles containing bath salts, lotions and scents. The floor was polished marble, the towels soft, well warmed and vast. The valet waited for his clothes, which he carried away with a faint air of disgust that any man could have contrived to get himself so dirty.

The warm water made Flight's foot sting, but by the time he was out again, wrapped in his huge bath-sheet and feeling not unlike a Roman emperor, he found that the bleeding had stopped, and there on a wide dressing-table was a roll of adhesive bandage.

His clothes were hanging outside the bathroom door, sponged and pressed. He put them on and walked back in his stockinged feet to the big studio. His host asked, without turning, "Did you get clean socks?"

"Your man had laid a pair out for me. The only trouble is that I have no shoes. I knew that I could climb better without them."

"Well, you most certainly can't wear mine. I have the smallest foot of any man I know. Years ago, Peel's fitter said to me, 'Your feet is—are —almost a deformity'. Poor fellow, I don't doubt that he meant it as a compliment, but I never went to him again. We must see what Passepartout can find for you. And then what do you propose? While you were in your bath a fellow came here asking if I had seen you. A great impertinence! He described you as being about five feet seven, having light brown hair, light eyes and a fair skin. He said that you were wearing a dark-blue suit. This only goes to show how little people actually observe. I remember the late Sherlock Holmes once saying the same thing. You are five foot nine, your hair is a *warm* brown, not light, your eyes are grey, and your skin—now that the dirt is removed—is not fair but rather sunburnt. That suit is not blue, the grey predominates, and there is a very faint red line running through it. He asked if you were here. 'Don't be foolish,' I replied. 'No one is here except my servants, my aunt, and a window cleaner.' He asked if he might see the window cleaner. I said, 'Certainly not! I pay the man by the hour and I will not allow him to lose time; he is busy now on the bathroom window.' Then he said, 'I will go in the bathroom.' I replied, 'You will do nothing of the kind, my aunt from Nantes is taking a bath!' He opened his eyes in the manner of these uneducated fools, and said, 'But you said that your aunt was taking a bath—your aunt from Nantes.' 'What,' I said, 'has it got to do with you where my aunt comes from?' He gaped, his foolish mouth half open. 'But your aunt—and the man cleaning the windows. Is your aunt in the bath?' 'That,' I replied with dignity, 'is a matter which concerns only my aunt and the window cleaner. Please remove yourself, you smell most objectionable.'"

His massive face was completely serious. Flight wondered if he were mad, or was he merely a comedian—what was he?

He said, "It is most kind of you to show such interest in my affairs. I am grateful—deeply grateful."

"Interest? Not at all. The only interest which ever concerns me is to make sure that I get a safe and certain four and a half per cent on my money. Young man, I am puzzling you? I puzzle many people. This"—and he waved his hand towards the table where the metal in process of engraving stood—"is a sideline. My work is at the Quai d'Orsay—does that mean anything to you? I don't suppose so. How do you suppose the finances of Europe are controlled? By the banks? Tut, tut! There are seven men—only two live in England, and neither is the Controller of the Bank of England. Another is in New York at the moment, a fourth in Lisbon. The sixth has gone to Ireland, and the seventh remains in France.

"My young friend, your Hitlers and Stalins, your Chamberlains and Churchills, your Benito Mussolinis don't make war. They decide to have a war—and that war must be financed. As a system it is barbarous, out of date, fantastic, but—it still exists. So your old, decrepit, self-indulgent friend, Maurice Gold is quite safe. If the Germans come, they will be civil—or reasonably so. If the British come, they will say, 'Neveh heard of yer! Better enquirah into this!' They will enquire, and they will be told to mind their own business. That old Maurice Gold is harmless, and must be left alone."

Flight stared at the handsome, placid face before

him. "And you mean to tell me that you—make wars—to all intents and purposes?"

"Tut, tut, make wars! My friend, I and my friends make money. That money may be used in various ways; some of them very excellent ways, let me assure you. Great dams, immense bridges, world-wide canals, experiments of a most costly nature. Not only—wars. Tut, tut! What a very limited outlook. I should be bored in a week. At the moment I am dreadfully, hideously bored. When you have left me I shall continue my engraving of the bridges over the Seine—it will be charming. Or I shall write a few pages of my book . . ."

"Your book? When will it be finished?"

"Never—and even if it were I should tear it in pieces. That is a pity. My handwriting is not only characteristic but exquisite." Then suddenly he became practical and gave his orders crisply and succinctly. Flight found that he was being instructed what to do and exactly how to behave.

He was to leave the house, leaning heavily on a stick. "Not a valuable one, so do not trouble to return it." He was to make his way to the end of the street, turn right, and then right again. There was a very shabby antique-shop, he was to stand there looking into the window. He would hear a soft whistle, and turning quickly, would get into the car which would be waiting immediately behind him. A rather old-fashioned car painted a drab shade of brown.

"Write down the address to which you wish to

go. Is there a back entrance? There is? Good!"
Obediently Flight wrote down the address and
handed it to Gold. He read it, his lips moving
silently, then without the least sign of surprise he
said, "So you know La Spero?"

"Yes—and her son Jules . . ."

"Will you be so good as to convey to her my
respects, and sincere compliments? Had I known,
I should have sent her flowers by you. However, I
send her so many she is probably bored by them.
Very well, here is your stick." He leaned forward,
rang the bell, and when his servant came, gave him
some rapid instructions in a language which Flight
did not understand but which he imagined might
be Polish. They shook hands, Gold smiled and
said, "Next time you call upon me, I recommend
the door, Mazaltov!"

He was shown out through a small back door,
which they reached through a little paved garden.
Flowers were blooming in the beds, despite the
lateness of the year. Passepartout said, "All the
year we have them. The soil is warmed by pipes
under the ground. My master got the idea from
some millionaire in New York."

Flight forced himself to walk boldly along the
street, fighting down a wish to hurry or slink along
by the wall. He turned right, and right again,
found the shabby antique-shop, and stood staring
into the window at the multiplicity of uninteresting
objects which it contained. He felt that he had been

standing there for an hour, that the eyes of every passer-by must be watching him, that the people in the houses opposite must be speculating on the identity of the man who stood staring at broken ear-rings, old false teeth, tarnished photograph frames, and odd packets of valueless foreign stamps with such intentness. Then he heard a whistle, soft and clear, and turning, moved to the car door, swung it open and got in.

The car rolled on. It was old, and rattled a good deal, the driver sat staring stolidly at the road ahead of him. They turned into Boulevard Haussmann, past the Opèra, and a moment later the Madeleine, turning off the Place de la Concorde. The car turned into a smaller street at the back of the Champs Elysées, slowed down; the driver glanced at the paper in his hand, drove on again, then stopped.

Flight asked, "We have arrived?"

"Two entrances farther along. Please descend quickly, monsieur!"

Clutching his precious bag and shoving a note into the driver's hand, Flight got out and made his way to the back entrance of the house of "Susan" Matot.

Part Three

1

ANN looked at the great Christmas tree, and said, "It's wonderful, Matron! I don't know how you've managed to make it so beautiful."

"We couldn't have done it without your generosity, ma'am."

Ann's eyes twinkled. "And the gifts from the working party, eh?"

The Matron sighed. "I don't know what the boys will say to them!"

"They'll send the American cloth animals home to their children and say they made them themselves, they'll send those awful socks home and say they're 'just the thing for Dad' . . ."

"Yes, but penwipers? What can they do with them?"

Ann giggled. "I shouldn't ask, or one of them might tell you!"

She continued her tour of inspection of the Christmas decorations; her trim figure gave every man who watched her from his bed a certain satisfaction. After all she was Lady Claverley; one day she'd be the Duchess of Alcaster, until that littlest boy—he was smaller nor what his brother was, although he was older—got married. Then she'd be Ann. Dowager Duchess.

"Chalky" White said to "Dusty" Miller, "What 'cher say 'er father was?"

Dusty replied, "Ole Nosey tole me—wholesale grocery! Rich as Cerebos, Nosey said!"

"Why's Cerebos so bloomin' rich?"

"Coo, like the salt! full of food stuffs, calories an' all this. It's suthing they always say, 'Rich as Cerebos'!"

"Funny one o' them kids havin' a fancy name like Sholto, an' the other just William, eh?"

Dusty sniffed. "Don't you know as the eldest son is allus given the same name? The old Juke's called Sholto; when this kid 'as a kid, it 'ul be called Sholto."

Chalky answered, "Might not be—might be a girl, see?"

Ann nodded to them all as she passed, from time to time making some comment on the excellence of the decorations.

"That's very good, who made that? You, Buster? And only a month ago you were telling me that you never expected to use your hands again! Look at that piece of gorgeousness!"

Buster, purple in the face, was understood to give the credit to, "'Lectric treatment wot I 'ad, that done it, ma'am."

Another man, pallid and unbelievably thin, scarcely moving even his eyes, whispered, "Just goes to show, eh, ma'am?"

She nodded, smiling. "Wait until we really get going with your treatment, Wells! There was a man over in B.5, far worse than you are. Worse! You could have broken him in two pieces, with one hand held behind you! You should see what it's done for him!"

The man whispered back, "A-ah? Well, I'll try anything once, ma'am."

On and on, through the great rooms which once had been filled with beautifully dressed women, where laughter had sounded, where splendid banquets had been given, where music had been heard and people had danced beneath the light of the great cut-glass chandeliers. Those rooms, now cleared of their fine furniture, with two rows of beds with their bright blue blankets, and a slight smell of disinfectant hanging over everything—beds filled with broken men—men who, if possible, must be mended, healed, cured, so that they might go back and "begin all over again".

Next time they might not come back—next time they might find the struggle too strong for them, and might stumble and fall in the mud, the snow, the sand, the hungry water.

She remembered one black-haired young Welshman, who had stared at her with hard, dark eyes, as if he resented having to die.

He had said, "Once, twice, three times—sometimes oftener—you can dodge it! Only, mark you, you're playing with Death, and Death holds nearly all the trump-cards, and is a fine player."

She had answered, "Learn to beat Death at his own game, Taffy!"

"That iss easy to say, ma'am, but less-s easy to do."

She walked out of the last ward; some man was being wheeled back to bed after an operation, the heavy smell of anaesthetics reached her, she caught a glimpse of a yellow face, distorted by the gag in the mouth, the lips curled back—the man looked dead, finished—in some macabre fashion—comic. A travesty of a man, who had fought, dealt out death, until Death had almost caught him in revenge.

The surgeon who followed halted for a moment. Ann nodded towards the moving stretcher.

"Who is it?" she asked.

"Came in two days ago. One leg had to go, I tried to save the other, but it was too badly smashed. Hard luck."

She answered, her eyes following the wheeled stretcher, "It's a heart-breaking business sometimes."

The surgeon smiled. He was young, full of ideas and hope. "Not always," he said. "There are some very bright things happen." His pink, freckled face cheered her, even the upward tilt of his nose seemed to speak of hope and determination. He added, as if to convince her, "Some remarkably bright and cheering things, Lady Claverley."

When people spoke to her in that tone, with that implication that they could say a great deal more if they wished, she knew that her heart always began to beat heavily, she always thought, "What if he is

going to tell me that there is news of Sholto?"
Trying to "break it gently", to minimise the
shock? He might say something like "And a very
cheering thing has happened today when the Duke
had a message from the War Office . . ." He didn't.
He just nodded, and said that he must be getting
back to the theatre.

She walked out into the garden; it didn't look too
untidy, even though they only had three gardeners, because the rest had gone to be soldiers.
Old Bateson, who was really too old for work anyway; Mackintosh—always called Mr. Mackintosh
because he was not really a gardener at all,
but a specialist who did marvellous things with
fertilisers and pollen and chemicals, in his little
room behind the conservatories; and young Matt,
who was Bateson's grandson and couldn't fight
because he had a false foot. A reaper had cut it off
when he was six.

The men were very good; once they were out of
bed, able to go out, some of them were always to be
found raking the gravel, or helping Mackintosh to
do what he called "A wee bit potting", or sweeping
up leaves. They liked doing it, took a pride in the
work.

December the twenty-fourth, 1941. More than
eighteen months since they had heard that Sholto
would not come home. The man he had helped
down to the boats, and another private soldier from
Dorset, as well as a Colonel who was in charge of
embarking or disembarking—Ann never knew

which—had testified to Sholto's courage. They had all written to her. The soldier's letter had been less stilted than the Colonel's, she remembered. Later she had gone to London and driven to the Palace, and had thought how very yellow the King's hair looked, and how any woman would have liked to have hair that colour, like ripe corn, only brighter, more shining. She had thought, "Poor souls, they can't be having much of a time, either of them."

The King had given her Sholto's medal and said, "I liked him very, very . . ." and then had stammered a little, and Ann said, "I think that most people did like him, sir." And the King nodded, and looked, she thought, grateful, because she had dared to interrupt him.

Eighteen months—soon it would be nineteen months—and the boys could almost walk safely alone, and grew more and more naughty every day. They weren't handsome children, Ann thought dispassionately, but Sholto hadn't been handsome either. He'd had a "snubby" face, she had always told him; he had stammered, and had been very obstinate about it too, when you tried to speak the word for him.

"All right, all right, I c-can s-s-s . . ."

Then she would laugh, and he'd say, without the trace of a stammer, "All right, you've won! I can't say it then. Who cares?"

Alcaster was a dear old thing. He adored the children, both of them equally. He never appeared to get over the fact that Ann had produced two children, and both boys. "And both, mark you" —he would say—"strong as lions! Lions! Whew! strong as elephants! Samson was a baby compared with those two!"

Everyone was astonishingly kind to her. Alcaster was always rummaging about in drawers and safes, sending to the bank for this piece of jewellery or that, and producing it shyly, saying, "Just struck me, Ann, that this might amuse you." He always thought that things might "amuse her". Her father and mother never ceased sending things for her; her father loved to discover "that I have an odd case of *pâté*—hope it's all right. You might enjoy it." Her mother sent more knitted clothes for the boys than they could ever hope to wear. Eleanor wrote long, often amusing, letters. Eleanor's spirits had returned since George was hit in the foot and sent home, because some of the tiny bones were shattered and would take months, perhaps years, to get right again. Old Charlton had returned to Harrogate.

She entered their own wing of the house and climbed the stairs to the nursery. How warm and comfortable it was after the cold air of the garden, how fresh and clear after the smell of disinfectant and dressings. The two boys were rolling on a wool rug before the big brass-topped fire-guard.

Nurse said, "Now, now! come, be good boys. Speak to your mama!"

The nurse had arrived, fairly bristling with recommendations and certificates of efficiency. She had stood before Ann and asked, "And what does your Ladyship wish me to call the two little gentlemen?"

Ann said, "I know what I should call them, very frequently, if I were in your shoes!"

"M'lady, I mean the elder, do you wish him to be 'y'lordship' and his brother, Lord William?"

"Good Lord, no! They're Sholto and William —Bill if you like! We can't begin treating them like belted earls at fifteen months old!"

"Certainly, m'lady."

But she hadn't really approved. She'd have enjoyed saying, "Now, m'lord, eat your bread and milk," and "Now, Lord William, don't lick the paint off the dog, if you please."

She sat down, said, "Come on, Sholto! come on, Bill! be civil."

Sholto smiled like a snub-nosed cherub and flung a wooden brick in her direction. William shouted with laughter and hurled a stuffed rabbit towards her. Ann said, "Couple of real jolly boys, you two!"

Nurse said, "Very high spirited, m'lady. Full of fun!"

"So long as they're well, Nurse, we'll teach them decent manners later. All right, good night, chaps! I'm going."

Then they flung away their toys and rushed towards her, clutching her round the knees,

406

yelling, "Mumm-ee!" at the tops of their voices.

She stooped and gathered them to her, feeling their hard little bodies, inhaling the smell of their smooth, clean skin, the touch of their soft downy hair against her face. She glanced up, and said to Nurse, "They're rather nice, I think, don't you?"

Nurse replied, "Full of fun, m'lady! and high spirits."

In her own bedroom, she sat before the glass, staring at her reflection. She decided that she liked her face, liked the pleasant oval shape, the dark hair, and the wide apart, clear eyes. The mouth was full, but it lifted a little at the corners. Her skin was clear and delicate.

She nodded at the face in the glass, saying. "You're not bad, my girl."

She slipped out of her uniform and turned on the water in the bathroom. Thank heaven, it was really hot! In these days the hot water was not always as "unfailing" as it had been a year ago.

Lying in the soothing water, Ann relaxed and allowed herself to indulge in speculations. During the day she was far too busy, people were always asking to speak to her, "Could she spare a minute?" The men liked her to spend a moment with them as she passed through the wards; there were forms, applications, endless letters to be sent off. Only when she came here, to her own room, and either lay in her bath or on her bed, could she be certain of no interruption.

Tonight, she lay staring at the slim, softly pink

body which lay stretched before her in the water. Slowly she raised first one arm, then the other, then lifted each leg, then slid suddenly down into the water and said, "Damn!" very clearly, but with complete good temper. They were good legs, good arms, her body was a pleasant shape, her stomach flat like a boy's. "Far flatter than either Sholto's or William's when they lie in their baths," she murmured.

It would soon be 1942, and she would be twenty-two. Twenty-two was still quite young; there must be all kinds and sorts of adventures, incidents, even romances, waiting for anyone who was reasonably good to look at and who was only twenty-two. She was a widow, the mother of two small boys, one of whom would one day be the Duke of Alcaster.

Sholto had left her a great deal of money, several houses and a large amount of land; left it unconditionally, without stipulation as to what she did with her life. "Of course," Ann admitted, "darling Sholto couldn't tell what was going to happen at that damnable Dunkirk." She didn't particularly want to marry again, there was not a single man who had made any appeal to her since Sholto died—except one young Air Force lad who was so extraordinarily amusing that she laughed immoderately whenever he opened his huge, wide mouth with its humorous upper lip. He had told her that he was married to a "smashing girl and had a smashing house in Whitby", and Ann asked if

Whitby were a smashing town? and he had answered, "Whitby? Whitby's smashing!" She got out of the bath; the water was chilling, and in these days you mustn't keep filling it up with hot water, it was wasteful! She dried herself slowly, frowning a little.

Sholto had spoiled her for other men. He hadn't been very clever, he certainly hadn't been handsome. She paddled into the bedroom and looked at his photographs in the double frame. He had said, "One with hat on; the other c-complete change of c-costume! same gent, without hat."

They had laughed, Sholto because he really believed that it was funny, Ann because she wanted to please him. And now here she was, twenty-two years old—a widow.

Holding the photograph frame, she stared intently at his pictures.

"I don't believe you'd mind, really," she thought, "because you were such a very 'fair' person, and it isn't fair to expect me to live all alone for—perhaps—sixty years, is it? Anyway, whoever I married, they would never have just that little 'extra something' that was yours. You were the first, my sweet, and in a funny way you'll be—the last. I shall never laugh with anyone as I laughed with you. I never could. You see, you weren't only the first man I ever slept with, you were the first person I went to the South of France with; bathed in the Mediterranean; spent money rather wildly and stupidly; the first person who insisted that I must have a maid, that I must be looked after like a princess. But more than that, when I used to watch you frowning and so intent over agents' reports, when I came to understand that the state of some old cottages in Buckinghamshire did worry you and make you determined that they must be put right at once—and not only because they would let better—but because you were ashamed that Sholto Claverley should be taking rent for places which were not hygienic and water-tight. That was when I began to understand that, although you wanted to have a good time —you wanted and intended to—you had a duty, you were going to do it, and what was more, you were proud to have it there to do."

She began to dress, her thoughts still going on, still thinking about Sholto.

There must be hundreds of young men like him in England, decent, clean young men, not very clever, indulging in silly escapades, in even sillier flirtations and "affairs", but who, deep in their hearts, had the same sense of duty. Not all with great estates, with whole villages where their word was law and where they could either accept their responsibilities or shelve them on to the shoulders of some agent, who, with the best will in the world, couldn't do much on his own initiative.

Smaller men—men with farms on which there were, possibly, ten or twelve cottages and lesser farms, men—like her dead brother Flight—or was Flight dead, she wondered?—who employed perhaps half a dozen people, packers, receptionist, secretary ... He had been proud to boast that although their tea was served in the basement, it was decent tea and a decent basement, where they could sit in comfort if only for half an hour a day. He had fussed about their little cloak-room, had a special liquid soap container installed; paid for clean towels to be delivered twice every week. That place, the Galleries, meant as much to Flight as Sholto's estates had meant to him.

It wasn't the actual size, it was the feeling they had towards their dependents.

It wasn't "patronage", it wasn't doling out new roofs, new gates, new wash-basins and clean towels as a kind of charity, as a concession—it was all part of the work. If you were a masterman in whatever strata of society, you must justify yourself, and your right to that position. She had gone over Wilberforce Cummins' works once, she remembered, long ago, before the war, and had never liked the man since. True, there had been well-equipped washrooms, rest-rooms where the tables were covered with newspapers and journals, a room with a billiard-table and a ping-pong table, a fine spacious canteen, but—in his own handsome room, with the heavy mahogany chairs, and fine desk; its thick carpet and cigar cabinet, its well-made sideboard which held bottles and glasses, he had spoiled it all for her.

"It's a marvellous place, Sir Wilberforce," she had said.

411

His little eyes twinkled. "Like it, little lady?"
She had been sixteen then. "Like it? I don't! My
father washed his hands, if he washed 'em at all,
under a tap in the yard; he brought his dinner with
him in a tommy-tin, or wrapped in a red handkerchief; he read the evening paper and nothing else.
As for billiards—he left that to his betters. We're
spoiling them—men and girls—pampering
them!"

"Then why provide these things?"

He chuckled. "Because they"—he jerked his
broad thumb in the direction of the works, from
whence came the dull, muffled roar of machinery
—"believe that it's reducing my profits a bit—and
they're such a mean-spirited lot, that pleases
'em! They're clock workers, they're 'pay packet'
workers. All they care for is football, dog racing,
football pools, and beer. That's the Working
Man of England today—from one who knows!
from one who was at one time a working man
himself."

She had flushed, she remembered, and said, "I
can't quite believe it."

"Wait until you're older; wait until you marry
some poor devil of an employer, little lady. You'll
learn that all I've said is gospel truth—and a great
deal more into the bargain."

Now, brushing her hair with a pair of ivory-
backed brushes which had belonged to Sholto, she
still said to her reflection in the glass, "I don't
believe it! I won't believe it either. My boys shan't

412

grow up to believe it!"

That evening, seated opposite to her father-in-law in the library, which was now their dining-room, she waited until he was leaning back in his chair, his glass of port at his elbow, his cigar drawing well, until she said, "I want to talk to you, Noble."

At first she had called him "Noble Duke", now it had become merely "Noble".

He inclined his head towards her, but a little sideways, in the courteous manner which she liked, even though she found it a little affected, Sholto would have said, "Do you? What world-shattering thing is coming now? Stand by for the crash!" She would have giggled, and then begun to speak, having, as it were, paid her small tribute to his wit.

She watched the grave, good-looking face, with its grey hair—hair which had been quite white at the temples for over eighteen months now—and said impetuously, "He wasn't like you, was he?"

The Duke never pretended not to know what she was talking about; that was one of the things which was so pleasant about him, he always seemed to be walking in step with her.

He said, "No, not in the least. He was the image of his mother. I wish you'd known her. She was Jane Fotheringham. The first time I was intro-duced to her, at old Bess Mowbray's in Park Lane—everyone who was a 'nob' lived in Park Lane in those days—I thought, 'So her name is

Jane, is it? Plain Jane, by Jove!' I danced with her; light as a feather, I remember, though she was a biggish girl. She didn't chatter. If she had anything to say, Jane said it—if not she didn't speak at all. There was something about her that—well, it got you. Got you! Charm, I suppose; she radiated it, and—she always listened to whatever you said. Great gift, to be able to listen. A week later—just a week, mark you—I ran into young Melford, he said, 'You're in a hurry!' I said that indeed I was, in a deuce of a hurry. I was going to ask a girl to marry me. He asked who the lady was. I said, 'Jane Fotheringham.' I can see him now, very tall chap, good figure, had a broken nose—he was killed at Arras—he gaped, and said, 'By Gad! you've picked the nicest girl in London!' And, m'dear, I had. She liked me to call her 'Plain Jane', and when Sholto was born I said, 'My dear, you've given me a brat who has no more pretensions to beauty than you have!' She laughed so much that the nurse pushed me out of the bedroom."

Ann nodded. "Sholto's and mine couldn't be called exactly a pair of Adonises, could they?"

"No; plain children. Good shape, nicely made, but plain as pike-staffs. Healthy, though, so the nurse tells me."

"Noble, dear," she asked, "would you mind dreadfully if I married again? Oh, not yet . . . I've not met anyone I should even like to marry, but if I did—would you?"

He examined the end of his cigar with great

attention, lifted his glass and sipped the wine with appreciation. Then, after touching his lips delicately with his napkin, he said, "Not provided the man conformed to certain things. And I imagine that if he didn't, you wouldn't want to marry him. I suppose, just faintly, and at first, I should in my secret heart regard him as something of an interloper, but that would be both unfair and foolish. I should get over that. I'm not young, I'm getting past being able to help you in bringing up the boys—and they'll need some bringing up— I'm too nervy, too tired, too—oh! a great many things. But, no; I think that you ought to marry again—if you can find the right fellow."

She rubbed out her cigarette, scrubbing the ash over the shining surface of her dessert plate. "What kind of man—would be right?"

"First, don't marry a man and tell me that 'he vaguely reminds me of Sholto', because it will be so damned vaguely that at the end of three months you'll realise that he bears not the slightest resemblance to my son—and after all, why should he? Don't marry a man who is retrogressive, or one who is so progressive that you get a mental headache keeping up with him. Anyway, there are plenty of old things, old ideas, old methods which are worth preserving. You want a man who will take an interest in the place, without assuming that every damned inch belongs to him. Give the tenants what they've a right to have—decent homes, decent roofs—and don't try to make them

415

get wildly enthusiastic over things they don't want but that you'd like them to have. They don't like electric geysers. They don't want central heating, they don't want patent-this or patent-the-other. No. Ann, m'dear, you want a man who will make a job of it, looking after the land and the folk on it. Who will, incidentally, look after you as well. You've got nearly twenty years' stewardship, before young Sholto—if God spares him—can take over." He rose and stood smiling at her over the table. "The type of man on the lines of a modernised Albert, the Great and Good, only let the adoring come from him! There, I'm going up to bed. Don't sit up too late." He went out, then re-opened the door and said:

"Oh, Ann! when I said that your boys were plain as pike-staffs . . ."

"Yes?"

"I've an idea that I ought to have said— pike-*staves*. Good night!"

Alicia Masters had leave for Christmas; they had drawn lots, and she had been one of the fortunate ones, the rest would be on duty all through the Christmas season. She sat in a corner of the railway carriage, a pile of papers at her side, too tired to bother to read. The work seemed to grow heavier as the War continued, there was less informality about it, more forms for this and that, additional regulations, more mobile canteens to be driven; and to drive them through streets which had been bombed was no easy work. Night after night—or when she was doing night duty—morning after morning, Alicia returned to her flat, to find Deborah Miller waiting, always grumbling, but never failing to provide her with food, hot drinks, and, in some miraculous way, scalding baths.

"'Ow many more hours a day are you going to work, Miss Alicia?" she would ask. "Seems ter me we'd better arsk the Almighty ter put in a few extra every day, so's you can work a bit longer. I'm a wreck!"

"I feel one, Deb."

"You! You're young and strong and 'ealthy —leastways you *uster* be 'ealthy, before you started this silly rubbish. Nice thing if you have one of these nervous breakdowns. I shan't know what to do for you. I knew a woman 'oo had one, she went com-ple-tly barmy, kep' saying that she saw little 'ens with pretty 'ats on! 'Ens, mind you, in 'ats!"

Well, she was free of it all for five days. Free to lie in bed late, to go to bed early, to wear civilian clothes, spend time on her hands, forget what the steering-wheel of a heavy car felt like under her thick dogskin gloves; forget what canteen food tasted like—even though the grey-faced, almost exhausted Commandant, always said cheerfully, "This is exactly the same food as the men get—only better served and probably better cooked!"

She would forget the flat, and Deb, who had

gone off cheerfully to visit some relations in Wakefield.

"Not seen 'em for twelve years," she told Alicia. "It will be nice to meet them again."

"I don't see why it should be, I've always 'ated the lot of 'em."

She would forget—she moved restlessly, picked up a paper and tried to read, she threw it down again. She couldn't forget, it was no use trying.

Flight—even now she thought of him as "dear Flight"—even now she loved his memory, but memory was a cold thing on which to base your life; a thing which grew more and more dim with every month that passed. At first, to think of him had been to call up an exact picture of him; often she had felt that she could visualise him, standing in the doorway of their flat, hear his voice quite clearly, listen to every loved inflection. Then had come the time when she caught up his photographs and scanned them eagerly, almost fearfully, as if she tried to impress his image on her mind, when she examined the pictures of him minutely feature by feature.

That wide forehead, the way he used to wrinkle it when he was worried or puzzled, that good, straight, if faintly melancholy nose; his mouth—a very tender mouth, but firm—how often had it been pressed to hers, how often had she lain in his arms while he kissed her gently, murmuring that she was beautiful, wonderful—his!

In those earlier months, after such an analysis,

she had lain down the photographs with a kind of satisfaction. "No, I am not forgetting. Everything is clear. I remember—everything—everything."

She closed her eyes and leaned her head against the cushions of the carriage, thinking—half desperately, "I must see his face if I close my eyes—I must keep still—concentrate. Flight—Flight." She saw nothing, no pictures came to her; only vague shapes and colours, mists swirling past, twisting balls of light with movements which were purposeless and aimless.

At first she had been stunned. That telegram, "missing". Slowly the sensation of being numb had left her, and she had been conscious of actual physical and mental pain. That had been when, tired after her work, she had still been unable to sleep, had paced up and down her room, saying again and again, "It's not true—it can't be true! He will come back—he must, must, must."

One of her fellow-officers had a son who was missing. She talked to Alicia in those early days, told her how clever he had been—Derek was his name, "But I'm afraid we always called him 'Poggy'"—how keen on his work, liked by his brother officers, popular with his men. He was posted as missing before Dunkirk, when the Army had been told to fall back on the line of the Scheldt.

She showed Alicia his photograph; a pleasant, ordinary-looking boy with a nice smile.

Yesterday, after mess, she had touched Alicia's

419

arm and said, "I've heard. 'Missing, believed killed'."

Alicia had turned quickly and whispered, "Oh, my dear! I am so sorry."

The other smiled, a queer wintry smile, and answered, "Really it's almost a relief, you know. I'm on duty at Waterloo Bridge. See you after Christmas. Happy Christmas!" she added, as if it were an afterthought.

That restless living on Hope from day to day, assuring herself that, "Today I am bound to hear," or "Perhaps when I get home he will be there waiting for me." All that had passed and a dull acceptance had followed. Flight was missing— there was nothing to be done but wait. She knew that Edward Masters had interviewed men who had come back, had paid money for their railway fares, had visited them in hospital, had taken them out to lunch and dine with him in an effort to discover someone who had seen Flight. She knew that; knew, too, that he had found nothing of any value, only the man Flight had helped down to the boat, who said, "T' yoong laady gie'd the Cap'n t' charnce ter cum wi' uz. 'E jest shook 'is 'ead and larfed, waved 'is 'an' and went orf agen." Edward discovered that the girl lived near Folkestone. She came to see him in town; a slim, attractive creature, with short hair and a firm chin.

"I only saw him when he and another soldier—a private—brought this other man down. The other man was wounded, not very badly. I asked

420

him—your son—to come with us, he shook his head and said the boat was sufficiently full already. I said, 'Good night, sweetheart!' and he waved his hand and said, 'Sweet dreams, Angel face!' and went back. Went just like that—'with a smile and a flip of the hand'. That's all I know. It was pretty hellish there, and getting dark."

When she left Edward, she said to him, "If he comes back, I wish you'd let me know. I should like to see him again."

Edward asked, "Do you think that he will come back?"

She shrugged her shoulders. "You never know—can't tell. Good-bye."

And, last of all, the young officer who had lunched with Edward at his club, with one foot still in plaster of Paris, and a crutch to help him. He said, "Oh, I knew him, sir—not awfully well, but I knew him. I was one of the last lot—sheer luck that I got away at all. We thought the last of the boats had gone. Getting dark, too. I spotted this boat and shouted to some chaps, 'Come on! for God's sake, come on!' We ran like mad and on the way I saw Masters—your son, sir—lying on his face, with another long, thin chap close to him. I stooped down and gave him a shake, I said, 'C'on, Masters, old chap! there's a last boat, stir yourself!' but he didn't move and I saw that he was bleeding—I couldn't say exactly where. The blood was all plastered over his thigh. The other type was definitely dead, he was shockingly—I beg your pardon, sir. He was dead, the other type."

"And your opinion is that my son was dead also?"

The young officer assumed an air of great cheerfulness. "Oh! I say, sir, I shouldn't like to say that. You never really know, do you? I mean I was lying waiting for them to come and find me—a mine got me, in the middle of a field, away from anywhere—well, you might say almost away from anywhere. I was lying there for simply ages—ages. I shouldn't like you to think that—that is, to think anything too drastic, if you get me?"

Edward shook hands and said, "Thank you very much indeed. I am grateful to you. Good-bye!"

He watched the boy swing off on his crutch and thought how easily it might have been Flight . . .

She had heard all this from Edward, who had come up to town to tell her, and had tried to make it all sound as hopeful as possible, but that was months ago. Since then—silence.

Long evenings when she was off duty, days spent in trying to sleep, to get rest when she knew that she must go out to face the long nights; sleeping badly, wondering, speculating, trying to come to a decision.

A decision—she sat upright in her corner and opened her eyes wide, forcing herself to watch the passing landscape with feverish interest. Almost saying, "That's a pretty house—nice garden there—how cold the woods look, leafless—there might be some snow—the sky looks heavy—'A white Christmas'—'with every Christmas card I write'—she hadn't sent any this year—what did Christmas matter? A country church—Norman, I believe?—badly restored—this mania for restoring things!" A decision—about Chris. He had come to see her, kindly, sympathetic, and friendly.

"Thought that I'd look in, 'Licia. Mustn't shut yourself away from us all. I know it's a bad show, my dear, but I shall be out there too in a few days. Will you write to me sometimes, 'Licia? After all, I might be unlucky, too, you never can tell."

That had been in the very early months after Dunkirk.

The night before he went, he telephoned and asked her if she would dine? She hesitated, and he begged her to do so.

"Lonely work, being alone on my last evening," he said.

"Why did you come down from Baddock?"

"Because I've got to be off early, my sweet! Also because I didn't want to join the 'binge party' and set off in the morning with a head like the bottom of a parrot's cage. Come on, 'Licia, come and dine with me."

She had promised, and when she told Deb was surprised to meet with nothing but approval.

"You go, Miss, you go! Life's fer the living arfter all, not them as is parsed on, with their troubles all be'ind them. You can't spend your life in this state of—well, not knowing which side o' the fence yer livin' on, as you might say. Neether wife nor widder. I remember once readin' a buke, lovely buke it was, called 'Nor wife, nor maid'—well, that might be you, almost."

She had gone with Chris, and he had been charming; looking very well in his uniform, very spick and span, well-groomed. It was pleasant to have someone "taking care" of her again, consulting her wishes, making suggestions, praising her dress, the way she had done her hair. He asked about her work, expressed the belief that it was far too strenuous, and then asked if she would dance?

She had been confused—showed her confusion—and Chris had noticed it.

He said, "Now listen to me, 'Licia! and if I sound brutal, try to remember that I don't mean to be. I'm only trying to talk sense. Flight is missing, there's a chance that he may be still alive—I hope to God that he is; on the other hand he may not be alive and we have to face it. If he's alive—there's no earthly reason why you shouldn't get a little enjoyment out of life; if he isn't—well then, you're young, and men are dying every day and . . ."

She said, "Chris, don't."

He said, "My sweet, they are! I'm only trying to be sane and logical. I'm only trying to show you that by living this life—the life which you are leading—you're helping no one, certainly not poor old Flight. You see . . ."

She said abruptly, "Very well, I'll dance."

The next morning she had seen him go away. He had laughed and asked if she really would write to him. "Nice letters, not just starchy formal things—oh! and, Alicia, can I have a photograph? After all, you are my sister-in-law."

He had been sent, finally, to the North of Scotland, and six months later came to see her again. As they stood drinking a cocktail in the flat before going out to dinner, Chris asked, "Glad to see me?" and slipped his arm round her. She had twisted away and said, "Chris, don't do that!"

He had laughed, smiling his impudent smile, his eyes very bright, and dancing with amusement. "Why not—you like it?"

"Please, Chris! I don't like it at all. Don't do it again!"

But that evening when they drove home after dinner, after dancing, she knew that he held her very tightly to him and whispered all kinds of foolish, loving things; she knew, too, that she liked hearing them. That was the first time, she remembered, that she realised that she was forgetting exactly how Flight looked, as if someone had breathed on a mirror in which his face was reflected. As she undressed, she lifted his photograph and stared at it anxiously, then pressed her lips to both the pictures, whispering, "Flight, my darling!"

She had seen Chris twice again during his leave, for he spent some days at Baddock St. Mallory, and she was tied to London.

Since then he had been twice to London again, once on leave, and the other time on some business or other connected with the camp where he was stationed.

The last time had been a month ago, and he had grumbled that he was unlikely to get Christmas leave. "On duty, curse it!" he said.

"I shall be going home. I've got five days' leave."

He sipped his cocktail, watching her intently, and at last she laughed nervously, saying, "Don't watch me all the time!"

"I can't help it. I'm in love with you," he said, "'Licia, we've got to get this straight. I'm going overseas. Probably North Africa. Are you going to let me go—like this?"

"What can I do to change—anything?"

He set down his glass, took a step towards her, and said very coolly, "What you did—before. Only then—I wasn't in love with you, I was desperately attracted. Now I am frantically in love. Well, what have you got to say?"

"I wasn't married then . . ."

"You were engaged to my brother."

"I know, it was wrong, dreadful."

He laid his hands on her shoulders, and shook her gently. "Darling, do face the facts! Of course it wasn't wrong or dreadful. You were engaged to a man—oh! I'm not going to say anything detrimental about him, poor fellow—a man who was all full of ideals and dreams, and things that don't apply, and never will apply, to people who are flesh and blood, who have impulses and reasonable appetites." He paused, took his hands from her

426

shoulders and walked away, saying, "Which you and I have."

She put her hands up and covered her face. Chris watched her from the farther side of the room, his mouth lifting a little at the corners, his eyes very bright.

Finally she said, scarcely above a whisper, "Chris, you see it's all different now. I'm married to your brother."

"How do you know?" he demanded. "How do you know that he isn't dead? Eighteen months, and not a word. Posted as missing. One morning the next message will come—'believed killed'. By that time I shall be among a lot of stinking Arabs, getting sand-fly fever or something choice of that kind. You see, 'Licia, my sweet, I want to marry you. I will marry you one day, I swear. Flight isn't coming back. I *know* it."

"You don't know," she cried passionately, "you can't know, how can you?"

"I just do know," he answered stubbornly. "One of those things . . ."

"Wishful thinking—wishing your brother dead . . ."

"Don't be hysterical, sweet! I don't wish him dead at all, I only wish that he wasn't your husband . . . or that if he's dead, he never had been married to you. 'Licia, if you heard that Flight was dead, would you marry me? Now answer truthfully—and don't say 'After a proper interval' because if you do I shall scream!" She did not reply, and he repeated his question, "Would you marry me?"

She raised her eyes and met his. "Yes—yes, I would."

He laughed, pulled her to him and kissed her. "And yet I'm to go away with nothing except that promise, eh?"

She laid her head on his shoulder, she liked the feel of the hard cloth; beneath it she felt his strong, broad shoulder. His arm was round her, holding her to him.

"Eh?" he said. "Tell me!"

"I don't know . . ."

He kissed her again and let her go. "Get your bonnet and shawl and let's go out to dinner. I enjoy being at the Savoy with the best-looking woman in town. Gives me a sort of *cachet*!"

2

THE train drew up at Baddock St. Mallory, Alicia gathered her hand luggage together and stepped out, beckoning to the old porter, who came along at a kind of clumsy hand-gallop.

"Get my suitcase, will you, Gibbons? Merry Christmas to you!"

"An' ter yew, Miss 'Licia! The Rector is y'ere, waiting in the car, it's that cold on this y'ere platform; I doan't s'ppose as theer's another platform as cold as w'ot this y'un is, not i' t' length an' breadth o' England. Noa, I doan't!"

Her father was waiting in the comfortable Daimler. As she entered she felt the sudden rush of warm air on her face—foot-warmers, of course, she could imagine Belton filling them before the car left.

Her father leaned forward and kissed her, his voice was richer and fuller than ever.

"My dear girl," he pronounced it "gairl". "This is de-lightful! We were a leetle afraid that your duties might keep you in London, but everything has turned out for the best—in this best of all possible worlds."

She frowned. "The best of all possible worlds,

Papa? Surely that is something of an over-statement?"

"No, no! I believe not. We have our blood brothers with us, fighting shoulder to shoulder; it is admitted that our aircraft numerically outnumbers that of Germany, before . . ."

"Against which," Alicia said, "you have the loss of the *Prince of Wales* and the *Repulse.*"

"Ah, my dear child, losses are inevitable. To use a very homely phrase—you can't make an omelette without breaking eggs. But—let us talk about happier things, shall we? You look tired, I think. You're working too hard. Still, your mother and I are proud that you are doing your duty, very proud. Your mother is working tremendously hard, very handsome she looks too in her uniform, I admit. Masters is still very active with his Home Guard; not that I think for one moment—not for one moment—that the Germans would ever dare—dare—to attempt to invade these shores, still the spirit is admirable, oh, admirable!"

"They're all well?"

"Yes, yes—I saw them at Morning Service last Sunday. I suppose"—he dropped his voice, as Alicia remembered he always did in the Litany when he came to the passage ". . . for all those who travel by land or by water." That was spoken firmly, bravely, confidently, then came the drop, the voice speaking as if he uttered some intensely private and personal matter, "all women labouring of child." Then louder and more cheerfully as he

430

reached "All sick persons and young children . . ."

Now he said, "I suppose—that there is—no news?"

Alicia said shortly, "None at all."

"Ah well, no news is always said to be good news . . ."

They turned in at the Rectory gates. The drive seemed to be as well kept as ever, Belton was waiting for them, he said, "A merry Christmas, Mrs. Masters," and she said, "And to you, Belton."

Her father boomed, "Is Lady Sophia back yet?"

"Her ladyship asked that the car should be sent to the hospital for her immediately on your return. It would appear that there is some difficulty with her Austin, sir."

Alicia said, "You keep two cars now, eh?"

"No, no. The Austin is your mother's own property, what I call her 'official' car. She uses it to drive backwards and forwards to the hospital. It is most necessary, most. Imperative, in fact."

Back in the softly lighted green drawing-room—Flight had always loved this room—Alicia lay back in her comfortable chair and wished that Belton would bring tea. Surely they were not going to wait for her mother's return? She thought of the mess in London, where women scrambled for thick cups of tea and large pieces of bread and margarine, where, in the middle of the turmoil, the Commandant arrived and sank down in an armchair saying, "For God's sake, someone, give

431

me a cup of tea, I'm half dead! Thanks." And while she sipped the scalding tea she asked questions, a pad of paper fastened on to a board about a foot square resting on the arm of her chair. "Brownsmith, is that canteen ready to go out? Not! What's wrong with it? I thought you were a mastermind regarding machinery? Get it done, for heaven's sake, get it done! Leach, you'll have to take Harris with you, Morrison is sick. 'Flu she thinks—a cold in the head, *I* think. You might see her, Doc? Where is the QMS? Masses of stuff lying about out there, it ought to be checked in at once. All right, if she's off duty, tell the Corporal in the stores to do it. There, take this cup somebody, I must be off. Feltham, I'll see you at the Transport Offices at six. Yes, outside."

That was all so clear. She could see the faces of the women—Feltham, who was always so immaculate; Leach, who might have the buttons of her tunic cleaned twenty times a day, but they still remained dirty and dull; little Brownsmith, who had pretty fluffy hair and wide blue eyes, who looked as if she were in a perpetual state of astonishment at finding herself in uniform. The room—with its uncomfortable armchairs; the one near the window had the arm broken, young Tenfield had done that one evening, demonstrating something or other. The green baize-covered board, plastered with notices, the Commandant was always glancing at it and saying, "Alison, keep those notices up to date." Alison always answered

432

in a tone of hurt surprise, "Of course, ma'am," but she never touched them. That was all so clear, so astonishingly clear. Yet—she couldn't remember the tones of Flight's voice, couldn't see his face if she closed her eyes.

Perhaps she didn't want to so desperately now? Perhaps it was easier to remember two eyes which danced with amusement, a big wide mouth which smiled, a strong chin, and a firm, thick neck, tanned as far as the collar line, then almost startlingly white. Hair which grew ruffled so easily, and could only be persuaded to keep in proper position by the applications of some pleasant-smelling stuff out of a tall, narrow-necked bottle. A voice which could speak roughly, which could say ordinary things in a tone which made her realise that she was being made fun of. All these things she could remember, all these things gave her a queer sense of excitement; excitement mixed with fear and uncertainty.

"Missing, believed killed," or ". . . is found to be a prisoner of war in the Stalag 724." Which was it going to be?—and she shivered—which did she really hope might come to her?

Her father said, "My dear, I am sure that you are over-tired? You look quite pale."

"What I really want is a cup of tea, Papa. I'm dying for one."

He looked pained. "I always wait for your mother, my dear, always."

"Does she come home to tea every day?"

"Practically, unless someone comes down from HQ to inspect the place, then of course she takes tea with them. Ann Claverley was over last week. She was visiting at Little Manor, and called in at the hospital. Your mother was *not* very favourably impressed, I'm afraid. Neither was she, I am afraid, when she visited Alcaster. She found the discipline most lax, most. Ah! here she is! Well, my dear, our wanderer has returned."

Lady Sophia entered, she looked remarkably handsome in her uniform, held herself upright, and moved forward smoothly and easily to greet her daughter. She embraced her with just that hint of restraint which Alicia remembered all her life.

"My dear! this is very pleasant! You're still in uniform?"

"I didn't change, Mama, because I wanted to have tea first."

"Ah—and so you shall. Here is Belton bringing it." She began to pour out tea. Alicia, looking at the pale fresh liquid, said, "Can I have the last cup, Mama? I like it very strong. Is that China?"

"My dear, you know that I always have China tea."

"Yes, I remember . . ."

Lady Sophia turned to her husband. "Who is taking the service at the hospital tomorrow? Oh, Mr. Taddlestone—oh, dear! Well, I suppose that it can't be helped. He is so *noisy*, and the hymns he chooses are so apt to make the men *shout*. I still feel that it was Gerald Beamarsh's place to remain here,

434

and not to contrive to be sent to some RAF camp in the north of Scotland."

Alicia said, "Is young Beamarsh with the RAF?"

"Yes, somewhere in Scotland. The same camp, I believe, that Christopher Masters was at. Did you know that he had gone to North Africa? Oh, you did? No"—and again that strange dropping of the voice as if something faintly indecent were going to be uttered—"news, I suppose, darling?"

"None. May I have another cup of tea, Mama?"

Slowly, with great care, Lady Sophia gave her daughter such news as might be of interest. Everyone was well, Eleanor Masters was living in that queer old house with her husband, he still limped badly. Oh, yes, a very good fellow, George Charlton. Careful, and, to a certain extent, clever. Sir Morlett Browning who had come down, "at my special request, last week, really praised Charlton whole-heartedly! Won-der-ful surgeon, Sir Morlett." Mrs. Masters—"a good little woman that, a very good little woman"—was doing a dozen things. Lady Sophia's own opinion was that it was better to do one thing superlatively well than ten indifferently. Still—there could be no doubt about it, Mrs. Masters worked very hard. Her own work—"My dear, don't ask me about my own work! My work is doing everything that other people are too stupid or too inefficient to do. Yes, there is Matron"—she laughed softly—"a Scots-woman! She has been overseas. She appears to

435

regret having come home. As if a wounded man did not need the same care and attention here in England, as he does in North Africa! I told her today, I said, 'Matron, forgive my saying it, but there are times when I feel that you would like to be back again?' Of course, we know that the Scots are sentimental to a degree, but, my dear, her eyes filled with tears. She said, in that odd, dogmatic way the Scots have of speaking, 'Lady Sophia, when Ah remember awe we did over yonder—with naething, or scarcely mair then naething . . . Ah just feel ashamed at the easy life Ah'm leadin' ower here!' I'm afraid that I replied somewhat coldly, that if that was how she felt, she had better apply to be sent back. She was—no, I may be wrong, she may only have been nervous—'An' that's just what Ah've din! They sent me back home after hauf a dozen goes o' malaria. Ah'll know better this time then let them know that Ah've got the wretched thing. Oh! Ah must away back.'

"I expostulated, I asked her if she thought that she was fit to go? She is an excellent matron—though there are times when I wish that her discipline were better—she said that the Medical Board would decide that, adding that she didn't doubt that she could pull wool over the eyes of 'yon old haverers'!"

Lockwood smiled. "I suppose that one must commend the spirit, it shows . . ."

His wife replied coldly, "The spirit is not the spirit for wartime, my dear! Obedience is the first,

436

and almost the last thing—obedience and discipline. Now, Alicia, dear, if you have finished your tea, would you like to come upstairs and change?"

Alicia sat at her window, staring out into the darkness. Her first evening at home had dragged its interminable length to an end. She admitted that she had been bored, unutterably bored. Once, after dinner, she had said that she would like to stroll out for a breath of air; her father had pursed his lips, her mother had said, "Go out, Alicia! Oh, I don't think that I should! You see there are soldiers quartered at Mexford, and they come over by the 'bus with late passes. Some of them have made friends here—*how* I don't know—they are apt to be noisy."

Alicia said, "I'm used to walking about London alone, Mama!"

"Ah! but in uniform! Even the roughest soldier respects a woman in uniform, remember. No, dear, I don't think that I should go out."

Her father had read *The Times*, he had merely scanned it in the morning. Her mother, glancing at the clock, said, "Ah, nearly nine! I think that I must go down to the hospital. Or tonight—I might possibly telephone." Instinctively Alicia felt that she telephoned nine evenings out of ten. She heard her voice, crisp and business-like, saying, "Yes—of course! And tomorrow . . . ? quite! Yes, quite! Well, good night, Matron. Make them get on with the decorations, I want them all up and in order by half past eleven in the morning. I have the

Press photographer from Mexford coming. Yes. Good night!"

Her father lowered *The Times*. "You might play something, Alicia."

"I haven't played for months, Papa. I've forgotten all my music."

"A pity, my dear, a pity! Such a nice accomplishment. After the War . . ."

After the War! What then? What would happen if Chris came through? What would happen if Chris didn't come through? Could she, Alicia Masters, ever come back to live here, to sit night after night in this beautiful, still, safe room? Could she face living here, going to London at long intervals to stay either in Portland Place or at Claridges, dining with the Hortons, spending a few days at Rusmere, visiting that horrible house in which her grandmother lived, with everyone pretending that she was "eccentric", and knowing very well that she was as mad as a hatter?

At nine o'clock her father rose and turned on the wireless. "The news," he explained. The same smooth, unemotional voice, the same precise enunciation, the same news—she moved restlessly in her chair and sighed.

The news ended, her father switched off the wireless and returned to his chair, saying, "Ah! it might well be worse. I am ve-ry hopeful." At half past nine Belton arrived with a tray on which stood glasses, hot water, a bottle of whisky and a syphon.

Lady Sophia asked, "Do you take your hot water every evening, dear?"

Alicia said, "No, I find that a whisky-and-soda does me more good. Thank you, Papa—right up."

He gave it to her, but she felt the sudden chill which ran through the room. Meeting her mother's eyes she found them critical, disapproving.

"Mama, surely you don't mind my having a whisky-and-soda? After all I am a married woman—possibly a widow!"

"Really, Alicia!"

She drank her whisky, put down the glass, kissed her parents and said that she was tired. She thought, "The moment the door closes behind me they'll discuss me, say how I've changed."

"What time in the morning, my dear? For your tea?"

"Oh, just let me sleep, I'm dog-tired. I'll ring. Good night."

She stared out, the stars had come out and were shining like lamps, there must be frost in the air. Stars—were they shining everywhere? In North Africa? She pushed that thought away from her quickly. What did it matter? She was here, home again—only it wasn't home at all, it was a strange, beautiful old house filled with fine furniture and lovely things which held not the slightest interest for her.

She rose and looked at Flight's photographs again, wondering why she had brought them?

Photographs of a man she could scarcely remember! Where was he? And tomorrow evening they were asked to dine at Little Manor, to make a festivity, and all the time when his mother spoke gently, or his father hopefully, of Flight, she would feel that she had betrayed him—betrayed him with his own brother. That morning before she left London there had been a letter from Chris, no different from his other letters, simply cheerful and matter-of-fact, hoping that she would have a good leave, and like the present that he had sent her.

Even the thought of his presents did not disturb her; he sent presents that were more impersonal than any she had ever known. If he sent her a bag—and how hideous most of them were—from Algiers, then his mother, Eleanor, and Ann each received one, differing only in colour. Rugs—the pattern varied, but the value was obviously the same; covers for foot-stools, covers for books, slippers—they never fitted anyone—and so forth. Once he had sent them all large dried lizards, with the same note attached to them all. *These are specially treated and quite sanitary. C.*

Each time a letter came from him, Alicia held it in her hand, hoping that this time it might contain something more personal, something which would assure her of his affection. Again and again she had grown angry with disappointment. He had said that he wanted to marry her, and yet his letters told her nothing. She was just "a girl he wrote to", "a girl I slept with when I was on leave". She turned from the window and got into bed, thinking furiously "I detest him! How could I have been such a fool?"

She rose the next morning still feeling tired, and, what was worse, bored by the prospect of the day which lay before her. There were presents by her plate at breakfast. Alicia thought how much rather she would have spent an extra hour in bed! Although they were very nice presents, beautifully packed and obviously chosen with care. She handed out her own, and received smiling thanks. "My dear, how very charming!" and, "Thank you, Alicia, exactly what I wanted—most acceptable."

Letters, cards—and at the bottom of the pile, one from Chris. She made herself read all the others first, examine all the cards, and now and again make suitable comments upon them; then she took a knife and slit open the thin paper folder.

Chris might be a good business man, might have had a first-class education and have done well, but his writing was deplorable. She compared it with Flight's—Flight's, which had always been so clear, so easy to read, and always conveyed the impression that he had taken time and trouble over what he wrote. This was scrawled in indifferent ink, and difficult to decipher. Alicia read it, insisting upon being critical.

Angel Face—[he probably said that to every girl he met]—I hope that this will reach you on

441

Christmas Day. I hate Algiers except for a bar called the "Pigalle". The stuff they sell is no better and no worse than anywhere else, only it costs more. I wish that I were home with you all. But I shall be home sometime and then we'll dance again and—dance again. My love to you. Ever Chris.

She crumpled the letter in her fingers. That was the best he could do when he wrote to her for Christmas! Only that "dance again and—dance again" was in the least different from what he might have sent to his sister Eleanor. And that—that dash, was it really the remembrance of wonderful hours, or was it merely—Chris?

She went to the Morning Service walking beside her father, silent and absorbed. The church smelt of evergreens and hot-house flowers; Alicia disliked the heavy smell of the one and the acid tang of the other. People looked at her—curiously, she felt—as if they speculated as to whether she were a wife or a widow? She longed to turn and say to them:

"I don't know myself. I wish that I did."

There was Wilberforce Cummins and his wife, there to praise God for the benefits which were showered upon them because their factory was turning out munitions; there was Wilfred Horton and his thin, aristocratic wife; and the Masters —Edward and his wife, Flight's father and mother; Eleanor was with them—she had given up

442

playing the organ since her marriage—with George Charlton, still limping badly.

Her father took the service alone, for his only curate was ministering to the souls of the men in hospital, where Lady Sophia had gone early that morning, seated in the Austin, surrounded by parcels of all kinds and sizes.

Alicia listened to the service, conscious of nothing except the beauty of the words and phrases of the liturgy. None of it actually meant anything to her. She enjoyed the words, spoken in her father's fine, if somewhat affected, voice. She liked the old church, it was part of her life, a place which was built into the structure of her existence. She had stood there, at those altar rails, when she had married Flight, when lifting her eyes, she had seen Chris watching her, amused, quizzical, unrepentant.

She remembered then that she had felt nothing but a sudden spasm of anger, she had wondered how he dared to stand there, with laughing eyes and an air of complete amusement? Had he been sure of her even then? Had he known that, even if Flight had not been missing after Dunkirk, she would have capitulated to him sooner or later?

And in her bag, where her fingers could touch it if she wished, lay his last letter. "Angel Face!" Not a single word which made any reference to his love for her—she wondered if he had any love for her?—nothing to tell her that he missed her, that he longed for the time when they might be together again, only that brief phrase. "We'll dance again and—dance again!"

She moved restlessly, wishing that her father would end his comfortable platitudes, and that they might all leave the church. What good were these sermons, delivered by men who had never known what it meant to suffer distress, uncertainly, indignity? These smoothly-spoken sentences, these quotations and extracts, these assumptions that all was fundamentally well with the world! Why not stand up and tell people the Truth? That Britain, the Empire, freedom, decency, liberty of speech, even food itself, were in danger? Why not tell this congregation the truth concerning how men died—"died gloriously" —"gave his life for his country"? Making every man out to be a hero, pretending that in death they were noble—as they had been in life. Why not speak truthfully, and admit that the night before, this young "sub", that captain, the other major, had held some girl in his arms, had drunk too much, had told bawdy stories, and that the last thing of which he had thought had been Religion or anything connected with it? And then, why not admit that if, on the eve of a day which might mean Death—extinction—their minds had turned to having "a good time", a "binge", a "first-rate party". The fault lay with the people who had failed to make Religion real, actual and vital to them.

"The Majesty of Death"—she had seen death

444

sufficiently often in the streets of London, Hull, Birmingham and the rest, to have any illusions regarding the "majesty" or the "dignity" of death. Smashed, crumpled, sprawling bodies, often obscene in their postures, horrible to the sight. That was how much dignity and majesty there was about sudden death!

She raised her eyes to the East window, given by Wilfred Horton in memory of his mother—an old lady who had been disliked whole-heartedly by everyone—where in a horrid conglomeration of violent reds and painful blues, with a yellow which set one's teeth on edge, the figure of the Suffering Christ hung on the Cross, pallid, and anæmic.

She thought, "You're badly served, you poor Soul! They depict you as hanging there dead—and dead they let you remain."

Her father was using that special tone of voice which denoted that he was reaching the end of his sermon, "And as the Wise Men came from the East, where they had seen the Star, so today do we turn our eyes towards the East—from whence cometh our Help."

Irritably, Alicia thought, "That was the Hills, not the East!" Thousands of little yellow men in the trees, hidden in the undergrowth, flying, guiding torpedoes, burning, pillaging—that was the East to which we must look!

His voice was even fuller now. She waited, and knew for what she waited—"We shall fight on the beaches . . . We shall never surrender!" Good

445

words, fine words, but words which applied to the men who were sweating in the desert—are you safe, Chris?—to men who were battling through swamps; through snow, ice, struggling up mountain-sides; men who were flung into the icy water and fired on by smiling Huns from the safety of firm decks. They weren't words to be bandied about to a well-fed congregation, every one of whom slept in a comfortable bed and was going home to a very excellent Christmas dinner.

"And now to God the Father . . ." and the usual rustle of good material, and the flutter of the leaves of hymn-books as people sought for "O Come, All Ye Faithful".

Then the sight of her father, taking the offertory bags and holding them in a rich heap of scarlet velvet on a large silver salver (given to the Church by Wilberforce Cummins as a "thank offering for the merciful recovery of his beloved wife after a serious operation"), raising his arms as if he wished the pale Christ on the Cross to notice how nobly the congregation had responded that morning to the oratory of the Hon. and Rev. Stanley Lockwood.

Alicia smiled and said, "A Happy Christmas to you," with varying inflections, and thought how she hated it all, and wished with a kind of violence that Chris could come pushing his way through the knots of people, and say "Hello, Angel Face . . ." and then remembered that she was saying, "A Happy Christmas, Mrs. Masters," and that

446

Mrs. Masters was Flight's mother as well as Christopher's.

She looked older, Alicia thought, but she smiled and spoke to everyone and praised the decorations in the church and said what a very excellent sermon the Rector had preached; while her husband stood near her, leaning more heavily on his stick than Alicia remembered. He said, "Hello, Alicia! torn yourself away from London, eh?"

"Five days' leave," she said. "We're dining with you, aren't we?"

"Yes, and there's an immense parcel from Chris, which I suppose contains new horrors from Africa. If this War goes on much longer I tremble to think what the average English home will be like. Noakes showed me a table-cloth sent by his younger son—the elder is a prisoner in Germany, poor chap—never in my life have I lied my soul away to such an extent. Silk, with the family life of Arabs depicted in detail." He shivered. "Terrible!"

She asked, "Did Chris send you shoes? He sent me a pair."

Edward nodded. "Indeed he did! Mine are made of camel hide, I believe. They weigh several hundredweight and the heels bang on the floor when you try to walk."

She laughed, surprised to find that with Edward she could laugh quite easily. "Mine were white kid decorated with gold eruptions. No one but a baby could have worn them. Deb—my maid—uses

447

them for what she calls a 'hair tidy'."

"Sounds revolting. Well, see you all this evening. Irrespective of how we feel, we are going to immolate ourselves on the altar of Christmas Festivity. I am not sure that I shan't ask the Rector to read 'The Christmas Carol'."

Alicia whispered, "No, please don't."

"Why not?"

"Because," she whispered again, "he *would*. He'd love to!"

Luncheon passed drearily and Lady Sophia announced that they were all going to the hospital to take tea there. "It will cheer the boys up so wonderfully. We had the offer of an ENSA concert party. I, personally, was against it, but apparently the boys were so anxious, that . . ." she shrugged her shoulders.

Her husband said, "I hope that their—their material is carefully chosen. In keeping with the Spirit of the day."

His wife raised her hands as if denying any part in the affair.

"My dear—I can do nothing! We had one part and when I suggested that they might sing something pleasantly quiet—a little part-singing for example—one of them laughed . . . laughed quite openly, and said, 'D'you mean a spot of close harmony?' I told her that I had no idea what 'close harmony' was. She laughed again and said, 'Better leave it to us, we'll give them what they want.'"

At four o'clock they drove down to the hospital.

Lady Sophia was wearing uniform, but something had made Alicia wear what she considered her most attractive dress. Her mother said, "Darling, surely that is just a leetle—well, elaborate, isn't it?"

They made a tour of the wards; Lady Sophia stiffly upright, wishing the men a "Merry Christmas" and assuring them that she knew they had enjoyed a wonderful time. Some of them appeared to be less certain than she was.

"And what present have you got?" she asked one man with a snub nose and china-blue eyes.

He answered, "H'among h'other things, m'am, a pair o' knitted bedsocks, an' very tasty they h'are too, but they'd be reely usefuller h'if I 'ah h'any feet ter put 'em on, if yer get what I mean? I mislaid mine in Greece."

She answered, "Oh, how very sad!"

"Not h'altogether, m'am, I shall never git chilblains again. I uster suffer 'orribly."

Alicia laughed. Her mother turned sharply and said, "Alicia, dear!" The snub-nosed man caught Alicia's eye, and winked. She wondered if he had really lost his feet. She hung behind her mother and when she passed to the next bed, asked, "Have you really lost your feet?"

He nodded, "Betcher life! Ondly what I say is s'no use crying over lorst feet. They fit yer with noo ones, simply lovely. Imagine never 'aving cold feet again."

The man on the other side of him called, "Now,

Miss, tell 'im he's *wonderful*, that's what he's angling for. Aren't you, Shorty?"

One man lay on his side; he had a lock of hair hanging over his forehead which momentarily reminded her of Flight. He half-opened his eyes when she paused at his bedside, looked at her, then said, "Oh, thank God!"

"Why this piety?" she asked.

He opened his eyes wider, they were dark and half obscured by long lashes. He seemed either too weak or too indolent to open them fully.

"Because," he said, "it's such a relief to see a decently dressed, good-looking woman. Oh! lots of the nurses are pretty girls, but they are always rushing about at such a rate. The rest—oh, Lord! Can't someone teach them some new phrases, can't someone make up a handbook—'Conversations with Wounded soldiers'? We're not all bloody heroes, we're not all suffering like hell—I am exceedingly comfortable, except for a burn on my leg, which really doesn't hurt except when they dress it. I've plenty of cigarettes, I don't eat chocolate, and I've all the books I want."

She said very calmly, speaking as she would never have done a year ago, "You're a nice, pleasant, grateful little bastard, aren't you?"

He opened his eyes wide. "*What* did you say?"

"You heard!"

"Well, I'm damned!"

"That is more than probable, I imagine. I suppose you're a gentleman ranker, are you? Public school and the 'Varsity. I like the other kind better." She was moving away, when he said suddenly, "I say, don't go! I'm sorry. I didn't mean to be beastly. Only if you knew some of these old dears—'old drears' would be more suitable—you'd have some sympathy, you would really! I know they mean well . . ."

"Of course they mean well. They've plenty of their own work to do, half of them have sons fighting . . ."

He shook his head. "No, my child, not the mob that come here. Not on your life!"

"Well, nephews or something of the kind; homes to look after, but they sacrifice an afternoon to come here. They might stay at home, put their feet up on a sofa, snatch half an hour's sleep . . . even go to the cinema. Instead, they come here, and superior little beasts like you sneer and talk in that unpleasantly patronising fashion."

He said, "I say! I didn't mean to be so beastly. I'm sorry. I promise that I'll be awfully nice to all the ENSA artists. I will really!"

Alicia watched his face. He was a good-looking lad, she thought. "Not quite as good-looking as he thinks he is, but quite pleasant."

She said, "I'm sure the artists will be tremendously gratified."

"You're still annoyed with me? That's not awfully kind, when I have tried to apologise handsomely—is it?"

Alicia realised that that moment she wanted

451

nothing so much as to talk to someone. Not to discuss the War, or the political situation, but just to talkly and ordinarily.

He might not be a very pleasant person, but he was, at least, sufficiently real to comprehend all the boredom, the falsity, the endless dragging-out of the war—visiting sick men, and so on.

She said, "I know I ought not to have spoken as I did. But like you, I'm 'browned off'. There are times when I only want to kick, and kick hard. So—I kicked you."

He grinned, looking years younger. "That's all right. It's very pleasant not to have someone who talks to you as if you were going to arrive at the Pearly Gates tomorrow morning. I'm not really 'public school and the 'Varsity'—I'm a medical student and I went to Marchester Grammar School —because I won a scholarship. My father keeps a very good ironmonger's shop in Marchester. Now —can we start again?"

Alicia nodded, and pulling forward a chair sat down beside his bed.

"You're married?"

She longed to say, "Yes, my husband is missing, and I'm having an affair with his brother." Instead she nodded.

"Am I allowed to say that he's a lucky fellow?"

"He's missing . . . since Dunkirk."

"Whew! Bad luck!"

A sudden bustle announced the arrival of the Concert Party. The Rector mounted the small

452

platform and told everyone how grateful they ought to be to the artists, and how much they were going to enjoy the show, and what a proof of good Fellowship and Christmas Feeling it was that these people gave up their Christmas to entertain the men who had done so much to help them. "Never has so much . . ." the Rector boomed and quoted the words of a Prime Minister.

The man in bed groaned, and said, "Now do you wonder that we get sick of that kind of tripe?"

She answered, "Frankly, I don't! That's my father who has been speaking."

A girl sat down at the piano and played—played very well as a matter of fact—"The Warsaw Concerto". That ended—and the men liked it, or their good manners were sufficient for them to pretend that they did—she was joined by a tall, thin man who sang "Trees" and "The Devout Lover".

A girl replaced him and played various unrecognisable tunes on a huge guitar, she closed her act by crooning, to her own accompaniment, "All the Things you are". The applause dwindled.

Alicia asked, "Are they always like this?"

The man answered, "More or less."

The men were restless, inattentive, when suddenly a small, fair-haired woman propelled herself on to the stage. She was not very young, she was not particularly pretty—Alicia thought that she looked rather like a very attractive, blonde Pekinese. A man in the next bed said, "Coo—

453

know 'oo she is? That's Dot Doreen . . . one o' the famous Gallimore fam'ly."

Alicia had never seen that remarkable thing—an unsuccessful bill saved by the appearance of a single act. She knew that she was held spellbound. The little woman stood there, staring at the boys, frowning at this one and that one, as if she had seen them before, then unexpectedly she said, "Happy Christmas."

They laughed. Alicia found that she was laughing too, and yet she could not have said why.

The woman on the stage demanded, "What's there to laugh at? Isn't it a Happy Christmas? I hope you've all copped nice cushy ones that 'ul keep you here for a long time." She began to patter, told some long story about a General, which kept wandering off into by-paths until the original story was completely lost. Her jokes were never actually dirty, but they were certainly "near the knuckle", and she put them over with an air of wide-eyed innocence which reduced her audience to tears. They rocked, they hammered their hands on their knees, they made noises which were inarticulate, but indicative of mirth. She danced —even Alicia knew that as a dance it was not particularly brilliant—but there was such vitality in every movement that when it ended the applause was deafening. She sang a song, no sillier than twenty others, but they hung on every word. She knew a dozen "army" jokes, jokes which held no meaning except for soldiers, but which made them

454

roll in their beds or wheeled chairs. Something about General Wavell and a dish of rice pudding —another concerning Rommel and a certain lady—one which centred round some Brigadier at Aldershot—incomprehensible to any but soldiers, but to them—wit of the most exquisite kind.

She made them sing a chorus, new in those days, about a certain "Lily Marlene". She told them the history of it . . . "So we pinched it from the Huns . . . we'll pinch a good deal more before we're through."

They roared the chorus, they demanded it again and again, until the little woman flapped her hands and panted, "Have a heart! I want my Christmas pudding," and left them.

The medical student lay back exhausted. He said, "I've never seen anything like it. She took that show in her two hands and lifted it right up. Marvellous!"

The man in the next bed said, "Ah—I've seen it 'appen once or twice. It's 'quality' as does it. That liftin' a bill. Marie Lloyd could do it—Florrie Forde, she could—so could Nellie Wallace. It's 'quality' as does it. She's one o' the Gallimore's —there you 'ave it."

Alicia offered her hand to the young man.

"Good-bye, get well soon."

"Shan't I see you again?"—

"I'm only on five days' leave. Then I go back to London."

"Try," he begged, "will you try to come in again?"

She nodded. "I'll try."

3

ALICIA looked back on the dinner at Little Manor as a kind of nightmare. True, the food had been excellent, Frances Masters as kind as ever. Edward assuming that slightly pedantic manner which his children had always regarded as wit, had been moderately amusing. Ann Claverley had driven over and brought the Duke with her. Alicia watched her and thought that, while she herself had grown harder, coarser, less pleasant, Ann had broadened, grown more tolerant, and essentially kinder.

It was obvious that Alcaster adored her, his eyes followed her whenever she moved, he hung on every word she spoke. Everyone had been cheerful, but there was a sense of strain which persisted all the time.

Chris had sent them all bags of hide, heavy as lead, and made in the usual slip-shod Arab fashion. Alicia's was no different from any of the others, and for a moment she longed to fling it from her and say, "I don't want it. I hate that rubbish Chris sends home."

All through dinner Ann had chattered, told them amusing incidents which had occurred at the hospital; Lady Sophia had contributed her quota, relating stories which usually reflected some minor

457

discredit on either the Matron or the nursing staff.

Ann laughed and declared, "My Matron is a gem! I don't know how they carry on day after day! Every one of them ought to be given OBEs or something."

Lady Sophia smiled, slightly acidly, and said, "Yes, but, Ann, dear, I happen to be a stickler for discipline."

"It's my opinion," Ann retorted, "that the less all this blasted discipline obtrudes—the better."

Alcaster said, "Ann, is it necessary to be so coarse?" but he smiled.

She answered, "Noble, there's a War on."

All the time Alicia felt that, however they might laugh and tell amusing stories, there was a sense of guarding against mentioning either Sholto or Flight. Someone began to speak, and it was as if suddenly a sign-post appeared, bearing the word "Flight" or "Sholto", and immediately another road was taken quickly, as if they all swerved away from the thought of those two men.

Only Ann seemed to have the courage to mention either of them. She said, "How Sholto adored rum sauce! He'd make a perfect pig of himself over it." Or—"I'm thankful Flight isn't a patient in my hospital . . . he'd have been so temperamental he'd have driven everyone crazy." Otherwise the two men were never mentioned.

Only when, in the drawing-room, Alicia found herself standing in the big bay of the window with Edward Masters, did he speak intimately. He said,

"Alicia, my dear, I don't wish to hurt you in any way, but if—remember I say *if*—the only news of Flight we receive is the worst, I want you to know that neither his mother nor I wish you to contemplate going through life alone. You're young, you're very lovely, and you must live your life, not go through it hugging a memory."

"No," she said. Then, "No, I understand."

"I wanted to say that, because—well, eighteen months is a long time."

She said, "Yes—yes, it is a long time."

They walked back to the Rectory, scarcely speaking. In the green drawing-room, Lady Sophia gave it as her candid opinion that Alcaster was rapidly entering his dotage. Really, the way he listened to everything that Ann said, as though she uttered pearls of wisdom, was preposterous. And for a girl of her age and in her position, to swear, as she apparently did, habitually, was little short of disgraceful.

Alicia listened, bored and indifferent. What did it matter if Ann swore like a trooper or Alcaster hung on her every word? She knew that she had in some way grown out of her home, grown out of her parents. Trying to criticise herself, she admitted that she had not improved; she had grown no more kindly, her tolerance was actually less tolerance than mental indolence. She accepted everything—people might do as they pleased, live as they pleased, hold what opinions they wished. She was not sufficiently interested to care. Her own life was complicated and difficult enough. She supposed that she was in love with Chris, but there was no actual tenderness in her feeling for him. She knew that frequently she disliked him, disapproved of his easy acceptance of everything that she gave him. Her kisses, her embraces, her body, were all part of the elaborate game of "being in love". He had wanted her, when she was engaged to his brother, not because he loved her, but because her looks attracted him, and because he had accustomed himself to taking whatever appealed to him. In London he had spoken the truth when he said that he enjoyed dining with "the best-looking woman in London".

That night Alicia went to her room feeling that she was one of the world's misfits. She had been born into a home where everything was regularised, where even opinions and ideas were subjected to a certain amount of mental inspection. She looked back on the years which she had spent there. They had been happy enough; happy, because they were not actively unhappy. Since she had married, since she had worked in London, toured the bombed and blasted cities, she had come to understand that life might be uncomfortable, dangerous, unpleasant in many ways, but at least it was—life. Whatever happened to her in the future, she had learned to live. Perhaps not to live in any very exalted sense; the average conversation in her mess did not reach a particularly high level. Until Chris had arrived and had come into her life, battering his way into it, she thought, she had met comparatively few people.

Her hours of work were irregular. Often when she returned home she was far too tired to bath, change and go out to dine or dance, and slowly people had let her drift away into her own channels. Even so, though she had been lonely, too tired even to care that she was lonely, her life had not been a merely negative business. At the Rectory it had been acceptance, negation, happiness, because it was not active unhappiness; now it was affirmation; when things were difficult then unhappiness was something real, definitive.

Again she stood at her window and looked out into the velvet-black night. She tried to make a mental assessment of herself. She was not a nicer person for her months spent in London, but she was incomparably stronger. Her attitude towards morals and beliefs was not more tolerant, she merely felt that life belonged to each individual, and provided they did nothing which was violently antagonistic to the general well-being, they had a right to live their own lives. Too much was at stake as the moment for individuals like Alicia Lockwood to stand still in their tracks and criticise the morals of other people. Alicia Lockwood—she paused and remembered with a kind of mental start, that she was, after all, Alicia Masters—had too much to occupy her to have time to occupy herself as well with the doings of Tom, Dick and Harry.

She had married Flight—she still thought of him with an almost unbearable tenderness—filled with hopes, ideals, and the belief that together they were going to make a perfect marriage based on a perfect companionship. The interlude with Chris was to be pushed forcibly away into the dark, inner regions of her mind; she wished to forget it completely. Only Flight really mattered. The other—that had been a momentary madness, something which was outside her comprehension —an incident, or a series of incidents, which must be forgotten.

She remembered her two perfect days with Flight in Paris, the things they had bought, the way they had laughed at trifles; their journey to Italy, the beauty of the Lake, the tranquillity and peace, the realisation that they were actually growing to "know one another", and that with that knowledge came a very real and firm sense of "liking". Their visit to Milan. That pleasant little man in the immaculate clothes, with his obvious devotion to his "Master"; his whole-hearted admiration, his trust and belief. Their luncheon with that young man who was English and yet bore an Italian name, who had married an Italian wife. The wife herself, magnificent, full-blown, charming; and the small, grey-haired man whom they had called "Gillie". Those were pictures which remained clear and vivid in her mind.

"But I never want to go back," Alicia thought. "That is all over. Flight will never come back. If he did, he'd find me different, harder, coarser. I doubt if even he, with all his sweetness, could take me back to being what I once was. I've moved on too far along another road. Chris never walked side by side with his brother. Yet I found it easier to walk along the road that Chris took, than along the one that Flight followed." She shrugged her shoulders and turned to get into bed. "No, I'm not a very nice person. Ann Claverley, with all her 'blasteds' and the rest, is far nicer than I am. Well, I am as this war has made me. I was not sufficiently strong to take a line of my own, I've gone the easy way." For the first time she stared out into the night, and smiling said, "Good night, Chris, my dear."

Boxing Day was, as Boxing Days always are, an anti-climax. Everyone suffered from over-eating, the excitement had died away, and all that lay before everyone was the prospect of writing a number of letters saying "Thank you" for gifts, which, nine times out of ten, they had neither wanted nor appreciated.

Alicia wandered into the garden, found it very cold, and returned to the house for a heavier coat. Her mother was down at the hospital, her father busy with Parish matters in the library. She walked out down the main street, wondering what on earth to do to pass the time.

At the back of her mind was the recollection of the young soldier, of his churlishness, of his apology, and his request that she would visit him again. She smiled as she remembered him. He was young, impudent, probably self-satisfied, but he was alive.

She caught sight of the bright brass plate which announced that William Charlton, MD, was ready to see patients from nine until ten-thirty, and again in the evening from six to seven. Below that statement another brass plate had been fixed, bearing the name of George Charlton, with the same letters following but with the addition "FRCS" Alicia stopped, stared, and decided that she would call and see Eleanor Charlton.

In the long narrow hall, with its white panelling and old hunting prints in maple frames, she found an atmosphere of peace. The whole place smelt pleasant, as if dried rose leaves and lavender had been touched for a second with a modern disinfectant. The two-hundred-years-old chest shone with much polishing, and against the wall hung a series of "horse tokens" polished until they shone like gold.

Eleanor came out to meet her, saying, "Alicia, my dear, how nice of you to come!"

Alicia said, "Not really, Eleanor, I was so bored . . ."

The other woman nodded. "I know, it's the transition. The leaving behind a life where there is never sufficient time to do anything, and coming to one where there is far too much time, and no way in which to spend it. Oh, I do understand. Come in,

464

there's a good fire here."

Compared with the Rectory, the room was simple in the extreme. True, the furniture was good, if not very valuable. There were some portraits on the walls, none of them particularly noteworthy. No chance here for anyone to say, "They tell us that this is a Reynolds, for it was obvious that they were the work of very modest artists. Pleasant, rather bucolic faces, against backgrounds of red plush curtains; decent, hardworking people, with a pardonable wish to leave behind some memorial which might be lasting. Some pleasant farmhouse Chippendale chairs, a good dining-table, one or two pieces of china —again obviously handed down—and the result was, to Alicia, something which breathed solidity, security and completeness. Eleanor said, "We don't have the drawing-room fire lit in the morning. I'm always busy, George is out on his rounds and"—she laughed—"coal is expensive."

Alicia remembered that she had never in her life considered whether coal was expensive or not; whether it was worth while lighting a flare or waiting until the room was going to be used. She said, "Do you like it, Eleanor?"

"Like—what? Being married to George? Working?—I do a great deal of his dispensing, you know—running a house? My dear, I adore every minute of it. Of course, at first it all seemed small after Little Manor, but after all, one can only live in one room at a time, and these old houses are well

465

built and comfortable. George's foot bothers him a little, but ..." She stopped, laid her hand on Alicia's arm and said impulsively, "My dear, I'm sorry."

Alicia, with that sudden sense of feeling stunned and unreal, which she always did when anyone referred even vaguely to Flight, said, "Oh, that's all right, Eleanor."

"I know"—she was evidently distressed—"but we—who have been lucky, who have our husbands back with us, even if they are a little maimed, forget what you others have to face—we get careless, we don't watch our words."

Listening, watching the anxiety on her face, Alicia thought, "What a sham, and at this moment I don't feel anything. Not only Flight, but nothing for Chris ... nothing at all. It's as if I were quite numb."

It was pleasant to sit by the bright fire with the light winking on the polished brass, the copper kettle on its stand, and listen to Eleanor's even tones. Soothing—as if someone laid a cool hand on her heart, assuring her that she must rest, tranquil, that she must not fret and delve, that sooner or later her emotion would wake again and life would be normal and sane. Now, it was as if she passed through a nightmare, a desert in which was nothing but sand, dry and unfriendly, stones which bruised and stung her feet, and above all a sense of unreality. The calm, kindly voice continued. Eleanor was talking of simple, ordinary matters—the car, George's ability to drive because the damage had been done to his left foot, old people who were so pleased to have him back among them, his kindness and sympathy, and yet that ability which was his to galvanise them into life, to force them to make efforts to further their own recovery.

"Small things," Alicia thought, "and yet are the things which go to make up my own life any larger, more important? Aren't all our lives made up of trivialities? Is it any more important that I drive down to East Ham taking Malcolm and Brownleigh with me, than that George Charlton turns out at two in the morning, with the temperature below zero, to attend some old woman at Parson's Farm who is suffering from colic?

"I'm in love with Chris—or, when he is there, I believe that I am—I'm married to his brother, we don't know whether he is alive or dead. I'm going this afternoon to talk to a young man in hospital, because he has an impertinent manner which amuses me; I shall probably flirt abominably with him and finally have to pull him up—'short and sharp'—what does it all amount to, anyway?" She heard Eleanor's quiet voice speaking, knew that she comprehended what was said, and that she answered at intervals, saying "Yes" or "No, I agree . . ." but in reality she was outside it all, thinking her own thoughts, and deciding at last "I'm pretty certain that I dislike myself sincerely." She did not realise that when she left the flat-fronted Georgian house with its shining brass plate, Eleanor Charlton watched her go, and, turning back into the security of her own home, thought, "Poor Alicia! She's got into a mental muddle. I wish I could help. She has found a new personality, and she can't make up her mind how, or on what lines, to develop it."

That afternoon, when luncheon was over, and the Rector asked if Alicia would drive with him to visit the Hortons, she refused, saying that she thought she might go down to the hospital and return with her mother.

The Rector smiled, indulgent and approving. "That's very kind of you, my dear, to devote part of your well-earned leave to visiting those poor wounded fellows. Your mother will appreciate it very deeply—as I indeed I do."

She walked down to the enormous house which had once been inhabited by Wilberforce Cummins. "He'll probably get a peerage for what he has given to this hospital," Alicia decided. Lord Cummins of Mallory, or Lord Mallory of Baddock. How she disliked the man.

Her mother, cool, immaculate and efficient, was seated in her office. She glanced up and said, "Ah, Alicia, this is very nice."

"I'd nothing to do, I thought that I might wander round the wards."

"I am certain that the men will be delighted to see you. Come back here and we'll drive home together. Oh, the work! Forms, without end. I am always deciding that I must have a secretary, but the majority of them are such fools."

She walked along the long corridor where acres of canvas, indifferently painted, hung in large, heavy gilt frames. "Reputed" Constables, "Accredited" Gainsboroughs; immense vases, monuments in ceramic, hideous, and notable only for their size; here and there a white marble bust, shining spectre-like against the dark wall-paper. Over all hung the faint smell of antiseptics.

She pushed open the door of the ward, knowing very well that she had no wish to talk to the men. She had come there to spend half an hour with one man—a medical student, educated at Marchester Grammar School, whose father kept an iron-monger's shop; a young man who had been badly burned in some engagement, who had a heavy lock of hair which fell over his forehead, and whose voice was intolerant and faintly impertinent.

With intent, because she sensed that he knew that she had entered the ward, she stopped to speak to the Sister on duty; she stood by the bed of a soldier who was busy making a tablecloth, using a combination of colours which set her teeth on edge. She praised his work, he nodded and told her, "Ah live i' Manchester, an' yer can do wi' a bit extra colour there, tha' knaws, Miss."

She moved on and stood talking, her voice slightly louder than was usual, to a good-looking lad with his arm in a splint.

He said that it didn't really hurt. "It's just awfu'

i' the road, ye're conscious o' it awe the time, ye ken."

Moving on again, knowing that the boy with the heavy lock of hair was pretending, as she was pretending. She wondered if there were any real emotions left in her, if she had ceased to be an actual person and had become only a strange, half-mechanical thing?

Why on earth had she come? What did it matter if she ever talked to this young man again or not? Surely he had no actual interest for her, or she for him? Just two people, who in a strange way titillated the senses of the other. He, because his attitude was almost brutal in his indifference, she because that queer brutality, that disregard for convention, reminded her vaguely of Chris.

She stopped beside his bed. "Good afternoon."

He said, "Good afternoon. So you did come, after all."

"Obviously."

He nodded to the empty bed on his right. "He was discharged this morning. You can sit on his bed if you like. Your mother being the Commandant, no one will say anything about it. Well, we had a beautiful Christmas, everything the heart could wish for . . ."

Alicia sat down and looked at his thin, nervous face.

"If you're going to talk like that—just being superior and 'clever-clever', I'm going, because it doesn't amuse me."

"And you only enjoy being amused?"

"I don't like being bored by inferior sarcasm."

"Ah!" His eyes brightened. "I must mend my manners. First, I know who you are, because Sister told me, with a proper amount of awe. I cannot demand any such awe—my name is—it's a disgusting name, by the way—Faust Mallison. Yes, really! it is Faust. My father had a passion for the opera and the play—so I was given that awful name. I have . . ."

She interrupted, "I know, you're going to tell me that you made a bargain with the Devil years ago. That you have done your best to live up to your name—and so forth."

He nodded. "I was going to. None of it would have been in the least true, but I rehearsed it last night—I felt that it might amuse you."

"Last night? You thought that I should come today? Let me tell you just why I came, shall I? I was bored, bored, bored. Tell me more about yourself—Faust."

He lay back smiling. He was really a very attractive young man, she thought, only far too conscious of the fact. His eyes were very bright and intelligent, his mouth curved easily into a smile.

He told her about Narvik, of how he had been caught in the machinery and had watched the boiling, thick oil creep nearer and nearer to where he lay; it was all vivid and horrible. Alicia wondered how these men contrived to remain sane, or did they slowly creep back to sanity after long weeks of semi-madness?

She asked him. He said, "Oh, I think at first most of us are mad. Burning isn't pleasant; there's such a delightful sense of doubt as to how much has been burnt, where, and if it can be saved or not. For weeks I looked like a nigger. Then slowly they peeled the stuff off, and—there I was, handsome as ever. Except this confounded leg. That's taken a long time. I didn't mind *much*. Now I want to get up, want to be discharged, to go to London and —ask you to come and dance with me."

"How do you know that I shall be in London, or that I dance . . . ?"

"Or that you'd be willing to dance with me, or—a dozen other things? I don't. I'm taking a chance. I've always believed in taking chances. You'd probably expect to go to some frightfully expensive place, I should have to pawn my watch, but—it would be worth it."

"And if you were disappointed? If I danced abominably . . ."

"Then we'd sit out all the dances, and visit the bar at intervals. Have you ever been to the Palais de Dance at Hammersmith?—no? I thought not. Or the Palais Royal in Bloomsbury, or the Dancing Doll off Holborn?—no? I know the kind of places you've been to. Never mind, we'll go to one of your places one night, and one of mine the next. That's fair."

She laughed. "Don't you think that you're going rather fast?"

472

He nodded. "I daren't waste time." He moved restlessly. "'I wasted time and now doth Time waste me . . .' Tell me about yourself."

"There isn't anything to tell. I've lived here all my life, with visits to town for the Season. I married, went abroad for my honeymoon, came back here and then, after Dunkirk, I went to London to drive. Not a very interesting story."

He frowned. "Not as you told it. It might be if you hadn't cut it down to a bare recital of facts. I wish I knew what you were really like. Oh, I don't mean just to look at, you're divine to look at. But—*you*. Does anyone know—you?"

"Faust, I don't know myself. I wish that I did."

He watched her gravely, then said, "I wonder if anyone ever knows anything about people like us? I doubt it, because we're—in common with a great many more of our kind—fakes. We aren't real people at all. Oh, we eat and sleep and drink, and possibly make love, but we're not real people. We're sensationmongers. That's why you're here this afternoon, that's why I was waiting for you with my heart pumping hard. We both wanted to savour a new sensation.

"I'm a young soldier, I speak rather more grammatically than most of the fellows here, I was impertinent—and you're not used to people being impertinent to you. The experience was rather amusing. I'm not used to talking to young women who are miles above me socially, who have aristocratic relations, who are obviously the product of

473

a class of which I know nothing. It was amusing to assume a kind of impudence, to assume that you'd meet me again in town. My dear, I could no more afford to take you out to dinner at one of *your* places than I could fly! No, we're both pretending, we're both fakes—imitation people."

She listened, nodded and said, "I wonder if you're right?"

"Of course I'm right. Oh, the War is partially to blame; people like you and I have lost our bearings somehow. Maybe we weren't sufficiently stable to begin with. 'Shorty' over there he hasn't lost his. He's the same chap that he was when he first joined the Army. I'm not, I don't suppose you are the same person as you were before you began to do 'war work'? I believe that making ourselves 'real' again is one of the big things we've got to learn. It's not a question of being made of 'base' metal; tin isn't base, unless it tries to pass itself off as silver. We aren't base, we're just rather silly, not terribly 'worth while'—fakes, imitations. Don't you agree?"

"I don't know," Alicia said slowly. "I've never listened to anyone assuring me that I was a 'fake' and so on before. I suppose you—well, intrigued me."

He said almost sulkily, "That's a damned silly expression people use—intrigued."

She laughed. "Look here, Faust, I can't talk to you if you're going to interrupt me. I'm not one of those brilliant people who can talk easily. Particularly to a young man I've only met once before, and who was as rude the first time as he has been the second."

"That's the kind of glib stuff I hate," he retorted. "It's all part of this elaborate verbal flirtation. Oh, I know that I'm being rude, damned rude. I know that I could quite easily let myself fall violently in love with you. What would be the use? It would only make me acutely miserable, and, God knows, I can find sufficient misery without going about looking for it."

"Poor Faust," she said, and for the first time she began to realise that this whole visit was futile and stupid. He was right, this young man, the impulse had been unworthy. She had been bored, he had been the only man in the ward who seemed attractive, and she had looked forward to—exactly what he had said—a verbal flirtation.

He shrugged his shoulders. "Oh—poor!"

"I think we're all learning to snatch," Alicia said. "It may be the feeling of insecurity, of not knowing what may happen tomorrow, or even if there will be a 'tomorrow' for any of us. It's a poor way of living, I suppose. You're right when you say it's unworthy. I apologise for having come this afternoon."

For the first time he smiled, looking immediately younger and more attractive.

He said, "That, Mrs. Masters, is very handsome of you."

"But when you're better I should like to see you in London . . ."

He said, "What, proudly wearing the stripes of a Corporal, and Army boots . . ."

"Yes. I don't mind, why should I? And we will dance . . ."

"At some stuffy hole in the Tottenham Court Road . . ."

"Wherever you like—again, I don't mind. You're being bitter, you're assuming that I am even more unpleasant than you have already assured me that I am. I've offered you an apology. The least that you can do is to accept it."

"You really mean that you did—come here because . . ." he paused.

"Because I was bored to extinction, because I was—sorry—intrigued. And because—I really am eating, not a slice, but the whole humble pie—I thought it might be amusing to indulge in a little, very harmless flirtation with a rude young man."

"And now—what are you offering me?"

"The right to telephone me when you're in London to ask me if I'll go out to dine or dance or—well, whatever will be amusing."

"You really mean that?"

"Yes."

"And if I get annoying—what's your word for it?—ah, I remember, tedious? What if I get tedious?"

"I think you can rely on me to—cope."

"You're in the telephone-book? I shan't forget.

476

When do you go back?"

"I think that after your lecture I'd better go back tomorrow, don't you?"

He laughed. "I'd much rather you came to see me."

She walked home, making an excuse to Lady Sophia that she needed exercise, and as she made her way along the quiet country lane, with its bare hedges on either side, her mind went back to the young man she had left in hospital. Was he right? Were they all growing to be imitations, fakes, snatchers at every passing emotion? Did the attraction which she felt for Chris Masters consist only of that craving for excitement, of a kind of conceit which made her long to be of first importance in the life of some man?

Flight had been different. Flight had talked of his ideas, his plans and hopes; Flight had proved that his feeling for her was not merely a great physical attraction, not merely pleasure at being in the company of a pretty woman. Then came the doubt as to how long she would have been happy with Flight. Did she really long for his return, so that they might begin their life together once more, or was the idea faintly disturbing? Was she the same Alicia Masters who had lived with him on the shores of Lake Como, who had been amused and delighted with the *naïveté* of Guido, and the time spent with Iva Alfano, her husband and that little grey-haired man called "Gillie"? Would Flight be able to satisfy her, or would she find his quiet, rather gentle outlook, his idealism, and his thoughtfulness, dull and faintly boring?

Had life during the past eighteen months coarsened her, perhaps brutalised her mental vision? Made her appetite turn from the fine, sensitive things which Flight loved, and prefer rather the stronger flavours of the life which Chris Masters lived with such gusto?

She walked on, frowning a little. The thoughts were disturbing. She felt apprehensive, fearful of what the future might hold. She had gone too far and yet was not prepared to go completely along the road that would cut her off from the life to which she was accustomed.

She knew that Chris attracted her powerfully; how much of that attraction could be called "love" she did not know. He excited her, he seemed to carry her forward with him into a tempestuous sea, at which they both laughed, as it buffeted them. There was a reckless courage about Chris, a disregard for everything except that the present moment should be lived fully and completely with the greatest possible amount of enjoyment. Whatever he did he enjoyed, or left it alone. He loved good food, movement, laughter; he drank with appreciation and actual pleasure, he warmed "both hands at the fire of life" and saw to it that the fire was kept burning brightly, and continually.

He had wanted to make love to her when she was engaged to his brother, not because he wished to wrong Flight, but because she was young, lovely and desirable. Now, when it was uncertain as to whether she was his brother's wife or his widow those same sentiments continued. He had said to her once, when she had expressed the belief that they were behaving disgracefully in continuing the love affair on which they had embarked, "You get such muddled ideas, 'Licia. I don't want you more, or less, because you may be my brother's wife or his widow—I want you because you are you, and I am I. I'm not good at analysing my emotions, I distrust emotions anyway. But if I were given to it, if I could take out all the things I feel and think, and stick them on pins and watch them wriggle, I should say that I believe there is sufficient evidence to prove that I love you. It may not be of the quality that the World's Great Lovers possessed. I didn't know any of them and I suspect that they were average bores anyway, but—it's good enough for me. When it is possible, I'll marry you. I'll be good to you, I'll work for you—whether I shall always be faithful to you, I don't know. I should think it's more than probable that I shall. If you like I'll run away with you now, only there's the damned Army, and the blasted War, to make it insuperably difficult. Would you run away with me—if it were possible?"

She remembered how she had sat, her chin on her hand, listening to him, watching his clean-shaven, good-looking face, his powerful shoulders and strong neck, and tried to decide what her reply should be.

He repeated, "Would you?"

"No," she said at length. "No, Chris."

He had flung back his head and uttered that ugly barking laugh, which indicated that he was growing angry, and demanded, "Why? I'll tell you. You haven't got the pluck, have you?"

"No," she said again. "No, Chris, I haven't got the pluck."

"But you have the pluck to live with me—so long as no one knows?"

"Yes—that isn't pluck, that is self-indulgence, my dear. I'm a coward, and I know and admit it. I don't pretend to say that you are doing wrong, though I suppose it is wrong to take another man's wife . . ."

"Not if he can't hold her," Chris objected.

"Flight isn't in a position either to hold me or to let me go," she said. "I don't know that you're doing anything very wrong, you're a person without moral scruples, aren't you? I'm not. I'm ashamed of being in love with you, ashamed of living with you, ashamed of the lies I tell Deb."

"In short," Chris said, and smiled, "the whole business isn't satisfactory to you—beginning with me, and ending with yourself and your own moral doubts?"

"I don't see how it can be. Be honest, Chris."

This time he laughed. "I like that. I am honest, my sweet. I'm desperately, completely honest. You're the little coward, the piece of walking dishonesty. If you're not satisfied—chuck the whole business. I'll walk out of your life and stay out."

She remembered her sudden feeling of actual distress, of helplessness; how she had made a little gesture of despair with her hands and said, "But I couldn't—I couldn't let you walk out of my life, Chris!"

He rose and came over to her, knelt down beside her and put his arms round her, saying as if he were talking to a child, "Little idiot, I know that. Do you imagine I should have talked as I have been doing if I'd imagined there was the slightest chance of losing you?"

She stared at him, her eyes still perplexed and worried. "Do you know that's one of the very few nice things you've ever said to me?"

He nodded. "I expect so. I'm not very good at saying nice things."

The next day she went back to London. She knew that she had failed to fit into the life at the Rectory, knew that her father and mother were distressed because they realised that she was no longer the daughter they had known, and of whom they had approved.

From her flat she sent a note to Faust Mallison. She wrote simply, without affectation, and asked him to telephone her when he was next in London. She looked for his reply. Days passed and it never came. Years afterwards she thought that she caught sight of him in the Strand, but he had passed before she could speak to him.

She asked about him when she wrote to her mother and was told that he had been discharged and sent to some convalescent hospital in Wales. That was all she ever heard of him.

Her work went on, hard, trying, but it served to keep her from thinking and speculating too much on her own affairs. Chris wrote that he might get leave at the end of March, but in February Edward Masters wrote to tell her that he had been wounded and was in a hospital in Alexandria. *Not seriously wounded*, Edward wrote, *but, naturally, we are worried and anxious.*

Chris wrote her that it was nothing, that he had only managed to get several pieces of shrapnel in his thigh. Two days after she had his letter she received one from the War Office, stating that in spite of all investigations and enquiries, no trace of Flight had been found. They regretted that he must be "assumed to be dead".

Part Four

1

FLIGHT moved forward as quickly as his injured foot and heavy bag would allow him to do. He had that sensation of trying to make himself as small as possible, and the result was that he felt about eight feet high, and conscious that everyone must notice him and regard him with hostile eyes.

He tried to push open the big wooden doors, and finding them locked, rang the old-fashioned bell. In the distance he heard it tinkle and presently heavy steps could be heard coming over the courtyard. The door opened. A man, old and ugly, peered out, his expression full of suspicion.

"Yes?" Nothing more, only that brief question. It came like the shot from a gun.

"Is it possible for me to speak with Madame Matot? My name is François Pascal. I am a friend of her son, Monsieur Jules Matot."

The surly old voice asked, "How do I know that you're speaking the truth?"

Flight smiled. How indeed could the fellow know? He ought to have prepared proofs. He held out his bag, saying, "I will unlock this. Take it to your mistress; what she finds there will convince her that I am an honest person." He longed to laugh at that remark. To hand over a bag

485

containing clothing which had been stolen by a German officer; pictures which he himself had virtually obtained by false pretences, and a number of duplicate receipts for stolen goods, was scarcely the best proof of integrity.

The old man said, "Come in, and be quick about it. How do I know who is watching us?"

Flight entered, the big doors were closed and barred. He stood in a small courtyard, covered with old stones between which grew little bunches and sprigs of greenery. He saw a tiny patch of "London Pride", and felt his heart warm suddenly. The old man jerked his head in the direction of the house and said, "Come on. Oh, you're lame? Give me that bag."

In through a back door, along a passage paved with the same type of stones as those in the courtyard; they reached a swinging green baize door, against which the old fellow set his shoulder, and again said, "Come on."

He almost pushed Flight into a small room, where a plain table and two chairs stood. He said, "Wait there," and closed the door behind him.

Flight heard the key turn in the lock; he sat down and waited. He knew that he was terribly tired; tired, not only physically, but mentally and spiritually. He seemed to have been living a life of constant watching, pretence, and deception for years. How long ago was it since he had lain on the beach at Dunkirk? since he had nudged a dead man and urged him to "Come on, make a move." Years and years. He had grown accustomed to assume first one personality and then another. He had walked, hidden, spied, listened and pretended —and now he was tired of it all. He was waiting for "Susan" Matot. Three years ago that knowledge would have excited and pleased him, now—he only wished that she would come quickly, and either give him a bed on which he could sleep or throw him out immediately.

He had information to give, he had pictures to hand over to the proper authorities. He knew so much that he realised that he was an important person, that he had done excellent work for the people who were his friends and—he was too tired to care. He sat there on a hard wooden chair, his whole body slack with intense weariness, his hands hanging loose at his sides so that his fingers almost trailed on the floor.

Even his ability to hate seemed to have been dampened, as a fire may be damped with fine coal-dust, so that only the very heart remains glowing and hot. At that moment he felt nothing. Had the fat Marshal entered, could von Ludbach have walked in, or that unpleasant creature who called himself "Mademoiselle Jamais" have appeared, he thought that he could have summoned up only sufficient energy to nod to them, without even attempting to speak.

He blinked his eyes, they felt gummy, in spite of the wash that he had enjoyed at Maurice Gold's. His whole body felt as if it itched with weariness, his foot was giving him considerable pain, he felt in his pockets hoping to find a cigarette. Crumpled and broken, he discovered one lying there; he took it out, tried to smooth it with his fingers, found that it had burst in several places. His disappointment was so intense that he knew that tears stung his eyes.

Then the door swung open and Madame Matot said, "Well, this is a surprise. Have you heard that the road between here and the place where the German Marshal stayed last night has been blown up? No? Unfortunately they—whoever 'they' were—miscalculated the time, and he wasn't hurt. I hear that he has arrived at Headquarters, looking ghastly. They say that someone tried to poison him?"

Flight shook his head. "No—not poison. That's not true. It was only a severe purge. Tell me, the aeroplane going to Algiers . . . ?"

"With a general on board. It came down. They were all killed."

He said, "I liked him, he wasn't a bad chap. He'd been dreadfully—dreadfully disillusioned." The words felt actually heavy in his mouth. Susan Matot watched him intently. His head was falling forward on to his chest, he kept forcing himself to keep awake; jerking his head with a motion which was almost epileptic.

She leaned forward and laid her hand on his; he started, and stared at her as if he tried to remember who she was.

She said, "Listen—you are going to bed—'immediately'. It will not be a very elegant room, for I suspect that these people may come looking for you. It is quiet and the bed is comfortable. This bag . . . ?"

He said, "Yes—that bag. I have the key here, take it. It must be hidden somewhere—there is a Clouet in it—and some others. Papers . . ."

"Yes, it shall be taken the greatest care of." She spoke soothingly, as if to a child, "Now, first, tell me—your name?"

He spoke like a parrot. "My name is François Pascal. I am a native of Paris, a traveller—you understand—in office equipment. Inks, pencils, and so on. I am nearly twenty-three years of age."

She nodded gravely. "You have your papers?"

"Yes, Madame." His hand went to his breast-pocket.

Opening the door, she called softly. "Henri —you are to help this gentleman to—The Room. See that he has all he requires."

Stumblingly, Flight followed the bad-tempered old man along a corridor, down some stairs, into what appeared to be a cellar. The old man shuffled his way among wine-casks, boxes, and packing cases, and fumbling with his fingers against the wall found what he evidently sought. A section of the wall moved, the bricks opened, and before them was a small room, containing a bed, chairs and a wash-basin.

He said, "You'll be all right here. I'll shut the

489

door when I go. If you want anything urgently, ring that bell. Don't go ringing it for nothing, I'm too old to keep running backwards and forwards. Get some sleep. I'll call you when Madame orders. There are towels; the place is air-conditioned. Oh, she is practical, that one."

Flight flung off his jacket, slipped off his shoes —vaguely he remembered that they weren't his shoes at all, and before the old man had closed the brick door, he was asleep.

How long he slept he did not know. He awoke to find Henri standing by his bed, a newly-pressed suit hanging on his arm; an electric light was burning, shining on his face. He rolled over, flinging his arm over his eyes to keep off the glare. He fought wildly with his memory. Where was he? how had he come here? was he still in the dirty little room making a rope of grimy sheets? He opened and shut his eyes.

Henri said, "She opened your bag. This is a clean suit, the one you were wearing is a disgrace. I am to examine your foot at once." He turned back the clothes, grumbling as he did so. "Tut, tut! always there is something to do. Now I must examine the foot of a man I do not know. Ah, it is not so dirty as I feared. This is a very fine table napkin. I wonder where you got this?" As he talked, complaining and criticising, his hands were at work, surprisingly soft and gentle. "Are you rested? you've slept long enough! It is very late, but she wishes to speak to you. Remember,

490

although you may seem to be alone with her, I—Henri—shall be very near. Don't try to be clever, most emphatically it will not pay you. I have a nasty way with—unpleasant people."

Flight said, "But I don't think that I am an unpleasant person."

"Huh! This is your opinion—it may not be mine. Now wash yourself, and come with me. Keep your mouth shut, and only speak when you are spoken to, you understand?"

Later he was escorted upstairs and shown into a room where a table was laid for dinner. Madame Matot came towards him, smiling. "You're rested, poor fellow? Later you must tell me all that you have done. I have been through your bag. I have placed the pictures—and very lovely they are, a magnificent haul—in safety, and your papers. Already"—her eyes twinkled, and Flight thought how attractive she was, even though the years had aged her—"I have had a telephone conversation concerning you. Oh, don't worry, there are ways and means by which the all-conquering Hun is circumvented. Money can do anything, and the man who asked for news of you has"—she shrugged her shoulders—"all the money in the world—Maurice Gold."

Flight said, "Oh, he is charming, isn't he?"

"I tell him that the good God intended him for a saint, and that he made himself a wicked old devil. He made me laugh with his account of your arrival in his *appartement*. But Maurice always makes me laugh. Now we must eat, and then there is a great deal of business to be discussed. Jules, your old friend, will be here presently. He is going south in a few days; I think that you must go with him. Things are moving very quickly, my dear. Next year is going to see many, many changes."

Then, as dinner was served, she ceased to speak of his travels, of dangers and political matters, and became—as he had known her before the War—a charming hostess, her conversation light and amusing, her comments often caustic and vastly entertaining. He asked if she were acting. She nodded, "Of course, it is necessary for the morale to be kept up. I have found a young man, one of the most brilliant young men I have ever known—his name is Armand Erdodi. That, of course, is not his real name; what that is—one does not enquire. He has written two plays, both of which have been submitted to the German Kommander. He expresses himself as delighted. They go to prove how fine the German ideal is, how misjudged they are, in short what magnificent people this race has produced, and how fortunate France is to have such generous conquerors. One is called 'Quel Coeur Généreux', the other—which we hope to produce in a few weeks—'Tirez le rideau!' Never have I read such exquisite irony, never such delightful cynicism. Do they see it, these 'Puddenheaded' people?" She used the English dialect word—"No! They actually believe that we play seriously, that I, Susanne Matot, feel every word that I speak. I do," she laughed, "I do indeed, but not as they imagine.

"My dear, on the first night of 'Quel Coeur Généreux!' no one believed that Maurice Gold would come out of the theatre alive. My friend Olympia sat next to him and she assured me that she trembled, because, in the pathetic scenes, Maurice swelled with suppressed laughter like a bull-frog."

She went on to tell him how the German High Command had sat in their boxes with tears glistening in their eyes at the wonderful portrayal of the "True German spirit of goodness and true kindliness."

"When it is all over," she said, "I shall be called a collaborationist—not by the French, but certainly by the British and the Americans. You see your German has trained himself to be so metaphysical that he analyses too deeply, so deeply that he goes below what is the actual truth. So these plays of Erdodi seem to them to be filled with deep truths, as a matter of fact they are the most delicious—I use that word because they are literally like something which tastes good—comedies."

How pleasant it was to be seated at a dinner-table where the glass and silver were not stolen goods, where the napkins did not bear the monogram of someone from whom they had been pilfered. To drink wine which had not been taken—almost by force—from the people who had made it and preserved it. How additionally pleasant to listen to

493

a woman speaking in a cultured voice, speaking lightly, laughing at danger, ready to take risks and—still smile.

He said, "Please tell me about Jules?"

"He has done very well—but it is invidious to speak in that way, they have all done well." She leaned forward and laid her hand on his. "I have no doubt that you have seen dreadful things, so have I. What many of these men—and believe me, I am sure that you were one of them—have suffered, are ready to continue to suffer, makes one's heart beat with pride. Everywhere, in every country where Nazism or Fascism exists, there is this army of people—men *and* women, my dear, as I know only too well, all banded together for the sake of Liberty. When it is all over—and there can and will be only one end to it—can nothing be done to keep that spirit alive for ever? It is too precious to be allowed to sink down, become extinguished, swamped, or caught up in quarrels which are only political."

She talked, and he watched her, conscious that with every moment she was pouring her own vitality into his mind. Vaguely he wondered how old she was? Jules was his own age, Susanne Matot must be at least forty-three, perhaps older; and yet her energy, her enthusiasm and her faith were so vigorous and all-embracing.

She said suddenly, "What are you thinking, Flight?"

He said, "Quite honestly, I was thinking how

much I had missed hearing a woman talk. All those months in the farmhouse, Madame spoke very little, she was old and tired. Sometimes I spoke to a girl in a café, sometimes to a prostitute—they often know so much, those women—but to sit at a decent table, to listen to an educated voice, to hear a woman laugh again—it is like heaven."

"And your own home? You were going to be married, yes?"

"I am married," he said, "I have tried by every means to get messages through; if some of them have reached my wife—I have heard nothing from her. At first, I thought that I should go mad, I dare not even think of her. Now, it still hurts to remember that she may be suffering, believing that I am dead, or that she herself may have been killed in the bombardment, but it is a queer kind of dull ache, as if part of me had been battered into unconsciousness."

"I know, I understand that feeling. You love her very dearly?"

"Alicia? I adore her, she is everything that is wonderful. Very beautiful, not perhaps very intellectual, but charming and—gracious. That is the word—gracious."

"Poor Flight. Soon, very soon we shall be able to get messages through, and yours shall be one of the first. Oh, yes, I have plenty of good friends. Maurice Gold shall help us."

They sat together talking over their coffee—coffee which Susanne made herself—until Henri came and whispered to her. She rose and signed to Flight to stay where he was, then went out closing the door softly. He sat there, relaxed and restored; conscious that she had filled him with a sense of reality once more. The past months had been unreal, fantastic. Again and again he had wondered if he was quite sane, or if indeed he was the same man who had once lived in a country house in England?

His whole habit of life had been altered, not changed slowly but disrupted violently, as if he had been flung into a new world where the old ideas did not exist. Cleanliness which he had once regarded as a mechanical business, as necessary as food and drink and sleep, had been relegated to the position of a luxury, even regarded as something of an eccentricity. If it were possible and safe to bathe in a stream or secluded pond, one bathed; if not—one was content with a wash in the old tin bowl in the back kitchen of the farm. Clean clothes were not a matter of regularity; if your shirt became too dirty, you asked Madame Peloux if she had a clean shirt in the press.—It was not your shirt, it was only a communal shirt which happened to be washed and ironed ready for use. You rarely scrubbed or specifically cleaned your nails. If they needed cutting then you opened a clasp-knife and hacked them to a convenient length. Shaving was not an every-day occurrence; razor-blades were unobtainable, and Pierre's old "cut-throat" razor was in the nature of a mediaeval torture no matter how long or how hard you stropped it.

True, while he was living with the Germans he had been given more opportunities, baths had been regular and hot; von Ludbach, when in a good temper, had pressed upon him oppressively scented soap, talcum powder and expensive tooth-pastes. The men had only observed a superficial cleanliness, such as was necessary to give them a smart appearance when von Ludbach held an in-spection; then their faces had shone with soap and the close application of razors, their hair was always kept short, so that the skin of their heads showed through. In most cases their personal habits were filthy.

He let his mind go back over the past months. It seemed incredible that he should have done the things which—as they occurred—he had merely accepted as being part of the daily routine. He, Flight Masters, had with his own hands strangled a German officer, had disguised himself as a French prostitute in order to do so. Why? He had no sense of moral disgust that the German should have wanted to visit a woman, he had done it because his own hate and anger had blazed up suddenly, because the German had struck him—unjustly and needlessly. To kill a man for that. To risk your life in order to satisfy a sense of revenge. He had done this thing. He who hated to see any small beast in the fields maimed or suffering, who worked himself into a fever when one of his dogs had been ill, who hated blood—both the sight and the smell.

The terrible artificiality struck him so forcibly that he felt his mind reel. This hatred, it wasn't a real thing, it was manufactured and fostered, and with each encouragement it became more and more easy. The day they had buried Father Maurice—when they had bundled his body into a grave, as they might have buried potatoes which were to be reserved for winter use. Yet they had all liked Maurice—no, they had loved him, for his patience, his courage, his apparent inability to grumble at anything, however dangerous or difficult. Flight remembered that they had scarcely spoken of him again; only Pierre had mentioned him once. Jacques, Shaff, even Madame Peloux had never spoken his name.

War itself was artificial; that it was wasteful and illogical he had decided long ago, but now he realised that it was an unreal thing. A huge machine which caught up people—men and women—and whirled them into a state of mind which was completely foreign to their original natures. It was the crowning piece of artificiality following on the heels of such fantastic ideas as Nazism and Fascism. A kind of manufactured fire, such as he had read that men made in the prairie in order to avert another fire; it must be made to blaze and burn in order to avert another fire; it must be made to blaze and burn in order that these conflagrations endangering the peace of the world might be overcome.

Madame Matot interrupted his thoughts, she

came back and told him that he was wanted. "Two men are waiting to see you," she said. "One is known as Number Seven, the other is X. They are two of our must successful and courageous agents. They will give you your instructions."

He followed her into a small room at the back of the house. The curtains were drawn, but he noticed that the windows were closely shuttered. The two men sat at a plain kitchen table. The one who was Number Seven was small, insignificant, with a sharp nose which looked as if he suffered from a perpetual cold in the head; the other was heavy shouldered, bullet-headed, with strong, ugly jaw and small bright eyes. They nodded to Flight, and Seven said, "Sit down. You'll stay, Madame? Yes, better to hear everything he has to tell us."

The bullet-headed man began to question; there was no attempt to praise, the queries were merely shot at him like bullets. Now and then Seven interpolated a question in a small, snuffling voice; when he spoke the bullet-headed man drummed with his fingers on the table as if unable to restrain his impatience.

They both seemed to know a great deal concerning his movements, and to have very exact information. For example, when the bullet-headed man asked, "How far was this farm from Matrec?" and Flight answered:

"Roughly—twelve kilometres, I should say."

The little man, sniffing as a preliminary, said, "Twelve and a half."

499

"Shaff? What was his other name?"

"I don't know. I never heard him called anything except Shaff."

"His Christian name is Ernest—don't you know that?"

"I tell you I never heard his Christian name. If you know, why bother to ask me?"

X narrowed his small eyes until they almost disappeared. He said, "My friend, we're not here only to find out how much you know, we're here also to show you how much *we* know. A kind of warning, you understand? So that you should be very exact in your replies."

"In other words," Flight said, "you are both trying to—catch me out?"

Seven sniffed, as if in appreciation, and squeaked, "Ah, ah! that's right, that's right!"

Only when he told them of the sudden illness of the German Marshal did they become slightly more human. The thickset man so far forgot himself as to beat softly on the table with his clenched fist, muttering, "Magnificent! but truly magnificent!" while his companion not only produced a blue-and-white checked handkerchief with which to blow his nose, but he wiped his eyes and rocked gently backwards and forwards. Susanne Matot having laughed immoderately, said suddenly in English, "Nay, lad, give over do—ha' done!"

Bullet Head asked, "Did you know that we nearly got your fat friend?"

"I heard so . . ."

X rapped back, "Who told you?"

Flight said with studied nonchalance, "I forget —someone or other."

"And this General with whom you talked—did you hear that his 'plane had crashed?"

"Yes, I believe I did hear that. As I said before, he told me himself that it was likely to do so."

Susanne laughed. "X, he's beating you at your own game! He's all right, we shan't catch him out. And if you can't—no one can, that's certain."

X nodded. "I think you're right. We'd better send him to the south. He certainly can't remain here, too many people know him. The Marshal persists that he was poisoned, even talks of reprisals, here in Paris, to revenge himself. They say that he has lost seven kilos."

Susanne answered, "He can afford to—even then he'd be overweight."

"Yes"—he tapped his front teeth with a pencil—"yes, he'd better go south as soon as that foot is better. I'll get him some papers; we'll baptise someone else—François Pascal." To Flight— "You know the south?"

"Not particularly well. But—is there no possibility of my getting to England?"

Seven shook his head. "At the moment, not the slightest. Later . . ."

"Can I get a message through?"

"Possibly—it's still difficult. Once we begin sending odd messages through—there'd be no end to it. The Vatican do what they can, but the

Germans are very worried, and so they are very sharp about such things. Better to wait a little longer . . ."

X said, "Remember, they've got quite a number of people looking for you. Incidentally they got Shaff this morning. My report says that he has been sent to Germany."

Flight, startled, and furious at the matter-of-fact tone, cried, "My God! you mean to say they've got Shaff? Can't something be done?"

X stared at him. "If something can be done, my eager young friend, we can safely leave it to Shaff to do it. There isn't a prison built that can hold him. They might shoot him—but it's not likely. He's much too valuable. No, he'll probably turn up in a few months wearing the uniform of a German general, or disguised as Hitler, or some damn thing."

Seven leaned forward and whispered. "We don't need to worry about people like Shaff, you see. Yes, the south will be best for you. Keep him here, Madame, until we get his papers made out. What name shall we give him?" he giggled, "something attractive, eh?"

They went, nodding their "good nights". Susanne slipped her arm through Flight's and together they went back to her drawing-room.

She said, "You didn't like them much, eh?"

"Frankly, I thought that I had never met a couple of more unpleasant brutes."

"They're neither of them decorative, I admit.

But they are both tremendously single-minded, incredibly brave, and as honest as any men I have ever known. X was a schoolmaster before the War, Seven was an accountant."

She talked to him of the whole Movement. Slowly he came to understand the extent of its work, how the elaborate network reached to the borders of France, pushed over into Italy; how, even in Germany, men and women were to be found planning, contriving, scheming to further the day when Liberty should return to the world. He remembered how he had felt at the farmhouse —that Jacques, Pierre, Madame Peloux, Shaff and Father Maurice were the whole Movement; that they, with a few other "moles" constituted practically the main army of the Underground Movement. Now he came to realise that they were merely a tiny outpost, a diminutive section. As Susanne talked of the exploits of some of the men who were working, of their hairbreadth escapes, of the incredible dangers which they had run, and of the magnitude of what they had accomplished, he saw his own place in this immense scheme for what it was—small, unimportant, insignificant.

He said, "I don't wonder that they didn't think much of me."

"That's where you're wrong. It's like a hymn I learned when I was a small child about a 'little candle burning in the night'; it ended 'so we must all shine, you in your small corner and I in mine'. That is where so much of the power comes from—the tremendous number of people, *all* working, all doing whatever work comes to their hand, no one thinking that they are too important to tackle the *little* things. Those men didn't intend to belittle what you've done—indeed, when I was talking to them before you came in they both spoke in the highest terms of what you'd done. Remember they are interrogating people, sifting evidence, studying reports, from early morning and through most of the night . . ."

The door was flung open and she sprang to her feet, crying, "Jules, my dear, you're back! Look—look whom we have with us!"

Flight scarcely recognised him as the Jules he had known. He was thin to the point of emaciation, his dark eyes sunk deep in his head, his cheek-bones seemed to jut from his face, his clothes hung on his thin frame.

Only when he smiled did Flight feel that this was indeed his friend.

Jules said, "I have heard of you, the story of the Marshal is all over Paris. They say that Maurice Gold is furious that he cannot pretend that he organised the whole thing. However, he has added all kinds of picturesque details, which he swears you told him. And now you are to come south with me. Ah, we'll have some amusing times. I met Seven, he is already thinking out a name for you—I suggested Riom Corbin. He likes it. Do you?"

He told Flight that he was a clerk at the moment,

working very hard in a Government office. He added, "I have not been there long, but I have made an excellent impression; my Chief promises me a rise in wages shortly. Poor fellow, he will be heartbroken when I show him the letter from 'my poor old mother who is nearly starving in a village among the hills above Cannes'."

They sat late that night in the little underground bedroom, talking and making such plans as were possible. Jules told Flight, of the activities of Louis Lara, of the courage of Olympia, adding, "If only we could persuade Olympia that she is not invisible! She walks out in the evening and does some really shocking things, believing that no one either sees her, or, if they do, recognise her. It worries poor Louis terribly. A few weeks ago, she watched a German Colonel go into a certain house; she got into conversation with his chauffeur, and actually sat in the car with him, one arm round his neck, while she searched with her other hand in the pocket of the car for papers. She found some too—only the papers belonging to the car, but they had a certain value. Ah! that Olympia!"

"And that little man in Milan—Guido Maroni?"

Jules shook his head. "I have no idea. Perhaps fighting in the Italian Army—perhaps a prisoner, perhaps killed, who knows?"

"Do you hate the Italians as you hate the Germans?" Flight asked.

Jules frowned, for some moments he sat swinging one foot, encased in a very shabby patent-leather walking shoe with a large crack over the toe, then he said, "Listen—I don't think that I hate any nation as a nation, because I regard that as illogical and—yes, a little unworthy. I hate Fascism, I hate Nazism, and all that goes with them both. In the case of your German nation, you are faced with a most difficult problem. They are a stupid people—oh, yes! tremendously painstaking, immensely thorough, careful, industrious, but they remain—*stupid*. Because of this ability to throw themselves into any project, any experiment, any research, they become fanatical over it. They cease to have the power to think of anything else.

"Take, for example, their chemists—once they get on the track of a new discovery, they think of nothing else; they eat, drink, and sleep with their discovery. No effort is too great, no time is too long. The longer they take over it, the happier —really—they are. No one but a German would have named a drug '606', with a kind of pride that he had made 606 experiments in order to perfect it! To him '605' would have been a *little* less meritorious.

"Now comes Hitler to these people—who, like all stupid people, were *weltering* in their self-pity, their inferiority complex. He shows them his 'new discovery' and demands their co-operation in its development. What is the result? Their co-operation is immediate. Not only do they join in working at Hitler's scheme, but a number of specialists—or if you prefer to call them savages, semi-lunatics, sadists or thugs, it makes no matter —join hands in this immense task.

"One works at a series of experiments regarding warfare, another at various methods of torture, invents elaborate instruments to administer this torture; another regiments the whole nation— children, boys and girls, men and women. They invent a 'Youth Movement', they invent another movement by which young people shall find 'Joy through Strength' or 'Strength through Joy'— the 'tickets' were really immaterial. The whole great series of experiments were proceeding splendidly."

Jules laughed suddenly, poured himself out another glass of wine. Flight thought that he was looking better, younger than he had done an hour or two ago. He said as much. Jules nodded.

"I am better. I am always better when I am under the same roof with my mother. The very fact that I am breathing the same air is like a tonic to me. But let me get back to my discourse"—he winked—"I'm a clever fellow, eh? Poor old Flight, how bored you must be! but you will be unselfish and remember that I love to talk. Where was I? Oh, yes! the great German experiment! Another was the extermination of the Jews in Germany—no, I'll go further, they wished for the extermination of the whole Jewish race, and began to put that into operation in a most excellent and efficient manner.

507

So now we have the Nazi System really 'getting on its feet'—and here is the difficulty about it all. The German people being, as I say, stupid (I often wonder if that is one reason they disliked the Jews so much? For whatever the Jews may be, at least seventy-five per cent of them are intelligent), painstaking, and being very absorbent, actually became, with the exception of possibly one per cent —oh, less than that—Nazis. They have ceased to be Germans, they are Nazis. And unless the whole world is on its guard when this War is over what will be the result? No one who *thinks* can have a doubt that your German, having failed to make a lasting success of the experiment of Nazism, will begin another experiment. What it will be, who knows? Now"—again he laughed—"I am going to answer your question about hating the Germans. I don't hate the Germans, I hate the Nazis, and as all Germans have made themselves Nazis—with the exception of less than one per cent—well, you have my answer! But my ethical reply would be that I hate Nazis, but I don't hate Germans. Unfortunately the one is the synonym of the other."

"And the Italians?"

"Not an *absorbent* people, my friend! Fascism has been superimposed; a very good solid, thick layer has been spread over the Italian character. Your Italian loves his country, as long as she does not ask him to defend her. Strange what a difference there is between the reaction of various

508

nations to a declaration of war, eh? You British are pugnacious, no one is going to 'walk over my cabbage patch'; you don't really sentimentalise over your country, you sentimentalise over your enemies, once you have defeated them. I've heard Englishmen say, when I cried out in admiration of your lakes or hills, 'Yes, it's not a bad place, this England!' An Italian will rave about *Mia bella patria* for hours, but I wonder, in Italy when war was declared, how many men over military age went and *lied* about their number of years so that they might join the Army again? Not many! But in England—oh! the lies that were told by old gentlemen who dyed their moustaches and bought *toupées* and tried to pull wool over the eyes of the doctors!

"You see, deep down in their hearts, Italians are Realists, they are not fundamentally Romantics. I wonder how many of them really had complete faith that Fascism was the solution to their problems? Taxes went up, the cost of living went up—oh, yes, trains ran to time—but the war in Ethiopia was not really popular; certainly the Spanish war was not, and they didn't appreciate the arrival of hordes of Huns who swaggered and swanked and wanted to get as much as possible and spend as little as they could. Oh! they're in the War, we know, but I wonder how many of them have their hearts in it? Damned few! I wonder how many are deserting and going back to their homes? A damn lot of them! They know that they've

509

backed a loser—and they're going to cut their losses if they can."

He rose, stretched his arms high above his head and yawned. "I must go to bed. Tomorrow I must be at my desk by half past eight. Ah, we work in my department, I can tell you! My chief will hand me papers which—though they are not as important as he likes to imagine, still are—important. He will blink his silly, kind old eyes—he is really dead, but no one has told him officially that he is, so he continues to walk about—and say—'These are important. I want copies—three. I know that I can trust you, can't I?' I say, 'Monsieur, need you ask that question?' and he says, 'No, no! *mon brave*, no!' So I make four copies, and give him three of them. Poor old man, often I feel a pig! There—Good night, sleep well."

2

FLIGHT remained hidden in the house of Susanne Matot for ten days. Each day he sat for long hours reading in his little underground room, for Susanne was rehearsing all day and he only saw her in the evening. Sometimes old Henri came in to talk to him, usually to grumble that he had too much work to do, or that he was growing old and suffered from rheumatism. Only when he lowered himself into one of the hard wooden chairs very slowly, as if he feared that his old bones might break, and then sit with gnarled hands on his knees, talking of his mistress, did his rheumy eyes brighten.

"This one," he would say, "is unlike any other woman in the world. She is forever working, working, working. Yet with all her goodness and charity, remember, she is practical. Ah, she has suffered! One day perhaps she will tell you. It is a story to make one weep."

"Did you know Monsieur Matot?" Flight asked.

The old man raised his hands. "Did I know him? You ask this? All France knew him, he was the laughter-maker of Paris! An actor, but of what distinction. Decorated on the field of battle by Marshal Foch and kissed by him on both

511

cheeks—both cheeks, monsieur!"

"He was killed?"

"He was murdered, monsieur—murdered by the Germans. Tortured, so that he crept home. We heard the noise and thought that it was a dog whimpering. We brought him in, he lived for twenty-four hours. I never wish to watch such suffering again; but borne like a hero. That was what he was, this Jules Matot—a hero!"

"And you have been with Madame ever since?"

Henri scowled. "Do you imagine that I should leave her? Of course I have been with her, so have Teresa and Marie. So was Jean, but he died; he was old, that one. Old and bad-tempered."

In the evening when Susanne returned from rehearsals she would send for him, and together they would sit in the quiet room, talking and listening with their ears close to the cabinet, to the hidden radio, either to England or to one of the French underground stations.

Flight liked to watch her as she talked, to note the change of expression, to listen to the tones in her voice; he thought that it must be the most perfectly modulated voice in the world.

That evening, as they sat alone, he said impulsively, "I wish that I knew more about you."

She looked up, startled, then said, "There isn't very much to know."

He said, "Old Henri was talking about your husband this morning. He says that he was a hero."

512

Susanne laughed. "The obvious reply to that is—any man who married La Spero would have to be a hero. But no, Henri was right. He was adorable, amusing, kind, and oh, what a divine actor!"

"Were you married for a long time?" Some impulse made him long to ask questions, he had a desire to know, he was conscious of a strange sense of frustration because he knew so little of her life.

She met his eyes squarely, then said, "I was married to Jules for about ten minutes. We were married in his bedroom just before he died. I'd lived with him for three years, three of the happiest years any woman was allowed to spend. Why am I telling you this, Flight? I don't tell many people, Jules knows, of course, but Jules is like his father, a person of great understanding. Jules—I am talking of my husband now—had not seen his wife for years, at last she divorced him; I was married too, my first husband had not lived with me for years, he was killed in the war, fighting with the British. It's all a queer story, my dear. We're all inclined to think that our own story is strange, interesting, absorbing, but I think that I have some excuse for believing mine to be all those things."

He said, "It was kind of you to tell me so much of it. I'm greedy, I want to know more, all. You're an absorbing person, aren't you?"

"Not particularly. I'm a first-class actress, I'm not unattractive physically, I'm practical, and I have an average amount of courage. But in many ways I'm hard—hard and unforgiving, unrelenting, bitter."

That night when Jules came home he brought the news that they were to leave in the morning. Their clothes were ready—peasant clothes—and a market-cart would be waiting at a place appointed in the morning just at dawn. He would tell Flight all their plans as they travelled. Flight saw Susanne's face lose its colour, fancied that she caught her breath, then she smiled and said, "You'll be glad to be off again. How did your old man at the office take the news?"

Jules said, "He is inconsolable. He—poor old man!—gave me five hundred frances to spend on my 'poor old mother' when I get to her. I felt such a cad!"

As the sky was turning grey the next morning they set out. Flight had slept very little, he had studied his papers until he knew their contents by heart. Riom Corbin—he was twenty-four years of age, his parents had lived near Sangatte. His trade was that of railway porter, and he had been employed at the Gare du Nord before the war broke out.

Susanne was waiting for them in the entrance hall; Jules was to leave first and Flight to follow ten minutes later. She was very calm, she held her son to her, kissed him repeatedly, and Flight heard her say, "Darling, may God have you in His care always."

When he had gone, she begged Flight to have another cup of coffee before he left. "It may be weeks before you get a cup of good coffee again."

As he sipped it, she began to talk very softly, her hands clasped tightly. "Flight, I don't want to try to make you hold yourself responsible for Jules; I don't want you to protect him, he can look after himself, but—will you try to make him take whatever care is possible of himself? He is ill, I know it, though he does not know that I have any knowledge of it. I am very, very afraid for him. If I could keep him here, feed him well, see that he did not wear damp clothes, it might be different, but—as things are, I am afraid."

He said, "I'll do all I can, I promise. Now give me a promise in return. Don't run risks. Don't let Olympia Lara drag you into any wildcat stupidities."

Susanne laughed. "Darling Olympia! What a crazy person she is!"

Flight insisted, "Never mind that. Will you be wise? Will you be waiting for us when we come back, just as you are now? You're a very precious person, you know, not only to Jules, but to me also."

"I'll try, dear Flight! Now you must go. God bless you."

She leaned towards him and kissed him on both cheeks. He stood staring at her, feeling suddenly lonely, forlorn, and rather apprehensive as to what the future might hold for him. He was going away, he would perhaps never see her again, and the thought filled him with a sense of desperation. He

515

put his arms round her, drew her to him and kissed her as he had kissed no woman except Alicia in his life.

"My God! I hate leaving you," he said.

She pushed him away, gently, but quite firmly. "Flight, dear . . ."

He said, "Susanne, forgive me, I'm sorry!"

He watched her smile, that enchanting provocative smile, widen. "How British!" she said. "No Frenchman would ever have said—I'm sorry."

The tension had gone, he was able to smile back at her, and said, "Very well then, I'm not sorry. I'll come back one day and do it again."

"Get along with you, you'll be late. You're an impudent young devil, for all that disarmingly serious manner. There, you must go."

Their journey was long, wearisome, and often dangerous. During it, Flight came to know Jules very well, and with each day admired and loved him more. He was gay, in spite of discomfort, he laughed at danger, and his inventive ability was extraordinary.

He talked to Flight one day as they were tramping along a road which was frozen into hard ridges, where the little streams at the roadside had turned to hard lanes of ice, and the trees overhead looked bleak, bare and unfriendly. They had slept the night before in a barn, had eaten very little, and both of them were hungry.

"Do you remember me once telling you that I

516

wanted to be an actor? How strangely things happen! Here, because of the War, I virtually am an actor. Jean Morbeau, who was lately employed as a clerk in a Government office, and is going to find his poor old mother near Cannes. Could any man ask for a more difficult and complicated rôle?"

"And after the War—what then?"

He fancied that Jules looked at him quizzically before he answered. "After the War? Ah, my friend, I may not be here—neither may you for that matter! I should like to act with my mother. She might consent, once the Germans are beaten. She wanted me to be free for the War, that was why she never let me be on the stage—that, and I think because she didn't want there to be a second Jules Matot. Not that in all probability I should have ever been as good, or anything like as good, as my father."

"You didn't know him?"

"Me? No. I was born seven months after he died. He died at Matrec. My mother had taken a villa there during the War. He is buried there. I have seen his grave. He and my mother were married in his bedroom, he was dying, they both knew it. They both longed to be married, and they knew that my mother was going to have a child. It must have been a strange, rather terrible scene. There were two nuns there, the doctor, the priest and, I believe, the mayor—I forget. There was my father, with his fingers all bound up because the Germans had broken them, his mouth cut

517

and bruised, bleeding from his wounds, slowly bleeding to death.

"They were married. My mother pulled an old ring which had belonged to her mother off her finger, my father couldn't put it on—his bandages prevented it. He did manage to scrawl his name—Jules Matot. They were both very gay. My mother sent for wine. My father said, 'I am the most lucky man in France—success as an actor' —he was very conceited about his acting, and with good reason—'I have been decorated by Marshal Foch, I have married the loveliest woman of all time—Susanne Matot. Now I shall drink her health in the best of wine, produced under the direction of the greatest widow of all time— Madame Cliquot!' Very gay, you see! He drank my mother's health, and—phew!—he died. Not a sad story really. But yet sad because, through it, my mother's life has been darkened, and in her flames a bitter, fierce hatred for the Germans, the people who tortured him."

"She never married again?"

Jules shook his head. "No, so far as I know she never even took a lover. She is marvellous, my mother. How old would you imagine her to be?"

"She *looks* about thirty-five, but you're twenty-two or three. so she must be forty, possibly more."

"She's more than forty, my friend. Not really, for she is ageless. Oh, how hungry I am! Is it possible that there is a village over there? There is! Now we will drink some atrocious coffee and eat some disgusting bread and—thaw. I am completely frozen."

That night they slept in the little attic of an old woman in the village. They were very cold, for some of the tiles were missing, and the wind whistled miserably; she had done her best, but her blankets were wretchedly thin, the straw mattresses as hard as the boards would have been. They slept in all their clothes and still were unable to get any degree of warmth.

Flight lay staring into the darkness, while his thoughts turned again and again to that strange scene of which Jules had told him. He could imagine it so clearly, the actor lying with his bandaged hands, Susanne being "very gay". He could picture her laughing at her husband's jokes and compliments, knowing all the time that death was creeping nearer and nearer to snatch away the man she loved.

Susanne—La Spero—was beginning to assume tremendous proportions in his life. He was not in love with her, he knew that in all probability if he could be again with his wife, with Alicia, fully realising her beauty, her charm, La Spero would sink back—if not into the limbo of his thoughts, at least into something which was a memory, tangled, as were so many other memories, in the fantastic life he now led.

Alicia was miles away in England, living a life which had nothing in common with his present mode of living, except perhaps the danger that they shared. He had not seen her for so long, and although he could visualise her with perfect clarity, yet she appeared to him as someone, something, so far removed from him that one day he would have to regain her. He had known and loved her. Fate, destiny, events, had separated them; one day he would return to his old life—if he were not killed —and slowly, even painfully, come to know and understand and love Alicia again. The love, the understanding, the admiration still existed, it was in no way diminished, rather it was safely buried, and when the time came it would be exhumed and emerge from its temporary grave, as real, as strong and as beautiful as before.

La Spero was different. She had played little part —except for one long conversation with him in her house in Paris when she had talked of the coming war—in his former life; it seemed to him that she had never ceased to be entangled, in a greater or lesser degree, in his present way of living.

She had won his admiration, he had been conscious of her artistry, of her courage and her ability; she had welcomed him, had even confided in him—and that morning when he left he had taken her in his arms and kissed her. Lying there, in an attic without warmth or comfort, he remembered the immense wave of content that had swept over him. It was natural, he assured himself. He was lonely, deprived of women's society, except such society as had never been acceptable to him; his gratitude had overwhelmed him, carried him off his feet. It was all explicable, understandable. Yet, as he tucked his thin blanket more closely round him and tried to make himself as compact as possible to retain what small amount of warmth his body still generated, he remembered too vividly the softness of her cheeks, the acute sensation of happiness when he had kissed her lips, the faint scent that clung round her, and the tone in which she had said, half-laughing, half-rebuking, "Flight, dear . . . !"

During the months that followed, and they were incomparably the hardest Flight Masters had ever known, the memory of Susanne remained with him as something which cheered him, gave him fresh heart, and a greater capacity for endurance.

They made their way to the mountains; not until then did they join an organised band of "Moles", they were under the control—if such a word could be used concerning them—of one Bragadin, sometimes called Le Blanc for no good reason that anyone knew. His great asset was that he could pretend to be a half-wit, to be deaf and dumb, so perfectly, that even when he had been captured by some German soldiers, they had turned him loose with nothing worse than a few hearty kicks. He said, turning his quiet grey eyes on the person to whom he spoke, "I have played at being a half-wit, being deaf and dumb for so long in so many places, that there are times when I believe that I am an idiot, that I am deaf, and when it becomes difficult for me to utter a word."

He had a girl with him, a tall, splendidly made creature with wild hair and very strong white teeth. They called her Demi-Tassie, no one knew or bothered to ask why. She adored Bragadin, and would sit beside him all night when he slept, or if he were working at night, she scarcely left his side during the day.

There was Georges, who had been a prize-fighter, and who told magnificent stories of his successes—Ghent, Nat-ion-al Sporrt-eng Klubb, Lon-don, Albairt 'All, Noo Yark, and so on. He had always been splendidly victorious, yet not one of his companions had ever heard of him.

Bragadin said to him one day when they lay hidden, sleeping in snatches, smoking their cigarettes—made, as Jules said, "of everything under the sun except tobacco"—"You, Georges, with all these victories, what's your other name? Carpentier?"

Georges, who was very stupid, blinked and said, "No—why?" then when they laughed, he grinned, for he was the best-tempered fellow imaginable, and said, "No, my name is—Jak Dem-sie!"

He too had a woman with him, thin and wiry, with a tight-lipped mouth, who could handle a gun as well as any man, and who could shoot the pips off playing-cards while standing twenty paces away. Georges said that he had met her in America, and when he demanded that she would confirm this statement, she curled her thin lips and said,

"Yeah—what you say, baby!" Georges called her Maimie; she never talked, but she looked after Georges in her cold, efficient, half-sneering fashion, and never failed him.

Le Haye hated her, and she hated Le Haye. He said that he was a poet, that when the War was over he was going to electrify the world with his poems. He had longish fair hair and very beautiful hands, a mouth like a pretty girl from which could issue such a stream of filth and obscenity that even Georges would order him to keep quiet. Jules told Flight that he had never known any man capable of such cruelty. He said that one night when they had ambushed four Germans, Le Haye planned such deaths for them that Bragadin reminded him. "We're not Huns, Le Haye. We're Frenchmen, fighting for France—or perhaps you're not, eh?"

Le Haye had been furious, had rushed at Bragadin with an open knife, and Georges had knocked him down, which didn't make Le Haye feel any more kindly towards either Georges or Maimie.

They had two boys with them called Romulus and Remus. They were about seventeen and devoted to each other. Both of them had soft, gentle voices and smiled easily. They were very clean and went to endless trouble to wash not only their thin young bodies, but their clothes. They were very obedient, and invaluable because they had the trick of moving noiselessly through the woods and undergrowth.

Flight asked where they had come from, and Bragadin shook his head.

"Riom, I don't know, and I don't ask. They are good boys and their love for each other is beautiful. It is not only wishing to hold hands, it is a longing to do service, one for the other. They have, somewhere in the mountains, a secret hiding-place. They told me this, and if one of them is caught, the other is to escape there. Not to come back here, you understand, because that might implicate the rest of us. No, they are two good boys, I love them very much indeed."

Madame Kalt, the third woman of their band, liked them too. She shouted at them—but then, she shouted at everyone. She was like a sergeant-major, a big, broad-shouldered woman with huge freckled arms and a stride that carried her without apparent effort for miles. She permitted no grumbling. In her eyes it was not permissible even to say, "Whew, how cold it is today!" She would roar in response, "Cold! Ah! It is colder in the grave, my friend!" When Le Haye complained that he had a cold in his head, she stared at him as if he had insulted her, and replied, "In your head! How fortunate still to have a head on your shoulders in which to procure this cold! *Cochon!*"

Their life was desperately hard. Food was often very short; it was inadvisable to light large fires, for the Germans were everywhere. Stores were sent to them at irregular intervals, and their clothes were almost falling to pieces. Romulus and Remus had discovered a cave, and there the whole band lived during the worst of the winter; the men slept by day, while the women watched, or, in the case of Madame Kalt, sallied out alone, often bringing back information which was valuable. For all her bulk, her heavy footfall, she could when it was necessary move like a giant cat.

With the spring came longer days, and nights when there was less darkness, when danger was increased. There were days on end when the rain poured down, when men coming back from a distant expedition arrived soaked and shivering, not only with cold but with intense hunger and fatigue.

On the longer raids, men might be away for days without a sign that they were still uncaught or even alive. They talked very little of what they had done; raids were planned by Bragadin and Jules Matot, by common consent they were the "brains" of the concern. Together they would sit huddled over their maps, working by the light of a flickering candle or a smoky oil-lamp. Only when the plans were complete would Bragadin lift his long, rather sheep-like face with its strange eyes and say, "Come here, Riom and Georges," or Le Haye or even Madam Kalt or Demi-Tassie. In whispers their instructions were given, and they would slip away without a word. Only Georges ever said good-bye to anyone, and he never omitted to embrace Maimie fondly, while she stared at him, her lips twisted into a smile that was almost a sneer.

One beautifully warm evening towards the end of May, Flight had returned from an expedition which had taken him and Jules—though they moved separately—down through the Col du Montgenèvre, to Aiguilles, and by the Col de Vars to Barcelonnette. It had been a long and difficult journey; again and again they had to take to the rough country, sleep in the open, and take their chance of getting sufficient food. Jules lay on a pile of dried bracken and leaves and longed for nothing so much as sleep. Flight, weary though he was, found that sleep would not come to him. Madame Kalt came over and squatted down beside where he lay. She was frowning and twisting her hands together.

He said, "Something wrong, Madame?"

"Wrong? There can be nothing wrong! But those boys—they have been away for four days. They were only going to St. Michael, not very far from Vallores.Four days—I should have expected them to be back. It will be five days tomorrow. Pah! Riom, I grow very silly, old and silly!"

Flight said, "Oh, they'll turn up all right. They always do."

The five days became six, and still neither of the two boys returned. Bragadin looked worried. Demi-Tassie suddenly burst into tears one morning and said, "Those two little boys—it's dreadful!" Maimie shrugged her shoulders and answered, "It's all part of this game, isn't it?"

Madame Kalt stood before Bragadin, stiffly upright. "Have I your permission to go and find them, Commandant?"

He said, "What—alone?"

Still braced like a soldier, she answered, "A man called Keepleeng said, ''E travel festest 'oo travels alone.' You comprehend when I speak English? Good! I await your permission."

He nodded. "Very well. How are you going?"

"On my feet, and as what I am—an old woman!"

She went off looking like a typical, sturdy peasant.

Flight walked with her for a short distance, wished her good luck, and said, "Keep your heart up."

She returned savagely, "Tell me, when was *my* heart ever down?"

She was away for nearly a fortnight. Bragadin said again and again, "I ought never to have let her go. It was madness!"

Le Haye said, "That one is mad, anyway."

"A madness which I should like more people to suffer from."

"Ah! Meaning me, eh?"

"If you like!"

One breathless morning in August, a morning which gave promise that the day would be unbearably hot, Flight sat cleaning his revolver with a piece of oily rag. Everyone was away on some project or other except Maimie, and she rarely spoke to anyone. He started, therefore, when she laid her hand on his shoulder and said, "Riom, look! Someone is coming!"

He followed the direction in which she pointed, stared and exclaimed, "It's Madame Kalt! Alone! Oh, God!"

Maimie said, "Go and meet her, Riom. She's all in, I guess."

He ran towards her, reached her, and said, "Madame—what news?"

She stared at him with red-rimmed eyes. She looked ten years older than when he had seen her last, the lines on her face seemed to have been engraved more deeply, her hair hung, matted and wispy, she was very dirty and travel-stained.

She said, "Ah, Riom!" in a hoarse, dull voice. Then, as if she were not sure that she had spoken, she repeated, "Ah, Riom! Yes, I've come back. I've brought Remus with me, he's in that little hut half a mile back. I couldn't carry him any farther. I had to come on to ask for help." She twisted back her lips in a kind of snarling grin. "Not often I ask for help, eh?"

"You carried him? He's not—dead . . . ?"

"No, I wish that he were dead. Let me sit down for half an hour and I'll go back with you. He's asleep. He sleeps a great deal. Perhaps one day he'll die in his sleep, that will be very good."

He took her arm and helped her back to the cave. Maimie was unexpectedly gentle and helpful. She made some coffee and laced it heavily with cognac. Kalt drank her first cup in great gulps, the second she took more slowly. Then she began to speak, disjointedly, as if every sentence were wrung from her.

"They were caught, but Romulus got away. That hiding-place they had—you remember? They took Remus. They questioned him for thirty-six hours. No food. Nothing to drink. 'Where is your friend?' He refused to speak. They have an instrument for pulling out the finger-nails. They used it. He did not speak. They broke every finger with a rubber truncheon. At last he spoke. Poor boy! he is only seventeen, and he was very tired." Flight thought that he had never heard such divine pity in any voice.

"They went to find Romulus. They put Remus to bed, gave him hot milk and sent a doctor to attend to his hands. Later they let him wash. Promised him very good food, praised him for betraying his friend. He cried bitterly. He felt as St. Peter when the cock crew. Poor child! They gave him food: wine, new bread, butter, salad and meat—good fresh meat. Then they said that he might see his friend if he wished.

"They took him to where Romulus lay dead, stripped naked. On his buttock was a great wound. Remus cried, 'He's wounded!' They didn't answer except to say, 'He's dead—and that wound—well, did you enjoy your excellent dinner?' They laughed, laughed very loudly. After that he doesn't remember. Perhaps he escaped. It may be they turned him out because he was mad. I think that

529

these primitive people—and they are primitive people—are afraid of lunatics. Who knows? I found him wandering near their old hiding-place. They had once confided its situation to me. I have brought him home—to die, I hope."

She rose stiffly, like an old person. "Let us go for him. Tell the others, will you? I don't want to have to repeat that story again."

They found the boy lying with his head on his arms in the little hut. Madame Kalt knelt down beside him and said, "We have come to take you home to your friends. Come, Remus—you're safe!"

Flight said, "That's all right, Remus. You're all right."

He licked his lips, opened and shut his eyes, then whispered, "Ah, Riom—it's you! Do—you—know—what I did?"

"I know that you're a grand, plucky fellow and we're all waiting to welcome you. That's all we know—or need to know."

The boy sat upright, holding out his hands with their dirty bandages. "But you *must* know, I must tell you! I am something so terrible . . ."

"You shall tell us—one day. Now Madame is tired, she wants to get some rest. Let's help you up."

They half-carried him to the cave, and in the farther corner laid him down and watched beside him until he slept. Slept uneasily, whimpering like a frightened dog from time to time.

530

The others returned. To them the story was whispered, while all the time Madame Kalt sat beside Remus, scarcely moving her eyes from his face. Georges, the big prize-fighter, went out and stood, his arm flung up over his eyes, sobbing, completely abandoned to his grief. Maimie stood beside him and they could hear the murmur of her voice, gentle and kind.

For three days they nursed him; there were times when he seemed to have forgotten, when he smiled and said, "It is pleasant to be back again." Other moments when he beat them off, furiously crying, "Don't come near me! I'm unclean—filthy —abominable! You don't know—you don't know!"

On the morning of the third day he died. Madame Kalt rose to her feet as if she had flung a great weight from her broad shoulders.

They buried him, much as Flight remembered they had buried Father Maurice in the barn, only this time there was less haste, and Demi-Tassie and Maimie both sobbed bitterly. When it was over, Madame Kalt returned to the cave and went to her own particular corner. Flight watched her going through her small stock of clothes; wandering over to her, he said, "You look as if you were packing, Madame."

She nodded. "Yes, I'm going, Riom."

"But where? Why?"

"I'm going," she answered, "to where Remus came from, and I'm going there because I have business to do. Immediate business."

"Alone?"

For an instant he saw the flicker of a smile touch her lips. "Don't you remember what I said to Bragadin when I went before? I said—in English—in the words of the English Keepleeng, "'E travels fast-est 'oo travels al-one'."

Later she talked long and earnestly to Bragadin. Flight watched his disturbed expression, saw that once he laid his hand on her arm as if he begged her to stay. She shook her head and smiled.

"Have you any money?" Flight heard him ask.

"Sufficient. I don't suppose that I shall need a great deal."

"It will be dangerous for you to carry arms—a civilian."

"Who said that I was going to carry arms? These are all the arms I need," and she held out her great muscular arms covered with freckles. "They are good weapons," she added, and opened and closed the fingers of her two hands and laughed.

That evening she set out. She shook hands with them all in her firm, masculine fashion. Flight thought that she looked younger, happier. Bragadin asked if they would hear from her, and if so when they might hope for news.

She grinned back at him. "Don't be silly, my Commandant! I've been very obedient, I've tried to be a good soldier; now—I'm a free-lance. How long I shall be free . . .?" She shrugged her shoulders. "Well, *au revoir*, since you like to be a crowd of sentimentalists!"

Turning away, she went marching into the dim obscurity of the forest. They stood watching her in silence. When at last she disappeared—she had never looked back—Bragadin said, "That's a grand woman! D'you know, even hating the Huns as I do, I have it in my heart to be almost sorry for those who run across Madame Kalt!" He added inconsequently, "That's not her real name, of course."

Jules asked, "What is her real name?"

"Her real name—since none of us are likely to meet her again, and if we do, then it is understood that we make no reference to it—is Leone Leah Brachmann. She was born a Jewess, her husband was a Jewish banker of immense wealth, long before Hitler and his thugs were heard of."

For many days they watched the woods for sight or sound of her, but she did not return, and slowly she became only a memory to them.

Life went on. People came and went. Several times Italian partisans managed to get over the frontier, and Flight, Bragadin and Jules crossed over to the mountains near Aosta and spent two months there. The whole business was becoming better organised; means were found to provide them with food for the winter, clothes were smuggled to them, boots, and munitions. It seemed to Flight that the danger increased, that every day they heard news of German patrols searching the woods, and finally Bragadin held a council-of-war and declared that the time had come for them to move on.

"There are too many of us in one concentrated place," he grumbled. "If we were scattered about in the hills we could still communicate, but in a mob like this it's too dangerous. We ought to be in regular communication with the Italians, not just trusting to visits at long and irregular intervals."

The early days of November found their cave empty, they were scattered. Flight was sent south; Jules to a position near Cannes; Le Haye, Georges and Maimie despatched to various other points. Demi-Tassie cried so bitterly that Bragadin consented to take her with him.

"It's not been too bad," Bragadin said on their last evening. "We've done a tremendous lot of work; apart from everything else, we've scared the Germans in this forest so that they can scarcely bear to walk on the very fringes of it, because they get heart disease. Well, good luck, everyone! One day—who knows?"

3

FLIGHT and Jules made part of their journey together; during that time Jules gave Flight his instructions.

"It is quite possible that we may meet. There is an amusing job before us. You will, on arriving at Juan-les-Pins, get in touch with a Monsieur Flurrey. He lives in a villa called 'Les Chênes', he expects you. I am going to move in higher society!"—he laughed—"I am to go to the house of an Englishwoman, Lady Frances Melfort. Here is sufficient money to carry you on, and Flurrey will give you more. Now we'd better move on separately."

Flight said, "Look here, Jules! I wish that you'd take care of that cough. I don't like it."

Jules said, "You silly idiot! Do you imagine that I like it? It's nothing—nothing that this bright winter sunshine won't cure. *Au revoir*, I shall see you later, my friend."

He turned off down a side road, and Flight stood for a few moments watching him. He looked too slim, and although he held his head high, you felt instinctively that it weighed heavily.

Flight continued down the other road. After two days he arrived in Juan-les-Pins. The place looked deserted and neglected, the people stood about in small groups; groups which dispersed every time a German soldier appeared swaggering down the street. The shops were empty, the people looked pinched and hungry. Flight entered a small café and ordered a cup of coffee, quite the worst he had ever tasted. He felt lonely, homesick for the Cave, for his companions; he knew that his mind was turning to things that were better forgotten—to Romulus and Remus, to Madame Kalt. He was indulging in speculations concerning her, her whereabouts, her—fate?

The woman who served him was immensely stout; she moved softly, like a big cat; her eyes were very bright, her moustache was heavy and grey. There were huge bags beneath her eyes; they were stained a dark unhealthy brown. Flight thought, "She's big, but she's unhealthy. I think she suffers a great deal."

He rose and went to the counter, leaning his arms on its stained surface, for the whole place was dirty and neglected.

He said, "Madame, could you direct me to a villa called 'Les Chênes'?"

Her heavy eyes flickered, but her voice was cold, even unfriendly, when she answered, "Why do you wish to go there?"

He stared at her. His eyes wide in assumed innocence. "Why, Madame? Because monsieur is a friend of my uncle in Rouen and has promised to try to find some work for me."

"What is the name of this friend of your uncle in Rouen?"

"His name, Madame, is Monsieur Flurrey."

"You know him, this Monsieur Flurrey?"

"No, Madame, my Uncle Henri told me to go to him after he received a kind letter from Monsieur Flurrey. I have never seen him."

She leaned forward over the counter; her huge breasts were flattened against it into a fantastic shape, she spoke in a hoarse whisper, "This man is very clever, but I warn you, play no tricks on him. *Whoever* you are, play no tricks. I have warned you—I, Mère Toutine."

Still wide-eyed he said, "No, Madame, naturally."

"You had better go to the back door. You are scarcely presentable to go to the front one. Monsieur is very elegant. Leave here, turn left, the first on the right, and 'Les Chênes' is the third villa on the left. Tell him that you have been here and that you found the coffee disgusting. Now, go!"

He walked out into the strangely deserted street, turned smartly to the left as if he had no doubt as to which direction to take, and in five minutes arrived at a hideous, but obviously luxurious villa. The paint had grown shabby, the garden was untended, but evidently it had been a place of importance at one time. Deplorable taste, but possessing great comfort and costing a tremendous amount of money. He made his way to the back entrance and asked for Monsieur Flurrey. The elderly man-servant eyed him coldly, and asked why he wished to see his master? Flight produced a dirty slip of paper on which he had scrawled, *Sent by Henri Corbin, of Rouen, the friend of Bragadin the deaf and dumb man.* Taking the paper between his finger and thumb, the man nodded coldly and disappeared. He returned in a few moments and motioned to Flight to follow him.

The interior was as ugly as the exterior. The carpets were thick and rather dusty, everything was over-elaborate, the door-handles were formless convolutions of shining metal, the walls were hung with bad paintings in very bright gold frames. Between them were mounted antlers of beasts which ranged from immense stags to minute mountain deer.

A door was flung open. Inside was a second door of heavy green baize; that being opened, Flight found himself in a room which held one of the largest and least pleasing collection of carved furniture he had ever seen. Even the ceiling was carved with heavy swags of fruit and flowers, and over everything hung a faintly musty smell of dust and stale air.

A man with a purple face and a completely bald head was seated in a large armchair; the chair was covered with carved bosses, to such an extent that Flight wondered if to sit in it was not acute torture? The owner of the purple face wore a large red and yellow silk handkerchief as a cravat, and a dressing-gown of brilliant scarlet satin.

He spoke in a high, petulant voice. "Ah! so you're Henri Corbin's nephew, eh? You can go, Philippe. Shut the door quietly. You hear me, *quietly*. And what's your name, young man?"

"Riom, monsieur."

"A silly kind of name. How is your uncle? I never liked him a great deal—inefficient. I dislike inefficient people. I am most efficient."

Flight thought that he must be listening to a madman, for Flurrey continued telling long and pointless stories of his youth, when he and "Henri Corbin" had been at school together; going into long explanations as to why he, Ernest Desfontaines Flurrey, had made such a success of life, while Henri Corbin had remained—"What is he, this uncle of yours?"

"A tailor, monsieur, a working tailor."

The two puffy hands were raised. "Ah, a tailor, a working tailor, and here am I surrounded by every luxury, the friend—if not of princes—at least of the Great Ones of the world—or if not of the world, at least of the South of France! And how is my friend Bragadin?"

"He was well when I saw him last."

"When was that? Four months ago! And his deafness?"

"It appears to be incurable, monsieur."

"And the impediment in his speech?"

"So bad, monsieur, that often it is difficult to believe that he is not completely dumb."

"Ah! a disaster."

Slowly he began to realise that he was being tested; to see that those heavy eyes were, in reality, remarkably bright; the wide, thick-lipped mouth very firm, the chin obstinate. Flurrey rose and deliberately kicked a stool out of his way. He rubbed his hands, almost gleefully. "You must change those clothes . . . let me see your papers? Ah!"—as he turned them over rapidly—"a railway porter, umph? But a clever boy all the same, one who has educated himself. You are passionate concerning wireless, you understand? Wireless!"

"Monsieur, except that I know how to find the various stations and one or two very minor particulars, I know nothing about it."

"No?" Flurrey was completely undisturbed. "I shall give you some excellent little books on wireless. You will study them, you will make diagrams, on the tables of cafés. on the backs of envelopes. You are doing your best to revolutionise the wireless. Do you know anyone in Juan?"

"I have only just arrived. I spoke to one lady who sent you her greetings—La Mère Toutine."

"Ah! a nice woman. She is growing old and I dislike her moustache. It is so heavy. A mere trace, you understand, gives a certain fascination, but who wishes to kiss a Grenadier? Or if they do," he laughed, "they have no right to. You might do worse than stay with Mère Toutine. Her shop is filthy, but upstairs is clean enough." Again he laughed. "I can promise you that. Do you smoke?

540

Ah, you do! I advise you to break yourself of the habit, because they will not allow you to smoke—or smoke much—in the prison camp."

Flight sprang from his chair and stared at the fantastic figure which stood before him. He knew that his forehead was wet, but with a great effort he contrived to speak calmly.

"Monsieur, if this is a joke, then it is a poor one. I am not in the least afraid. My papers are all in order, I have friends who can speak for me. I shall now take my leave of you. Let me bid you a very good afternoon."

He moved towards the door, when Flurrey held up his hand.

"Stop, stop!" he said. "My good Riom, what is the matter with you! You misunderstood me. Sit down; compose yourself . . ."

"I am perfectly composed, and I have no wish to sit down."

"Then," Flurrey snapped suddenly, "stand up! But listen to me. Here, I am going to give you money, for which you will give me a receipt. I am going to give you several books on wireless, which you will study. There they are. Now, I am going back to my chair—a beautiful piece of work, isn't it?—and you are going to take a glass—possibly two glasses of wine with me."

Flight said, "I'll do so when I've seen you drink yours."

Flurrey nipped back to his chair and settled his feet again on the stool. He smiled. "Tut, tut! what

541

a suspicious young man. Ring the bell for Philippe, will you?"

He gave the order for wine, he chatted lightly about the state of France, of the civility of the Germans, of their respect for him, and finally, when the glasses were set before them and the door closed, he said, "Pour out the wine. Oh, yes! watch me drink mine first by all means. It is a beautiful wine—beautiful. Now relax, and listen with attention, please. To prove to you that I know all about you, that I am to be trusted, I will tell you that your friend Morbeau has gone to Cannes; his real name is Jules Matot, he is the son of La Spero. I know Maurice Gold, I know Bragadin and Georges—I even know the farmhouse of Madame Peloux. Now—listen . . ."

Slowly he gave Flight his instructions. He was to go to Mère Toutine; a tailor would come there to make the necessary alterations to a suit which Flurrey would send over. Flight was to go out every morning, always with his precious books about wireless. In cafés he was to study them, to make sketches; sometimes he might leave the sketches behind him, crumpled up and thrown down. "You are full of ideas," Flurrey told him, "they come rushing through your mind like water over a mill-wheel."

Near Juan-les-Pins the Germans had an experimental station—a wireless experimental station—and they were anxious to get prisoners who were wireless experts. The others, they could go to camps in Germany, but here, somewhere near the Col d'Allos, they had this camp.

"One evening," Flurrey continued, "when Colonel Wolheim did me the honour of dining here—for I maintain that I am 'international', like my friend Maurice Gold—he drank rather more of my excellent wine than was, to a narrow-minded person, perhaps—strictly good for him. He confided to me that they are on the brink of a great discovery. A discovery which, he asserts, will revolutionise all the aerial affairs of the world." He waved his hands. "A ray, a beam, a shaft, some kind of harnessed energy. I know nothing of these things and I gather that Wolheim knows little more than I do. Their great expert is a certain General Ulruch. He was sent to investigate some experiments in Germany, and Wolheim was sent here from Lyons. He wants to make good, to gain promotion, to make a success of his experimental station. He wants technicians and he doesn't much care how he gets them. We—on the other hand —wish to find out how much truth there is in this discovery. We want sketches and diagrams. Very well. Do have some more wine, it *is* good, isn't it?

"After a time, you will be noticed. I am afraid that your papers will not be *quite* in order, which is to be regretted, but cannot be helped. You will be taken inside. So, I may tell you you will meet that young man, Jules Matot, because you are both very clever young men, and necessary. Is that all clear?"

Flight shrugged his shoulders. "Clear enough, but once we're in?"

"Then it will be the duty of someone, or of yourselves, to—get out—once the work is done."

"It's asking a good deal to send Jules and me into a prison camp."

Flurrey said easily and even soothingly, "From the reports which reach me, it is not at all a bad camp; small, you understand, and not too rigid with regard to discipline."

"And we are to get hold of the plans and designs and take them—where?"

"Oh! that will be arranged, believe me. I think that you will find it all much easier than you imagine, my young friend. Ah! your glass is empty again, fill it, please. I cannot tell you more, except that Colonel Wolheim replaced General Ulruch—I don't think that he has ever actually seen Ulruch. If he did, it was only a brief interview."

Flight emptied his glass. "Except that I know practically nothing about wireless, and I doubt whether Jules knows much more, the idea seems excellent."

"If, in a week, you—both of you—cannot learn sufficient from those excellent text-books"—he shrugged his shoulders—"you deserve to be shot."

"I imagine that we are both likely to get what we deserve then."

If ever Flight Masters hated anything, it was the sight of those two text-books. For hours he pored over them; he managed to get drawing-pins and string, and on the top of the table in his little bedroom at Mère Toutine's he worked out diagrams and drew designs. Slowly he began to see light, began to get some idea as to how, and why, a radio set produced sounds; of how various stations affected various other stations. One day Mère Toutine staggered in with an old oven. She said, "That Flurrey is a kind-hearted man. He wishes me to bring this, and if we can light it, you will have additional heat in this room."

The thing was rusty in the extreme and Flight stared at it in contempt.

He said, "Good God! that thing's no use," and swung open the oven door to prove that the old thing was as dirty inside as outside. Inside he found a radio set. From that day he made actual progress. He took the thing to pieces, put it together again, experimented with it and slowly became absorbed in its workings and mysteries.

Three weeks after his visit to Flurrey, he ventured out to a café, ordered coffee, and sat there making sketches on the top of the marble table. He gained confidence and went farther afield. He chose not only the modest places, but ventured into the larger cafés frequented by German officers. Once on raising his eyes, staring round him, frowning, as if he strove to solve some difficult problem, he found that two German officers were watching him intently. He returned to his work, and when he left—as if in a fit of exasperation—he crumpled the paper on which he had been working, and flung it on the floor. He went out and returned a few moments later for the glove which he had purposely left behind. The proprietress gave him his glove; he thanked her, and as he went out again, he noticed that the little crumpled ball of paper had gone.

Two days later he saw Flurrey, seated in a corner of a café. They made no sign that they knew each other and Flight again began his endless diagrams and designs. Later, Flurrey was joined by a man in plain clothes, who, Flight felt certain, was no Frenchman, but a German.

Later, Flurrey came over to him and said, "You will forgive me, I am sure, but my friend and I could not help being interested in the intent manner in which you are working on your—designs—are they?"

Flight looked up and said with what he hoped sounded like youthful eagerness, "I'm something of a designer, sir. Not by trade, you understand, but for the love of it. I'm trying to work out a problem."

"With regard to . . . ?"

"Radio, monsieur."

"Ah, radio! How interesting. Forgive my curiosity."

"But of course, monsieur."

Two days later, Mère Toutine came into his

room to tell him that there were three German soldiers and a lieutenant waiting below, and that they wished to speak to him. Flight's heart beat heavily, for despite all Flurrey's assurances, the prospect of a German prison camp did not make much appeal to him. At that moment he longed for nothing so much as to escape, to make his way out through the back door, swarm up the wall and—run. He walked downstairs, conscious of a strange shaking in his stomach. The officer came towards him, asking his name; Flight gave it. "Your papers?" He handed them over. The officer —he was an elderly man with a heavy, stupid face—turned them over, reading their contents aloud. "Corbin—er—Riom? Umph! railway porter—ah! railway porter at the Gare du Nord, eh? Umph, umph! Hello! no, no? this won't do— this won't do!'

Flight said, "My papers are all in order, surely, sir?"

The German continued to grunt over the sheets which he held. At last he said, "Whether they are in order or not, is not for you to decide, eh? You can come with us!"

"But where? Where are you going to take me?"

"You ask too many questions. It is for a soldier to obey."

"But, excuse me, I am a civilian."

"French civilians are only alive thanks to the tolerance of the German Army. Understand that. Bring him along."

Flight stared round him wildly, he hoped that his acting was sufficiently good to deceive them. He cried, "But my drawings, my books, my designs. I cannot leave them, they are my whole life's work!'

He thought, "I've overdone it there. 'Life's work' wasn't good!"

The German, however, nodded to one of the soldiers. "Go with him, and let him collect his designs. See what else he has hidden up there."

He went back to his room, the soldier marching behind him. He gathered together his note-books and papers, his textbooks, feverishly, and then pointed to the old oven. "Can I take that—my wireless set? No! it is not connected, I am only making experiments with it. Can I take it with me?"

A long argument followed. Stolid, on the side of his soldier; impassioned on that of Flight. Finally the officer was appealed to; he came rushing up the stairs, examined the wireless set, demanded to know where the "prise" was, which connected it? Flight disclaimed the existence of one, and finally it was taken with them.

They drove away. The morning was bright but cold, the sun shone with a chilly brilliance; the colours of the countryside through which they passed were beautiful, the air clean and fresh; they were heading for the mountains. Almost feverishly Flight tried to memorise the road, whilst again and again, the thought came to him that quite possibly he might never travel this road again. They might discover that he was a fraud, an "ignoramus" who had learned a few elementary facts, who could reel off a list of technical terms and draw a simple diagram which he barely comprehended. Despite the chill of the morning, he wiped his forehead.

Once, the officer, touching the old oven which held the radio set, with the toe of his boot, asked, "What stations can you get with that?"

"None, it isn't connected with anything. It is only for mechanical experiments."

"You don't expect us to believe that, eh?" Then after a pause:

"Have you ever listened to the lies the English tell?"

"I can't, I assure you . . ."

"Only the German radio tells the truth. Remember that!"

Wilder country, where great rocks shot up out of the earth, where snow lay in sheltered places, hard and crusted; the truck shook and jolted horribly. Flight knew that his depression was growing with every mile they covered. They swung so suddenly to the left that they were all flung in a sprawling heap; the officer cursed the driver. They entered a thickly-wooded region, winding in and out until finally they came to a clearing where, behind a barbed wire fence, Flight saw wooden huts. The truck came to a standstill. The soldiers scrambled out, and the officer followed them. Flight came last, and between two soldiers, was marched along a narrow, sanded path to the Kommandant's office.

As the door opened, he felt the delicious rush of hot air as it touched his cheeks; they tingled. His fingers were frozen with cold; he blew on them in an attempt to warm them. The soldiers watched him scornfully. One muttered something to the other that Flight could not catch.

Then he was pushed forward into the office. The Colonel seated behind the desk, he took to be Wolheim. He was handsome, heavy, and although still fairly young, was already running to flesh. His face was anxious and not unkindly.

He said, "Your papers are not in order. It would be possible to shoot you for this. I suspect that you are a spy. Are you a spy?"

"No, sir. I am a railway porter."

"You don't look like one. Why did you conceal a radio set?"

"I did not conceal it, sir. It was given to me and I used it for working out my diagrams. You can see my diagrams, they are here."

He laid them on the desk, and from the moment Wolheim looked at them Flight realised that here was a man whose ignorance was even more profound than his own. The air of attentive interest was overdone, and the pencil which followed lines on the paper, did so without purpose or any sense of direction. The Colonel grunted once or twice, then said, "Ah! interesting. Have you ever heard of the name of Ernst Jungbrech?"

Drawing a bow at a venture, Flight said, hesitating a little, "Sir, you mean the man—the man who has the theory of the new band?"

"New band? New—all kinds of things . . ."

"Yes, yes!"—eagerly—"Frequency and intensification. The—the idea that will revolutionise radio."

"Well," Wolheim leaned back in his chair. "Unfortunately this clever young man is dead. He was only thirty-two, and died of scarlet fever. He left drawings, and so forth. We have a certain amount of men, technicians—working on them. We need more. Do you think that you could understand them?"

"I could try, sir, it would be an honour." He hoped that he was making both his eyes and his voice sparkle. "I should, if you permit, like to work with someone, so that we might check each other's ideas. It is considered better to work in this way."

"That might be arranged. I have a young man here. What is his name?"

The lieutenant supplied it. "Morbeau, Jean, Colonel."

Flight, still eager as a young girl at her first dance, cried, "Oh, it is not possible. Jean Morbeau! a clerk in Paris? Oh! he is so clever, this one. He is far more intelligent than I am. Imagine that I find him here! He is wonderful at this experimental work. I remember once . . ."

The Colonel listened, smiling tolerantly. He was

amused at the excitement of this young man. These fellows and their damned radio. To hell with it all! He was sick of it—wires and valves, switches and everything.

He said, "What you remember is of no great importance. But if you know this fellow, I see no reason why you should not work together . . ."

"We had a little experimental circle in Paris. Oh, quite modest, but Morbeau was always the leader, and we—his humble followers. Once when . . ."

"My good young man, spare me these eulogies! There, take him away, and set him to work with Morbeau. Mind! don't imagine that because there are two of you working together you can try any monkey tricks. I shall know how to deal with any nonsense—very quickly and *completely*. You understand?"

"Yes, oh, yes! To work with Jean Morbeau."

As he was marched out he heard the two men laugh. The lieutenant said in German, "I think he's half-witted."

The other replied, "No, more likely a homo-sexual in love with this Morbeau. I never saw such excitement."

There were twenty camp beds in the hut into which Flight was taken. The place was certainly not excessively clean; on the other hand, it was not offensively dirty. He was given prison clothes, which smelt unpleasant, and felt scrubby and harsh; the underpants and vest were like thick boards, and the boots at least two sizes too large.

He was given a tin plate, a small bowl and a spoon. To everything he said, 'Oh, thank you, thank you!"

The guards grinned and mimicked him. They came to call him, "Thank You".

A long trestle table ran the length of the room, and soon after Flight's arrival the other prisoners marched in. Jules was the tenth. He looked thin and his eyes seemed too big and too bright; he did not smile when he saw Flight, merely nodded his head.

Flight said to one of the guards, "May I sit next to Morbeau?"

"If you like!"

"Oh, thank you, thank you very much."

The guard roared with laughter and said, "Get along with you. 'Miss Thank You'!"

He sat down next to Jules and began to talk to him in a high whisper.

For a second he watched Jules' eyes widen; then they stared back at him and he said, "Hello! you, Corbin."

Later, after a meal which consisted of a bowl of very thin soup, with a small stringy piece of meat floating in it like a pathetic island, and a piece of dark-coloured bread, Flight contrived to exchange a few words with Jules.

Jules said, "I'm always taciturn, do you see? Sulky, unresponsive. That's my rôle. Yours—and it's very good—is the eager student."

Flight said, "Oh, I am so happy to be with you."

Jules grimaced at him. "How hateful it sounds to hear you talking in that damned silly voice. But it's good, stick to it."

Their life in the camp was not desperately hard. The rooms were insufficiently heated, the food was poor, and the beds terribly hard, with thin, well-worn blankets. Most of the men slept in their clothes, and in the morning the atmosphere of the place was suffocating.

In spite of Flight's nervous, affected manner, the others liked him; they detested Jules, who scarcely spoke, but pored for hours over diagrams and designs. Flight, contriving to speak to him in whispers as they worked, asked, "*How much do you really understand? My own feeling is that if we connected this wire—here?*"

Jules answered, "*I understand more than I could have believed possible. We'll try that connection. I'll tell you one thing, that once we're out of here, I never want to see or hear a radio again!*"

So they talked always, interspersing their own conversation with details concerning their work. They were given copies of the designs of the dead Jungbrech; Flight gazed at them in admiration. Jules grunted and growled.

"He was less clever than I had believed him to be," he told the lieutenant.

"Then improve on his ideas, Morbeau!"

"I have already done so, Herr Lieutenant."

Their difficulty was not to make copies of the designs, but to find some place in which to hide

554

them once they were completed. During the copying, it was sufficiently easy to lock them in the drawer of their work-table, and to hand the key, with considerable ostentation, to the lieutenant in his office.

Indenting for metal for making some special part of the new model, Jules had contrived to cut a key which opened the drawer. They had nowhere to hide anything. They decided that their best plan was to keep their copies locked in the drawer, and trust to luck to be able to extract them if the opportunity for escape offered.

They were both satisfied. They had all the information that Jungbrech had supplied; much of it, it was evident even to their unscientific minds, was very valuable. They began to debate the chances of an escape.

The early days of 1943 were hard, travelling would be difficult, there was a good deal of snow in the mountains, tracks would be plain, easily followed by pursuers. Jules, shivering in his overlarge greatcoat, counselled waiting until the frost broke. Flight was impatient.

From time to time their guards gave them news. The British had been totally defeated in North Africa, Alexandria was in German hands, Rommel was victorious everywhere. Wavell was dead and Auchinleck was dying of his wounds.

A new tank had superseded the Mark IV, called "General Chairmain". It had been smashed to pieces by the German guns, the Allies had run short of steel, the tank had been found to be made of three-ply wood!

Jules listened and said afterwards to Flight, "Things are evidently going better for the Allies."

Later, when Jules was in bed with a dreadful cold which he seemed unable to shake off, Flight felt such depression as he had never known. He sat on the edge of his bed, his elbows on his knees, staring at nothing, allowing his mind to race back to England. He could see the dining-room at Little Manor so clearly; he thought that he saw his mother enter, with Eleanor, to put the last touches to the decorated table at Christmas. He could see his mother turn to Eleanor and smile, almost hear their voices—and because he was underfed and ill-nourished he imagined that the smell of cooking came up from the kitchens as the green baize door swung open. The usual Christmas dinner, which never varied. Very small helpings of clear, rich soup. The turkey—immense, brown and dignified, even when served on a huge dish—the sausages—did they still get those fat, stocky sausages, burst and crisp, in England? Chestnut stuffing! Eleanor would have come over to make that, it was her speciality. His father saying, "Now—lights out. The great moment is at hand!" Sudden darkness, and the pudding borne in, darting pale blue flames. The lights on again. The search for the "souvenirs" which were always hidden in the deep, dark richness of the pudding—a silver button, a thimble, a horseshoe, and a three-penny piece. Mince pies. His mother's voice. "Oh, you must have a mince pie! You know every one you eat before New Year's Day means a happy month!" She had said that every year since he could remember.

Toasts. His father's firm voice. "My dear wife and my family—wherever they may be. God bless them all!"

Alicia—was she sitting there? He could visualise only his mother and father and Eleanor completely. Alicia must be there. He experienced a sense of panic. Why could he not visualise Alicia? Again and again he tried to go round the table, slowly, painstakingly naming everyone. The sense of panic almost overwhelmed him.

My father—on his right, Ann. Yes, Ann! she might be Duchess of Rusmere by this time? I can see Ann, very "alive", laughing a great deal, being cheeky, even if she is Lady Claverley. George Charlton next to her, not laughing a great deal, but his eyes twinkling and his lips softening. Then—my mother. Very, very pretty still, smiling and showing her teeth a little when she laughed. Next—his own Alicia?

He put his hand to his forehead and found it damp. The effort he made to visualise her was almost too much for him, he felt weak, drained.

"Alicia, Alicia, let me see you! You're there? You're turning to speak to my father—my lovely Alicia! God, why can't I see you? . . ."

He flung himself down on his bed, his hands clenched, the sweat running down his cheeks. He felt suddenly lost, abandoned, without any definite place in the whole world. He was lost—he would never be heard of again—years would pass, and he would be here, or in some other prison camp, eating his heart out. Sooner or later Wolheim would be replaced by someone who actually did know more than the merest rudiments of radio. He and Jules would be discovered. Fakes—cheats—impostors! Then it would mean a move to some prison camp where punishment would be waiting. That old play-acting idiot down in Juan, he had talked airily enough about getting away, he didn't know—the crass fool!—what an escape in the mountains in winter was like.

Jules said, "Are you awake?"

"Yes, do you want anything?"

"No, only wondering what you were thinking about?"

Flight laughed unhappily. "What most of us are thinking, I suppose. Indulging in a flood of sentiment and despair, and—longing!"—he laughed again—"I have gone through the whole Christmas menu at my father's house."

Jules said, "And I! There would be a Christmas tree! My mother always has one. She decorates it herself, takes so much pains, and it is beautiful when she has finished . . ."

Eagerly Flight said, "And my mother too. Go on!"

558

"Presents for everyone. She loves giving presents."

"Yes, yes, and my mother also!" They were like children, each eager to tell their own story. "The table too, that is decorated, holly and mistletoe, crackers—bon-bons—everything shining and gleaming . . ."

"Wine standing in wine-coolers; wine bottles with their necks covered in gold paper—very aristocratic bottles! My mother looking magnificent, wearing her pearls, and with her hair beautifully done—perhaps just a *leetle* too much make-up, because she is rather tired? No, it is not too much, it is perfect! Who will be there? Louis Lara and Olympia—she certainly has too much make-up—and Maurice Gold. I believe that he wants to marry my mother. I have thought so for a long time! I wonder if Emmanuel Gollantz might be there? or Guido? Or Iva Alfano and her husband? However, that does not matter! They are all very gay, they drink toasts and laugh, and eat beautiful food, and drink exquisite wine. 'Allow me, Monsieur, to give you some more *pâté*?' 'Olympia—this Strasburg pie is excellent!' 'Susanne my dear, where did you get this duck—it is perfect! . . .' 'Being a Jew, I shall take some more sausage!' That is Maurice Gold, of course! 'Louis, dear, my husband's favourite wine—Cliquot!' The doors are closed, the windows shuttered, my mother turns on the radio, and says, 'Listen!' and faintly it comes—from London, perhaps:

"Adeste Fideles,
"Læti triumphantes,
"Venite, venite in Bethlehem . . ."
He lifted his hands and laid them over his eyes.
Flight heard him catch his breath in a sob, and
leaning nearer heard him say, "Oh God, and
perhaps by this time—it isn't like that at all?"

Flight lay, long after the lights were put out, his
eyes closed, trying vainly to "see" Alicia. Instead
he saw Susanne Matot, her head thrown back a
little, her eyes shining with the tears she would not
let fall, listening to a Christmas hymn.

4

THE wireless operator passed the table where Flight and Jules sat working at their endless diagrams. He liked Flight, who had made "an improvement" on his receiving set. The operator knew nothing about the actual working of the radio, he knew only enough to take down signals in Morse. Because he liked Flight he had sworn by the "improvement"—which had, in fact, nothing to do with the mechanism at all—being merely a small brass screw with a piece of fine wire attached to another screw, having no bearing on the radio at all—and had praised it to Wolheim as being "masterly".

He flicked a tiny ball of crumpled paper on to the table before Flight as he passed. Without moving, Flight allowed it to lie there for a few moments, then unrolled it and read the message, *General Ulruch arriving at any moment*. He pushed it, under the cover of a tin box, to Jules, who in his turn read it.

Jules said, "God, 'at any moment'! Pass me that rubber, bone-head. Looks as if our game is up. Not that one, the other, fool!"

Flight said in a whining voice, "Don't be so unkind! No chance of getting away. It stopped

561

snowing this morning at six, nothing has fallen since."

"They'd track us for miles. We might try to bluff it out."

"Ulruch's an expert. Oh, don't keep on *asking* for things."

"We'll try it. If it's no go—well, we've had a run for our money."

The door opened. Wolheim looked in, grunted, and went out again. They heard the sound of voices, the guards said, "Get on with your work, now! 'Miss Thank You', be sure to speak nicely to the General."

Flight said, "The General. Oh, I will, I will, really!"

"The General won't want to speak to you," Jules growled.

The guard, a big, blond North German, said, "Well, no one would want to speak to *you*, Gloomy Face!"

Jules scowled and bent over his work. He whispered, "If—it's the worst, I'll manage to get in here. I've a box of matches at the back of the drawer, I'll set fire to the lot and then hand in the key. If I can't—you must. Light a match and spill the others in the drawer."

"Right."

They bent over their work, intent, watchful; their ears straining for every new sound. The door opened. Neither of them moved, though Flight knew that his heart beat so heavily that it made his pencil move in jerks across the paper.

"Morbeau and Corbin, immediately! Bring those designs!"

Jules sprang to his feet. "Ours, or the old ones of Jungbrech's?"

"Both, better bring both. Come on, the General is waiting."

Jules gathered together the drawings, and with steady hands placed them in the folders; mechanically Flight made an effort to keep in his assumed character. He whispered, "Oh, dear—don't crumple them! Oh, fancy, the General."

Jules glowered sullenly, "Oh, shut up, 'Miss Thank You'."

They went out, across the yard where the snow was trampled and already turning to grimy slush. Flight thought, "If the luck turns against us, this may be the last time I shall walk over here." He did not feel particularly afraid, rather strangely excited, even elated. The air was fresh and sweet in his nostrils, the grey clouds were clearing, a little patch of blue sky showed, and he remembered, "If there is enough blue sky to make a pair of sailors' trousers—it means fine weather"—some nurse or governess had told him that.

The guard entered the office, closing the door behind him. Flight whispered, "Shall we make a bolt for it?"

Jules answered, "Not a chance! Good luck!"

"Good luck."

The door opened, the guard motioned them to enter.

Colonel Wolheim sat behind the desk in a straight-backed chair, whilst in the big armchair lounged a small, thick-set man, wearing a long grey military overcoat with the collar turned up to his ears.

Wolheim said, "These are the men, sir, who have been working on the designs of Jungbrech."

A deep, hoarse voice said, "Ah, clever devil, Jungbrech. Let's see them!"

The designs were laid before him, he peered at them, then smote the paper with his hand. "I've seen these damned things," he said. "These are Jungbrech's unfinished designs. I thought these fellows had been completing them? Or have they only been sitting biting their nails and picking their noses all this time?"

Wolheim glanced at Flight, as if seeking assistance; it was evident that he did not know one set of designs from the other.

Flight said, "If the General will permit, well, the designs on which I and my friend have been working—only he is much more clever than I am—he is Jean Morbeau of Paris, where we used . . ."

The General uttered a kind of stifled bellow. "What the devil! Where did anyone find this?" He pointed a stubby finger towards Flight, staring at him with small, angry grey eyes. Flight thought that his heart had stopped beating. General Ulruch was—Shaff.

He allowed himself to start back as if dismayed.

Wolheim said, "He's a queer, nervous fellow, sir, but they've worked well. They're clever . . ."

Shaff snarled, "I'll tell you how clever they are, when I've seen their work." He bent again over the sheets, grunting from time to time; once he raised his head and demanded, "Where did you get this idea?"—tapping with his gold pencil on the design.

Flight said, "That was Jean's—I beg your pardon, that was Morbeau's idea."

Shaff scowled at Jules. "Umph! It's the only time I've seen that done! It's—by Gad—it's astonishing! If you behave yourself, young man, you've got a future. This arrangement of the valves—an improvement?"

"I venture to think so, sir."

"Got a model?"

"Not fully completed, sir."

Shaff returned to the drawings. Again and again he smiled; once he actually rubbed his hands, and as he did so gave a sharp cry of pain. With his face twisted he turned to Wolheim, "Damned arthritis in my hand! Keep forgetting it, and go and do something idiotic like rubbing my hands, or trying to write a letter—phew! Ever had it? Horrible thing. Ought to be on a strict diet but, confound it, life wouldn't be worth living, eh?" He turned again to his examination. Once be beckoned Jules over to him, and pointing to a line followed it with his pencil, saying, "There? Eh? Umph, I see! Yes!"

Finally he leaned back, puffed out his cheeks and said to Wolheim, "Well, you've done very well! *Someone*—you know to whom I refer—will be very much pleased about this. This pair have stumbled on something—ve-ry good, ve-ry useful. D'you hear that, you two?"

Flight said, "Oh, thank you, sir! Thank you!"

Jules said, "Allow me to suggest, sir, that these ideas will revolutionise radio."

"Gather up those papers—yours and Jung-brech's—I'm taking them with me. I'll sign for them, Colonel. Just get a receipt drawn up, will you? I propose to take these two men with me. I want to get the complete new model made. One on a full scale. I've got everything at station 709. I wonder if we really want Jungbrech's? Yes, better take them. I'll be glad to take luncheon with you, Colonel. It's a long drive back to 709. Tell these fellows to get their things together. I'll leave in three-quarters of an hour."

The Colonel said, "Here is the receipt, sir. I hope that you'll exonerate me if there is any question of allowing the drawings to leave the place—and the men?"

Shaff glared at him. "Good God, man, you know me! Let's sign this receipt." He took up a pen, suddenly yelped with pain, and growling and grunting like a wounded tiger, scrawled his signature. "No one will be able to read the damned thing! Oh, my cursed hand! Better add: 'Signed in my presence by General Eitel Ulruch', and put your own name. That's right."

In the huge staff car, they sat opposite to Shaff. Wolheim had offered to send them in a truck to follow him, but he objected, saying that he was pressed for time, and couldn't hang back for a lumbering truck.

A glass partition separated them from the driver. Shaff leaned back and smiled contentedly. "Nice car, isn't it? Old Ulruch likes the best. Surprised to see me? Flurrey put me on to your track. Nicely arranged. Congratulations on your inventions and improvements. I've never seen so much"—and he used a regrettably coarse word —"in my life. Still, Jungbrech's ideas are good, very good. We'll get them copied nicely and send 'em to England. Like to take them, Pascal? Oh, I suppose you're not Pascal any longer, eh? Well, whoever you are, we might send you. Like to go?"

"Can we get to England now, Shaff?"

"It's not easy, but it can be done. A lot's happened. I'll tell you tonight, when we've collected new types and number plates and other oddities."

Jules said, "You were taken prisoner, weren't you?"

Shaff nodded. "Umph! Nasty, sticky business. After the Goering affair. We made a mess of that road. Remember, Pascal? Well—I'm going to sleep. So keep quiet, both of you. Here, have these cigarettes. I've plenty more."

They drove on through the still forest, by long, deserted country roads; passing tiny villages where people stared at the big car, as if they prayed that it might not stop. Again they turned into heavily wooded country, and stopped at last before what appeared to be a woodman's hut, against the door of which a tall, heavily built peasant stood, smoking placidly.

Shaff woke the instant the car stopped, blinked his eyes twice, and said, "Ah, we're here!" He got out, and spoke to the peasant, who nodded.

Shaff said, "This is Maltby—RAF type. Called here 'Malice'! He's all right. How are the General and his pal, Maltby?"

Maltby sighed. "Been makin' a hell of a row. Knocking on the door, and promising me everything except the kitchen stove if I'd play ball. The other car's round the back; I've changed the tyres, and the plates."

"Good, let's have a look at the General. I'm no oil-painting, but he's a damn sight worse."

Maltby said, "See that he doesn't slide out as you slide in."

The interior of the hut was dim, and smelt stuffy and damp. As they entered two men sprang to their feet. One an elderly fellow, wearing the insignia of a general, the other tall, slim and good-looking, in the uniform of a captain.

Shaff said, speaking in German, "Hello, how's things? Now, I can't stay long. If I did right I should shoot the pair of you—especially you, 'Eric von Stroheim'." Neither of the men, Flight noticed, showed the slightest change of expression. Shaff continued, "I shan't, because I don't like killing cold. But I'm afraid you're both going to have a long, cold walk. It's a long drive, and walking—well"—he shrugged his shoulders— "however, I'll give you some rations. You're the Ruling Race—for the moment—and I don't doubt that you will land up eventually. You—'Eric von Stroheim'—had better change clothes with my friend 'Malice'. We want your uniform. Just change, Maltby, will you?"

Maltby said, "My clothes smell abominably. It's my opinion they need delousing."

"Our elegant friend will see to that, no doubt. Look slippy! Auguste's got the other tyres changed? Right."

The General said, "You realise, I suppose, that this is both irregular and abominable?"

Shaff said, "Go on! D'you really think so? Aren't they funny people, Maltby?"

Maltby, who was struggling into the captain's tight tunic, said briefly, "They're simply bloody, if you ask me—unspeakably bloody."

Within half an hour they were on their way again. Shaff had insisted that the door of the hut should be fastened. "But fastened so that with a little patience and ingenuity, you can both get out—in time. There's food. Oh, of course that's enough, this isn't the 'Adlon'! I have all your papers? Yes. Well, good-bye, remember me to

569

Wolheim! Quite a fool, but a pleasant, honest fool. Good-bye, 'von Stroheim', when it's all over, you'd make a fortune in Hollywood! Say that I sent you. Shaff—that's the name. Good-bye!"

They drove away, the daylight faded, and Flight ceased to attempt to notice where or in which direction they went—he sat alone in the big car with Shaff, for Jules was driving with the man called Maltby—and allowed his mind to wander. Shaff had said that "They" would send him to England. He was to go back, to see his own country again, to talk to his own people, to hold Alicia in his arms again, feel her kisses, realise fully and completely her beauty and her love for him. He closed his eyes and felt that tears were making them smart; hot tears which slowly and painfully forced their way between his lids. He lay back, relaxed and almost exhausted. He knew that the past few years had taken their toll of him. He was no longer the young Flight Masters who had found life exciting, beautiful and wonderful. He had always known fits of depression, they had attacked him when he had suddenly felt uncertain of Alicia's love, or when he had believed himself to be unworthy of her; now he felt neither elation nor depression. Work had to be done, danger to be faced, but there was little or no joy in either achievement or failure. Laughter, real laughter, which bubbled up through the clear water of joy, seemed to Flight to have gone from the world. Such men as Shaff derived a kind of grim humour from desperate situations, but they did not appear to feel fury against their enemies, or any great affection for their allies. It was as if they played a huge and dangerous game, a game which meant safety for the victor, and death or torture for the vanquished.

Laughter, joy, real mirth. Would he ever experience them again? Had he known any of them since that afternoon at Dunkirk?—how many years ago—June 1940. And here he was, driving through France in a German staff-car, seated beside a man disguised as a German general and it was March 16, 1943. He had last seen England— the soft green of the lush grass, the trees where the leaves were beginning to turn to red and gold, where the great white clouds had sailed through the sky, thrushes and blackbirds were singing, little villages huddled under the leeside of the rolling Downs—in the late September of 1939.

He had been nearly twenty-one; newly married, home after a wonderful honeymoon—and the war clouds had burst. "You will be fighting evil things," the Prime Minister had said on that Sunday morning. Well, he had seen, watched, and schemed against some of these "evil things". He believed that he had done quite a number of evil things himself.

And now—Shaff told him that he might be going home.

They drove for hours, and at last stopped in a small market-town. The driver demanded the name of the best inn. Shaff lowered the window and bawled in atrocious French, asking if there was a German Headquarters Staff in the place?

The Frenchman, looking terrified, shook his head and said that the place was empty of Germans; they had been there, but the place was small, unimportant. It was as if he offered an apology for the modest nature of the town. There was an inn—"The Golden Lion"— old-fashioned, yes!—clean, honest people.

Shaff roared, "All right, man, all right! We shan't eat you! D'you imagine that we're monsters?"

The man's expression appeared to indicate that this was exactly what he did imagine, but he managed to smile in a rather sickly fashion and directed them to the inn. It was an old-fashioned place; plainly the Germans had taken everything that was worth taking, and the elderly landlady and her equally elderly husband looked strained and harassed. She gave them a meal and promised to make up some beds—"although I have only sufficient sheets for two beds; not more, General!"

Shaff gave his orders. He spoke to his own driver, "How far from Paris?"

The man replied, in pure Cockney, "Bi my reckning, abart coupler 'ours. That's keepin' ter the side roads."

Shaff said, "Here, you stick to your French, my boy!"

"Orl rite, guv'nor!" And he burst into a flood of correct, but mutilated French, while Shaff roared with laughter.

"And yet, somehow," he said, "he gets by! Don't you, Bill?"

Bill grinned. "Blimy, guv'nor, when I talk nachural they don't know what blinkin' langwidge I am perishin' well talking! I've gotter a nice quiet place in me mind, ole broken dahn 'chattoh' it is, where you can change. Then wotter we all do? All disperse an' wander, like wot the ole song says?"

Maltby yawned. "What about the buses? Pity to lose them, eh?"

"Set them alight. They're no use to us, we've stopped being carriage folks."

They slept, dead with fatigue, and were roused by Shaff before it was light the next morning. He had been up hours, he told them. "Had to shave off that remarkable moustache I wore yesterday. Pity, I'd grown fond of it."

About three miles out of the town they overtook a body of German soldiers. Flight knew that his heart was in his mouth. Shaff grinned like a wicked idol. He said, "Stop when you reach them, Bill."

Bill returned, "Right-cher, guv'nor!"

The car drew level with the soldiers. Shaff shouted for the officer in charge.

A young, fresh-faced sergeant strode to the car and saluted.

"Where are you going?" Shaff demanded.

"To Vermenton, my Colonel!"

"*General!*" Shaff bawled. "Dumb-head, have you no eyes? What is the road like to Tonnerre —the direct road? Indifferent? What do you mean? Bad?"

"Yes, General, very poor indeed. To reach Paris . . ."

"I have no wish to go to Paris. I wish to reach Troyes. Very good."

"Thank you, General."

Salutes, heel clickings, and they moved off. Shaff said, "Sorry, Bill, but we're less likely to meet anyone on a bad road. I had meant to go the other way. We'd better take the road to Tonnerre. Never mind your 'chattoh', we'll find somewhere else to change."

In what had once been a farmhouse they changed. Shaff gave them their orders. "You, Matot, can find your own way about Paris, you'll go to La Spero. Pascal, go to Maurice Gold. He'll get in touch with Number Seven, and find you new papers. You'd better be Pascal again. Join Matot."

"And the drawings?"

"You take one set. Matot takes the other."

"And, Shaff—what about England?" He felt timid and shaky as he put the question.

"Oh, blast it, give me time to breathe! I'll arrange that. You sit quiet. Maltby, you've got your orders. Bill, you'd better come with me. All got sufficient money? Sure? Don't run short, Maltby, as you did in Dieppe."

"That's OK," Maltby answered. "I've got oodles."

Shaff apologised for the clothes. "They're a bit creased. I managed to get them to that damn hut and then we buried them, waiting for the old boss Ulruch to come along. He was two days later than we expected. Better bury this German clobber; might come in useful sometimes, one never knows. Maltby's clothes are a bit on the small side—not Saville Row cut, are they? Well, off we go. Get cracking on those cars."

Two burning cars, into which Shaff had thoughtfully flung some odds and ends of German equipment, being particularly insistent on the General's cap being left where the flames could not reach it, and five men scattering in different directions. Maltby loping off towards the west, Shaff and the Cockney turning north-west, and Flight and Jules moving off towards Paris.

Jules said, "What a couple of days! He's a living dynamo, that Shaff!"

"I thought that my heart stopped, before I recognised him, and saw him begin to look at the drawings."

"And I! Whew, a very nasty moment."

They tramped along the hard road, talking very little, each occupied with his own thoughts. Indeed, they never talked a great deal, they seemed to have lost the ability to talk easily, their sentences were short and clipped and unless there was something important to be said, they remained silent. By the late afternoon, Jules' face looked drawn, his steps were dragging, and Flight suggested that they should take a train into Paris. Jules was doubtful, but Flight insisted, and presently they were sitting opposite to each other on the hard wooden seats of a third-class carriage. Jules lay back, his eyes closed. Flight watched him. Presently the eyes opened, and in them Flight thought that he detected some of their old sparkle and glint of amusement.

He said, "Well, we've got through so far, eh? We've done nothing terribly spectacular, but we've thrown a few spanners into the works, I think? I wonder why we do it? Oh, I know why I do it, I'm French. I've been brought up to believe that my destiny was to make life unpleasant for the Boche when the time came, but you . . . ?"

Flight said, "Don't be an idiot! It was either getting away or going to a prison camp. I didn't fancy that. Once I got away, once I landed at the farm, I had to—well, justify my existence—hadn't I? Some of it has been great fun, some of it's been very dirty and unpleasant."

"Does it strike you," Jules asked suddenly, "that we're both talking as if the job was finished? It's not, you know! There's a lot of ground to be covered yet. We might have asked Shaff to tell us how things are going? We don't know a thing but, then, in a war, no one does actually *know* anything. Half the people in the world just know 'there's a war going on'! They know that the Hun wants to trample over the world, that he doesn't want only a place in the sun, but he wants the whole ruddy sun itself. They don't know at what exact moment, or for what exact reason, the war between Britain and Germany began. Then we all go to fight. I don't believe that most people *like* wars, but I do believe that most people like living in rather excited, well-drilled herds. Most of us are lazy. We're quite willing to let other people think for us. You and I don't question Shaff's right to say 'Go here!' or 'You go there!' It relieves us of responsibility. What are you going to do, if Shaff manages to get you back to England?"

Flight said, "Deliver these drawings. Then—well, see my wife, my people, have a look at my Galleries."

"And suppose," Jules said very gently, "suppose—that when you got back everything was different? Suppose things were all changed? London can't be the same as when you and I knew it."

Flight stared at him, then drew a deep breath. "You're trying to suggest that—people might have been killed, eh?"

"No, no, only I want you to remember that you're going back after a long time, a time packed full of incidents, incidents of a violent and dreadful kind, and you must go prepared. Even then, are you the same person who left in 1939? Don't go back hoping to find London just as you left it, to find people just as you knew them. They won't find you the same, you know!"

"I do try to realise that. Ever since Shaff said that they might get me back, I've lain awake at night wondering what I should do, if . . ."

Jules leaned forward and laid his hand on his friend's knee. "You'd do what we all do—*go on*! Will you come back to us?"

For the first time Flight looked startled. "Why, yes. I mean, it never occurred to me to imagine doing anything but—come back."

"You could join your own army; that's what they'll want you to do."

"But I shan't go over as Flight Masters."

Jules laughed softly. "You might find 'Flight Masters' asserting himself once he arrived in London. Look, we're nearing Paris. I'll get out here and go on by foot or get a lift."

"*I'll* get out," Flight insisted. "You're not the boss of this show. Stay where you are, I know my way into Paris."

Jules grinned. "All right, 'Miss Thank You'; you seem to have shed some of your femininity."

Flight laid his hands on his shoulders and shook him gently. "Listen, if you ever tell anyone about that, I'll—blast it—I'll murder you!"

Lazily the other said, "Tell anyone—who should I tell?"

"Your mother, possibly . . ." Flight said, and for some inexplicable reason, could have bitten his tongue out for speaking so quickly.

"No, I won't tell my mother."

The little local train rumbled and jolted to a standstill. Flight opened the door and, looking back, called "*Au revoir!*" then disappeared into the darkness.

It was late that night when he arrived at Maurice Gold's house. The servant admitted him and he was ushered into Gold's studio. The vast man held out his beautifully manicured hand, saying, "Ah, you've come home to roost, eh? I suppose," he continued, "that you want food and drink, and a bath and the loan of a razor?"

Flight said, "Thank you, I have a razor. It belonged to a German general—Ulruch. Shaff presented it to me when he went through his 'effects'."

"Ah! Shaff kill him?"

"No."

The huge face expressed silent disapproval. "Umph! Shaff's losing his nerve. Well, what instructions has he given you? You understand that I am only a wretched pawn in Shaff's game? Kings —when there were any—Dictators—when they began to grow like mushrooms—Diplomats and such might come to me crawling, flattering, begging for loans. Shaff—and I often wonder who the devil Shaff is!—says 'Do this!' or 'Do the next thing!' and I risk my highly valuable neck to obey him!"

As they sat over excellent whiskies-and-sodas,

Gold recounted all the news to Flight, told him of the happenings in North Africa, in Russia, in the East with the Americans; told all these things slowly, with a kind of rich appreciation. He said, "Much of that may sound depressing. That is because you will insist upon looking at what happens *today* and *here*, at some given point. This War is like a tremendous piece of tapestry. At the moment a small piece is worked here, another small piece there, some of it badly done, will have to be done again, slowly, when the time comes. The tapestry will be turned over, the ragged ends cut off, and it will emerge as something complete, following the design, which is the one worked out by a whole army of artists. Like a Walt Disney film, hundreds of small pictures, meaning little or nothing in themselves, but in the end— satisfactory, if not strictly beautiful."

"And then," Flight asked, "and then?"

"Then—ah, then!—some bloody blundering idiot will go and put his foot through it, and the design will have to be worked all over again. But that will not come until the War is ostensibly, won; and the greatest brains in the world, and a few honest men, will meet to discuss the rebuilding of the Universe. But not yet! Although this year is going to see remarkable changes—remarkable!"

The rather heavy, melodious voice rumbled gently on. Again and again Gold chuckled softly at one of his own jokes or satirical comments, while Flight, slouching in the great comfortable chair, watched him, thinking, "Can it be true that he wants to marry Susanne Matot? Could Susanne marry him?" Then, conscious of a feeling of irritation, he asked himself what business it was of his, and how it could affect him, what Susanne did or did not do?

Gold was talking of the plays which she had produced, chuckling at the recollection. "Laughter is so good," he said. "Not only is it helpful in making a new spirit, in restoring courage, but it is so destructive. It restores the one who laughs, it destroys—provided it is sufficiently strong—the person or thing against which it is directed. This is not a discovery made by La Spero, of course! Voltaire realised it when he wrote *Candide*. The last play, *Draw the Curtain*, was diabolical in its cleverness. Then the only one of the Big Bosses who, in my opinion, has any brains or artistic appreciation, came to Paris and attended a performance. That nasty little club-footed rat saw something that the others had missed. It was suggested to La Spero that she withdrew it.

"No actual reason was given. First, because it would have argued the complete stupidity of the others, who had been blind; secondly, La Spero, who has more brains in her little finger than the whole of the Big Bosses put together, would have argued that it was merely an 'attractive trifle'.

"I believe that was exactly what she did say, at the interview with this *abortion*. He suggested that, at this grave moment in the History of the

World—they always speak in capital letters!—something more serious was demanded. She replied that she had two admirable translations; he asked from what language? She replied, 'Irish! They are by Bernard Shaw'. He nodded. 'Provided that Shaw was sufficiently critical of the British, they might "prove of interest to be".' She sent him *Saint Joan* and *The Apple Cart*. He sent them back with no comment, but advised that her theatre remained closed until she found some more suitable plays! She says that he added 'that the Leader of frivolous plays did not approve'. The incident was closed. So was the theatre!"

Flight slept that night in unbelievably fine linen sheets; pale, exquisite china tea was brought to him by "Passepartout" in the morning; clean clothes, a selection of ties, were laid out for him; his shabby suit had been sponged and pressed. A large envelope with heavy seals was handed to him.

"My master's compliments. He trusts that you slept well. Please order what you wish for breakfast. My master never appears before half past eleven. He hopes that he may have the pleasure of meeting you in the near future." He broke the seals and found his papers, including one enclosed in another envelope, marked "Strictly Private". He was François Pascal again, but in the smaller envelope was a document stating that he was Flight Masters, who had escaped from Dunkirk and had since been serving with distinction with the Maquis. The notepaper bore the address of the

Free French Headquarters in Carlton House Terrace, London. There were two signatures. One *E. Shaff*, the other a name so important as to make him blink his eyes. He dressed and carefully made his way to the back door of Susanne Matot's house.

As he knocked and waited for Henri to admit him, his thought turned back to the last time he had passed through that door. Like an echo, he heard Susanne saying, "Flight—dear!" then his own voice muttering words which his memory did not record clearly; her laugh followed, and that provocative smile. "No Frenchman would ever have said 'I'm sorry'."

At last his own voice, clearly ringing in his head, "Then, I'm not sorry! I'll come back one day and do it again."

So long ago since that morning, since the moment when he had caught her in his arms, held her close, and kissed her again and again. His cheeks flamed, Henri opened the door. He growled, "Ah, it's you? You look well, I must admit. Come in, move quickly, for God's sake!"

He waited for her. Not this time in the little bare waiting-room, but in the small drawing-room, with her portrait looking down at him. He stared at it, rubbed his eyes, and frowned.

"Damn it!" he thought. "What the devil is the matter with me? I'm going home to my wife. My wife, who I adore, and yet I'm blushing like a schoolboy, my heart hammering against my ribs because I'm going to see Susanne Matot, who I kissed months ago! I'm behaving like a fool!"

She came in and stood smiling, holding out her hands.

"My dear, how good to see you! Thank you for bringing Jules home safely."

He took her hand and bent over it, brushing it formally with his lips. He said, speaking in a level voice, "I'm afraid that he isn't in very good shape. We had some tough times. Maybe he has told you?"

She nodded. "He's dreadfully thin, I don't like that cough. The specialist has seen him this morning, he wants him to get away to Switzerland. You know what that means?"

His first thought was, "Switzerland—she's going away! When I come back she won't be here. I shan't be able to get to Switzerland." Then his heart smote him that he could only think of himself, only think of his wish to see her, forgetting his friend, forgetting that he was going to England, and might not come back. He added mentally, "Might not even *want* to come back."

He said, "That's bad, but he's very tough, Jules. I've seen him go through things that would have laid anyone else out completely. Can you get to Switzerland? Can it be arranged?"

Susanne nodded. "Oh, I think so! Maurice will manage it somehow." She smiled. "Maurice manages to get everything—provided he wants it sufficiently!"

He said, "I'm going to England, you know."

"Jules told me. How marvellous for you! Do you think that you could manage to get a letter through for me to my brother? He may be fighting, I don't know—but his home is in Yorkshire. Colonel Crowther—Harry Crowther."

"If it's possible, I'll manage it."

"Now you'd like to see Jules?"

Jules was immensely cheerful. He looked better, his cheeks were less bright, his eyes less feverish. He was excited at the idea of getting to Switzerland. "I've had enough to last me for a time, of hiding and getting wet through, and killing people in nasty ways. Even soldiers deserve some leave now and then, eh?"

Two days later Flight was handed his papers by Number Seven. He liked the man no better than he had done at their first meeting, but it was impossible not to feel a certain satisfaction when Number Seven said, "You've done well! They're pleased. Particularly for an Englishman. Not many of your countrymen are so tenacious—you understand? They fade . . . wilt . . . wither."

Flight said, "Damn it, they didn't show much sign of 'withering' when I saw 'em last at Dunkirk."

"An exceptional case, no doubt. However, you have the drawings. You will deliver them to Broadcasting House, London. There you will ask for Mr. . . . um . . . what is his name? Ut-skinsond."

"Hutchinson? Is that what you mean?"

585

"That is possibly how *you* pronounce it. That is not his actual name. They will know when you hand them this card, it has been printed with great care, in the English style, very small, you see? Mr. Hair-bairt Goos-age. This is the club to which you belong. All Englishmen belong to clubs. This is the Savage Club. Savage—ferocious!"

"But, damn it, I'm not a member of the Savage!"

"That does not matter. You will make your way to a small place south of Dieppe, called Parnay. Get there at night, the day after tomorrow. Look, here is a map of the place, study it, but don't keep it. Go to this street, then the house where there will be a dim light behind a dark green curtain. Knock, and say, 'Excuse, your light is showing, this is not permitted.' Speak French all the time. Roll your drawings inside your shirt, in a piece of waterproof silk. Look, we have even provided that. If you are in the water and rescued—should anything hit you, contrive to get them out, if it is possible—or else take them with you, if you are not rescued. Is that clear?"

Flight said, "Admirably. It looks like being a charming trip."

"Report to Fred Grimes, fourteen Sout'ampton Street, third floor. He is a traveller in musical instruments. Have I made myself clear?"

"Delightfully."

"We shall hope to see you soon. Not, understand, that you are under any obligation to return, but it might be wiser. You see, we are—trusting you completely—Pascal."

"I am flattered."

He said that evening to Susanne, "Now that it's come, now that I know that, with luck, I shall be in England very soon, I don't know how to explain it all. I'm—yes, I'm nervous, afraid. I don't know what I shall find. They may be all right—all of them, but they may not like me—the Flight Masters that I am now? My wife—suppose that she hates me, finds me very different from the man she married—what then?"

"Your wife means a great deal to you?" Susanne asked.

He nodded. "Yes, yes, everything. She is beautiful—very beautiful. Very 'fine', you understand? Really fine. Perhaps that very fineness will make it difficult. No, I'm being foolish; everything is going to be marvellous. I must think out a way to let them know. I mustn't burst in on them. It might upset Alicia. It's a lovely name, isn't it —Alicia? I think that the best thing might be to get in touch with my sister, my younger sister. She is very practical, very sane"—he laughed—"I doubt if I shall be very sane by the time I get to England."

"I wonder if I shall ever go to England again?" she said. "Sometimes I think that I would give anything in the whole world to see the hills in autumn, purple with heather. To smell the warm, friendly smell of the byres as you pass on a cold

587

evening; the light going, and in the stable the sudden stamp of horses as they munch their evening meal. The sunsets, the lovely dim colours of the dawn. The springtime—when you can smell spring in the air long before it arrives. The lambs staggering about on long wooden-looking legs, the faint wisps of peat smoke rising from tall, old-fashioned chimneys. Then—I wonder? I've grown away from it all. I remember that I told my brother Harry so—years ago.

"But, oh, it's a friendly country, our Broad Acres. With age-old grey abbeys hiding amongst immense trees; with dignified cathedrals 'lording it' over small towns; the coast where the seas dash and rave, and try to bring terror into the hearts of fisherfolk—and never succeeded. People tell me that the towns with tall mill-chimneys are hideous. They're not, really. Where else do you find the neat little houses, with their sanded steps and well-washed pavements?

"The flowers—violets you have to seek for, finding them by the scent that betrays them; dim primroses with their furry leaves; the 'lords and ladies', sheathed in grey-green satin covers. The birds—the joy of seeing a kingfisher flash past, darting over the water like a piece of living flame. The thrush, the blackbirds—they're the sweetest of all—and the first sound of that silly cuckoo. Oh"—very seriously—"you mustn't be afraid to go back! I don't know what you'll find, my dear. Things have changed, perhaps people have changed, you admit that you are not the same; but the moors, the dales, the little fishing villages, the solid farmhouses, with their buildings gathered round them, where beasts are housed well, warmly and in comfort—those things don't change! Northallerton, Studley, Thirsk, Masham. Time hasn't touched them. Yarm and Acklam, Stokesley and Ayton—they're not changed, and the people in them haven't changed. The speech has scarcely changed, either. They use words that were old when Shakespeare wrote and Bunyan preached, and I'll lay you'd find one of the Blakeboroughs —for as long as there's Yorkshire there'll be a Blakeborough riding to hounds!—using the same words. Nay, you've no need to be flaid, my dear."

"Flaid?" he repeated. "No—I'll not be flaid." Then, rising, he came to her and took her in his arms. "Susan, Susan—if I were going home to you—there'd be nothing to be afraid of, my dear. It's going to be all right . . . it must be. Give me courage, darling, wonderful Susan!"

"It's so long since anyone called me Susan," she said.

His doubts and apprehensions were leaving him. He could have sworn that he felt strength and courage emanating from her. She made no attempt to push him away, but let him keep his arms round her.

He whispered, "Once—months ago—I told you that I should come back, that I wasn't sorry . . ." and he drew her face nearer and kissed her.

Again she said, "Flight—dear!"

He let her go, moved away and said, "I go early in the morning, as I did before, but I'll come back."

She nodded. "I know. And England, and . . . everything . . . is going to be all right. Come back to tell me that, my dear."

"I will," he said. "Good night, and God bless you!"

5

SOMEWHERE on the dark sea he was transferred from the little fishing-boat to a throbbing motor-boat. He was tired, for the journey to Parnay had been long and difficult. He had walked down to the long row of cottages which faced the sea, had found the faint green glimmer, had knocked and said:

"Excuse, there is a light showing! This is not allowed." A grim-faced fellow had opened the door an inch or two wider and jerked his head, indicating that Flight was to enter. A narrow dark passage, which smelt of the sea, a tiny room cluttered with fishing tackle, lobster-pots and great swathes of brown nets. The man spoke to him in a gruff voice, in a dialect so broad that Flight found it difficult to follow.

"We're going at once. Put on that black oilskin and sou'-wester. It's blowing up a little. God! it's as black as pitch. Well, if we can't see them, at least they can't see us. That's one comfort."

He poured out a small glass of clear liquid and handed it to Flight saying:

"That 'ul put heart into you! Drink it down."

Flight did as he was told. The stuff was like fire in his throat, some kind of very raw Schnapps he thought? He coughed and spluttered. For the first time the grim expression of his host softened a little.

"Generally makes folks cough—the first time or two," he said. "It's all right when you get used to it."

Together they scrambled down the beach, carrying nets and tackle; they pushed the boat off, wading knee-deep in the water to do so. Then levering themselves into it, the grim man unshipped the oars and they swung out into the darkness. They rowed in silence, Flight shivering a little, as his wet trousers clung to his legs. He thought if he took a turn at the oars, it might warm him.

"I'll take a turn if you like," he said softly.

The reply came back in a sarcastic whisper, "You? Huh!"

"I assure you that I can row quite well."

"Try it then!"

They changed places, and slowly Flight felt the circulation returning to his cold legs. On and on, into darkness which seemed to become more dense with every stroke of the oars. No lights were visible anywhere, no sounds except the whisper of the sea against the sides of the boat. Presently the grim man whispered, "Dip that oar in the water! The rowlock's squeaking like the devil. Can't you hear it?"

Flight had heard nothing, but he obediently plunged the oar into the water, shuddering at the sudden cold as the sea licked his fingers.

"What time is it?" he asked.

"Nearly ten. We ought to pick her up any minute now. We've been moving for nearly two hours. I'll take over. Keep your eyes skinned."

He sat staring into the blackness, turning his head to the right and then to the left; the gloom was impenetrable, like some great black curtain dropped down, cutting them off from the rest of the world. He remembered a story he had read once —who wrote it? Frank Shaw? Morley Roberts? he forgot which. A sailing-ship, which went on and on, while an old mad man kept asserting that "England had sunk at her moorings". That was what this experience felt like. They might go on and on for days, nights, and find nothing. He was trying to think—almost feverishly—about anything and everything, except his arrival in England. He had promised Susan not to be afraid—when had he begun to think of her as "Susan", and not as Madame Matot, or La Spero, or even Susanne? But his fears were returning, crowding round him in the darkness. What was he going to find? A battered London? The news that Alicia was dead somewhere among the ruins? His mother and father; Eleanor, Ann—Chris would be out somewhere fighting by this time. Perhaps Chris was dead too? A light flickered in the darkness, then disappeared.

He said, "I think that I saw a light over there —to the left?"

The man grunted. "To the left! Don't you know

which is port and which is starboard?"

Flight snapped, "No, I damn well don't, and why the hell should I? There it is again! See it?"

"Umph—that's her! Make the changeover quickly, I don't want to hang about near her thudding engine."

Out of the darkness came a dim shape and the beat of an engine. They were alongside. Flight heard someone say, "Give me your hand. Now!" He was on the deck of the motor-boat. It swung round. The fishing vessel disappeared into the night; the engines throbbed, the speed increased.

A man was standing beside him, holding his elbow. "This way, down here! Mind your head. That's it."

The door shut, every porthole darkened; Flight saw a young man, scarcely more than a boy, wearing a shabby uniform with a tarnished gold stripe on each cuff. He said, "Managed that nicely! Old Gaston never lets us down. Gosh! he's making a packet out of this racket, the old basket! Have a drink? My name's Harris—Jimmy Harris."

Flight said, "Thanks, I'd like a drink." He paused. "I'm hanged if I know who I am, I've had my name changed so often. Gossage, I think, is the last effort—Herbert Gossage. How long does this trip take?"

Harris drank deeply, wiped his mouth with the back of his hand, then said, "With luck, four hours. If they spot us—as long as our juice lasts."

"Do they often chase you?"

"So—so—not so much as they did. They've got their hands pretty full, y'know. It used to be quite exciting. It's getting bloody dull in these days. Have another drink?"

Later he lay down on the shabby, plush-covered settee, and tried to sleep. He lay with his eyes tightly shut, trying to force sleep to come to him. He counted sheep, and when he reached eight hundred and forty-three, gave it up, because he was becoming less and less sleepy. He tried to remember pieces of verse—Shakespeare, the Psalms, extracts from the church service—nothing brought sleep any nearer.

He worked out his plans for the time he arrived in London. First to get rid of the designs, then to see this man Grimes—Fred Grimes—who lived on the third floor of a house in Southampton Street, number fourteen. Then—then he would go to Alcaster House in Princes Gate and find Ann. Together they would plan his next move. Ann would know where he could find Alicia. She might have left London during the bombings. Perhaps they were still going on, though not so intensively. Alicia! He whispered the name and thought how wonderful it sounded. Grimes would tell him whether he was to report to the WO or not. Was he bound to the Maquis? He felt that he was, that whatever happened, he must go back, take up the life that he had been living for the last two years. Perhaps they'd give him the job of coming over to England to bring information? Perhaps he might get a job with de Gaulle? Perhaps—perhaps . . .

The door opened and Harris slid into the cabin.

"You've had a decent sleep, eh? I looked in twice, but you were dead to the world. We're creeping along the coast now. Nothing exciting happened—like a trip to Margate—'piece of cake' this trip. We might run into a mine but it's not likely. We'll be off Brighton soon. Passing Worthing and Shoreham—y'know? where all the 'pro's' build houses . . . Teddy Brown and Bud Flanagan. I'll tell you who has a place near here —'Gert and Daisy' . . . y'know, Doris and Elsie Waters. Their brother's Jack Warner. Y'know . . . 'Mind my bike' . . . that chap. If that damned engine wasn't kicking up such a row I'd give you an imitation of Jack Warner! It's pretty good! He once came to our place. They got me to do it for him. Know what he said? 'I honestly believe you're more like me than I am!' That's what he said. Funny, eh? Have another drink? One for the road . . . yes?"

"Are you landing me near here?"

"No—near Chichester. Brighton? Whew! not likely. Much too sticky. Nice little creek near Selsey Bill. Snug little place. Then, after we've been to the local for a wash and brush up, I'll take you along to some pal of mine and he'll drive you! If you're like the rest of them, you're not out for a lot of publicity? Oh! we've got plenty of Huns roaming about in UK. Slimy lot of baskets. But you'll be all right with Herbert, he'll land you right in the Heart of the Greatest City in the World . . . no prize offered for the answer."

Flight asked, "Is it—London—badly knocked about?"

The youth shrugged his shoulders. "Badly? Yes, I suppose so. Had some nasty smacks, here and there. But it's—all *right*. I mean there's still a hell of a lot of it left, if you get me?"

He cocked his head suddenly. "Hear that? We're into the shallow water. Another minute and your voyage, O Mysterious Traveller, is at an end!"

In a bedroom of a small old-fashioned hotel they washed and shaved, they ate a meal of bacon and fried eggs, drank tea which was so strong that it made Flight's tongue feel rough; they went out to a ramshackle car, and as it was growing light, bumped and rattled through the Sussex lanes. The boy drove rapidly and particularly badly. Whenever he crashed his gears he roared with laughter. "My theory is," he explained to Flight, "treat 'em rough, cars! They like it! Enjoy it, respect you for it! Just hop out and open that gate, will you? We're there, I've landed you. Not such a bad trip, eh? Come again, patronise the old firm, eh?"

An immensely tall man, a woman with beautiful dark eyes and a lovely smile. A house which was filled with charming things. Flight caught sight of a picture, a picture he knew. He stood before it, drinking a cup of excellent coffee. His hostess said, "You like it?"

"I do indeed!" He longed to say, "I bought it because I liked it, my dear lady! And if I didn't sell it to you myself, I'm a Dutchman."

"I saw it in a Gallery in Bond Street," she said. "Melton's Galleries. It's gone. Bombed, you know! I was so sorry, it was such a pleasant place. That's an Etty."

He said, "It's gone—has it? I've been out of England—I didn't know."

She glanced at him, then said quickly, "You're not well. Sit down. Herbert, give Mr. Gossage a drink."

He sat down, feeling shaken and rather sick. This was the first shock. His Gallery had gone! Had Mac seen that the pictures were taken away when the bombing began? What else would he find—gone? He protested that he was all right, that possibly he was a little tired. The tall man said, "Drink that. If you're all right it won't hurt you, if you're not, it will put you right."

Flight drank the brandy and felt surprisingly better. After all—what did it matter? If everything else was safe, everyone else safe, Alicia safe? The man called Herbert asked where he wanted to be dropped in town?

"I've got to go to the BBC."

"To broadcast?"

"Good Lord, no! I've got some—I don't suppose it matters my telling you—new designs for them. I haven't listened to anything but the News—and that tuned down until it was scarcely more than a whisper—for three years. You're not an actor, are you, sir?"

"Me? Heavens above! One in the family is sufficient. My wife's father. Did you hear him last night, Jimmy? Came over very well."

Jimmy said, "Go on! on the air was he? Good old Bransby."

"You don't mean Bransby Williams!" Flight asked, and they laughed, for into his voice had crept the tone of surprised respect which great names of Stage or Variety impose on people who still regard the theatre as a place veiled in mystery.

Jimmy shouted, "You bet they do!"

He said, "Thank you very much indeed. I hope one day we may meet again."

"I hope so. Good luck."

He stood staring up at the towering bulk of Broadcasting House. He went forward past the guard, and was stopped and asked what his business was? He said that he wished to see "Mr. Hutchinson". The man said, "Got your pass, please?" He faced a good-looking girl across a counter, and said again that he wished to see Mr. Hutchinson. He added that his own name was Herbert Gossage.

She spoke to someone on the telephone. He listened, half-amused, at the various inflections she put into "Yes!" and "No!"

"Someone is coming down for you," she said. "Won't you sit down?"

A pleasant-looking young man, wearing an excellent suit and a club tie, arrived, and said, with an upward inflection, "Er—Mr. Herbert Gossage?" Flight nodded. "Come with me, will you? The Chief will see you immediately." He chatted brightly as they traversed corridors, sprang in and out of lifts; he hoped that Flight had enjoyed a pleasant journey? Had he breakfasted? that was good! One never felt at one's best before breakfast. Was he going to do a broadcast? No! That was a pity, wasn't it? Listeners would be most interested.

Flight said, "That's exactly why I shan't broadcast."

Ah! The young man fancied that he knew what Mr. Gossage meant. Quite . . . too many listeners, eh? But after all, if he spoke about—er—his experiences, well, it would only prove to the Germans the truth of the old adage, that listeners never heard any good of themselves! He laughed merrily.

Flight thought, "Why the hell can't you *shut up!*"

The young man had stopped. He tapped lightly on a door, a voice bade him enter; Flight was ushered in.

An elderly man seated at a desk said, "*Good* morning! You are . . ."

Flight produced his card and said, "Herbert Gossage."

"Ah! a member of my own club. Curious coincidence?"

"It might be, if I were. I'm not. That is—one might say—my professional card. Who are you? Your name isn't Hutchinson, I know that."

The other gave a nod of dismissal to the young man saying, "Just wait outside, Kenneth, will you?" As the door closed he handed Flight his own card saying, "It is not always advisable, in these days, for all and sundry to know that I am in London! Is that card sufficient, or do you want further proof that I am—the man you have been sent to see?"

Flight answered, "No. The card, plus the guards and the passes, and that walking gramophone that apparently never runs down, who accompanied me to this room—will suffice. You know who sent me? Good! You know why I have come? Just tell me quite briefly, will you?"

The man behind the desk stared for a moment. This shabby-looking fellow—fairly young, wearing a deplorable suit and a tie which was evidently a Frenchman's idea of elegance; a shirt which looked crumpled; and shoes which had never been good and certainly had never known the existence of trees, was taking a good deal upon himself. Apparently the name on the card had not impressed him.

601

He said, "I can assure you that I am in full possession of the facts . . ."

Flight answered, "Good! I should like to be also."

"Mr. Gossage, I am not used to being spoken to . . ."

"Listen! I'm used to being blackguarded by Huns—from generals to private soldiers. I'm used to a whole lot of unpleasant things. I want that information or I'm going. Now, d'you mind if I sit down? Thank you! Before you begin to talk, just lift those receivers off their hooks, will you? If anyone wants to speak to you they must wait. Now—if you please?"

He listened attentively. The story was correct enough, except that he called Shaff "Shaft", once or twice, and frowned at Flight's insistence on the proper name. He ended and asked, "Are you satisfied?"

"Yes, all right." He unbuttoned his waistcoat and produced the packet in its covering of green watered silk. "There you are. I'll have a receipt, with the date and time on it, please. If there is anything you don't understand"—he laughed suddenly—"don't apply to me. I've spent months trying to pretend that I understood those damned drawings."

"Where are you staying, Mr.—er—Gossage?"

"I haven't the faintest idea. Have a look at those drawings before I go, will you?"

"Certainly." Flight watched the drawings being

unfolded. His mind went back to the room in the camp, where he and Jules had pored over them so often, where they had held whispered conversations and drawn on their own scanty handbook knowledge to help them to understand—even remotely—what they all meant. It was evident that this man understood them. He frowned, he smiled; once he uttered a long-drawn "A . . . a . . . ah!" Finally he looked up. "Revolutionary—positively revolutionary, Mr.—er—Gossage. Would you dine with me this evening—any evening?"

"It's kind of you. I can't promise to dine. I've all kinds of things to see to. I've not been in England since 1939, not seen or heard from my people —I'm sure that you understand. Now that receipt and I'll be off." Kenneth was waiting for him. "Just show me the way out, will you?"

"Of course. This place is like a rabbit warren, isn't it? In fact sometimes people who know it quite well—yes, this lift. Mind the step . . ."

As they were emerging from the lift, a woman wearing a Red Cross uniform was standing talking to a man. Flight heard the voice and said to Kenneth, "Quick! That woman with her back to us. What's her name? *Quick!*"

"That? Oh, the Duchess of Alcaster. She is doing an appeal for us, I . . ."

Flight stepped forward, and speaking in rapid French, said, "Excuse me, but I believe that we have a great mutual friend in La Spero?"

603

For a moment he saw Ann's eyes widen, watched every vestige of colour fade from her face, then she answered him. "But of course! We have met in Paris—when was it, before the War? You are—oh, I am so stupid about names!"

"My name, Duchess, is Goss-arge, but that is immaterial. Before I left Paris, La Spero charged me to deliver a message to you. But"—he glanced round him—"it is of a private nature."

"My car is waiting, perhaps I can drive you somewhere?"

He bowed. "That will be most kind. I shall be honoured."

She turned and spoke to the man who had been waiting. Flight noticed how crisply and decisively she spoke: there was no hesitation, no fumbling for words. He had been right when he decided to go to Ann, she would give him the advice he needed so badly. She was twenty-three, she looked older, he thought. She was the Duchess. Then the old man had died. Ann—his small, cheeky sister—a Duchess! Fantastic!

She said, "Now, Mr. Gossage, if you're ready?"

They did not speak again until he was seated beside her in the car and she had told the chauffeur to drive to Princes Gate. Then she turned and faced him squarely.

"My God! Flight!" she said.

"Yes, it's me," he replied.

"You were reported missing—then—officially —dead."

He smiled. "Sorry! That wasn't my fault."

She shook her head as if words evaded her. Then she whispered, "Flight, my dear!"

"Tell me," he begged, "tell me, how are they all? Alicia—she's well?"

"She's very well. Down at Baddock St. Mallory. Mother and Father—Eleanor—she's got a little boy. I've got two, Flight. You heard about my Sholto?"

He laid his hand on hers. "I saw him, my sweet. I was the last person to speak to him. Presently I'll tell you—I'm shaken a bit, Ann, meeting you like that. And I heard this morning that the Gallery has gone. I hated hearing that. Go on talking—give me—a chance to pull myself together."

She gave orders that on no account was she to be disturbed. When the butler began, "Your Grace, Sir George telephoned to say . . ." she interrupted him with, "I don't want to hear! Tell me afterwards. Remember—no matter who telephones, I am not to be disturbed. I want luncheon served for two in the small study in an hour's time."

"Very good, Your Grace."

"Telephone through to Alcaster, tell Matron that I shall not be back tonight. I shall probably be there tomorrow, I'll let her know."

"Very good, Your Grace."

"Now, Mr. Gossage."

He followed her into the room, closing the door behind him. She came to him and put her arms round him, kissing him, beginning to cry. He said, "Ann, dear, don't cry! I'm back . . ."

She shuddered. Then leaving him, walked away and stood staring out of the window. He said pleadingly, for there was so much he longed to know, "Ann, talk to me. I want to hear everything. I know it must be pretty hard on you for me to come back—when Sholto didn't. He was a first-rate fellow . . ."

She said with sudden bitterness, "Yes, I had some really magnificent letters about him. Poor Sholto! I did love him a great deal. But I have my boys at least, you . . ."

He said, "Darling, the Gallery doesn't matter. I'll build a new one. I've got Alicia, she's safe. When shall we go down? This afternoon?"

She came back to him, put her hands on his shoulders, and looked him steadily in the eyes. "Listen, Flight, this is going to hurt like hell. You'd better have a drink and sit down to hear it."

"She's not dead? My God, she isn't dead? Or hopelessly maimed? Ann, tell me! Tell me!"

"She's—married—Flight. She was married last August."

"It's not true! It can't be true! Alicia . . . ? Ann, it isn't true!"

She nodded. "It is true, my dear. She's going to have a baby in July."

He stumbled into a chair and sat there, a crumpled figure, his face hidden in his hands. She watched him, then went to the side table and poured out a drink, bringing it back to him, saying, "Drink this."

"I don't want it! Leave me alone. Damn you, leave me alone!"

She repeated, "Do as I tell you—drink this!"

Furiously he snatched it from her and drank it, saying, as he handed back the glass, "Now for Christ's sake leave me alone!" Then, almost piteously, "No, no, Ann! Don't leave me. Explain . . . I don't understand. Explain!"

"We had the official statement that you must be 'presumed killed' in February last year . . ."

He said, "She didn't lose much time!"

"I think she was very lonely. Puzzled, Flight. Alicia isn't a very strong character. Perhaps . . ."

He burst out, "Lonely? I wasn't lonely, was I? I wasn't puzzled, was I? Puzzled as to how to save my skin, how to avoid a bullet in my brain. I didn't run after every tart I found, and there were plenty. Always I thought, 'Alicia's waiting for me. I shall get back to Alicia.' Who has she married? Who is the bastard? What's his name? By God, I'll kill him!"

"My dear, you've got to see this straight! Alicia believed that you were dead—we all did—until February 1942. It's a long time. A long time for a woman to wait and hope and trust—even the strongest love wilts, you know. She didn't know—none of us knew. How could we? He—the man she has married—adores her. She loves him very deeply, I believe."

"What's his name?" Flight demanded stubbornly.

"Does that matter?"

"Does it matter?" he half shouted. "Does it matter? Good Lord, of course it matters! He'll have to let her divorce him. I don't care if he divorces her. I don't care how it's done, but she's coming back to me!"

"And the child—what about the child?"

"He can take the bloody child if he likes. What do I care?"

She shook her head. "Flight, my dear, dear Flight, you can't do that. She loves him, she herself told me so. I know more about Alicia than anyone—except her husband—in the world. She doesn't really like me, I don't care for her, but —she trusts me. I'm going to betray her confidence now, if there is no other way of convincing you that it is hopeless to try to get her back—by any means."

He beat his clenched fist on the arm of the chair. "Oh, get *on*!"

"Alicia was this man's mistress while she was engaged to you. Not persistently, but at intervals. When you were in France before War broke out, do you remember? It began then. There were times when she hated herself. For she did love you, remember. It's a strange, unhealthy sort of split in her personality, she's a schizophrenic. She loved your sweetness and gentleness. The other part of her loved his domination, his fierce passion for her, even his crudity. Am I—making you understand, Flight?"

"I understand that it's a lot of talk, talk, talk. Women don't love two men at the same time —they don't sleep with one man and promise to marry another!"

"She met this man—as a possible lover—after she promised to marry you."

He nodded. "Possibly. She's a bitch, but she's coming back to me just the same—or, by God, I'll make all England ring with the story! They'll enjoy that! Her old uncle Rusmere, her smug father and her rigid mother. They'll like the cheap news-papers making comments upon it, won't they? Now—what's the blasted fellow's name? Tell me that—or I'll go straight to Baddock and find out for myself. Now, Ann!"

She looked at him sitting there, thin, the marks of weariness on his face; saw how his hair was greying at the temples, receding a little from his forehead; his hand, which he stretched towards her, with its ill-kept nails; his wrists were bony and the veins stood out like cords. His clothes. His wretched shoes. His whole appearance told of hardship and privation. He was twenty-five—he would have been taken for a man of forty. He had been through so much, faced danger, privation, gone in fear of his life; and now—she was going to inflict more pain upon him.

She said, "His name is one of the reasons why you—can't do anything. His name—is the same as your own. It's Chris, Flight—your brother!"

He did not move. His expression did not change. Ann thought that he was stunned, beyond speech. He only allowed his hands to fall and hang loosely between his knees, as if all strength had gone from him. When he began to speak it was as if he uttered words mechanically, without feeling.

"Chris! Chris, is it? Chris—who promised to take her to play golf. It was Chris who I damn nearly caught one night in the Little Wood, when he was supposed to be playing a match at Raisley. Best man at my wedding! Chris! And now he's married her and she's going to have his child." He glanced up sharply. "Isn't he in the Army?"

"Invalided out—he was wounded in Egypt."

"Gosh! there isn't much justice, is there? Chaps I knew—Father Maurice, buried like a dog in an old barn; Romulus killed—poor bloody little Remus dead. Madame Kalt—God knows what happened to her. And none of them ever did any harm—do you understand, no harm—to anyone except the enemy. Jules, he's got TB. He may get well, he may not. Chris—that bastard, that thief, that bloody cheat—gets away with—everything!" He drew a long sobbing breath and said, "Ann, what am I going to do?"

She said, "You are going to do the biggest and bravest thing you ever did in your life. You are going to do—nothing!"

"But when I see Father and Mother? Eleanor, George, Alicia—herself?—they'll know—know

610

that she isn't really married to him. They'll know that this child is a bastard, that she's . . ."

Speaking very quietly, Ann said, "I know. That is why you are not going to see any of them."

He repeated, very slowly, as if every word were wrung from him, "Not—going—to see—any—of them? My God, I can't hide all my life!"

"Flight Masters can't—Herbert Gossage—or whatever other names you may have—can go back to where he came from. Flight, my darling, I know it's banishment. It's the end of your career here, but—Father and Mother are getting old. They've changed, they're almost worn out. They could never face the awful scandal—and awful it would be. There's Eleanor and George. A doctor in a country place—he can't afford gossip. She'd break her heart. There's me. I don't care a damn—but my boys, Flight . . . The 'county', the 'aristocrats', have never quite forgiven Sholto for marrying a girl whose father was a wholesale grocer, even if he loved her. Endless repercussions. People whispering, gibbering, *delighting* in it all. Darling, you can't do it!"

"It might be better if I killed myself," he said.

"Darling, you're young. You've got years before you. If I hurt you, I'm sorry. You married a woman who was weak, selfish, who lived on her senses . . . She loved to exercise power over you. She flung herself headlong into a whirlpool of passion and sex-satisfaction with Chris. If you had not gone away, if you had come home on leave at intervals

611

—how long would she have been faithful to you?" She sprang to her feet and paced up and down the room. This was the old Ann—tempestuous, indulging in one of her fits of fury. "You'd have come home to find some other man's brat foisted on to you, as yours! I've always hated Alicia—always! Cold—when she ought to have been warm and loving—egotistic, self-centred, mean—cheap! Ready to behave like some easy trollop because Chris was sufficiently animal to appeal to her. How often have I felt my fingers itch to smack her smug, superior face! Now—God, she knows now that I shan't betray her confidence; but she never forgets that *I know.*

"Coming whining to me. To me!—'Ann, I must talk to someone or go mad!' Bah! Whining hypocrite! I listened, I said damned little. She's never been near me since, she never will come near me again, or my blasted brother! We ought to be thankful that they've got each other, they can only ruin their own home. Let's hope they stick to each other. Mother, bless her, says, 'Ann, dear, I wish you'd go and see Alicia while you're here. She's very fond of you—very. She always says such sweet things about you!' I'm always too busy. I shall go on being too busy . . ."

Flight said, "Don't, Ann! It's no use. I wish that I could have seen Mother and Dad . . ."

She was calm and mistress of herself again. "Flight, dear, now only two people know—you and I. A secret which is known to more than two people isn't a secret any longer. How could you see them without putting them in an impossible position?"

"No. You're right. It's easy to say 'If only she had waited,' 'If only I hadn't got lost at Dunkirk.' Then it goes on, 'If only there had never been a War . . .' It's no use! Don't worry, Ann. I'll go back. It's got to be the greatest good of the greatest number. They'll take me on again; there's lots to be done still, and Shaff thinks well of me. Only—afterwards—when it's over . . . ? Sorry to be so materialistic—I've money over here, but I can't get that, can I? Or maybe it's all been divided by now. I left a will with Dad's solicitors."

For the first time she smiled. "You didn't really like Chris much even then, did you? Don't you remember that you left everything to be divided between Eleanor and me? You can have my share. I've more money than I know what to do with. Once the War is over, we'll arrange it. Don't worry. If you want more, you can have it. I'm going to be married again. I talked it all over with Alcaster before he died. What a darling he was to me, that old man! He's not like Sholto, there will never be anyone like him—never! But he's terribly kind, frightfully efficient about estates and cattle and leases and farming. He's rolling in money. Between us we shall stink of the stuff."

"And you love him, Ann?"

"Yes, yes, I love him—like that. The sun doesn't shine out of his eyes, I don't go weak at the

613

knees when I see him come into a room; but—he's real and good and decent." She knelt down beside his chair and put her arms round him. "Flight—dear, wonderful, brave Flight—when the War's over I'll come to Paris and see you. What will your name be?"

"François Pascal," he said. "Yes, François Pascal."

"You're doing something very great, darling, something tremendous. One day I shall tell my boys—pretending that it all happened to somebody else. Some day there might be someone —someone who'd be very good to you, who loved you, whom you loved—eh, darling? Might there? Wounds do heal, you know, and scars don't go on hurting for ever. I've learned that."

He leaned forward and kissed her cheek. "I don't know. One day . . . I don't know. I was afraid when I came over to England. I said, 'I'm afraid!' Susan said. 'Don't be afraid, Flight, don't!' I said, 'If I were going to *you*, to find *you*, over there, I shouldn't be.' Queer that she should have said that."

Luncheon was brought in to them on a wheel-table, silently, swiftly, by men who moved with precision, whose hands never fumbled. Flight watched them, his eyes heavy and full.

He sat down and ate, as he had eaten so often in France—not because he was interested in the food but simply because he was hungry, and his body was a machine which must be stoked with fuel in

614

order to keep on working. Once or twice he asked questions, mechanically, without any great show of interest in the answers.

"Your boys, Ann—nice, are they?" or, "Tell me about Father and Mother—they're well?" He listened to her replies, but did not pursue any subject further. Her bare responses seemed to satisfy him.

She tried to ask about his work; he shrugged his shoulders and gave the briefest of comments.

"It's often very dull. Dull, dirty, and I suppose sufficiently dangerous. I've met some grand people. You'd like some of them. You'd like Jules, he's La Spero's son."

"Tell me about La Spero. I saw her when I was over in Paris with Sholto. How attractive! Is she still attractive?"

She fancied, although his expression did not change, that his voice lightened a little when he answered, "I think she's the most attractive woman I've ever met. She's been very good to me. Jules—don't you remember Jules Matot, coming to Little Manor—hundreds of years ago?—we've been together a lot. I stay at Susan's—Madame Matot's—house when I'm in Paris. Hiding, you understand. She's something very important in the 'grape-vine' business."

"Women are in it too?"

"Lord, yes! Most unexpected women." He gave his queer short laugh, like the bark of a fox, Ann thought. "Olympia Lara, for example. Fat, charming, luxury-loving, utterly without fear—doing outrageous things. Madame Kalt—the old 'sergeant-major'. I wonder where she is—nowhere on this earth by this time. At least, it's better to hope not!"

"Tell me . . ." She longed to make him talk, to try to change that dull expression, to hear his voice sound young and excited and interested as it had done before.

He shook his head. "Some day—in Paris, eh?—when it's not so close." He finished his meal, pushed his plate away from him, took out a crumpled packet of cigarettes and straightened one out in his fingers. Then, as if he had suddenly remembered where he was, he said, "D'you mind if I smoke? Then I must be off. I've some people to see."

"Yes, smoke," she said, "but for heaven's sake smoke something decent! Here—in this box. Yes, give me one. Listen, you are going to rest—no, don't shake your head. I repeat that you are going to rest—more, you are going to take something to make you sleep. As for the people you have to see—let them come to see you."

He laughed at the tilt of her chin and said, "My dear Duchess, *you* may be a 'big noise'. I'm just a very insignificant member of the Maquis! I've got to see one of our people, and I've got a letter to deliver to a Colonel at the WO—Colonels loom large on my humble horizon!"

"Who is he, your Colonel?"

"Colonel Henry Crowther . . ."

Ann said, "D'you mean Harry Crowther? He's George's—the man I'm going to marry—greatest friend! Oh, Harry Crowther can come to see you! I suppose you're Gossage to him, eh?"

Flight hesitated. It was true that he longed for sleep, for oblivion. If only he could forget everything for a short time, he might gather sufficient strength to begin again. Now he felt bruised, beaten—and in some strange way befouled and ashamed as he had never done in those days of hardship and danger in the mountains, the woods, when he had lain hidden in barns, in attics with leaking roofs, on beds, which in themselves were filthy as well as old.

He said, "Yes, I'm Gossage to everyone. There's Grimes too, I have to see Grimes about—getting back. D'you think that Grimes could come here?"

"Scrawl a note for him; give me the address, I'll send a messenger. Grimes damn well *will* come here! Though I don't know that we shall bother Grimes to get you back. Let George and Harry manage something. Go and sleep, my dear—here, take these two tablets—they won't hurt you. I'll call you in time for dinner."

"Really?" He stared at her owlishly, stupidly. "That sounds too good to be true! Thanks a lot, Ann! I made up my mind to come to you first. I was right, eh?" He put out his hand and laid it on her arm, for the first time she heard a trace of genuine emotion in his voice. "Ann—you won't let me go—for good? I mean, when we all begin again, when life goes back to normal—if it ever does—you'll come and see François Pascal in Paris? You promise?"

"I swear that I will! Now Carrick shall take you to your room. Sleep well!"

6

CARRICK—who, Flight noticed—walked with one leg quite stiff, said, "Will that be all, sir? Nothing else I can get for you, sir?"

"Nothing at all, thank you."

The man hesitated; he was about thirty, Flight judged, fresh-faced and fair-haired.

Flight said, "Yes, what is it?"

"Only, sir, that I gathered that you were a French gentleman who had come over from France on a dangerous errand. I didn't want you to wonder what I was doing out of uniform. I joined up when the War started. I've lived on the estate all my life, I was his lordship's batman. Got my knee smashed at Dunkirk, his lordship was with me at the time. I've got a silver knee-cap, sir. Her lady—that is, her Grace—got me back when I was discharged. Excuse me, sir, I just didn't want you to think I was—well—dodging anything, sir."

Flight gave one of his admirable French bows. "I thank you for the honour you have paid me to speak in this way. Thank you."

"Thank you, sir."

He undressed and flung himself down on the comfortable bed, realising that his limbs ached as if he had been beaten. He felt old, tired, stunned by this thing that had happened to him. As often,

619

when he was physically exhausted, his brain began to work fast and with great clarity. He felt as if he took out, one by one, the characters in his own little drama, and placed them on a stage before him. Slowly they passed before him. How dreadfully clear they all were! He watched his mother, with her charming smile; his father, well groomed and upright—"The Major". Eleanor—he could see the little high-lights in her eyes as she passed with George Charlton, her arm through his, Chris —he watched Chris dispassionately. Yes, he could see where his attraction lay. Broad-shouldered, virile, the picture of health, loving life, greedy, lustful. Chris would always feel that if he wanted another man's woman, he'd a right to take her —"if the other chap can't hold her!" Well, he —Flight—hadn't been able to hold her, and no doubt Chris felt that his philosophy justified his actions. He felt scarcely anything against his brother now, a kind of fastidious disgust, a revulsion, as if he had witnessed something shameful and disgraceful. And lastly—Alicia. He could see her moving slowly, gracefully, before him, completely mistress of herself as she had always been, except that night when he had found her in the Home Wood, and even then she had possessed enough presence of mind to tell lies which were insufficiently convincing. He understood now why she had begged that there should be no enquiry; he wondered if Lady Sophia and the Rector had sensed her reason and so supported her objection. He smiled sourly. So they had not rated the intelligence of the county police so low after all!

If he could have had Alicia—alone! If they could have spent the whole of their life as they had spent the weeks of their honeymoon, he might have held her, made her content with the love and care which he had to offer. But Ann was right—being what she was, having to leave her whilst he went overseas—how could he tell? If it had not been Chris, then some other man might have come, like a pirate, sailing into her world, robbing and claiming a willing victim.

There were two Alicias. The one he had loved —fastidious, exquisite, the product of a careful upbringing, of a sheltered life and a conventional education. The other, a woman with the same curious strain that existed in her grandmother —the old woman who haunted the gaming-tables, and whose son, for all his apparent urbanity, went in constant fear that she might, even at her great age, create a scandal! Well, the wild, fiercely passionate, reckless Alicia had triumphed!

She could not, he thought, ever have been stronger as the woman he had known and loved, than she had been as the woman who had married his brother.

Well, it was over. Not only his marriage, but his life in England. Ann was right again. It was difficult, hard. He knew that his mind would inevitably go back again and again to his father's house, the quiet gardens, the dignified rooms and the pleasant family life. He knew, too, lying there, growing drowsy with the drugs that Ann had given him, that the full meaning of what he was giving up had not yet reached him. He was to begin again. A new life. Assuming a new name, a new identity, at twenty-five. Too young, and yet too old to adjust himself easily.

There must be days when the thought of home would hurt damnably. When, in the future, he heard from Ann that either his father or mother had died. When perhaps she would say, "We were all with her . . ." or, "He spoke to us all . . ." Only he would be missing.

He frowned. That was something very nearly approaching self-pity. If he were not there, whichever of his parents lay dying would believe that they were going to meet him again. He would have been for years "our poor Flight" or "our dear boy who was killed at Dunkirk". Neither of them would know that, somewhere in Paris—always supposing that he survived the War—a man called François Pascal was working and buying pictures, trying to make his Gallery look something like the old one in Bond Street.

Their life—pleasant, decent, successful—in their own way. His father growing old, content that his business flourished, as it would, under the management of Chris. His mother, gentle, not very clever, but essentially good, looking forward to visits from her grandchildren, to their birthdays

—his mother had always adored birthdays!—
Eleanor and her George, working hard, giving
their children good, sound educations, possibly
skimping themselves in order to do so . . . And
Alicia and Chris . . .

He pressed his hands over his eyes and lay very
still. Slowly sleep came to him.

Ann called him; the room had grown dark, and she
switched on the light at the side of his bed. He
opened his eyes and lay staring at her, scarcely
certain as to where he was.

She said, "Hello, Flight!" and stooped and
kissed him.

He said, "Hello, Ann! I say, what will your
servants think—your coming into the bedroom of
a strange Frenchman? And I'm not Flight, darling,
I'm Monsieur Gossage."

She said calmly, "Oh, let the damned servants
think what they like! I've found a suit of yours,
precious. That—charming person—sent on a box-
ful when she left your flat. Thought that they
might 'come in useful' for some of my hospital
blokes. She—'couldn't bear to look at them'!"

He said half-warningly, half-bitterly, amused,
"Now, Ann—now!"

"Anyway, there's a nice, almost new, suit, and
everything to go with it. I should think the other
one might be handed over to the dustmen, eh?
It's shocking—it really is. And there are darling
Sholto's precious razors—one for each day of the

623

week in a lovely ivory case lined with red velvet. Why do they always line cases with red velvet, I wonder? And Harry Crowther is coming along immediately to have a cocktail. The gin's not awfully good, but there is some real Vermouth left, and odds and ends. So when you . . ."

Flight lay watching her. He felt soothed, rested, relaxed.

"Your Grace is being most marvellously— ordinary, everyday and matter-of-fact. It's commendable! I appreciate it."

She said, "Oh, darling, and I thought I was doing it so well!"

"You are—superlatively well!"

"Don't make me cry, Fl—Monsieur Gossage!"

He dressed and went down to join her.

The man Carrick said, "In the small drawing-room, sir, if you please." He eyed Flight's suit, obviously thinking, "Another of her 'lame ducks' fitted out as good as new! What a marvel she is!"

Ann was standing by the fire, her foot on the polished steel top of the fender, talking rapidly to a very tall, good-looking man in uniform. Flight thought, "By God, I've seen some Hun officers wear their uniforms well, but when our men take pains they can beat them hollow! This chap's a picture—and, great Scott, he's Susan's brother! Think of it—me in my sister's house in London talking to Susan's brother! That takes some beating, I'll say!"

Ann said, "Harry, this is Monsieur Gossage,

who has a message for you. Monsieur Gossage, this is Colonel Crowther."

Crowther said, extending a large, well-kept hand, "This is very pleasant, Monsieur Gossage. You speak English? My French is—well, it might be worse, but . . ."

Ann said, "Might be worse! My dear Harry, impossible! Even now you said 'mongsewer'. Oh, yes, you did! Give Monsieur Gossage a cocktail, please."

Flight explained in careful English that he had recently come from Paris. Crowther laughed, showing magnificently white teeth, and said, "No need to tell me that. You see, Gossage, we're not completely ignorant—we do know something about you. A 'Very Important Gentleman' has expressed great satisfaction regarding your—er —work in France. Old Stick-in-the-Mud at the BBC is fairly gloating over some designs you brought over to him. Now . . . this message."

"It is a lettaire, my Colonel, from Madame Matot."

The Colonel stared; for a second Flight thought that he was going to drop his cocktail-glass, but he recovered himself and drank it quickly.

"A letter from Madame Matot? From my sister, Ann! Imagine it! You've seen her, Gossage? How is she? Pretty as ever? Ah, the letter! Ann, forgive me if I glance at it. I haven't heard from Sue since this show started. I remember in the last affair— when?—1916, was it?—I went to see her. Poor girl, lost her husband, gallant fellow—good actor too. Let's see. Ah! 'Dearest Harry'—imagine that, now—um-um—bless her! Dear little soul!" He finished the letter, wiped his eyes unashamedly on a huge khaki silk handkerchief, blew his nose and then said, "Might I have another cocktail, Ann? Upsettin'—pleasant, but upsettin'." He kept repeating, "Imagine it, little Sue! With a grown-up boy. Know him, Gossage?"

"Ver' well indeed! Jules is 'is name, Jules. A fine boy!"

"Just a youngster, eh? I mean much younger than yourself, eh?"

"That depends," Flight said, "'ow old, my Colonel, do you think that I am? Jules is, I t'ink, twenty-five—yes, twenty-five."

"Oh, I didn't mean that you were old, old man! No, not old. Not more than what—thirty-five, forty, perhaps?"

Flight smiled. "You flatter me, my Colonel!"

"I'm getting to be an old feller, y'know. Ann, m'dear, I'm ten years older than George. Let's see, how old is Sue?"

Flight smiled again. "Madame Matot is—wissout age, 'ow do you say . . . ageless. She is, and always will be, at the pairfect age for a voman." As he spoke he saw Ann's eyes watching him curiously, as if she speculated concerning this Madame Matot. He almost forgot himself, and said in his old eager fashion, "It's true—she really is! She's wonderful!" but his training held, and he

626

merely continued to smile.

They were joined by another soldier—a large man who, Flight felt, was all muscle and very little fat. He had smooth dark hair and eyes which appeared to be lazy, until he opened them wide and you realised that they were particularly keen and alive.

Ann introduced him. "Sir George Frensham." He wrung Flight's hand until he could have yelped with pain. He sat down and gazed at Ann, scarcely speaking, except to ask with startling suddenness, "What's the cultivation like in France, monsieur? People working, eh?"

"The peasant always works, Saire George."

"Umph! believe you're right. Not sure they aren't the backbone of the country. Industrialism—pah!"

Harry Crowther said, "Never mind the crops, George. This feller here wants to get back to France. Ann here has seen old Grimes—y'know old Grimes?—and she told him to leave it to us. After all, we owe monsieur a good deal. It can be arranged, eh?"

George said, "Oh, Lord, yes! When d'you want to go, monsieur? Soon—or going to stay with us for a bit? You might get the Duchess to show you round a bit. I'd be glad if you cared to see my little place. I shan't be there, but it's a pleasant spot, eh, Ann? Know England at all?"

"Not for many years 'ave I veesited 'ere, Saire George."

627

"Good country. We'll fix your trip . . . really, must you go so soon? Ah, too bad! Where to, Harry? Paris?—oh, that's simple! Well, we must make a move. Work, Ann m' dear, work! I'll telephone to you—or, better still, come round and tell you about the trip back. Good-bye, Monsieur Gossage."

Flight said, "Saire George, I am very deeply obliged. I 'ave 'eard that eet is possible that your wedding might be celebrated in the near time. I 'ave in Paris a small painting"—he held out his hands, as if measuring a picture to show its size—"eet might be of interrest to you—no? It ees by Troyon, the very good painter of cattle. Of returning-home cows in the evening. I should 'ave pleasure to send it to you. And also for Madame la Duchesse"—he smiled—"a little small Clouet. Oh, this is a dear picture! 'Ow do I say—wiss my devoted love . . . yes? Per'aps it might be arranged to send zeese? Oh, they arre —'ow is eet?—'fairly come by'."

Ann, Duchess of Alcaster, suddenly burst into tears and flung her arms round the neck of Monsieur Gossage.

George said, "Ann, my darling! . . . Ann, for God's sake!"

Crowther said, "I say—what's wrong? I say, Gossage, what is this?"

Flight smoothed Ann's hair softly. "It's all right," he said, "she isn't trained to this game as I am. Ann, dear, it's all up! I trust these two men.

After all, one is going to marry you, and the other is Susan's brother. Don't cry, poppet! Sit down and let's 'come clean'." He smiled at Sir George, who thought, "The fellow isn't as old as he looks, you see that when he smiles."

Flight led Ann to a chair and knelt beside her, holding her hand in his. Carefully and slowly, omitting certain details regarding Alicia and his brother, he told his story; and as he told it the pain seemed to die away, leaving only a regret that he must separate himself from his home, the people he loved, and the country where he had been born.

"So," he said, "Ann and I discussed it. It was obvious that although I had married a very charming, beautiful woman, she was not exactly the woman I had—shall we say?—made in my own imagination. Therefore the fault was greatly mine."

Frensham said, "And she's married your brother, eh?"

Crowther asked, "Did she know him before the show started, before you were in the Service?"

"Naturally, as my brother."

"But she preferred you?"

"Well, obviously, at that time. She promised to marry me."

"Did he seem to—like her—a great deal when she was engaged to you?"

Flight shrugged his shoulders. "I can't say that I ever thought so. No, definitely I should say—they didn't care much for one another."

629

Frensham said, "Well, love plays some funny games. Bad show. Hard luck. Suppose when you were posted as missing, she was lonely and fell for him?"

"I suppose so."

Crowther asked, "And you're cutting loose from everything?"

"Except Ann here—and, I hope, you, Sir George."

"I say, what about me! Can't I come over and see you when I come to see Sue?"

"That will be a great pleasure if I am in Paris."

Sir George squared his shoulders. His face was scarlet with the effort he was making. "Ann, m' dearest dear, now don't cry, my sweet, don't cry! ... You've got a damned fine feller for a brother and I'm proud to know him. I shan't talk. By God, it's too, too sacred a thing to chatter about. I know that Harry here feels the same—eh, Harry?"

"I do—emphatically I do! It's a damned fine show, a *damned* fine show! Trust us, we'll be dumb as oysters. Talking of oysters, Ann, I've had about a ton sent up to me this morning; if I send 'em round, what about asking us to dine? I'd like to hear something about this grape-vine business—if you don't mind talking, Goss ... Damn it, I can't go on calling you *Gossage*!"

Flight said, "Françoise Pascal is the name, my Colonel!"

Dinner was over. Together they had sat and smoked the good cigars that Ann offered them; she refused to leave them to talk, but sat there listening to Flight's stories, told undramatically and with restraint, except when he spoke of the achievements of his comrades.

She watched his thin, sensitive face, and thought, "How has he come through it all? Flight—so easily hurt, so tender-hearted, and yet—he's strangled a man with his own hands! It's incredible! But it's doing him good to talk. These two men, so solid, so unimaginative, so *sound*, are helping him. It was right that they should know. We can trust them. Dear George, the most honest thing that breathes, and Harry, as good as gold. Neither of them particularly brilliant, but—they're satisfactory!"

Now they were going, Flight was to hear in the morning what his movements were to be. George Frensham said, "Don't worry, we'll manage it all right. You'll be more comfortable than you were with young Harris. Good luck and—*au revoir*."

Crowther waited until Ann and Frensham had gone, then he came over to where Flight stood and laid one hand on his shoulder.

"Tell me, old man, what are you going to do—when you get back?"

Flight looked at him and smiled. "I'm going to tell Susan how much I love her, my Colonel."

"And you're *in* love with her?"

"I think—subconsciously—ever since I first

saw her. I didn't realise it until today. When I heard this—news—well, it broke me. Then somehow I understood that the Alicia I'd known and loved had never really existed. She wasn't a real person at all . . ."

"And when you've told Sue that you care a lot for her?"

"I don't know. I'm a man without a name. The man I once was is dead, he was killed at Dunkirk. He's going to remain dead. What the future holds for me will depend on Susan."

"She's older than you, surely?"

"You told me that I looked forty—and I told you that Susan had no age."

"Well, good luck. Hope I never meet that brother of yours. I should find it very hard to be civil to him. Damned hard!"

"No, no! Remember, you *know* nothing, my 'oyster' Colonel."

"Quite—oh, quite! Well, see you some time. Ritz bar, eh?"

"Grand. Good show. Good hunting. See you soon."

Crowther wrung his hand. "By Gad, you said that exactly like an Englishman!"

Paris again, with the "blue black-out", with the dark figures slipping past in the shadows. Shuttered shops, deserted streets, except for moving shadows and the tramp of German soldiers. Flight stood for a moment near the Place de la Concorde and thought, "Here François Pascal is born. A great moment, surely, in his life." Back in Paris. The 'plane leaving England, landing him in some desolate place near the coast, a mysterious car waiting to whisk him off, while the 'plane took the air almost before she had touched down. Everything had been worked with precision, swiftness and efficiency. The outskirts of Paris, the car moving off and leaving him to walk on alone. Now, here he was—François Pascal—at the moment of his birth as a Frenchman. He smiled and walked on. It wasn't particularly healthy to stand, deep in thought, in the streets at night. The Germans disliked it; they were suspicious, one might almost believe nervous, of people who stood, apparently lost in thought, particularly if they kept their hands in their jacket or overcoat pockets.

He knocked gently on the wooded door. Henri opened it and peered out.

"It's you, eh? Back again? You come back like a bad penny! Be quick!"

"Madame . . . ?"

"In the little salon. Monsieur Jules left for Davos this morning. The old fat one, Gold, is a fast worker."

He raced upstairs and entered the little salon. Susan sprang to her feet. He took her in his arms and kissed her, saying, "Darling, I'm back!"

She said, rather breathlessly, "But this— embracing—it's becoming a habit. It must stop!"

Flight said, "Darling—I want to introduce you to François Pascal. He is a decent fellow. Your brother Harry puts his age at forty."

"Have you gone mad?" she asked.

"No. Listen, I have a long story to tell you. Might I have a drink? No, nothing to eat. Thank you. Now listen." Again he told his story, while she sat, her hands clasped in her lap, listening and watching. Only once, when he recounted his meeting with her brother and George Frensham, did she smile and murmur, "Harry—just the same? He doesn't change!"

He ended his tale, sipped his drink, and said, "And now?"

"Harry and his friend are right," she said, "it is—magnificent!"

He waited, and she asked, "My poor Flight, did it hurt terribly? I am sorry, I cannot imagine—ah, to have done this to you!"

"It doesn't really hurt terribly now," he said. "It did at first. But, you see, all that had to be just cut away like the rotten branch of a tree. It had ceased to have any use, it was merely an encumbrance. I stood tonight in the Place de la Concorde, and said, 'This is the moment when I am being born—François Pascal. The other—Flight Masters—is a dead man. Officially and completely dead. Mark that—officially, legally dead.' Susan, do you love me at all?"

She stared. "My dear—do you know how old I am?"

"No—I know that I am forty. You don't look anything like as old as that."

"You're not forty . . . Harry's a fool. I'm . . ."

He stopped her. "I told Harry that you were ageless."

"My looking-glass is more truthful than you, my dear."

"Impossible! I ask you again—do you love me?" She flung out her hands in a gesture of despair. "I tell you—I'm old. Old . . . old. In another ten years—imagine what people will say—'old' La Spero! Snatching infants from their cradles!"

"Ten years," he said. "Please give me those ten years then, and at the end of them you will walk out with your old and tottering but still devoted François, and everyone will say, 'La Spero, who threw herself away on the decrepit old man! How foolish!'" She rose and walked about the room, feverishly, he thought, then turned and said, "Jules has gone to Davos—oh, you know? Henry chattering, eh? I saw Shaff this morning, he wishes you to escort me in two days' time." Then sharply, "Have you been talking about me to Shaff?"

"No, darling, not a word."

"He looked at me in a queer fashion, I thought, when he said, 'I shall detail Pascal to escort you.' He added that he wished you to have some leave, to rest—and then you are to go back. *Must* you go back?"

"If Shaff says so—of course."

"I don't want you to go back . . ."

"No?" He raised his eyebrows. "Now why not? You want me to do my duty?"

"Have you only a duty to Shaff?"

"And the Movement."

"No one else? Your father and mother, your sisters . . ."

"I have told you that I shall never see any of them again, except Ann."

"Then you—don't care what happens to you?" She was rapping out her words like a minute gun, standing tense beside him; he could see her whole body quiver with her intensity.

"Oh, I have no value . . . what does it matter?"

She flung herself on her knees beside him, caught his hands and held them against her breast. In another woman the movement might have been artificial, theatrical; in Susanne Matot it was beautiful.

"Darling . . . I am so old. My son is as old as you are."

He took her face between his hands and kissed her gently. "Susan, this question of your age . . . I can see it developing into a long and interesting subject for winter evenings, when we sit round the fire. You are being very foolish and unutterably sweet. I told your brother that I was going to tell you that I loved you, that I believed that I had always loved you. He shook my hand and wished me good luck. Susan—Susanne—La Spero— Madame Matot! . . . You've been so wise for other people. Now—be wise for yourself. It isn't

636

finished yet—but on the day that Paris is liberated, then—life can begin."

"But you are married?"

"You are confusing me with a man called Flight Masters, who came to see you in Paris once and fell in love with you, though he didn't know it. He's dead, poor devil!"

"The law . . ."

"We shall consult the law . . ."

"The Church . . ."

"The Church also . . . We shall present the case of a man we know who lives in Canada but is of French descent."

"But in ten years' time . . ."

He groaned. "Oh, now, dearest one, you begin to repeat yourself! That is unpardonable!"

Susan laughed shakily. "You know all the answers, eh?"

"I'm still waiting for one I don't know. Do you love me?"

"You do know that answer—you should have known it months ago. Do you imagine that I allow young men to embrace me—embrace me passionately? Remember?"

"No, not young men, only one elderly gentleman, who—is going to embrace you now. Darling, you told me not to be afraid—with you I never shall be afraid again. Oh, Susan . . ."

She said softly, "I must learn to call you François. And everyone else must learn to call me—Madame Pascal. I like it! Yes, frankly,

I like it!" He laughed. "You'll always be La Spero."

"Jules will be surprised when we tell him."

Flight shook his head. "Jules? Not he! He's known for a long time."

Via Leopardi. Milano. 1945.
Sirmione. Lago di Garda. 1946.

***Other titles in the
Charnwood Library Series:***

SEASON OF PASSION
by Danielle Steel

Kate and Tom were the original star-crossed lovers. Kate, a beautiful model, Tom, a successful American football star at the peak of his career. It almost seemed they were made to share their lives together. Then one day the bubble bursts. A gunshot ends Tom's career and puts him in a sanitorium—forever. Kate is left alone in a world with nothing to live for. And the fear that she will never love again.

NO LOVE LOST
by Helen Van Slyke

Pauline and Howard Tresher live in a twelve room apartment on Fifth Avenue. They have two children, a son called James and a daughter Lindsay. A quarrel between her parents—sparked off by Howard's many infidelities—is overheard by Lindsay who, at ten years old, is not quite sure what it is about but realises that something is radically wrong. Much was wrong at that time because it was 1930, the time of the Depression, and Adele, one of Lindsay's friends, was left fatherless by suicide. The story of Lindsay and Adele, James, Geoff the man Lindsay marries, their loves and fortunes through World War II and the strange twists that emotions and fate take, makes this an unusual and absorbingly readable narrative.

BLOODLINE
by Sidney Sheldon

Elizabeth Roffe was the only daughter of one of the world's richest and most powerful men. When, without warning, he died mysteriously while mountain climbing in the French Alps, she had to take command of the family-owned drug company, a giant international pharmaceutical manufacturer. As Roffe and Sons' new president, she discovers that someone unknown in the highest echelon of the firm is not only out to destroy the company, but is determined to kill her.

WOMEN IN LOVE
by D. H. Lawrence

This novel, which Lawrence himself considered his best, is the story of the lives and emotional conflicts of two sisters. Gudrun and Ursula Brangwen, who also appeared in *The Rainbow*, live in a Midlands colliery town. Ursula falls in love with Birkin (a self-portrait of Lawrence) and Gudrun has a tragic affair with Gerald, the son of the local colliery owner. These four, and such well-drawn characters as Hermione, the sensuous and intellectual hostess and Loerke the sculptor, clash in thought, passion and belief. The tale reaches its tragic conclusion in the Alps as the reader is gripped by the deeply held convictions about love and modern society.

THE MACLARENS
by C. L. Skelton

The first volume of the author's projected "Regiment Quartet", a saga which will take one family through nearly a hundred years of history, is a story of love, war and honour, spanning three continents. The Maclarens are a famous Highland clan. Andrew Maclaren, young, sensitive, is serving with his regiment, the 148th Foot, in India when the Mutiny of 1857 breaks out. After the shocking carnage, he discovers Maud, raped and homeless, who becomes inextricably involved in his life. But the good of the Regiment would be damaged by his marrying a sullied woman.

THE OSTERMAN WEEKEND
by Robert Ludlum

John Tanner, network news director, is looking forward to a weekend party with his closest friends—the Ostermans, the Tremaynes, and the Cardones. But then the CIA tells him that they are all suspected Soviet agents: fanatical, traitorous killers working for Omega, a massive Communist conspiracy. From this moment Tanner and his family are caught up in a nightmare whirlpool of terror, helpless isolation, violence and slaughter. Until the shattering climax, Tanner cannot know who are his friends, who are his implacable, deadly enemies . . .

ROUGH DIAMOND
by James Broom Lynne

Born two hundred million years ago, the 8-carat diamond was to mark the beginning of a long journey into fear and intrigue. Its discovery was destined to play the catalyst in the lives of many people. The reader is taken along the unique corridors of the diamond monopolies and into Central Africa; to Sierra Leone and across the Atlantic to Brazil and the murderous Quaqueros of Colombia, and to the urbane, but no less dangerous cities of London, New York and Geneva. A strong cast of characters tells the story of diamonds, from the mines to the glittering showcases of Tiffany's. But, between discovery and final polishing lies double-dealing, theft and murder.

THE FOXES OF HARROW
by Frank Yerby

Set in New Orleans and Louisiana State in the troubled days between 1825 and the Civil War, *The Foxes of Harrow* has a broad sweep and is charged with colour and action, with white-hot animosities, with strife and warfare and the clash of races. Dominating this fast-moving story is the figure of Stephen Fox, who is loved by three women, who has the face of an angel and a mind which can conjure visions of both beauty and evil.

CRUSADER'S TOMB
by A. J. Cronin

In relating the story of Stephen Desmonde—an artist so dedicated to his art, and of such integrity, that he is willing to sacrifice everything, fame, fortune, the responsibilities of a son and the loyalty of a citizen, in order to devote himself singlemindedly to his vocation—the author spans the first quarter of the twentieth century in a rich variety of settings in England, France and Spain with a colourful cast of characters.

NEVER LOVE A STRANGER
by Harold Robbins

The odds seemed stacked against him from the start, but Francis Kane was determined to come out on top. Born of an unmarried mother, raised by an orphanage in the New York slums, he never knew love, security or family life, and he despised them all. A natural leader with no scruples, he worked out his ruthless campaign against the society that had forced him into nothingness. Throughout the Depression and the hard times that followed, he never lost sight of his goals. But years later, when his cherished dreams came true, he realised his mistake—the pinnacle of power can be a very lonely place when men hold you in contempt instead of awe, and women only want you because you can pay them well.

THE MANCHURIAN CANDIDATE
by Richard Condon

Sergeant Raymond Shaw, secretly brainwashed and then freed with the rest of his patrol after being captured in Korea, comes home as a hero and winner of the Congressional Medal of Honour to be idolised by the whole of America. Only the Communists who indoctrinated him know when and where he will explode, and they alone control his actions as the fateful hour approaches. His mother, power-hungry behind the Washington scene, and his stepfather, an unscrupulous demagogue, are quick to exploit Shaw's sudden fame for their own purposes, while, implacably, the mechanism buried in his subconsciousness ticks away.

THE KING'S GENERAL
by Daphne du Maurier

There are only two main families who count for anything in Cornwall: the Arundells and the Grenviles. Honor Harris is a very unusual heroine: she is crippled in a riding accident shortly before her wedding to Richard Grenvile—the "red fox", and the King's General. This intriguing novel tells of her life during the Civil War years, her involvement with the Grenvile family and her love abiding for Richard.

79 PARK AVENUE
by Harold Robbins

Behind this story of the turning point in the lives of two lovers, one risen from the gutter and the other unashamedly drifting towards it, lies the ugly background of the seamy side of New York life. The story of the trial of Maryann Flood, a "model" at 79 Park Avenue, who has been arrested on charges of procurement, bribery and blackmail; and of the dilemma of Mike Keyes, who is conducting the prosecution. For fate seems to have played against Mike in offering him the chance of advancement in his career, through the trial of the woman he loves.

WATERSHIP DOWN
by Richard Adams

One dim, moonlit night a small band of rabbits leave the comfort and safety of their warren and set out on a long and dangerous journey. Not one of them knows where they are heading, only that they wish to find a new warren where they can live in peace. And once they have gained the longed-for place, then begins an adventure which makes all their previous adventures seem like child's play . . . This is a story of rabbits—*real* rabbits who act throughout in accordance with real rabbit behaviour and instincts, living their terrors and their triumphs with them.